WARHAMMER
40,000

OUTGUNNED

DENNY FLOWERS

BLACK LIBRARY

A BLACK LIBRARY PUBLICATION

First published in 2022.
This edition published in Great Britain in 2023 by
Black Library, Games Workshop Ltd., Willow Road,
Nottingham, NG7 2WS, UK.

Represented by: Games Workshop Limited – Irish branch,
Unit 3, Lower Liffey Street, Dublin 1,
D01 K199, Ireland.

10 9 8 7 6 5 4 3 2 1

Produced by Games Workshop in Nottingham.
Cover illustration by Jan Drenovec.

A CIP record for this book is available from the British Library.

ISBN 13: 978-1-78999-468-1

See Black Library on the internet at

blacklibrary.com

Find out more about Games Workshop
and the worlds of Warhammer at

games-workshop.com

Printed and bound by CPI Group (UK) Ltd, Croydon CR0 4YY

For all who yearn for freedom but do their duty.

For more than a hundred centuries the Emperor has sat immobile on the Golden Throne of Earth. He is the Master of Mankind. By the might of His inexhaustible armies a million worlds stand against the dark.

Yet, He is a rotting carcass, the Carrion Lord of the Imperium held in life by marvels from the Dark Age of Technology and the thousand souls sacrificed each day so that His may continue to burn.

To be a man in such times is to be one amongst untold billions. It is to live in the cruellest and most bloody regime imaginable. It is to suffer an eternity of carnage and slaughter. It is to have cries of anguish and sorrow drowned by the thirsting laughter of dark gods.

This is a dark and terrible era where you will find little comfort or hope. Forget the power of technology and science. Forget the promise of progress and advancement. Forget any notion of common humanity or compassion.

There is no peace amongst the stars, for in the grim darkness of the far future,
there is only war.

PREFACE

An Imperial propagandist's first duty is to the truth.

More precisely, their duty is to the Imperium's truth, the sacred creed preaching that humanity's manifest destiny is to rule the galaxy. In enacting that creed we suffer not the heretic, the witch nor the xenos to live. In their annihilation, we fulfil the will of the God-Emperor and the Imperial Throne.

Imperial records state that victory on planet Bacchus was bought in blood by the brave pilots of the Aeronautica Imperialis. More specifically, that the ork air offensive was blunted by the battered remnants of the 2208th Expeditionary Air Wing, spearheaded by the esteemed flight commander Lucille von Shard.

If a citizen were to dispute this account, and somehow avoid interrogation and execution, they could be directed towards the popular pict *The Glorious Martyrdom of the 2208th*. This sanctioned account of the war chronicles the 2208th's tireless crusade against the greenskin menace and contains actual footage of front-line combat.

I should know. I was the one who captured it.

But the pict is a lie. It does not tally with my recollections of the conflict, or the original data-files from which it was spliced, and bears scant resemblance to the truth.

Hence this account.

I do not scribe it for my own benefit. My memories of the war are perfectly preserved in myriad data-files. I could conjure any moment, relive any exchange, if I so desired. Nor do I write in recognition of the pilots and ground crew who gave their lives for the Imperium. Frankly, the sanctioned account portrays most of them in a far more positive light than they deserve.

And I certainly do not write it for Flight Commander Shard, who demonstrated repeatedly the scant regard she held for truth, propriety or the institutions of the Imperium. Her legend is founded on falsehoods and lies, her persona as crafted as any gutter pict. When I picture her now, it is as I last saw her. Her aircraft dark and silent, suspended in the cold void of space. Alone. At peace.

I write this because I am an Imperial propagandist, and an honest one at that. I draw scant solace from the sanitised account of the war. Indeed, I question if we truly serve the Throne by perpetuating such lies and falsehoods, however much they flatter or venerate.

Do we not owe it to the God-Emperor to speak the truth?

Even if, sometimes, it does not tally with the Imperium's Truth?

CHAPTER ONE

I cannot tell you when war began on Bacchus.

I could provide the date that Imperial forces were dispatched to the once prosperous agri world to combat the mounting ork threat. But greenskins emerged from the swamps years prior, local forces suppressing their numbers for almost a decade before their sudden plea for assistance. Many had already lost loved ones or limbs before official records decree the conflict even started. Their war began early.

My war began in a dingy cabin nestled deep within Orbital Station Salus, the monolithic space station suspended above Bacchus. I awaited authorisation to depart for the planet below, and had for over a day. There were either atmospheric irregularities or hostile forces operating in the area, depending on whether one believed the official account or overheard whispers in corridors.

With my meagre possessions and ample equipment already stowed, there was little I could do but wait. My time was occupied watching a tiresome recruitment pict, even though I had already endured it a dozen times or more. It was, after all, the reason I was there. The holo-display projected a grainy image of an ork warrior. A wiry creature, clad only in a scrap of loincloth, the greenskin was nevertheless imposing, its tusks bared in a snarl, a crude spear brandished with intent. It sniffed the air, like a blood-hound, before roaring and surging forward, intent on its prey.

'On the agri world of Bacchus, vile xenos beasts threaten the loyal citizens of the Imperium!'

As the narrator's voice crackled into life, the panned shot revealed an Imperial citizen fleeing, dragging a child behind her. Their attire was not in keeping with Bacchus, for the image had been cut from a far older pict and crudely spliced into the more recent footage. The work was sloppy, either that of an amateur or someone who cared little for their subject or reputation.

The woman stumbled, falling just as the ork loomed behind her, its spear poised for the killing blow. She tried to cover her child with her body, even as the boy glared at the ork with undisguised hatred.

I paused the playback, the image freezing.

The footage presented some classic archetypes: the mother embodying noble sacrifice, her child angry and defiant despite the xenos threat ably represented by the ork. I could see the intent. But the seams between the cuts were painfully apparent, noticeable to even the most dull-witted menial worker. The footage of the ork was genuine from what I could tell; the way its feet sank into the burnt-orange swamp would be difficult to simulate. Conversely, the woman had been deposited on a convenient stretch of rock in a crude attempt to disguise the pict-seam. She was beautiful in a restrained way, and I was sure I had seen her in a previous vid. *Beware the Foul Mutants!* perhaps, or *All Heretics Will Fall.*

'Restore playback,' I murmured.

The ork raised its spear, poised to impale both mother and child.

'But the God-Emperor protects the faithful. Look to the skies!'

The narrator's intransient optimism was grating. But at his words all three figures raised their heads, glancing upwards as if on command. Cue the roar of an engine, the pict zooming in on a distant spec hurtling through the sky.

The ork barely had time to raise its hand-hewn weapon before a las-bolt sheared off its head. It stood a moment, despite the absence of cranium, before pitching forward, the focus of the vid shifting to the mother and child. Both stood proud, her arms crossed in the sign of the aquila, her son offering a salute crisp enough to satisfy even the most stringent commissar.

'No matter how craven the xenos or foul the heretic, we need not fear. The brave pilots of the Aeronautica Imperialis are our impenetrable shield!'

An aircraft zoomed overhead, the shot cutting to the pilot, who returned the boy's salute even as his Thunderbolt fighter hurtled over the swamplands. The fighter's top speed is over one thousand miles per hour, and the pilot would barely have seen the child, let alone been able to plant a tank-piercing las-bolt between the ork's eyes. But here he was, finding time to make nice with the citizenry during his fly-by.

It was galling.

Of course, my peers would shrug and say, so what? The purpose of these vids is to reassure the masses, or inspire fresh recruits to enlist. It does not matter whether they are accurate, as in all probability none of the menial workers who join the Imperial Navy will ever get the chance to fly; that is the preserve of the nobility. All that matters is that the audience leave the vid flush with conviction and a desire to serve, and that enough enlist to fulfil the roles of ground crew, indentured workers and mechanicals.

But I maintained that such a poorly crafted vid could only encourage ridicule. And the recruitment figures suggested I was right.

The aircraft now swept over the swamp, its Avenger bolt cannons scything down an ork horde – a weapon that the standard fighter variant previously shown should not have had. Amateurs.

The orks' response was to hurl spears and insults, whilst the narrator continued to extol the inevitability of humanity's victory and the inferiority of the greenskins. It seemed the recruitment drive was focused on portraying the war as a thrilling adventure that could conclude at any moment, urging citizens to enlist before it was too late and the fighting ended. Not an inaccurate assessment, if one were to listen to some of the whispering in the corridors, but not for the reasons suggested in the pict.

By the Throne, it was tiresome. But I persisted, for what followed was the only shot in the pict worth a damn.

A second craft lurched into view, wobbling above the swamp at barely a walking pace. It was constructed from wood, though the rear-mounted engine looked to be assembled from scrap metal. It belched thick black clouds, the holo-display struggling to depict the smoke as anything more than static. Its pilot was a haggard-looking ork who appeared to be missing an eye and more than a few tusks. As the Thunderbolt fighter soared overhead, the ork attempted to fire a crude cannon mounted beneath its craft, but the recoil pitched it off balance and subsequently into the swamp. A rather impressive explosion followed, but I found myself winding back the footage until the ork flyer was visible again.

I had first thought it fake, the wooden aircraft spliced in to lighten the pict and ridicule the greenskins. But there were no seams. It was real, though the precise age of the footage was impossible to determine.

I frowned. I am no tech-priest, but it seemed impossible that such a craft could fly; I have used field latrines that were more aerodynamic. Yet somehow the orks found a way. There was something almost admirable about their ingenuity.

Admirable, and troubling.

The vox suddenly whined into life. I shut down the playback, opening the channel.

'Propagandist Simlex?' said a voice.

'Yes?'

'We are ready to depart, sir.'

'Thank you. I will be there shortly,' I replied, closing the vox-channel and rising to my feet. I should have felt elated, for finally my work would begin. But I found myself dwelling on that primitive ork aircraft. It was disconcerting seeing such a savage creature achieving powered flight. Humanity mastered the skies millennia ago, and our fighters and bombers have changed little since then, for the same sacred designs are portrayed in picts and murals stretching back centuries.

The orks on Bacchus began cobbling aircraft from scrap a few score years ago. Yet recent reports suggested they now possessed something akin to an actual air force.

As I departed, I found myself wondering if the greenskins' aspirations ended there.

The flight sergeant stood at the corridor's end, rigid as a sabre, his hair seemingly welded in place, his uniform unmarked by stain or crease. He was the model of an Imperial soldier, except for his face. Somehow, even when attempting to appear stern and sombre, he looked poised to break into a smile. As I hurried closer, he threw a salute so earnest it risked a head injury.

'Propagandist Simlex?' he asked.

I nodded.

'Flight Sergeant Plient, sir!' he said. 'Well, Acting Flight Sergeant Plient. Field promotion, sir, though I'm not sure the paperwork has been filed.'

He already sounded apologetic.

'My pleasure to make your acquaintance, acting flight sergeant,' I said, bowing my head. 'I take it we are ready to depart?'

'Yes, sir. I have your cases secured and stowed aboard the Arvus lighter. Just awaiting some last-minute clearance.'

I nodded, my gaze already drawn to the viewport behind him. From it, I could see a tapestry of glittering stars, each a priceless gem in the God-Emperor's Imperium. The scale was terrifying, but also strangely comforting. Suns blazed and planets progressed along predestined paths, ambivalent to the follies of man. It all seemed so ordered from such a vantage point, as though the galaxy were on the cusp of peace. The rim of the planet Bacchus was barely visible beneath, framed by a halo of violet light.

'Sir?'

I glanced round, having almost forgotten Flight Sergeant Plient.

'I've just been informed we have an opening, sir. Need to depart.' He gestured to the launch bay.

I nodded, following him through to the vessel. I had never ridden an Arvus lighter, nor even seen one before. It was a stub-nosed cargo shuttle, unarmed and seemingly unremark-able. Plient opened the rear doors, revealing an interior hastily refitted to transport human cargo. A trio of flight seats were bolted to the floor. My cases lay beside them, secured in place by mag-clamps.

'Please take a seat, sir. We will be departing soon,' Plient said, smiling as he slid the door shut behind me.

I glanced at the three identical chairs and, after a couple of false starts, opted for the seat on the left, closest to my cases. The flight harness was unfamiliar, and seemed intent on slicing through my shoulder. Plient's voice crackled through the vox-channel.

'All set, sir?'

'Yes, acting flight sergeant,' I said. 'Ready as I will ever be.'

'Nervous, sir?'

'A little. Though more excited. I've never made planetfall in a craft like this.'

'Understandable, sir. Though I should caution you that the shift between gravitational fields is disconcerting. Some nausea is not uncommon.'

'I'll try not to make a mess of your vessel,' I said, smiling. 'I suppose for a pilot such as yourself atmospheric re-entry is just another day's work?'

'That's what I should say,' Plient replied. 'But, between you and me, I never get used to it. It's magical, sir. Awe-inspiring. Except for the nausea.'

'I wish I could see the way you do.'

'I can arrange that, sir. You are not the first passenger to make such a request.'

Ahead of me, just above the cockpit door, a shaded pict screen lit up. I craned my neck, cursing myself for picking the wrong chair. My reward was a view of the now-familiar stars. They looked smaller on the pict screen, less significant.

'The ship has external viewers?' I said. 'Is that standard?'

'No, sir, but this vessel regularly ferried dignitaries before the war. Some of them enjoyed a view.'

'Thank you, Acting Flight Sergeant Plient.'

'I'm here to help, sir. Stand by for launch.'

My nails dug into the armrests. I willed myself to relax, taking a deep, slow breath, trying to unpick my apprehension. I had reservations about the journey, of course, but that was not the root of the unease. Nerves were not unknown to me; I felt positively queasy before arriving on the shrine world of Sacristy. But the pict I'd produced, a biopic of the life of Brannicus the Thrice-Maimed, had been received as my finest work. The infamous scene of the saint beating three hundred sinners to death armed only with his own severed leg is still regarded as a cinema-pict masterpiece.

But this was different. This time I would be on the front lines, obtaining live footage from an actual conflict, whilst balancing the whims of at least two masters. My unease was driven as much by the political pitfalls surrounding my work as it was by the prospect of imminent death on the surface below.

The craft shuddered, breaking out of the gravitational pull of Orbital Station Salus. A vast shadow blotted out the stars as Bacchus loomed into view. The moderately prosperous agri world was known for the quality of its wine but precious little else. Viewed from the shuttle, its surface was a dirty orange, with little indication of habitation or geographical variance. A casual observer might assume that deserts lay beneath them, the sands devoid of life.

They would be sorely mistaken.

A lurch. It was subtle now, for we were between gravities. But I felt my back press into the flight seat as the orange sphere swelled to fill the screen.

'Stand by, sir. It is about to get dicey.'

The screen flashed white as we commenced re-entry, flames lapping at its rim and seemingly consuming the planet below. They were purple, the tips edged in magenta, presumably a by-product of the atmosphere. A small sliver of me, the eternal propagandist, wondered how this might affect the project, whether I needed to adjust the lenses to minimise light diffusion, or should embrace the conditions to make my pict visually distinct.

The remainder of me was focused on holding down my breakfast, with mixed success.

'*Enjoying the ride, sir?*'

'It's a unique experience,' I replied, wiping my mouth on the back of my hand. The limb felt extraordinarily heavy, the craft's systems unable to fully compensate for the acceleration. 'Though I confess I am used to larger craft, where I suspect the ride is smoother.'

'*True enough, sir. But a larger craft makes for a bigger target. Our re-entry is less likely to be spotted by the orks.*'

There was something in his tone. A seriousness. But I assumed he was merely focused on his duties. I still pictured the green-skins as spear-brandishing brutes flying flimsy wooden planes, despite more recent reports. I could not conceive them posing a threat to a void-worthy vessel.

I would learn otherwise.

CHAPTER TWO

After the thrill of broaching Bacchus' atmosphere, the actual planet was rather banal. The landscape comprised one vast swamp, the monotony broken only by dank foliage. My research indicated the rest of the world was similar, barring the inhospitable poles. It was also the poorest planet of the subsector, lacking the stark beauty of Hedon or rich mineral reserves of Plutous. Though the world was habitable, its population was minimal, clumped on the few scraps of land that did not require permanent drainage. In fact, were Bacchus swallowed by a warp storm, Subsector Yossarian would be unlikely to miss it, at least until one of Hedon's nobles noted the wine-cask was empty.

We were low enough now that I could just make out the gnarl-vines threading through the lagoons. Their distilled fruits were the world's saving grace, the backbone of its economy and the only thing preventing it becoming little more than a vassal to its more prosperous neighbours.

As we levelled out, I was surprised to see a trio of fighters circling beneath us.

'Plient?' I said, my voice climbing an octave. 'What is that?'

'*Our escort, sir. Squadron Anisoptera. They were waiting planetside. Our Arvus lighter is unarmed, so we have three Lightning fighters accompanying us.*'

'Are you expecting trouble? I thought we were behind the front line?'

'*It's a precaution. We are far from the hotspots, but I'm afraid air combat does not have strict front lines. Still, it is only a few leagues to Planetary Governor Dolos' château. Don't worry, sir, I'll get you there in one piece.*'

'I have every faith in you,' I said, pleased my voice sounded steady.

'*Would you like a display, sir? The squad would be happy to demonstrate their skills.*'

'Thank you, but that is unnecessary.'

'*Are you sure? Our escort would be delighted to appear in the pict.*'

'My recording equipment is all stowed,' I replied, glancing to my cases. 'Perhaps, once I'm settled, we can arrange something.'

'*Understood, sir.*'

There was no change in his tone, but I wondered if I had offended him. Perhaps these pilots had hoped to be the focus of the pict, or at least prominent figures. But I had assumed the flight would be uneventful, and with my cases magnetically sealed I had no means of recording the journey.

Flanked by our escort, we soared over the endless lagoon, flying lower than I would have expected. I unpacked my data-slate, studying fragments of footage and the assorted files I had been given regarding Bacchus and its customs, preparing myself for our arrival. But the craft suddenly lurched right, almost causing me to drop the device. On the pict screen, I caught sight of one of our escorts moving into position ahead of us.

'Plient?' I asked. 'What's happening?'

'We picked up a little vox-chatter indicating a few hostiles may have slipped into our airspace. We're shifting formation, but giving them a wide berth. No sense engaging and putting you in jeopardy, sir.'

'Orks, I take it?'

'Yes, sir.'

I frowned, recalling the primitive wooden flyer. It seemed incongruous such beasts utilising actual aircraft, despite reported technological advancements. The idea such savage creatures could pilot functional war machines, let alone manufacture them, seemed absurd.

'How numerous are these forces?' I asked.

'Unknown, sir. My apologies, I need to liaise with command. Stand by.'

I nodded. A pointless gesture as he could not see me. Admittedly, being unseen is an advantage to my trade. I am neither a tall nor striking man, my hair dark and face unremarkable, the only notable feature a surgical scar tucked along my hairline. Anonymity suits me well enough, and I am content to fade into the background whilst others strut the stage. But I am used to observing the performance. Being trapped in a metal box high above an unfamiliar planet was disconcerting, and doubly so with hostiles inbound. With my equipment stowed, my perceptions were limited to what I could observe through the pict screen.

Which abruptly went dark.

The craft lurched right again, the flight harness slicing into my shoulders. I heard a sound a little like rain, assuming the cloud was a hammer. It pattered against the hull. First above, then to my left. But, besides a storm gathering to the far west, I saw no clouds during our descent.

My finger stabbed the vox-comm.

'Flight Sergeant Plient? What's happening?'

'Sorry, sir. Trouble out here. I'm pulling away. We have another squad inbound. There will be no–'

He cut out as the craft swung left, my stomach heaving as we spiralled into a corkscrew. I could not tell up from down, and with the screen blank I had no sense of the world beyond the cargo hold, which was beginning to feel like a jet-propelled sarcophagus.

'Flight Sergeant Plient, can you restore the viewer?'

'Yes, sir, but you do not–'

'Do it, sergeant. That's an order.'

It was my inaugural command: turn on the pict screen. Not the most inspiring first order an officer ever made, but I was not an officer, and my meagre authority was borrowed from Planetary Governor Zanwich, the most powerful man in Subsector Yossarian and my official patron. Yet he was no military commander, and, strictly speaking, the men and women of the Aeronautica Imperialis were not required to follow his or my orders.

Plient did not immediately respond, instead sending the lighter into another sudden turn. But momentarily the pict screen flashed into life, presenting the majestic image of a Lightning fighter. It surged towards our foe, wings swept forward like the pinions of an Imperial eagle. My heart swelled as its autocannons thundered the God-Emperor's wrath, whilst wing-mounted lascannons blazed with His glorious light.

Then it exploded.

For a moment I could not see the cause. There had been no telltale missile or energy discharge. But the perpetrator soared into view, its shadow eclipsing the flaming wreckage. There was no grace in its flight, the craft reminiscent of a rocket-propelled fist with crude wings welded to its flanks. Its myriad exhausts belched black smoke that stained the sky, whilst the weapons studded along its wings vomited a torrent of bullets. I recalled the sound I had heard before, the hammer of rain on the hull. I now knew the source.

The view abruptly shifted from the wreckage-strewn sky to rapidly approaching swampland, as Plient dived, our aircraft hurtling groundward. The blur of orange and brown rapidly condensed into rust-coloured water and twisted vines. Bullets pattered against the rear hull, and the land grew bigger. Closer.

'Plient! What the hell are you doing?!'

'*Sorry, sir. Situation has deteriorated. Stand by.*'

The swamp was seconds away.

I thought to pray, but all prayers left me. I kept dwelling on my magnum opus, the prized pict that would place me in the ranks of renowned propagandists like Pinmoth and Iwazar. It would never be completed now, the idea buried deep in the swamps of this backwater world, and me along with it.

But at the last moment Plient wrenched our nose up and somehow the craft levelled, skimming across the swamp water before banking sharply, the barbed vines clawing at the hull. I felt a shockwave behind us, followed by the thunder of an explosion. Our pursuer had not reacted as quickly. Though fast, his craft lacked manoeuvrability.

'Well done, Plient,' I managed, finding my voice again.

'*It's not over, sir. Three more are inbound.*'

He was right. As we levelled, I could see a trio of black smoke trails drawing in. They were some distance away, but accelerating.

'Where is our escort?' I asked as they closed in.

'*They did their duty, sir. They are with the God-Emperor now.*'

There was little I could say to that. Instead, I watched the attackers descend on us. Plient headed straight for them, resigned to the inevitability of our fate. I wanted to plead with him to flee, take us close to the ground. But the prospect of advising a flight sergeant, even an acting one, on aerial strategy felt foolish.

I could not speak, apparently finding certain death preferable to appearing a fool to a relative stranger.

But at that moment, the incoming fighters banked sharply, as though desperate to reposition.

It was too late. A scouring beam of light heralded our deliverance. It tore through the foremost ork aircraft, breaching its fuel reserves. The fighter erupted in an inferno, spraying flaming metal in all directions. Its allies lurched from the explosion's path, but it did not matter. A second las-bolt sheared across the closer craft, barely shaving the vessel's cockpit, and yet decapitating the greenskin pilot in the process. As he quietly tumbled from the sky, the last ork was still trying to engage the new threat. Though the greenskin fighters were quick and merciless, they lacked the agility for swift redeployment.

The vox-channel hissed into life.

'Plient? Who in the Throne's name let you near an aircraft? I thought you were confined to maintenance?'

The voice was curt, but at the sound of it my mouth was suddenly dry. It was her. I was sure of it.

'We were a little short-handed on the ground, sir,' Plient replied. 'Very decent of you to offer some assistance.'

'Don't flatter yourself, Plient. I was bored and wanted a scrap. I was hoping for some more challenging opposition, though. Perhaps the Bringer of Flame or Green Storm. Not a couple of barely blooded greenskins flailing about in the sky.'

'Still one left, sir.'

The remaining ork craft was coming about, rising to intercept. I still could not see our rescuer.

'Would you like to take this one, Plient? Actually contribute to a fight for once?'

'Very kind of you to offer, sir. But, as I suspect you are aware, my craft is unarmed.'

'Well, that's piss-poor planning on your part. Stand by.'

A score of las-bolts tore through the sky. Each only brushed the enemy craft, one almost taking its nose off, but none quite connecting.

'There now,' she said. 'You're even. Though I have to say the green fellow does not seem to be taking it well.'

It took me a second to realise what she had done. The fighter's silhouette was altered, and it now lacked the protrusions formerly adorning nose and wing. She had defanged it, removing its weapons without destroying the craft.

'He does appear agitated, sir,' Plient replied, as the ork's cockpit lurched open in the way an Imperial vessel's might when a pilot ejected. Instead, there was a flicker of movement, difficult to discern at such a distance.

'Hmm… You speak Orkish, Plient?'

'Can't say I do, sir.'

'I can understand a smattering of words. Well, I say words – it's more howls punctuated by obscene gestures. This one wants to communicate.'

'He's certainly making a gesture, sir.'

'Indeed. And he's now drawn his sidearm.'

'Can't believe you left him with that, sir. Seems sloppy.'

'I hate to agree with you, Plient, but you might be right. Still, perhaps he has learned his lesson. I imagine if we let him return home he will parley on our behalf, and we can put this ghastly war to an end. Wait… my mistake. He intends on ramming us.'

The ork craft was drifting from sight. Plient adjusted our angle, following. The sun flashed across the pict screen, forcing me to shield my eyes. Our rescuer had struck from above then, the light to her back. Perfect positioning.

'Shockingly unsporting of him, sir.'

'I know. I thought we'd established a genuine connection. Honourable *foes condemned to their roles by a glorious war, their rivalry a form of comradeship, their duels the stuff of legends.'*

There was no doubting the mocking tone, nor the derision dripping from every word. Still, it shocked me. The implication of any sort of comradeship with a greenskin, even in jest, was not what I expected from an officer of the Aeronautica Imperialis. I distracted myself with the pict screen, where the ork craft was thundering towards a formation of three Imperial fighters, presumably intent on mutual destruction. As I watched, the two flanking craft pulled away.

'It's getting quite close, sir,' Plient said, a hint of trepidation creeping into his voice.

'I know,' she replied. *'I was debating whether I could take the creature's head with my sabre. I'm sure it's here somewhere, I never fly without it.'*

The ork surged onwards, its craft now a jagged missile aimed squarely at our rescuer.

'Sir?'

'One moment, Plient, the blasted scabbard is stuck.'

They were seconds from impact.

'Sir? Flight Commander Shard!'

To say she pulled up at the last second would discredit her skill. It was less than a second, some micro-measurement of time known only to agents of the Ordo Chronos. Her fighter pirouetted from the onrushing ork, releasing a barrage of flares. They burst alight about the ork's aircraft, a number landing in the open cockpit. Smoke was soon accompanied by flames, and the xenos craft pitched from the sky, corkscrewing towards the swamps below.

'Were you saying something, Plient?'

'No, sir. Otherwise I might appear foolish.'

'Indeed. Well, I have exhausted available targets. Back to the château for some light refreshment. You had better tag along.'

'Thank you, sir. I have mislaid my escort.'

'Troubling. Though not as troubling as someone entrusting you with an aircraft. Our deficiency of experienced pilots must be worse than I thought.'

'I couldn't say, sir.'

'Did you at least collect your package?'

'I did, sir. He's safely aboard. Perhaps you'd like to speak with him?'

I heard her snort over the vox-channel.

'You always know how to make me laugh.'

She cut the vox. It was only silent for a moment before crackling back into life.

'Sir?' Plient asked. 'Are you all right back there?'

'Quite well, Plient, if a little shaken.'

'Understandable, sir. It was a little dicier than I'd have hoped. Fortunately, the God-Emperor was watching over us, for we were rescued by one of the Aeronautica Imperialis' finest officers, Flight Commander Shard.'

'Yes, I heard your exchange. She must have been broadcasting on all vox-channels.'

Silence.

'Yes, sir,' he said after a time. 'I apologise, sir, in the excitement I did not notice. I hope you did not find our words too shocking. Soldiers can sometimes be a little crass. The banter defuses tension, sir.'

'Not to worry, Plient. I found it illuminating. Besides, that is why I am here. I want to capture the true nature of the conflict, not the sanctified picts we normally produce.'

'You weren't offended then, sir?'

'I was thankful to get a glimpse of Flight Commander Shard in action. I do regret being unable to capture any of it, but I am sure I will have another opportunity.'

'I have no doubt, sir. Flight Commander Shard is our most skilled fighter ace.'

'I'm quite aware,' I said. 'Flight Commander Lucille von Shard, flight number six-one-six, has a most decorated history – hardly a surprise given her lineage. Her father, Colonel Horotha Shard, commanded the Verlaian One Hundred and Fifth Regiment, whilst her mother, Tazinia, was a tank commander in the Nauticium One Hundred and Twelfth. Both heroes and martyrs, too.'

'Sounds like you've done your research, sir.'

'I have researched the records of all the fighter aces currently active in this theatre. Shard, Gradeolous, even young Nocter. But hers was particularly fascinating, as is the entire family. There have been a few passable bio-picts on Horotha and Tazinia, but there is almost nothing of their seven children, despite all of them being prominent servants of the Imperium. I had the honour of working with Commissar Tobia von Shard following the Palatine Crusade, and I briefly met Confessor Maric von Shard in the aftermath of the Gigerian Cleansing. The former was even kind enough to provide a letter of introduction.'

'If you say so, sir.'

There was something off about his tone. I still did not know the man well, but he was not adept at concealing his feelings.

'Have I said something amiss, Plient?'

'No,' he replied. *'It's impressive that you have such a comprehensive knowledge of Flight Commander Shard's history.'*

'It's my duty. I have been commissioned to create a pict extolling the might of the Aeronautica Imperialis. The story needs a focal point, a lens through which the viewer can understand your world. Flight Commander Shard would make an excellent subject for my pict. In fact, I would be interested in one day overseeing her full bio-pict. When she eventually retires, of course.'

'Or is shot down, sir.'

There it was again, that edge to his voice. But it was not anger, or even insubordination. It was more a detachment, as though he sought to part ways with my sentiments without quite refuting them.

'You think that likely?'

'She is the best we have, sir. But even the best can miscalculate, or suffer misfortune at a critical juncture.'

'You sound rather morbid.'

'I'm a little shaken, sir. That was closer than I wished.'

I realised then my foolishness. I had only seen flashes of the conflict from the pict screen, and that had been sufficient to terrify me. How quickly I forgot my fears once Flight Commander Shard made her appearance. It all felt ordained, like the savage greenskins were lured into a perfect trap. But our escorts were dead. And I would never know how close we had come to joining them.

'Flight Sergeant Plient, I want to thank you,' I said. 'I am no expect on aerial combat, but I suspect if a less skilled pilot was at the helm I would not have survived. I owe you my life.'

'Thank you, sir. But it was merely my duty.'

'Still, at the very least I can immortalise you in the pict.'

His laughter was warm and genuine. *'I thank you, sir. Truly. I will help in whatever way I can, but I am more comfortable viewing the vids than appearing in them.'*

'You enjoy them?'

'Some of them, sir. I love parades, especially the music. It's nice to see the Imperium at its best and be reminded of what we are protecting.'

'You don't think I will see its best out here?'

'Well… it is rough, sir. We serve as well as able and praise the God-Emperor. But this is a swamp, and all is tainted and foul. The vids always seem so bright and clean.'

'Ah,' I said, and grinned. 'But this is to be a different sort of pict. I want to show real heroes, soldiers who wade through the muck to get the job done.'

'*Like Flight Commander Shard, sir?*'

'You tell me,' I said. 'Do you think her a hero?'

'*I have nothing but respect for Flight Commander Shard,*' Plient replied. '*She is a hero, but with all due respect, sir, perhaps not one best suited to a pict.*'

'We will see,' I said. 'I'd wager differently. She will be the most famous member of the von Shard family.'

'*If you say so, sir,*' Plient replied. '*Might I offer some advice?*'

'Of course.'

'*Refrain from mentioning her family.*'

CHAPTER THREE

Dusk encroached by the time we reached Planetary Governor Dolos' château.

Technically Bacchus' sun still hung in the sky, but foetid gases bubbling from the swamp water formed a mist that diffused any lingering daylight. The crepuscular light lent a certain gravitas to the towering edifice. The château's looming silhouette rivalled the tallest hab-block in size, and its shadow swallowed the grounds. The swamps and lagoons of Bacchus rendered conventional construction problematic, as structures of any substantial weight were swallowed by the quagmire. Indeed, the only indigenous fauna of any stature were the gigantic mandack trees, and that was solely due to how deeply the plant was embedded in the bedrock. A fully grown specimen's upper branches stretched nearly a mile, and its roots dug far deeper, extending for leagues beneath the crust.

Governor Dolos had elected to take one of the towering trees as her residence. The vast trunk had been hollowed, lights twinkling from a score of windows carved into the bark. The plant seemed alive enough, though the foliage was thinner in the mist-wreathed upper branches. A foyer extended from the tree's base, illuminated by lanterns filled with dancing fireflies, and through its arched doors a procession of officers and ground crew were in near-permanent migration. They were interspersed by servants clad in Dolos' personal livery: a winged insect picked out in iridescent shades. A squad of Imperial Guard hurried past, their boots churning the ground and crushing the last desperate stands of what once might have been a flowerbed.

'Here we are, sir. Planetary Governor Dolos' private château.'

I glanced to Flight Sergeant Plient, who was struggling under the weight of my cases, the larger of which he could barely lift off the ground.

'Private?' I asked, nodding to the doorway's unending procession.

'It was private until the war,' he grunted, setting the cases down beside me. 'The château drains the swamp water, making this estate one of the few locations within leagues where an aircraft can actually land. Given the needs of the military, Governor Dolos graciously donated it to aid the war effort.'

He nodded to a pair of rockcrete airstrips, carved into what was once the governor's lawn. Turf clung tenaciously around their rim, some enterprising shoots even seeking to pierce the rockcrete itself, but making little headway. It differed markedly from the picts of the estate I had viewed prior to arrival. They had shown meticulously manicured topiary with red flame leaves and sun-bright flowers, as well as dazzling water features that employed anti-gravity generators to craft skyward-running waterfalls. There were shoals of fish suspended in free-floating bubbles of crystal-clear water, drifting with regal grace through the artfully tended canopy.

But that must have been before the war, or at least before the military was in residence. Aside from the château itself, the grounds appeared nothing more than muddied fields crushed under a thousand bootsteps. Hydra flak batteries were embedded either side of the château, their long-barrelled autocannons trained expectantly at the sky. A hundred yards to our left the silhouettes of two Imperial bunkers marred the skyline. Despite Plient's assurances, it seemed the château was struggling to drain the land, for the fortifications appeared lopsided, as though slowly sinking into the foetid soil.

I glanced to him. 'Governor Dolos must be delighted to have so many guests.'

'She… understands the necessity of the war effort, sir,' Plient replied. 'Still, once the greenskins are crushed she'll be happy to see the back of us.'

'You think that will be soon?'

'Hard to say, sir. The local lads don't recall a time before the orks, but they were manageable then. It's only recently they've become threat enough that Governor Dolos requested additional support. But now reinforcements are continually inbound. That must mean we're pushing them back.'

'I'm sure their defeat is imminent.' I nodded, my gaze shifting to a servitor lumbering from the château. Remarkably well maintained, its mechanical components gleamed like silver, but as it drew closer it became clear that such care extended only to its augmetics. Its flesh was the greyest I'd seen on a servitor, and the skin around its implants was blistered and sickly looking.

It stopped afore me, its remaining organic eye fixed ahead. Its mouth opened to speak, but the lips did not move, the sound instead originating from a vox-speaker in its torso.

'Welcome, honoured guest. Confirm identity and destination.'

'Propagandist Kile Simlex. Guest suite,' Plient replied, speaking into the machine's torso before glancing to me. 'There you are, sir. Garrie here will take your luggage and escort you to your room.'

'Garrie?'

'I… I sometimes name them,' Plient said as the machine lumbered over to my cases. 'I don't know why. Silly really.'

'There's no harm in it,' I said, and shrugged, my gaze flitting to the runways. 'Tell me, will Flight Commander Shard be touching down?'

'No, sir, she will perform another pass. If those orks slipped through our perimeter it's possible there are more.'

'Ah.' I nodded. 'Of course. A pity, though. I would have liked to extend my thanks for our rescue.'

'You'll get the chance, sir.'

'Well, thank you again, flight sergeant. I imagine you have other duties to attend to?'

'Indeed, sir. Thank you for your understanding.' He smiled, bobbing his head. 'I'll get back to maintenance. We have a couple of fighters that need to be patched up.'

'You assist the tech-priests?'

'In a manner of speaking, sir,' he replied, his gaze shifting to his feet. 'The enginseers are stretched thin between the regiments.'

'I see. And you have been sanctioned to conduct repairs in their absence?'

'That's what they tell me, sir.'

It was not quite an answer, but I did not pursue the matter.

'Well, good day to you, Plient. I hope we meet again soon.'

'My pleasure, sir.' He nodded, throwing out a crisp salute before spinning on his heel and marching across the grounds.

I turned to find the servitor and my possessions gone. I glanced round, fearful, only to spot it entering the château's vestibule, cases in tow. I raced in pursuit, pushing my way through the press of bodies, struggling to keep pace. I caught a glimpse of it rising from the crowd, ascending a plush staircase. It was remarkably even-footed, plodding along at a steady pace whilst I found myself stumbling and tripping in my haste. Despite their gilded veneer, the stairs were rather uneven, the wood warped and cracked in places.

We ascended for what seemed an age, and I began to panic. Though hardly spritely, the servitor was tireless despite its load, and I fell further behind. At any moment I feared I would lose sight of it.

'Slow down!' I gasped.

But the machine did not respond. Mercifully, it abandoned the ascent at the next floor, veering down the leftmost corridor. It turned twice more before halting beside a door. As it attended the lock I leant against the adjacent wall, gasping for breath. The door was comprised of the same wood as the rest of the building, but I found myself wondering how its mechanisms functioned. The frame must have been cut, but it looked almost as though the wood had been coaxed into its current shape, the doorway an organic extension of the corridor, untainted by saw or blade.

The servitor was still struggling with the lock. It had inserted a key, but was unable to turn it. Tentatively I reached for it, wary the cybernetic servant might inadvertently break my fingers whilst fulfilling its function. But it released its grip, apparently pro- grammed to prioritise human safety, and I took hold of the key, working it back and forth, until eventually something clicked and the door swung open. As the servitor entered, my trunk clasped in its servo-claw, I examined the key. It too was wooden, though the hardness and texture were closer to rock. Still, it must have been ancient, the teeth worn by time's passage.

The servitor deposited my equipment, then turned and brushed past me, its duties fulfilled. As it disappeared along the corridor, I stepped into my room, closing the door behind me, alone for the first time since my arrival.

Except for my cases. The smaller was standard issue, containing my modest essentials. But the larger stood as high as my shoulders, and was at least twice their width. It was cast in obsidian, the dark metal emblazoned by bronze edging and an Imperial aquila of burnished gold. Within lay my eyes and ears, voice and memory, the tools by which I worked my art.

I rested my hand on the case, before glancing around the room, seeking the connection point with which to power the device.

There was only bark. Even the bed and furnishing were carved from wood, and light was provided by twinkling candelabra.

A search followed, until I eventually found a hidden panel, its brass hinges painted to resemble the wood's hue. Behind was an antiquated portable power unit which, mercifully, someone had had the foresight to charge. As I connected it, I found my gaze lingering on the crawl space behind the panel. There was an unpleasant sheen to the wood, and a faint scent of mildew. I picked at it with my nail, and was rewarded by a palm-sized chunk coming away in my hand. Beneath, the wood had rotted away, supplanted by tendril-like roots with tiny pink buds that quivered despite the lack of breeze.

Carefully, I closed the panel. Behind me the case hummed into life.

I rose, approaching the device and tracing a pattern across the concealed gene-lock. With an audible hiss it folded open, and I was greeted by the leering smiles of three servo-skulls. They stared at me from their housings, once-empty eye sockets supplanted with optic sensors and pict-cams. Each cranium housed an advanced cogitator, capable of processing vast streams of data, as well as interfacing with my own cerebral implant. Each also possessed an anti-gravity field generator in place of a spine, along with a series of spindly limbs and curious devices that, I confess, I did not fully understand.

I knelt before them, murmuring the Litany of Activation. As I did so I looked over the names inscribed beneath each.

Mizar, the Fearless.

Kikazar, the Patient.

And, of course, the renowned Iwazar, the Artisan.

Each was once a renowned propagandist, so dedicated to their craft that they continued to serve even in death. They were my seer-skulls, recording my encounters and spinning the memories into image and sound. Most propagandists were equipped with at least one such device, but to be entrusted with three was a rare honour. But I was in ascension, insisting I required such resources to capture the truth, rather than forge it from data-scraps. Faith had been placed in me, but I still had much to prove.

I inspected each in turn, ensuring they had survived the journey unscathed.

'Kikazar – engage data extract.'

The skull shuddered, its optic sensor blazing red. Slowly it rose, settling beside my right shoulder where it surveyed the room, its machine-spirit seeking the familiar or hostile. The abundance of bark seemed to confuse it.

'Kikazar, data extract,' I repeated, keeping my gaze fixed ahead.

Its cold metal limbs brushed against my shoulder as it sought the connection, my mind syncing with the machine's cogitator. The sensation was unpleasant, like having a stiletto scraped over one's brainstem, as the seer-skull began to transcribe my memories of the past few hours, reducing the subjective experiences to hard data. Images rose of their own volition: meeting Flight Sergeant Plient in the orbital station, the descent through Bacchus' atmosphere and greenskin attack. I re-experienced the terror and confusion, and the relief as our liberator arrived. Once more I saw Flight Commander Shard's Lightning soar into view.

'Kikazar, pause upload.'

The machine shuddered and I felt a stab of pain. But there it was, the image copied from my mind's eye. I could now see the craft in full relief. Its fuselage was a sandy brown, presumably to match the colour of the swamps, and its wings were adorned with the image of a black griffin on a red field, the symbol borrowed from the von Shard family crest.

'Zoom and enhance, grid sixteen by twenty-four.'

The image condensed into a close-up of the cockpit. The pilot was barely visible. Not a surprise; the craft had been moving too fast to capture a true representation. Even if it had done so, my memory was too fallible to preserve such a snapshot.

'Iwazar, access files designated "Shard". Project half-dozen assorted, random selection.'

The second servo-skull bobbed cheerily from its storage unit, tiny arms clicking as it flexed its joints. The projector in its left eye flared, spectral images materialising around me. The quality varied significantly. Here was a grainy shot of a scowling child, the data-source unknown. Beside it was an official holo-portrait, where a young woman with pallid skin and flame-red hair glared into the recorder. She would have been an adolescent, having just enrolled in the schola progenium following her parents' deaths. No doubt she still grieved their loss, but there was little sorrow in her eyes, only a cold fury. Her lip was unscarred then, the injury earned at some point during her studies.

I turned to the most recent image, captured a few months ago. It must have been taken post-battle, the squad celebrating their victory. They were cropped so only she remained, clad in full dress uniform, hand resting on the pommel of her sabre, the other cradling a glass. Her eyes were fixed straight ahead. She must have been aware the pict had been taken, but there was no smile, though the scar twisted her lip into something between a grin and a sneer.

Having now heard her speak, I wondered if the expression was a reflection of her disposition rather than an injury.

'Attempt data-splice.'

The seer-skull bobbed in acknowledgement, its inner mechanisms whirring as it began assimilating the various files. The blurred pict of the cockpit slowly condensed into something clearer, as the seer-skull mapped Shard's features onto the pilot. Her eyes were cold and calculating as she took the shot, but her mouth was stretched wide in a battle cry, as she basked in the savage joy of combat.

But it did not look right; the expressions did not tally. Though the technique was impressive and the final product convincing, it was artifice, an imitation spun from light and memory. I could not know whether it truly captured that moment, or was a facsimile born from data-scraps and my own preconceptions.

'Erase splice.'

The image vanished, though I wish the same could be said for the temptation. Splicing unrelated images to forge a sanctioned narrative was a propagandist's craft and trade. Indeed, before his interment and new life as my seer-skull, Propagandist Fiwel Iwazar had been renowned for his ability to weave image and audio with the flair of an artist and the precision of a surgeon, crafting stunning works from data-scraps. He could blend disparate images and sound until even the most talented propagandist would struggle to separate his facsimile from raw footage.

I respected the man's brilliance. But his methods seemed dishonourable to me, for through such trickery any lie could be framed as truth. And I believe in the Imperium, and the benevolence of the God-Emperor. It was His galaxy, and my task was to enlighten the doubtful by showing His truth, not forging my own. I would fulfil my commission and produce a holo-pict depicting the Imperium's superiority over the rampaging orks. But it would not be a manufactured tale to suit a narrative. Every shot, moment and encounter would be as real as possible. I would use her true face, not a crafted facsimile.

'Sir?'

The voice came from the other side of the door. I did not recognise it, though it sounded deferential, if not affectionate.

'All shut down,' I murmured, the images folding around me. 'Yes?'

'Pardon, sir, but may I enter?'

'Very well.'

The handle turned but the door did not open. I could hear the voice muttering and felt the shudder as a shoulder was applied to the wood. I had not locked it, but it seemed the door did not fit its frame.

Another shudder, but this time it abruptly swung open, pitching the servant to the floor. He rose swiftly, despite his advanced age, brushing down his lapels and smoothing what remained of his greying hair into place, masking his embarrassment with a look of practised contempt.

'Ahem,' he said, clearing his throat. 'Forgive the intrusion, Propagandist Simlex. I am Stylee, Governor Dolos' personal steward. We were supposed to meet outside the château.'

There was reproach in his tone, bordering on impertinence. But his manner was subservient enough, bowing so deeply I feared his face would collide with the floor.

'My apologies,' I said. 'I was anxious to get settled.'

'I understand, my lord, but this is an old house, and it houses old secrets,' he replied, his gaze shifting to the power cable running from the seer-skulls' docking station to the false panel. 'Who connected your unit?'

'I did.'

'I would ask you to refrain from doing so,' he said. 'There are… issues incorporating technology into this structure, and such matters are best left to the household staff.'

'I see. I will know for next time.'

'Indeed,' he said, his gaze falling to my hands folded in my lap. 'You did not… cut yourself?'

'No. Should I have?'

'Of course not, sir,' he replied stiffly. 'I merely wished to ascertain your safety.'

'Well, I am quite well,' I said, offering a smile. 'Is there anything else with which I might assist you?'

He looked at me as though I were an idiot. I suppose it was an odd question. I was the respected visitor, imbued with authority far beyond my meagre rank. To a servant, my words must have seemed a non sequitur.

'I am here to escort you to Governor Dolos' suite for dinner,' he said, looking me up and down. 'I apologise for interrupting you whilst you were dressing.'

'I was not dressing.'

'You intend to dine with the governor dressed in this manner?'

I glanced down. My garments were simple and unadorned, intended not to attract undue attention. Though on closer inspection, I had to concede they were caked in dust, and the hem of my robes dirtied from my passage through the mire.

'Perhaps I should change,' I said, once again glancing around my room. 'Is there a washing facility?'

Stylee gave a near-imperceptible sigh, raising his hand and clicking his fingers twice. Two bulky footmen entered, flanking me. Both were clad in the governor's livery, their faces hard and eyes cold. If either had carried a weapon, I would have taken them for guards or enforcers.

'Ensure the propagandist is washed and dressed, and be quick,'

Stylee barked, as the pair took hold of my arms and escorted me from the room. 'The governor will not tolerate undue delay.'

From his tone, it struck me that tolerance was not one of Governor Dolos' virtues.

CHAPTER FOUR

'I present Propagandist Kile Simlex.'

Stylee's voice had surprising depth. As he made the announcement his arm swept out, directing me through the doorway and into the dining suite. I took a step forward, trying to carry myself with a modicum of assumed nobility. But my ill-fitted robes caught on my heel, and I only avoided falling on my face by breaking into a half-run, jogging awkwardly into the centre of the room, Kikazar hovering at my shoulder.

It was an impressive space, the table organically grown like the other furnishings, the walls adorned with portraits and landscapes depicting Bacchus and its noble lineage. The room was spotless too, the wood buffed till it shone like burnished bronze. I could smell the floral notes of the wood polish, but there was something else too: a hint of mildew, unsuccessfully masked.

Aside from two footmen, the room was empty.

I turned but Stylee was already closing the door behind him, leaving me as the only guest, my host seemingly indisposed. A servant appeared beside me, pouring a glass of wine the colour of copper. I took it, nodding my thanks. The man bowed before retreating, reluctant to speak. This suited me well enough; small talk was not my forte. It would be poor form to sit before my host arrived, so I elected to stand by the window, watching the ground crew toiling. The fact that my pose mirrored the servants was not lost on me. Still, they could only serve the wine, whilst I at least could drink it.

I took a sip. It was good, which was hardly a surprise. Bacchus was lauded throughout the subsector for the quality of its liquors, and this was not the first time I had enjoyed a glass. Yet there was a faint aftertaste. Like the scent of mildew, it lurked beneath the delicate notes of honey-mead and sweet berries. But I could not ignore the faint but palatable bitterness. Though initially almost imperceptible, it was now all I could taste.

'Please welcome her ladyship, Planetary Governor Ariani Dolos.'

Stylee had reappeared without my notice. Perhaps his prior employment was as a purse-slitter or assassin. Regardless, he stepped aside, and for the first time I laid eyes on the governor in all her splendour. She was tall. Taller than me, the effect accentuated by tapered heels and a gilded headdress complete with half-mask that covered her eyes. The piece stretched a foot above her head and would surely strain the neck of the most bullish soldier. I kept expecting her to topple sideways, but she glided towards me with remarkable grace. Her amethyst robes were, like mine, laughably oversized, the opulent folds a traditional style designed to display wealth and prestige.

She was an arm's width from me before I remembered protocol, bowing as deep as I could with the blasted robes bunching around my waist.

'Please rise, Propagandist Simlex,' she said, painted lips forming a practised smile. 'I am so sorry for keeping you waiting.'

'Not at all, governor. I appreciate how busy you must be.'

'Always,' she sighed, taking a glass from one of the servants. 'But I was determined to make time for a man of your obvious station. It is rare we receive visitors from Hedon. I was surprised to find I would be hosting you.'

'I do apologise for the disruption.'

'How quaint. So far you are the only one of my guests to do so,' she said, eyeing the ground crew through the window. 'Still, when the request comes from Governor Zanwich's private office, how can I refuse?'

She sipped her wine, stiffening just a fraction as it touched her lips, before glancing to me.

'Tell me, do they still favour our wine on Hedon?'

'Yes, your ladyship,' I replied, truthfully enough. 'It still commands great interest and, if you will forgive me, exorbitant prices.'

She smiled. It seemed a little more genuine this time.

'Yes, people will pay for the best.'

'Indeed.' I nodded, taking up my own glass. 'Particularly given current shortages.'

I was not looking directly at her as I spoke, my gaze settling on one of the furniture-like servants. But from the way he stiffened, it was evident this was the wrong thing to say. I turned back, ready to offer the most obsequious apology, but she said nothing, merely smiling and raising her glass. If offended, she was exceptional at hiding it.

I ducked her gaze, taking a nervous sip of my increasingly questionable wine, its bitterness heavy on the palate. Was she the sort of noble who preferred to express their displeasure in private? Perhaps somewhere dark and hidden, where blood could be easily wiped clean?

'Yes, there has been a cut in production,' she said, glancing to the window. 'Regrettably, we must cater for the needs of the God-Emperor's armies. But it's comforting to know that this only makes our produce more desirable.'

'Quite so,' I nodded, though if a noble on Hedon had tasted that particular wine they would have tossed the bottle from the nearest window. 'It must be difficult running the estate with the military present,' I ventured.

She nodded. 'Indeed. Of course, I am happy to offer the Imperium's forces whatever assistance I can provide. But I confess surprise at how long it takes to resolve a trivial conflict such as ours. Frankly, were I in command, I would simply dispatch a platoon into the swamps and drive those filthy greenskins out. I am sure you have seen how inhospitable the terrain is. How many can truly scratch a living out there?'

'How long have they troubled you?'

'I have no idea,' she replied, her ignorance brandished like a shield. 'There have been stories of a few subsisting in the outskirts of the swamps for as long as I remember, though how much faith you place in those tales is your own business. But I do know a bunch of spear-wielding xenos should pose little challenge to the might of the Imperium.'

'They do seem a trifle better equipped than that. My escort was shot down on arrival, and I was lucky to escape.'

'Unfortunate,' she said. 'But an isolated incident. Those vile creatures have snatched a few craft lost by our more careless pilots. They are talented thieves, coveting our superior weapons even as they adorn them with crude glyphs. But a handful of ork fighters is a non-factor. To defeat them we merely need fewer planes to steal and more boots on the ground.'

Bile had crept into her voice, and it was not just directed at the greenskins. But she caught herself, masking her resentments beneath a well-honed smile.

'But I digress,' she said. 'We're really here to talk about you! Propagandist Simlex. A man with such vision that he enjoys the patronage of our cousin, Planetary Governor Zanwich. We are honoured to accommodate you, though I am a little perplexed as to why you are here. Charming as it is, I would not think Bacchus would hold much interest to the wider Imperium. Other than for our wines of course!'

She laughed, a braying sound reminiscent of a rutting grox. I smiled and took a sip to hide my discomfort, praying that the question was rhetorical. But the way she stared at me suggested that an answer was needed.

And I worried the wrong response might invite unpleasant consequences.

'My department has produced prior picts extolling the Aero-nautica Imperialis,' I said. 'But they are not our finest work. I am here to change that.'

'Commendable,' she said, nodding. 'But not the answer to the question I asked. Why here? There must be a million such conflicts across the galaxy. What drew you to Subsector Yossar-ian? Why are you on my planet?'

Her words were perfectly polite, her manner hinting nothing beyond a passing curiosity. But she overestimated her guile, a common failing among our aristocrats. They spend their lives surrounded by people who acquiesce to their every whim and laugh at their most pitiful jokes, and therefore struggle to accurately assess their own talents. The result is individuals of stupendous self-confidence but limited self-awareness.

But this was her planet, and offending her would be unwise.

'May I be candid?' I asked.

She nodded, as though granting special dispensation.

'I am here because I have a particular interest in the project. But this world was chosen because the governor of Hedon is, like you, concerned by how long this conflict has drawn out. And recruitment is suffering.'

'Surely that is what conscription is for?'

'It has a place,' I said. 'But it can be resource intensive. Why rely on conscription when we can instead inspire the loyal masses to throw themselves into the fray? And, where the Navy are concerned, it is skilled workers we seek, rather than simply strength in numbers.'

'So, you seek to woo more workers?'

'In part,' I said, nodding. 'But Governor Zanwich also desires a pict demonstrating that our forces are overcoming the orks, and that the sector should not be concerned by the conflict escalating.'

'Well, there we agree,' she said. 'Though perhaps the most expedient solution would be putting someone new in charge. I have no doubt Wing Commander Prospherous is a capable soldier, but I suspect he is out of his depth.'

'I could not comment. But, even were it within Governor Zanwich's power to dismiss him, I doubt the governor would support appointing a new commander. It might indicate the war is... not going as well as has been previously suggested.'

'Ah,' she said, glancing to the window. 'And Governor Zanwich fears that could impact on Hedon's coffers?'

I nodded. Hedon was a garden world, a meticulously terraformed paradise. It was a retreat for the elite of the Imperium, somewhere idyllic where they could bathe in crystal waters, survey beautiful landscapes, and enjoy the most exquisite food and company. If it were known Hedon neighboured a planet that was rapidly devolving into a warzone, it might discourage their clientele.

'Then you are here to show our inevitable victory?' she said.

'It was not quite put to me in those terms. But I suspect my role is, in part, to demonstrate the inevitability of victory.'

'I see,' she said, still intent on the window. I followed her gaze. There appeared to be a commotion, though from above it looked more like insects labouring than soldiers.

'And why you?' she said. 'Why are you the man for the pict?'

I smiled. 'I was fortunate enough to receive a recommendation from an influential commissar. I hope I can live up to his expectations.'

'But you are not from Hedon?'

'No, though I am told I have some familial connection to the planet.'

Her head tilted, as if she had registered a sound beyond my hearing. 'Simlex,' she murmured. 'Not a family known to me.'

'It is distant. I had not set foot on Hedon until a month ago.'

'Well, you must tell me what you saw there,' she said, suddenly jovial. 'Come, let us sit and eat. The fashions their nobles favour change like the seasons, and I do hate to be out of date.'

She stepped away from the window, but in doing so revealed flood-lumens now lighting the sky. They seemed to be coming from the bunkers, and there came a distant wailing too, the noise intensifying with every passing second.

'Governor, what is that?' I asked. But she did not reply, merely gesturing to the aircraft being drawn from the leftmost bunker. A crowd had gathered around, but it was too dark to see clearly, the glare of flood-lumens only serving to dazzle me further.

But I caught sight of a figure striding towards the lead craft.

'Mizar, on my sight,' I murmured.

There came a sharp twinge in my temple as the connection between our cogitators was established. The seer-skull shed its housing, sensors flickering into life. Through machine-eyes it surveyed my room, its gaze falling to the window that I had, regrettably, neglected to open. The glass shattered on impact as it sped towards the runway, Mizar's sensors effortlessly piercing the darkness. On the runway were three Lightning fighters, air superiority flyers known for their manoeuvrability and temperamental machine-spirits, awaiting their launch. But even through Mizar's eyes, the pilots were not visible. Perhaps the wing markings would be clearer. If one of them featured the griffin motif, then–

'Propagandist Simlex?'

I stiffened. Governor Dolos was seated at the table. Behind her, a footman had entered carrying a steaming tray. It smelt... good? With my perceptions split between Mizar and the meal it was difficult to be sure. I kept tasting promethium fumes.

'Is there something troubling you?' Dolos asked, this time making no effort to disguise her tone.

'No, governor – please forgive my rudeness,' I said, taking the seat opposite as the waiter poured a fresh glass of bitter wine.

Through Mizar's eye I saw the engines flare, the craft slowly lifting skywards before accelerating into the night. The seer-skull tried to follow, pushing its anti-gravitational engines to their limit, its telescopic lens straining to keep the vehicles in sight. But it was futile.

The Lightnings' afterburners flared, and with one final burst, were lost to the darkness.

CHAPTER FIVE

The fighters returned just as dessert was served.

I was the first to set eyes on them. Mizar's eyes, anyway. I had coaxed the seer-skull into abandoning its pursuit, a challenge given its rambunctious machine-spirit. It was left suspended high above the château, sensors sweeping the sky for any trace of the Lightnings. From this vantage point it observed a surprising amount of activity, though none of it attributable to aircraft. Insects swarmed across distant swamps, their iridescent armour shimmering lilac in the borrowed light of the twin moons. At such distance it was hard to judge scale, but I estimated they were at least the size of my hand, excluding the trio of wings sprouting from their backs.

The estate was no more subdued. Ground crew hurried about their business, relaying messages and clearing runways, while Dolos' servants fulfilled their functions and servitors hauled equipment. I spied three such machines heading for the château's rear, the moonlight glinting from their bladed limbs. I feared an assault was imminent, until they halted and set to work on the château's east wing, attacking a series of tendril-like roots emerging from cracks in the bark.

In other circumstances balancing reconnaissance and dinner might have proved challenging. Fortunately, Governor Dolos was happy to carry the conversation, regaling me with the glorious history of her household and the burden and joy she found in continuing their legacy. She spoke at length of the upcoming Harvest Banquet, the apparent jewel in Bacchus' social calendar, and made a point of apologising profusely for being unable to extend to me an invitation.

As our main was served – barbecued grubs drizzled in a jus derived from their progenitor's venom – she began discussing the military presence. Or, as she began to refer to it, the occupation. I pushed the food about my plate, nodding and making the occasional exclamation when it seemed appropriate. The questionable wine continued to flow, though primarily into her glass; I had endured all the bitterness I could stomach.

She was about half a drink from supine when Stylee entered, announcing the arrival of the dessert cart as if it were a distinguished dignitary. As a footman pushed it towards our table, Governor Dolos leaned forward, taking up her glass on the second attempt, sloshing wine about her fingers.

'I would make a toast,' she said, over-enunciating each syllable. 'To your successful project, and the end to this sorry little war.'

As I raised my dregs, Mizar chirped in the back of my mind. No visual yet, but increased activity among the ground crews. It also registered atmospheric distortion at their approach. The fighters were incoming.

I glanced to Stylee. He held a razored knife, and was poised to cut into a cake with suspiciously iridescent icing. The lilac colour was a little too reminiscent of the indigenous insects for my comfort, particularly given the decorative membranes, and the way the cake undulated was rather disconcerting.

The governor drained her glass, motioning for one of the silent footmen to replenish her.

I did not wish to risk offence by excusing myself, but I was desperate to greet the returning pilots, and finally meet Flight Commander Shard. Caught between fear and duty, I felt paralysed, and could only stare as the knife sank into the cake.

Something skuttled from the opening, disappearing under the table. That clinched it.

'Governor Dolos, I cannot thank you enough for this delightful repast,' I said, bowing my head. 'But I have just received word that our pilots have returned.'

'Yes, they are always doing that,' she slurred, gesturing with the glass and splashing wine over the attending footman. To his credit he did not react, his gaze fixed ahead as the liquid dripped from his chin.

'One has to ask why of course,' she continued, readjusting her lopsided headdress. 'So much back and forth. Rearming and refuelling. Poisoning my estate and crippling my planet's industry, just so they can go out and do it all over again. Why? Just send the Guardsmen in. There's a finite number of orks – it isn't as though they sprout out of the ground.'

'Quite so,' I nodded. 'However, it is my sworn duty to chronicle the conflict. Much as I would prefer to remain here, I must respectfully ask your leave.'

I bowed again. It was awkward whilst sitting, but preferable to maintaining eye contact. When I raised my head, she was still intent on me, though with her mask lopsided it was difficult to discern her expression.

'You're leaving now?' she said. 'In the middle of dinner?'

'Believe me, I would prefer your company to fraternising with the grunts,' I said, ensuring a hint of disdain crept into my voice. 'And I would never seek to depart without your permission. But before I left Hedon I promised Planetary Governor Zanwich that I would dedicate every spare moment to this project, and–'

'You spoke to Governor Zanwich?' She frowned, the slur suddenly absent. 'Why in the God-Emperor's name were you granted an audience? The man is practically a recluse. I haven't seen him in years.'

'It was brief, and only due to our family's connection.' I shrugged. 'Still, it was a great honour.'

She did not reply, though I noted Stylee had set the knife down, his expression darting between us.

'You are related to Governor Zanwich?' she said, incredulous.

'Only by marriage, and barely by that. I think we are cousins thirteen times removed? Or he might also be a distant uncle. Or possibly nephew – I confess the details escape me. I only found out after agreeing to the assignment.'

No response. Besides the blank stare. I shifted, uncomfortable. Even the statue-like footman looked awkward.

'Governor Dolos?' I eventually asked.

'Hmm?' She blinked.

'May I take my leave?'

'Oh… but of course,' she replied warmly. 'As I said, I fully support your project, as it would appear does Governor Zanwich. This does not surprise me – I always thought the two of us were of a similar mind.'

'Thank you,' I said, rising.

'Take dessert with you,' she demanded. 'Stylee, wrap him a slice.'

'Very kind, governor.' I bowed. 'But I am quite satisfied.'

'Wine then,' she said. 'Fill his glass.'

Stylee grimaced. 'Pardon me, Governor Dolos, but the glasses are part of a limited set that has been in your family for centuries. I worry one of the military grunts may attempt to snatch one if we–'

'A bottle, then,' she snapped, glaring at him. 'And don't interrupt!'

A bottle was pressed into my hands. It was best not to argue.

'I look forward to seeing you again soon,' Governor Dolos said from her chair. It seemed she did not intend to rise. Whether this was appropriate to her status, or because she was reluctant to test her equilibrium, I could not say.

I bowed for what felt like the hundredth time, my focus with Mizar. Through its eye, I watched the aircraft descend, their landing jets flaring like fallen stars, fuselages marred by the weapons of our enemy. A crowd had already gathered to greet the returned heroes. I hastened to join them.

As the door closed behind me, I could hear Governor Dolos demanding her servants fetch the genealogy tomes.

'It was coming up right behind me, and my lascannons couldn't pierce that damn hull. But then, just as the damnable greenskin was about to unload its incendiary missiles, I switched targets. Aimed for his payload instead. Not sure what orks use in place of promethium, but it was sufficient to consume not only his craft but most of his squadron. And that, my friends, is how an upstart greenskin colloquially known as the Bringer of Flames met his end, consumed by the fires of his making. And if you thought orks already smelt bad, trying catching a whiff of one that's chargrilled.'

A roar of laughter drowned all other sounds. I felt Mizar recalibrate its audio sensors, even as I approached the ever-expanding throng, still clutching the bottle I had been reluctantly gifted. I had debated disposing of it en route, but did not wish to risk Dolos' servants stumbling across it.

The press of bodies briefly parted, and I saw a figure reclining on the nose of a craft, lazily holding court. Then the crowd shifted, blocking my view. Someone yelled a question I could not hear.

'How many did I kill?' she asked, voice clear above the hubbub of the crowd. 'You think I keep track, Hikits? Do you tally the rivets you tighten each day? Actually, that's a poor comparison – you probably do.'

The laughter surrounded me now, as I was subsumed by the crowd. I still could not see her, nor could I navigate the press of bodies to get closer, and whatever voice I had was swallowed by the throng. I wanted to see her with my own eyes, but was forced to shift my focus to Mizar, who hovered high above.

She sat astride one of the two remaining craft, as servitors towed the others towards their hangar. She still wore her helmet, which was shading her face, but her flight suit was unzipped and had been pulled down to the waist, revealing bare arms and shoulders, the skin pale as moonlight. Like me, she had a bottle in her hand, though it held only dregs.

'You think you got the Green Storm this time?' someone asked, their voice audible through Mizar's sensors.

'Who?' She frowned, glancing to the speaker in feigned confusion. The crowd bellowed uproariously, though the reference was lost on me. Shard stared at the speaker a moment longer before slapping her forehead, suddenly remembering. The gesture knocked the helm from her head, revealing a close-cropped shock of hair that was such a rich shade of red that I initially thought Mizar's optics required adjustment.

'Oh, *that* Green Storm,' she said. 'Who knows? The greenskins all look the same to me – green.'

As she drained her drink the crowd howled again, the sound bordering on hysteria. I have rarely seen front-line combat, and only from a distance. But this phenomenon was not unknown to me. Post victory, fear recedes and laughter comes easily. Even the most stringent commissar may turn a blind eye to it. For a time.

Shard lowered the bottle from her lips, tossing it over her shoulder, where it shattered on the cockpit of the adjacent craft, spraying glass over the servitors who were attempting to open it. From within I caught a flicker of movement, and she held her hand to her mouth in mock surprise.

'My heartfelt apologies, Flight Commander Gradeolous,' she said, addressing the sealed craft. 'I really wasn't aiming, only scored a hit by chance. You understand – isn't that your dog-fighting technique?'

As the crowd cackled, Mizar's sensors sought to pierce the cockpit. I got the impression of a large man, his face dominated by a rigid moustache. His eyes blazed, mouth drawn in a snarl so vicious that even an ork might have taken note. But the cockpit provided exemplary soundproofing, and though his mouth snapped open and shut, and his fist thumped against the armaglass, I could not discern his words. It seemed likely he objected to Shard's comments, but trapped in the cockpit there was little he could do about it. Flight Sergeant Plient was endeavouring to assist, directing a pair of servitors to prise it open, but they were struggling.

Shard cupped her hand to her ear, as though straining to hear.

'Sorry, what was that?' she said with a frown. 'You'd like to finally concede that I am the greatest fighter ace of all time? Why, Flight Commander Gradeolous, that's very generous. Everyone else realised it ages ago, but it's heartening that you've finally caught up. Shame you can't do the same when we're flying.'

With that closing remark she vaulted from the fighter, landing lightly beside the aircraft. As the crowd parted I saw her make for the château, her path taking her straight for me. I blinked, departing from Mizar and returning to my own body. She was a few paces from me, bantering with someone in the crowd.

I took a deep breath and stepped forward.

'Flight Commander Shard?' I said. 'My name is Propagandist Simlex, and I am here to–'

'Sorry, I don't sign things,' she said, barely glancing at me. But as she turned away her gaze caught the bottle still clasped in my hand. She stopped, then took it, appraising the label. 'Hmm... Not the best but better than nothing,' she conceded, meeting my gaze. 'All right, I will sign one thing. Where's the quill?'

'Quill? No, I do not need anything signed. I am here–'

'Oh. Then thank you for your support.' She nodded, raising the bottle before turning away.

I called after her, brandishing a sealed scroll.

'Wait! I have a letter of introduction from your brother!'

She froze, glancing back to me, her smile absconded.

'Excuse me?'

'Your brother, Commissar Tobia von Shard?' I persisted, my voice faltering. 'I served with him on–'

She advanced on me, snatching the scroll from my hand and tearing the seal with her thumb.

'Hmm,' she said, barely glancing at the page. 'A shame. It seems illegible due to fire damage.'

'What? But I kept–'

Flames suddenly consumed the scroll. I did not see from whence the lighter materialised, but as she tucked it into her pocket the crowd roared in approval, even if they were unaware exactly what had transpired. She then pushed past me, her well-wishers flooding after and drowning out my protestations. As she approached the château she turned one final time, raising the bottle.

'My dear friends. And I mean both of you,' she said, to laughs from the crowd. 'Young Plient tells me my Lightning will require extensive repairs, so I intend to take some leave and continue the celebrations in my suite. I would invite a few of you to join me, but you've already begun to bore me.'

A cascade of boos and catcalls followed. She offered a low bow in response before departing, the crowd trailing after her. Behind me, I heard the servitors finally wrench the cockpit open. Flight Commander Gradeolous erupted from within, spewing curses in Shard's wake.

'You thrice-wretched cur!' he spat, gesticulating wildly. 'Come back here and face me! Coward!'

But she was long gone, and the other soldiers were returning to their duties, even as he continued to curse her name.

It was not the most auspicious of introductions.

CHAPTER SIX

I slept poorly, awaking in the early hours with frost crystallising on the shattered pane. Though I bound myself tighter under the blankets, sleep would not come that night.

Everything was falling apart before it had even started. I had utterly failed to engage with Shard, or any of the aces. I had no footage of worth and, worse than that, could not think how to obtain it if the pilots refused to speak to me. Even Mizar's sophisticated sensors could not track the aircraft with any reliability once in flight. How was I supposed to capture their aerial battles without their assistance?

Perhaps my predecessor was right. Perhaps it was better to splice images together, create preposterous scenarios where lascannons snipe orks and aces offer salutes to children. Better that than trying to barter with entitled pilots who thought themselves above me.

I rolled onto my side, my back to the window. I could feel the draught, the cold somehow penetrating the mounds of fabric.

I could not stop picturing her face. That disdainful expression, her scarred lip twisted into a sneer. She had looked through me at first, then regarded me with contempt. The rejection had stung, for I had envisioned our introduction in a different setting, some festivity or other event. I imagined her being excited at the prospect of the pict, flattered that I had chosen her as the focus. How stupid I had been. The whole thing was absurd. She was a soldier, her record speaking for itself. Her family had been loyal servants of the Imperium for generations. She was not a lowly civilian inspired to enlist by a stirring pict. It was likely she had never heard of me, and if she viewed a letter from her brother with such disdain, why should I expect any different?

I sat upright, dislodging the tangled bedding. It was still freezing, though a glance to the broken window suggested dawn was encroaching. But my anger had fortified me against the cold. For I was angry: a little at her, but mostly at myself. It was as if I had spliced a pict of my own before I had even arrived, fuelled by conceit and a thirst for acclaim. I had to move beyond that, deal with the situation as it was.

It was then I heard the siren's whine. It was faint, and probably would have escaped me were the window still glazed. I glanced to the shattered pane, seeing nothing, but the seer-skulls stirred in their charge-pods, sensing something unseen to me.

A second later it became apparent. A distant smoke trail framed by the morning light.

'Mizar,' I murmured. The seer-skull needed no further encouragement, disengaging from its siblings and streaking from the room. Through its eye I saw the craft veering towards us, its flight stilted, the left wing dipping towards the swamp below. It was a Valkyrie, a craft primarily utilised for troop deployment and ground support. One of its engines had failed, but the pilot was doing an impressive job keeping it in the air. It barely cleared the château, its fallen wing clipping the roof as it attempted to set down at the building's rear, its sole remaining turbofan straining to keep it airborne.

The landing was unfortunate. Such craft are capable of descending vertically, but the pilot must have considered this an impossibility with only one engine. Or perhaps they simply lost control. Either way, the Valkyrie pitched towards the dirt. On an industrial world no one would have survived the impact. But the well-trod quagmire offered a softer landing, the aircraft ploughing a furrow through the grasping mud. Its left wing was torn clear as it spun onto its side, the right wing now pointing skywards. Ground crews were already converging, their extinguisher-packs battling the erupting flames. The pilot was dragged clear, but from the way their head was twisted it was clear they had not survived.

Then the cargo hold was wrenched open. I did not immediately recognise the uniform of the figure emerging from the vessel, his garments bloodied and armour torn. His helm was missing, revealing a crimson gash that covered half his face, and his right arm ended abruptly in a bloody stump, but neither of these injuries prevented him from bellowing at his rescuers. Mizar's audio sensors were not sophisticated enough to capture the exchange, but one of the ground crew was soon sprinting towards the château, whilst the rest redoubled their efforts. Six more soldiers were liberated from the confines of the craft, and between them there were enough battered pieces of armour to discern their nature.

They were Tempestus Scions. The most elite human soldiers of the Imperium. Fearless, loyal and armed with the finest armour and weapons the Adeptus Mechanicus could forge. I had seen them before, though usually only as parade troops or escorts for a dignitary. But even then, with gleaming armour and freshly starched greatcoats, one look in their eyes told you they were not some ceremonial entourage. They were deadly warriors who had faced and overcome the worst the galaxy could offer.

These soldiers still carried something of that spirit, but few could walk unaided, burdened by their injuries. Most had not been inflicted by the crash, for they were already bound and bandaged. The gouges in their chestplates suggested bladed weapons powerful enough to rend carapace armour.

Orks.

'Lord Simlex?'

I almost jumped from my skin. My consciousness had been so bound with Mizar that I had forgotten my own body. It still lay upon the bed, but as I peered through my own eyes, I realised I was no longer alone. Governor Dolos' steward, Stylee, had the door half-open, though he cowered behind it, as if seeking to shield himself from my wrath.

'Please enter,' I said, sitting up. A sliver of my mind remained with Mizar, but there was little to report now. Instead, I focused on the servant.

He bowed low. It took me a moment to realise he did not seem intent on rising, apparently awaiting my command.

'Please, be at ease,' I said. Stylee bobbed once in acknowledgement before raising his head. I cannot say his expression was markedly more friendly than the evening prior, his eyes still hinting at something between bemusement and disgust. But his manner could not have been more courteous.

'Forgive the intrusion, my lord,' he said. 'Governor Dolos requested I periodically check in on you, and I wanted to ensure your rest had not been disrupted by... by the God-Emperor, the window!'

'Ah, yes,' I said as he rushed over to the glass. 'An unfortunate accident. I must apologise.'

'You are not at fault, my lord,' Stylee replied, glaring through the shattered pane at the rising sun. 'It is those thrice-cursed pilots. They fly too low and too fast, uncaring of the damage inflicted. This estate is not like the slums they are familiar with. We cannot simply insert a prefabricated pane, not with a living building. The wood must be coaxed into accepting the glass. It would be days of work even if we were fully staffed.'

I was no longer sure whether he was addressing me, the muttering having devolved into a mantra of resentment. I felt a stab of guilt for not admitting fault, but he would not listen anyway. Besides, he already held his prejudices against the pilots. It was not my place to refute them.

'It is quite all right,' I said as he fussed about the frame. 'We are at war after all. We must all make sacrifices.'

'I'm sorry, my lord, but this is not acceptable,' he said, turning to face me. 'A direct descendant of Planetary Governor Zanwich shall not abide in such squalor.'

'I am not a direct descendent–' I began, but it was too late. Obeying an unseen summons, footmen had already entered and begun stripping the bed linen, despite the fact I was still nestling in the sheets. Strong hands seized my shoulders, ushering me to my feet, whilst a servitor attempted to retrieve my case, though it seemed perplexed by how to close the lid.

'Stylee? What is the meaning of this? Where am I going?' I protested.

'Our governor has decreed you be given accommodation better suited to your status,' he replied, bowing his head. 'You will be transferred to the penultimate floor, and have the honour of sleeping directly beneath her.'

Governor Dolos was at breakfast when I was ushered into her suite, the bedding still draped across my shoulders as an impromptu toga. She was unmasked, clad only in silken blue robes, and for the first time I saw her face.

She looked young, her skin smooth, lips full. But that meant little. Rejuvenat treatments could extend youth and life for hundreds of years. And though the ravages of time did not show on her skin, some hint of it was carried in the eyes. She could have been older than my grandmother, may the God-Emperor preserve her soul.

She glanced up as I entered, feigning surprise.

'Kile,' she said. 'Please be seated.'

The use of my given name surprised me. Still, it was an order. I lowered myself to the chair opposite, and through bleary eyes marvelled at the décor. The room's colour palette was heavy on vibrant reds and burnished gold, including the gilded frames which housed numerous paintings. But I had little time to dwell on them, as I could not tear my gaze from the plant holding pride of place at the breakfast table.

It was tall and broad enough to almost obscure my view of Dolos, its leaves a vibrant green flecked with amber, its flowers pink and puckered, like tiny mouths. Each housed dozens of ripe berries. They smelt enticing enough, the skin a polished mauve and flesh an inviting shade of cyan.

It was these upon which Dolos breakfasted, though I was too befuddled to have much appetite. She held no such reservations, gorging herself on the fruit, the juice staining her chin. A footman stood beside her, cloth in hand, masterfully intercepting any droplets that would have stained her robes, as well as plucking fresh berries. I noted he wore chain-link gloves, presumably to protect himself from the plant's unseen thorns.

'Mmm,' she exclaimed, as the footman daubed her chin. 'Not hungry, Kile?'

'Not at present, I've only just awoken.'

'Shame, these are a rare delicacy,' she said, holding up a berry. 'They inspire the mind, and offer vivid dreams.'

'Good dreams?'

'For the most part,' she replied. 'The images are certainly breathtaking. What on earth are you wearing?'

'I did not have time to properly dress,' I replied, my gaze flickering to the door and the salvation it offered. 'Forgive me, governor. I will depart and not return until properly attired.'

'Nonsense,' she said. 'A man of your station can wear whatever he chooses.'

'Station?' I frowned, as one of the footmen poured me a blessed cup of recaff.

'Indeed.' She smiled. 'You know, you were quite rude last night.'

'Please, I did not–'

'Imagine concealing that you are a direct descendent of Governor Zanwich,' she continued, raising a hand before I could protest. 'I know, you were being humble, and that is commendable. But think of the shame I would feel had I discovered a blood relative of the governor was relegated to floor thirty-seven? Condemned to a suite better suited to an officer, or high-ranking servant? Why, I would not have been able to show my face in public.'

'Blood relative?' I frowned. 'I'm not sure that's correct.'

'It's quite correct,' she insisted, voice suddenly sharp. 'We maintain meticulous records. Admittedly, they did not contain details of your family, but after liaising with the Adeptus Administratum I confirmed you are, in fact, in line for Governor Zanwich's title when he finally passes into the God-Emperor's embrace.'

'Really? I had no idea.'

'Absolutely. Assuming his thirty-four remaining children, their various offspring and a score of cousins, nieces, half-siblings and assorted families expire first, you are next in line. Forty-three hundredth in line, according to our calculation.'

'I see,' I said, my gaze falling to the steaming recaff. Her words were both shocking revelation and frivolous trivia, had I but believed them. But I doubted my connection to the Zanwich family, long before I set foot on Bacchus. It seemed a little too convenient, and I knew from experience my superiors were happy to forge records when required. Still, I made no effort to correct her. After all, it was not a misconception likely to make my life harder.

'You will be the talk of the Harvest Banquet,' she continued, but I was not paying much attention. Mizar was needling the edge of my consciousness, the seer-skull's machine-spirit detecting something it considered of interest.

I ignored it, focused on the governor. Her repast seemingly concluded, she rose, a chambermaid draping a robe over her shoulders.

'So, besides this evening, what are your plans for the day?' she said. 'Do you need to set up a pict-recorder studio? Because I could clear the stables, the horses are all dead anyway.'

'No, my seer-skulls are all I require,' I said, and shrugged. 'Still, I do not know how to capture aerial combat. I prefer to bear witness as events unfold, but I cannot keep pace with their craft.'

'Well, they refuse to fly slower, believe me,' she replied, slipping behind a folding screen upon which was depicted the God-Emperor's victory over the Arch-Serpent, portrayed as a reptile writhing beneath his golden boot, its single eye bared banefully. A trio of servants followed her, brandishing bodice and lace.

'I need to be up there with them,' I said, keeping my gaze fixed upon the recaff.

'Can you fly?'

'No.'

'Well, even if you could, I doubt they would permit a civilian operating in their airspace. They even try and limit my excursions. Can you imagine that?'

I could, though I did not say so.

'Why not request they take you up with them?' she continued.

'I do not know how I would even approach something like that.'

'Speak to Wing Commander Prospherous,' she replied from behind the screen. 'It's his job to assist you after all.'

'I suspect he would not see it in those terms.'

'Immaterial. This is not his planet, it is mine, and I deem your work the priority. Frankly, the commander and those like him have been abusing my hospitality for far too long. I half suspect they are dragging out this war so they can take advantage of my wine cellars. It's time they provided a favour in return.'

She emerged clad in her finery, her billowing robes supported by her aides. Her new mask and headdress were fashioned to resembled storm clouds, the lightning framing her cheeks.

'We shall speak to Prospherous and inform him of your needs.'

'Are you sure he will see us?'

'He will see us when I tell him to,' she replied sternly. 'Now, get dressed. It is time to remind the wing commander who is truly in charge.'

Wing Commander Prospherous glared at me from across his desk.

It was not a pleasant experience. I would have described his gaze as predatory, except that would convey a sense of hunger or yearning, and I saw no evidence of that. His eyes were more like blades: cold, sharp and deadly in their indifference. I was relieved Governor Dolos was also in attendance, as it forced him to split his attention, his gaze skewering us in turn. The governor seemed immune, no doubt having experienced far worse in her time. But it had been years since someone of influence had regarded me with such ill-disguised contempt. Not since my apprenticeship, though I hoped that, unlike my former master, Wing Commander Prospherous would refrain from beating me about the head.

I cleared my throat. 'Sir, if I might–'

He raised his hand, the gesture silencing me as efficiently as a bullet to the temple.

'Propagandist Simlex,' he said. 'You will, I trust, forgive me for not having seen you sooner. But there is currently a war on. An actual war, mind, not a staged conflict for the pict screens that squanders valuable resources. This is reality, life and death.'

'Yes, sir. I understand.'

'Good. Then let me be clear. We are the only airfield for leagues and are currently supporting two offensives, both of which are seeing increased activity. I have just received word that an unseasonal storm front is drifting in our direction, and I am still awaiting resupply of our rocket pods. In addition, two of my craft are currently requisitioned to provide logistical support for Governor Dolos' banquet.'

He glared at her a moment before continuing.

'And all that was prior to this morning, when a Valkyrie nearly took the roof off the governor's château.'

Dolos stiffened at his words. Apparently, she had not yet been informed of the incident. He did not quite hide his smile at her discomfort.

'I saw,' I said. 'How are your soldiers?'

'They're not my soldiers,' Prospherous replied. 'Tempestus Scions are part of the Militarum Tempestus. Nevertheless, they are currently assigned here, ostensibly under my command. Why, are you hoping to procure some footage of their injuries for the citizenry to gawp at?'

'No, sir.'

'Good,' he said. 'Because those men risked their lives, and had they not... well, that is not for you to know. As it is, I am forced to scramble pilots and craft in response.'

He was at that. Mizar still hovered above the château. Through its eye I could see the ground crews swarming across the compound like insects, loading the Thunderbolts and Lightning fighters.

'I understand, sir.'

'Then you understand there is little else I can do for you. Feel free to take some picts of the aircraft taking off, and if you can find an off-duty officer and supply them with enough alcohol I am confident they will share a few anecdotes. I will, of course, require final approval of whatever you produce. Dismissed.'

His tone did not invite debate. I was already rising when Governor Dolos' hand thrust into my chest, pushing me back into my seat. She glared at Wing Commander Prospherous from behind her storm-framed headdress.

'Need I remind you, wing commander, that we are not your soldiers. This is my home. More than that, this is my world. You do not dismiss me.'

Prospherous glared at her.

'I am perfectly aware of that,' he said through gritted teeth. 'I was dismissing Simlex here.'

'He is not yours to dismiss.'

They stared at each other, two gladiators sizing up their opponent, the world beyond all but forgotten. I hoped they would forget me as easily, for I was anxious to be anywhere else. I synced with Mizar, scanning the sky, on the off-chance another Valkyrie was going to slam into the château and provide my deliverance. But I saw only the squads of Lightnings and Thunderbolts departing. The crashed Valkyrie had been retrieved, and a replacement was being prepped to launch, the ground crew loading the heavy bolters and refuelling promethium tanks.

The governor leant forward, resting her elbows on the desk.

'Wing commander, Propagandist Simlex is here on the behest of Governor Zanwich himself. He has been ordered to produce a pict on the Aeronautica Imperialis.'

'Is that right?' Prospherous replied, raising an eyebrow.

'My sources confirmed it, and you know how thoroughly I research such matters. He is here with the governor's blessing. More than that, he is here in his stead.'

Prospherous glanced between us, leaning back in his seat. He sighed, running a hand through thinning hair.

'Wonderful,' he murmured.

'Propagandist Simlex needs our support,' she said. 'I have assured him I will provide whatever resources are required to make it a success. Why, if need be, the entire grounds can be cleared of anything that does not serve this function. And though I may not command your troops, my voice carries weight across this sector, with countless nobles and Administratum officials alike, as well as innumerable officers throughout the Astra Militarum. I wonder how they would react to the discovery you oppose Governor Zanwich's project?'

It was a mild yet terrifying threat. I cannot pretend that I fully understand the division of power within the Imperium, but I do know any substantial campaign requires cooperation between its various departments. A single Administratum adept could, if so instructed, mislay the documents required to resupply the front line, and doom a campaign to failure.

Governor Dolos' casual threat bordered on heresy. At least, one could frame it that way. But she was also the planetary governor, appointed in the name of the God-Emperor Himself. Bacchus was hers to rule as she saw fit. Prospherous was but a soldier, a guest in her home and on her planet. Theoretically, he could arrest her as a traitor if she opposed the conflict. But it was just as likely she could blunt his offensive and ground his craft with but a word in the right ear.

I glanced to the window, still praying. But there was no sign of incoming respite. In fact, the other fighters were now airborne, only the Valkyrie still being prepped. Through Mizar, I spied a trio of aircrew approaching, clad in those familiar flight suits, Flight Commander Gradeolous at their head. Though he was no longer imprisoned in his cockpit, his expression suggested his mood had improved little.

'Simlex?'

The mention of my name tore me back into the room, where Wing Commander Prospherous was glaring at me.

'Yes, sir?'

'Governor Zanwich appears quite dedicated to this project. Unusually so.'

'Yes, sir,' I said. 'May I speak freely?'

He shrugged. I took this as consent.

'Certain parties on Hedon are concerned by the progress of the war effort,' I said. 'They feel it reflects badly on the subsector. This pict has been commissioned in part to assuage these fears and demonstrate that the Imperial war machine will triumph.'

Dolos kicked me under the table. I winced but Prospherous seemed not to notice. He was leaning back in his chair, gaze fixed on the ceiling. A strange noise escaped his lips, like something was caught in his throat. It took me a moment to realise he was sniggering, or attempting an approximation of it.

'Of course they do,' Prospherous nodded. 'When a planet is under siege the best approach is to commission a pict under-playing the threat. Not waste time with additional resources, or manpower, or even petitioning the Adeptus Astartes for assistance.'

He seemed lost in thought. I glanced to Governor Dolos, but she was quite still. As a noble she was accustomed to diplomacy, and knew when a cause was better served by bold words or pointed silence.

'What do you require, exactly?' Prospherous murmured. 'A quick parade? Some shots of aircraft zooming by? I can spare you a brief interview, but I refuse to discuss an active warzone with a civilian.'

'That is very generous, sir,' I said. 'But I do not wish to trouble you or disrupt the war effort. My assignment is to capture the truth of conflict, not an orchestrated spectacle.'

'The truth?' he said. 'Have you seen war's true face?'

'I have been on battlefields, sir.'

'During the conflict?'

I paused. 'Adjacent to it, sir.'

'And this pict of yours, this accurate depiction of war, this is what the governor wants?'

'It's why I was chosen.'

'Hmm,' he said, not quite believing me. That was fair, as Governor Zanwich had not provided details concerning his cinematic preferences. During our brief discussion he had dedicated the first few minutes to ranting about how the damnable gloom-mongers were depressing trade in the sector, and that he needed a pict to silence them. He spent the remainder admonishing his servants for permitting the sun to set so early, and demanding his residence be remodelled and neighbouring buildings demolished so his balcony enjoyed another hour of evening light.

Still, it was true he had approved the project and bestowed upon me his authority. I had his hastily scrawled signature on the commissioning papers to prove it.

'I read your file, Simlex,' Prospherous said, retrieving a data-slate from his desk.

'Sir?'

'You have something of a reputation. I confess I saw a couple of your picts, and one was actually used in training as an exemplar. But from what I saw, you arrive when the fighting is over. You see the aftermath.'

'That's true, sir.'

'Real war does not follow a script. There is chaos, unexpected reversals, and opportunities. Even in a ground war, you could not absorb the scale of the battle. How do you expect to capture a war fought thousands of feet above your head, at speeds you could not comprehend?'

'I admit it is a challenge. But I am a slender man, and I am sure I can squeeze–'

'You think our aircraft just carry spare capacity?' he said. 'Every ounce is a burden, affecting speed and range. You intend to tuck yourself into a corner? What happens when the craft sees combat? You will be nothing more than a smear on the inner hull, assuming your broken body doesn't strike the actual pilot. It is out of the question.'

'What about the Valkyrie?'

He glared at me. 'What about it?'

'I understand it has a significant transport capacity? From what I can see the squad embarking is under-strength. Perhaps there is room for one more?'

He stared at me. His expression shifted. Maybe it was respect? More likely suspicion.

'And how do you know this?' he asked.

'I have eyes outside,' I said, for Mizar was intent on the soon-to-be-departing aircraft. Ground crew were undertaking final weapons checks, whilst beside the vessel Flight Commander

Gradeolous stood rigid, hands clasped behind his back. He threw a crisp salute, wielding his hand as deftly as a swordsman's blade. His back was to the craft, and I could not see to whom he directed his salute. Possibly he was practising form, for he repeated the gesture with subtle inflections.

'Do you have any idea where those soldiers are going?' Prospherous asked. 'What they will face? The probability they will return?'

'No,' I replied. 'And I do not need to. I just wish to see those loyal servants of the Imperium in action. I am happy for you to review the footage, erase anything you feel compromises the war effort. All I desire is the opportunity to show the bravery and skill of your soldiers.'

'You have no idea of the dangers involved.'

'That is true, sir,' I said, nodding. 'But, if it is as awful as you suggest, I will likely be dissuaded from requesting anything further from you. And if I die you need no longer cater to my whims.'

'Indeed?' he said with a slight smile. 'Because if Governor Zanwich finds out I was responsible for–'

'I will sign an oath confirming I used his authority to take the assignment, and accept full responsibility for any consequences. Including, but not limited to, my untimely death.'

As I spoke, Governor Dolos leaned in.

'We need to consider this,' she said. 'Mr Simlex's work is vital, but I do not think Governor Zanwich would want to risk his life.'

Wing Commander Prospherous did not reply. His brow was furrowed, and he seemed to be weighing his options.

'You will take full responsibility if anything untoward occurs?'

'Yes, sir.'

'And whatever footage you capture, I can review and censor as I deem fit?'

'That's right, sir.'

'And if you die this all goes away?'

'Yes, sir,' I nodded. 'Though I have faith in Flight Commander Gradeolous' skills.'

'Be that as it may, it is not a...' He trailed off, the frown sinking deeper into his face. 'Did you say Flight Commander Gradeolous?' he asked.

'Yes, sir. He is outside. I assume he is piloting the craft?'

'Gradeolous!' Wing Commander Prospherous roared, rising and thundering towards the window.

Through Mizar's eye I saw the flight commander stiffen mid-salute. He turned to the window, repeating the gesture as Prospherous' head emerged from the château. We were at least fifty floors up, but his bellow easily carried.

'What the hell are you doing out there, Gradeolous?'

'Sir! I was preparing to head out, sir.'

'You don't fly Valkyries, Gradeolous. Not after last time.'

'Sir! That was not my fault! The landing strip had been tampered with, no doubt to sully my good name. I am not responsible for the damage–'

'I don't want to hear it. Dismissed.'

Mizar watched as Gradeolous offered a less-than-crisp salute and stalked away. Like all good propagandists, I avoid empathy with my subjects so as not to compromise my work, but I could not help but feel a twang of sympathy for the man.

Wing Commander Prospherous ducked his head back into the room, slamming the window. I felt Governor Dolos tense beside me at the sound, but the glass held.

'Emperor preserve us,' Prospherous murmured, before glaring at me. 'The Valkyrie will be departing in thirty minutes, assuming I can find a pilot. I want your signed oath in my hand before you board the craft, and once it is in the air you will follow orders without question. Clear?'

'Yes, sir.'

'Good. Now, if you will excuse me, I need to find out who authorised Gradeolous to fly.'

As we rose he retrieved the vox-handset from his desk.

'Get me an administrator to draft a Warrant of Sacrifice – we will be having some extra weight on this mission. And someone wake Flight Commander Shard. Tell her that downtime is cancelled, she's flying a Valkyrie today.'

CHAPTER SEVEN

I hastily signed the Warrant of Sacrifice, barely glancing at the text. An unthinkable act for anyone with a rudimentary understanding of the machinations of the Administratum. But I feared any delay would be deemed an excuse to depart without me. The ink was still wet as I sprinted across the estate, conscious of the ground crew's eyes upon me. The mud grasped at my boots as Mizar bobbed behind, its anti-gravity impeller humming in an almost cheery manner. I caught sight of Flight Sergeant Plient, who was overseeing a clean-up crew. He waved, but I could barely nod in response, my focus on the Valkyrie.

The Tempestus Scions were already embarking. There were four, five counting the Tempestor who led them. I assumed the squad fresh, tasked with avenging their fallen comrades. Then the Tempestor's greatcoat slid from his shoulder, revealing the stump that had once been his right arm. They were the same soldiers who had crashed hours earlier, still clad in their battered armour.

The Tempestor watched as I scurried over, faltering as my stamina waned.

'Propagandist Simlex?' he said.

The tone surprised me. I would have thought him irritated by my presence. Perhaps he was, but no hint of it registered in his voice, and his eyes betrayed nothing. I nodded, not trusting myself to speak, my breath still coming in gasps.

'I am Tempestor Taton. I will lead this mission. For its duration you will follow my orders.' It was not a request.

I nodded again, managing a rasping 'Yes, sir.'

He tilted his head in acknowledgement, beckoning me into the Valkyrie's transport bay. There were twelve seats within, but even at half capacity it was cramped, the air slick with sweat, the stench of unwashed bodies mingling with the stench of the swamp. The Scions sat in silence, though I noted one's lips were twitching as he wordlessly intoned an unspoken hymn, a string of prayer beads clasped in his hand.

I passed, brushing against their legs in the tight confines, Mizar bobbing behind me. I made for the far end, closest to the cockpit, my fingers shaking as I secured the flight harness. There was no means to secure Mizar, so I cradled the skull in my lap, my arms wrapped around it like a protective mother, its mechanical appendages protruding into my thigh.

Slowly, the pounding in my chest abated, my breath returning to something close to normal. As I awaited the hum of the craft's turbofans, I felt a smile form unbidden on my lips. This was it. This was the moment I would look back on. My first flight.

Minutes passed. Ten. Twenty perhaps. I felt my smile slowly subside, my foot tapping on the flooring, until one of the Scions stilled it with a glance. It was not quite a glare, but close enough to send a message.

Still, we waited. The other occupants seemed unconcerned,

content conducting a silent vigil. I found their gaze unsettling, and my own drifted to the craft's rear ramp, which still hung open and afforded a view of the grounds.

Through the waning mist I spotted Flight Commander Shard. She was advancing towards the craft. Or trying to. Her path was broadly directed at the Valkyrie, but she would periodically meander off course, as though her legs had separate operators with only limited means of communication. She almost tripped over her scabbarded sabre, blundering into a group of loitering ground crew. As they helped her to her feet, she snatched a lho-stick from the nearest and inhaled, before grabbing a steaming cup of recaff from another. She took a long swig, splashing the remnants in her face. I winced, but she did not react to the scalding liquid. Not until she attempted another draw on the lho-stick and realised it had been doused. The subsequent expletive was audible even from the confines of the Valkyrie.

One of the ground crew spoke to her. I could not hear his question, but her response startled him. He stepped back, brow furrowed, but she beckoned to him with both hands, her mouth twisting into a sneer.

He slapped her across the face.

Instinct kicking in, along with a gallantry I did not know I possessed, I surged upright, or attempted to, but the flight harness pinned me to my seat, its strap nearly garrotting me in the process. Shard, meanwhile, was staggered by the blow, but righted herself, glaring at her attacker.

She said something. He shook his head, raising his hands in protest, but she insisted, presenting her cheek and tapping her lapel, where her rank was prominently displayed.

He sighed and struck her again. Harder this time, the blow almost lifting her from her feet. She would have fallen had she not caught hold of his uniform, hauling herself upright, until they were face to face.

She nodded, patting his shoulder in thanks, before turning and lurching towards the craft, her path a little straighter, the pale flesh of her cheek stained red by the slap and steaming recaff. She stumbled from my field of vision, but a moment later I heard the cockpit open, accompanied by a barrage of curse words and threats, until the navigator had the good sense to close the vox-channel.

As the rear ramp rose, I glanced to the Scion opposite. For but a heartbeat his stoicism slipped, and something between incredulity and resignation flashed across his eyes. When he caught my gaze the expression vanished, supplanted by the steely resolve of his comrades.

Still, as the craft shuddered awkwardly into the sky, I couldn't ignore that the pious Scion clutched his prayer beads even tighter.

I know not how long we flew. There were no viewports, no updates or conversations, no means to mark the passage of time. Still, despite my reservations, Shard seemed capable of operating the Valkyrie. Certainly, she manoeuvred it better than she had her own legs. Our journey was smooth, perhaps soporific in different circumstances. But the flight harness dug into my chest, and Mizar kept fidgeting, its appendages clawing at my legs.

I found my gaze lingering on my fellow passengers, though this did little to put me at ease. I kept glancing to their battered armour and dressed wounds. It had been but a few hours since the crash, yet the squad was heading back out despite grievous injuries. What could be that important?

More to the point, why could nobody else be dispatched?

The latter was simple to deduce: this was a mission that could not be entrusted to the common soldiery. But then why was I permitted to accompany them? I had not questioned this prior to departure, but now, two alternatives presented themselves. One, that whatever secrets this mission involved were so beyond me that I posed no threat of uncovering them. Or, two, I was certain to die, thus eliminating Wing Commander Prospherous' little problem.

I shifted, trying to relieve my aching buttocks, and found my gaze meeting the cold, hard eyes of one of the Scions. A third option suddenly presented itself. On completing their mission, the team would simply dispatch me and leave my corpse for scavengers. After all, I had signed a Warrant of Sacrifice.

I wondered if a short pict would be made celebrating my work. It was fairly common for propagandists to honour their peers in this way, though given my current luck it would probably be given to Propagandist Capsula, a man infamous for describing the glorious heraldry of the Adeptus Astartes as 'too garish for the pict screen'.

The vox crackled into life.

'–more of that God-Emperor cursed wine,' I heard Shard mutter sourly, before putting on a slightly more positive tone. 'Greetings, all. We are a couple of miles from the rendezvous spot and should be there in a few minutes. Might I enquire what to expect on arrival?

Silence.

'Anyone?' she asked. 'If we are expecting a squadron of ork aircraft it would be nice to know in advance.'

More silence, though a couple of the Scions exchanged glances. Then again, given their seeming inability to form human expressions, I am not sure what this was supposed to convey.

'Still waiting,' Shard persisted. 'I wasn't even supposed to be flying this morning. Not until that idiot decided to get himself shot down. What was his name? Peckared? Pekari? Oh, I remember now – I don't care.'

One of the Scions glanced to Tempestor Taton. 'Sir?' he said. It was the first word they had spoken since I embarked.

Taton glared in the direction of the cockpit.

'Hello? Is anyone actually in there? If this is some jest and I'm carting around an empty cargo hold I shall be most displeased.'

'Mission is retrieval,' said Taton, clipped and pointed. 'One package to collect. Secondary objective is to rescue our operatives, but they are expendable if required, as are we. Now be silent and get us there before I have you shot for insubordination.'

Her laughter crackled across the vox.

'Relax. We have arrived.'

The rear ramp suddenly spilled open, the daylight blinding. I shielded my eyes, but the Scions were unconcerned, unfastening harnesses and snapping helmets into place. I could barely hear them over the roar of the Valkyrie's turbofans, and the fresh stench of swamp water nearly turned my stomach.

Mizar twitched in my lap. With a whispered command I released the seer-skull. It slipped past the Scions, taking position by the rear ramp, and through its unblinking eye I finally beheld our destination. Before me lay the familiar burnt-orange swamp that extended indefinitely across Bacchus. It was far from lifeless, though: barbed gnarl-vines threaded the mire, their geometric layout suggesting previous cultivation. But now the plants were spreading unchecked, the vines infecting the surrounding swamp like a tumour. Insects, some the length of my arm, skittered between the thorns, their proboscises dragging through the foetid waters as they supped upon the filth.

From within the craft, I heard Tempestor Taton bellow his orders. I did not understand the words; some battle code known to his soldiers. But two of them dropped into the waters without hesitation. It was deeper than I had expected, almost reaching their chest, forcing them to hold their weapons high. The pair moved out with practised precision, the multi-spectral occula mounted beside their helms scanning the swamp.

I heard one exclaim something right before a tentacle reached from the depths, binding his arms to his sides and dragging him beneath. A third Scion had already leapt from the craft, knife drawn. He plunged into the swamp, his still-standing colleague covering him as the blade stabbed at the limb. The two troopers emerged from the water, one sheathing his knife, the other returning to his vigil as if nothing had occurred, despite the suction marks now adorning his chestplate. Between them, I saw an amorphous shadow bobbing in the water, its blood staining it an inky black.

I vowed then I would never willingly set foot in the swamp.

The three Scions spread out, a fourth dropping in behind them to guard their rear. Only Taton remained within the Valkyrie, intent on his auspex. He was scanning for something.

Mizar's sensors encompassed most of the electromagnetic spectrum. But neither its heat sensors nor structural surveys were much use in the swamp. The waters either teemed with life or contained such volume of dead matter that it registered as organic. Either way, it was a difficult environment to analyse, and I imagine Taton's auspex interpreted the surroundings as one vast, ill-defined life form.

I synced with Mizar, struggling to comprehend the dizzying visual options presented as pictographs. It struck me I had barely used half of them; there seemed little point when I sought footage visible to the human eye. I drifted through various spectrums, experiencing some fascinating colours that tasted of copper and half-forgotten dreams. But none meant anything to me, and I cycled through them until something caught my eye.

There was a light in the water a dozen feet from us. A bubble picked out in blue, perhaps four feet in diameter and entirely submerged.

Within it, something glimmered with a vile green light.

I withdrew from the seer-skull. Before me, Taton was still intent on his scans.

'I… There is something in the water.'

He did not acknowledge my words.

'It's hard to see,' I continued, as Mizar drifted over the seemingly arbitrary spot in the swamp where the energy registered. 'I can't tell if there are life signs. But there is a bubble, and something inside it. A power source, maybe, but… I don't know. I can't make sense of it…'

I lapsed into silence. I am not a priest of the Adeptus Mechanicus and only profess a passing knowledge of their arcane science. But I saw through Mizar's eye often enough to know the shape and texture of Imperial technology. The green light was wrong. It was raw and primal, though no less potent for that. The power was unstable, more an inferno than a hearth.

I thought Taton had not heard me, until he gave a barked command and two of the squad suddenly convened on the spot where Mizar loitered, sinking deeper into the water. The lead handed the other his weapon, his shoulders barely above the swamp now, before unsheathing his knife and diving into the quagmire. He seemed submerged for an age, only his helm permitting him to breathe. The remainder of the squad were still, watchful.

The vox crackled into life. Shard's voice, but without the sardonic edge.

'We have incoming. Couple of miles out. But getting closer.'

'Aircraft?' Taton murmured.

'No. Ground-based. Assuming this sinkhole qualifies as ground.'

'We need more time.'

'No problem. I'll just engage our chrono-field and construct some more time for you. Would you like a couple of minutes, or shall we mosey back a few millennia and watch the Unification of Terra?'

He did not respond. The Scions sank lower into the swamp, only their heads and weapons visible, as their submerged colleague continued his labours. Through Mizar, I saw him hack at the blue bubble, his blade struggling to pierce it.

Something moved within.

'They are accelerating. Two minutes until they are on top of us.'

I compelled Mizar upwards, scanning the surrounding swamp. An oppressive layer of mist clung to the gnarled vegetation, and the seer-skull's lenses struggled to pierce it until it was above the brackish canopy, surveying the horizon.

I saw smoke. It rolled from the mists in great belching clouds that dirtied the sky. I employed Mizar's telescopic lenses, and caught the silhouettes of crude airboats propelled by massive turbofans, not dissimilar to those outfitted to the Valkyrie. There was no unity of design; each seemed assembled from repurposed scrap, but there was no doubting their speed. Between the spray and smoke it was difficult to identify the occupants. They were far broader than a man, and I saw flashes of green skin.

'Orks,' I whispered.

I did not think anyone was listening to me. But the vox crackled into life.

'Come again?'

'Orks,' I repeated, wishing my voice were steady. 'They're riding some form of airboat. Four vessels, maybe five. I can't be sure, there's too much smoke.'

'Who is this?'

'Propagandist Simlex,' I murmured as the craft raced onwards. 'We met yesterday, albeit briefly.'

'What the hell are you doing here? Did you get on the wrong aircraft?'

'It does seem that way.'

They were closer now, the smoke trails visible to Taton. He glanced at me from over his shoulder.

'Are they heading for us?'

'I think so.'

'What colour's the smoke?'

'Black. No, there is a green tint.'

'Marvellous, a signal. You realise we are exposed here? If a squad of ork fighters spots us we are dead.'

Taton ignored her, addressing me. 'Perform a perimeter sweep. Are more incoming?'

I synced with Mizar, its sensors sweeping across the swamp.

'Yes,' I said. 'There are more airboats coming from... that way. East. I can't tell if more come from the west – the storm clouds make it hard to see the smoke.'

I felt strangely calm, as though the danger were not quite real. It was not the first time I had experienced this sensation. I suspect it is a by-product of perceiving the world through Mizar's unblinking eye, its cold rationality steadying my human frailty. But as they drew closer I heard the whirr of their engines, like buzz saws carving through stone. Worse was their battle cry, a score of guttural voices united in joyous bloodlust.

It was then I felt fear, my mouth dry, bladder full.

Taton stowed his auspex, drawing his sword, the blade crackling with the faint glow of a power field.

'Flight Commander Shard,' he said. 'Retrieving the package is the priority. Once it is secured on board, depart immediately.'

He leapt from the ramp. Through Mizar, I watched him land and begin wading a path towards his soldiers. The submerged Scion was still struggling with the blue bubble. Taton called an order and the Scions spread out, weapons trained on the distant orks. He raised the power sword, plunging into the foetid waters, which churned and bubbled at his blade's passage. I manoeuvred for a closer view but Mizar resisted, for it now had the orks in visual range.

These were not the knock-kneed brutes from the poorly spliced pict. Despite their stooped shoulders they stood over seven feet tall, and more than half that wide. Their faces, if that was the word, were comprised of bony foreheads, thick enough to repel small-arms fire, and slab-like jaws infested with tusked fangs. Each wielded a thick-barrelled ballistic weapon. No two firearms were alike, but all were large enough that a human would require a gun carriage to survive their recoil. The orks had spotted the Scions and already opened fire. Though out of range, their weapons resonated with the fury of an artillery barrage.

'They're too close. Those idiots are not going to make it.'

The Valkyrie lurched, but my senses were entwined with Mizar, and I was unsure what was happening. At my urging the seer-skull swung back to the Scions, just as Taton pierced the bubble.

I don't know what I expected to emerge. But it was not another Scion.

It was difficult to be sure because of the mud and mire, but the shape had the same silhouette as Taton. The soldier's helm was firmly in place, permitting him to breathe whilst submerged. But he moved with a horrible hunched posture, as though his spine were compressed. He cradled something to his chest, but the waters shielded it from my view. Taton assisted him with his one good arm, the two powering as best they could through the swamp water towards the Valkyrie.

Which shifted, then accelerated away from the dropsite.

'What are you doing?' I screamed. I have no idea if she heard me, or merely did not think I warranted a reply. Either way, as the craft retreated I confess to mixed feelings. I was relieved to be fleeing the onrushing orks, but I felt shame at abandoning our comrades, and disbelief that Shard would be so callous with their lives and the mission.

The Valkyrie suddenly banked hard, accelerating as it curved around the incoming horde. It slowed to an abrupt halt, the nose spinning right, the momentum tugging my flight harness tight.

Ahead, the greenskins were moments from the Scions.

The Valkyrie surged forward, straight for the ork flank. It was a dozen yards away when Shard fired the rocket pods, the barrage of fragmentation missiles disappearing into the water, and wrenched the nose back. The turbofans screamed in protest, unleashing a gale that almost toppled the lead airboat.

Then the warheads detonated.

The swamp erupted in a deluge of filth and shrapnel. Orks were flung from their vessels, the lead boat capsizing. Another tried to turn to face us, but the airboat had no means of braking. In its enthusiasm the ork helmsman swung into the path of the rearmost vessels, the resulting explosion pitching the remainder into the swamp.

We were blessed with a moment's silence before the first ork rose sluggishly from the mire, still brandishing its weapon. It roared, a dozen more emerging around it. Several bore wounds, burns, but showed no signs of slowing as they surged towards the Scions.

The Valkyrie swung about, bringing its heavy bolters to bear. Rocket-propelled shells ripped apart both ork and airboat, the Scions adding a barrage of las-bolts to the equation.

But the beasts would not fall easy. Though clad in little more than fur and scrap they waded through the barrage, flesh scorched by a dozen las-burns. One lost its head to a bolter round, but still managed a dozen steps before its body finally accepted death. Had it been open ground they would have torn the Scions apart, but the swamp was our saviour, slowing their charge to a crawl and clogging their weapons.

Mizar captured every moment: the Valkyrie providing covering fire as Shard manoeuvred it behind the squad, the rear ramp yawning open. As Taton assisted his injured comrade into the craft, the Scions picked off the greenskin stragglers.

'You want me to leave now, or should I wait for the rest of them?'

Taton grunted something in response, but Mizar was calling to me. Through it, I saw distant smoke trails drawing closer, each heralding another swarm of greenskins.

'There's more coming,' I said, as the last Scion clambered up the ramp. 'From both sides.'

'Go!' Taton roared, and the Valkyrie surged upwards, pivoting on the spot before soaring away.

'Wait!' I screeched. 'What about Mizar?'

'Who?'

'My seer-skull. You can't leave without it!'

'I'm pretty sure I can. In fact, I'm fairly sure I just did.'

I did not reply, could not by this point. My consciousness was still synced with Mizar, and through it I saw the Valkyrie ascend, even as more orks swarmed in, drawn as much by the gunshots and explosions as the green-tinged smoke. As the Valkyrie accelerated Mizar tried to follow, its machine-spirit seeking to maintain our ebbing connection. But its anti-gravity engine could not keep pace with the attack craft's turbofans. As the distance stretched between us, the connection spluttered, the image flickering like a corrupted vid. There was a pop in the back of my skull, my cogitator seeking in vain to retrieve the lost signal.

My vision swam, and I drifted at the edge of consciousness.

When I could open my eyes I saw only the transport bay.

Mizar was lost to me.

CHAPTER EIGHT

I could not speak at first, so great was the shock.

The Scions were also silent, though Shard was in good spirits and decided to regale us with stories of her glorious victories and daring skill. I was relieved when Taton closed the vox-channel, though I could still faintly hear her voice reverberating through the hull.

As we sped homeward my gaze lingered upon the injured soldier they had dragged from the swamp. He was in a sorry state, unable to even secure his flight harness without aid, his fingers too weak for the clasps. There was little they could do for him. He tried to remain as stoic as the rest, gritting his teeth as we were buffeted by tailwinds. But he could not quiet his rasping breath, nor mask a plaintive sob when we suffered particularly violent turbulence. The other Scions averted their gaze, perhaps embarrassed by his momentary weakness, or sparing him additional shame by pretending not to have heard it.

He was dying, and not just from his injuries. His wounds

were grievous, like the rest of them, but more alarming was the exposed flesh of his forearm. It was infested with purple lesions, the surrounding skin swollen and cracked. We all stunk of swamp water, but his weeping sores had a sickly-sweet scent that over-powered even that. It was known to me, and it meant only death.

I wonder if I should have recorded him, shown a true glimpse of true sacrifice. But there would be no point; the Imperium preferred its martyrs portrayed as tall and proud, not riddled with disease, even if they suffered in the God-Emperor's name. Besides, I had no means of recording anything without Mizar. It was a relic, irreplaceable, its loss reflecting poorly upon me. The seer-skull possessed a rudimentary guidance system, compelling it to seek me out were we separated. But over such distance and hostile terrain it seemed a forlorn hope that it would blunder back into signal range. I reminded myself I still had the others, but neither had Mizar's advanced optics or bold machine-spirit. Worse, neither possessed footage of the conflict I had witnessed.

The dying Scion coughed, his spittle visible. I froze, watching it arch across the hold, suddenly mindful that I shared a con-fined space with a very sickly man. I turned my head, wrapping my sleeve around my mouth in an attempt to block the foul humours. I thought the gesture discreet, until I noticed Taton glaring at me. But when he spoke his tone was soft, almost gentle.

'You need not fear,' he said. 'It is not contagious. Not through the air anyway.'

'You know what ails him?'

'Vintner's Blight,' he replied. 'It's a mycological infection. The workers suffer from it if they spend too long in the waters. Fungus grows quick here – something about the climate. Or the water.'

'Can he be cured?'

'If the God-Emperor wills,' he said with a shrug. 'If not, he served with courage and faith. He will be remembered, and there will be a place for him at the God-Emperor's table. Just like Harkins.'

He spoke as though recanting a passage from a field manual, so it took me a moment to realise the significance of his words. There were five Scions seated in the transport bay, just as when we had departed. But that was before we took an additional passenger.

We were missing a soldier.

Harkins. That must have been his name. Perhaps he carried the prayer beads, for there was no sign of them now. I had not seen him fall; a wild shot from the orks must have found its mark. I felt very foolish all of a sudden, pining for a relic whilst these soldiers mourned their comrade. And they would soon lose another.

My cheeks reddened. I looked away, gaze falling upon Taton's missing arm, sheared off below the shoulder. His good hand clasped that strange device the submerged Scion had guarded with his life. It was covered by a cloth, as though for modesty's sake, but it had fallen away, revealing a lump of scrap pressed into a vague sphere. It was bonded with rivets the size of my thumb, and did not look forged by human hands. But there was a curious familiarity to the parts. It was the same with the ork airboats. Each was a crude, ugly thing, cobbled from scraps and with only a rudimentary resemblance to its sister vessels. But the similarity between the Valkyrie's turbofans and the airboats' propulsion system was stark.

I sat back, recalling the battle between the greenskins and Scions. It would have been easier with Mizar present, but I could perfectly picture images of the savage creatures. They were huge, terrifying beasts, nothing like the skinny, spear-brandishing green-skin from the poorly spliced pict. Could that bow-legged beast truly be the ancestor of the orks we faced today? I did not know when that pict had been commissioned, and the image of the ork could be taken from an even earlier source. Still, how many generations had passed for the spear-wielding primitive to evolve into the monsters we had faced? Centuries? Decades?

Their own rapid biological development was alarming enough. But the fact they could repurpose Imperial technology? Debase it and turn it against its masters?

That was terrifying.

No lavish reception awaited our return. Instead, a fresh squad of Scions stood to attention at the dropsite. They had arrived too late to undertake the retrieval mission, but their dour presence dampened any enthusiasm the ground crew might have felt for our return. The common soldiery were not privy to the nature of our mission, or the dangers we faced. All they knew was a squad of Scions had smashed a Valkyrie into their headquarters, requisitioned a replacement, and jetted off on yet another classified assignment, leaving the lower ranks to unpick the chaos left in their wake.

The fresh squad of Scions gleamed, armour spotless despite the filth, and stood rigid as statues despite the unyielding heat and encroaching humidity. I've heard tell that Scions are forged by training so demanding that few common soldiers could even survive it. The way they stood spoke of an inherent sense of superiority. What made it worse was they were justified in such sentiment.

I have heard Scions dismissed as glory-hogs by our more urbane troopers, and worse by those with coarser tongues. Once, I might have smirked at such insults. I knew of many who garner favour through privilege and rank, avoiding the dirty, inglorious tasks that the rest of us undertake, with little gratitude or recompense.

No longer. Not once I'd witnessed those bloodied, broken

men staggering from the Valkyrie, their comrade draped between them. I like to think he somehow survived, that a chirurgeon stemmed his wounds and healed his sickness. But I did not see him again.

The Tempestor leading the relief squad saluted, Taton returning the gesture with his remaining hand. The package was retrieved and promptly sealed in a gene-locked cask. Both squads wordlessly departed, leaving the ground crew to tend to the Valkyrie.

'You're welcome.'

I glanced to the open cockpit. Shard was lounging in the flight seat, staring after the departing Scions. Behind her the navigator dismounted the vessel, tearing his helm from his head.

She caught my gaze and frowned, arching an eyebrow.

'Something bothering you?' she asked. 'You have a face like a kicked dog.'

I hated her then. The smugness. Did she know I had lost vital footage, as well as a prized relic? It did not matter, for it was not as though she would care either way. I rounded on her, but the rant died in my throat, for I suddenly saw the empty seats on the Valkyrie, and remembered the soldiers scrambling through the swamp to retrieve their dying comrade. None of them had uttered a word of complaint. Why should I?

But she would not let it be, calling after me as I turned away.

'Hello? I asked you a question. Manners dictate you provide an answer.'

I froze, fists balled. I had no idea what I expected to do with them. It was years since I had thrown a punch, and I knew a trained soldier would effortlessly dismantle me.

Of course, that realisation just made me angrier.

'My problem?' I said. 'My problem is I am supposed to be producing a pict on the glorious Aeronautica Imperialis, the heroes who defend our skies from xenos and heretic alike. I came to bear witness to their trials and victories. I came here for a true picture of war.'

'And how is that progressing?'

'Poorly. I have limited means of capturing the conflict, just lost one of my most valuable assets. My boots are sodden, despite the fact I stayed in the transport hold the entire mission. And worst of all, I had intended my pict to venerate Flight Commander Lucille von Shard, the renowned fighter ace and hero. But I find myself flying with a drunken braggard who, from what I can tell, respects nothing and no one besides herself.'

'Sounds like you've found the truth to me.' She shrugged. 'Mission accomplished. Is there anything else?'

'Yes,' I said, glaring at her. 'Despite my warning, you gleefully abandoned a priceless artefact in the middle of that swamp. That seer-skull once belonged to Propagandist Taina Mizar. Do you know who that is?'

'By the Throne!' she whispered, flinching. 'Taina Mizar? I had no idea. Such a loss.'

She sounded sincere, her eyes bright and earnest. But the scar across her lip made it look like she was sneering.

'Truthfully?' I asked.

'Absolutely,' she said, nodding. 'My life would not be what it is without Mizar. She is the one who lifts my spirits when I falter, the one who presses my uniform every morning, the one who brings me my recaff when–'

She caught my expression and frowned.

'Sorry, I'm thinking of Milania, my chambermaid. Who, incidentally, is fantastic. Don't think she knows much of the propagandist arts, but my bedsheets are always soft and clean. Still, sorry you lost your toy. If only one of the Scions could have sacrificed their life to preserve it. How selfish of them.'

She smiled. It did nothing to dispel the mocking tone.

'Do you find yourself amusing?' I asked.

'As much as anyone,' she replied. 'So, do you plan to obtain a replacement? Or are you going to branch out? Maybe a ribcage on tank tracks?'

'A relic of that nature cannot be simply replaced.'

'Funny that,' she said, vaulting from the cockpit and dusting herself down. 'Aircraft, soldiers, citizens are all eminently replaceable. But Emperor forbid someone loses a hollowed-out cranium with a bunch of wires protruding from where its brain should be. I mean, where on earth would we find another propagandist's skull?'

She tapped her chin, as though lost in thought, still wearing that sneer.

'Taina Mizar is a legend,' I said, glaring at her. 'She braved the most dangerous warzones to show humanity's triumphs in a hostile galaxy. Through her efforts millions were inspired to enlist in service of the God-Emperor. It was said she had the potential to be the greatest propagandist of all time. Do not mock her.'

'So, what happened?'

I frowned, not understanding.

'What happened to her?' Shard persisted. 'You said she had great potential, why wasn't it realised?'

'She... was a little overzealous. Tried to get a close-up of a dying genestealer before it had fully expired. Still, she was the youngest ever propagandist to be posthumously honoured by being fashioned into a seer-skull.'

'And what greater honour could one ask for?' Shard replied, picking an invisible piece of dust from her collar.

'Forget it!' I snapped. 'Forget all of it. I will make this pict and it will be a triumph. But there will be no mention of your name. I had intended you to be the focus, but that is done. Your comrades can be immortalised whilst you will be forgotten, erased from history.'

'How disappointing.' She smiled. 'Still, I draw a sliver of solace from the fact you would be dead twice over without my assistance. So, in a sense, your pict could never be completed without me. But you frame history to suit your needs, because I don't care. And that's the truth.'

Her words were well chosen. There was nothing I could say. Instead, I stalked away with whatever dignity I could muster, telling myself that the unpleasant stench that clung to me was merely the swamp water, and not the rank odour of hypocrisy.

CHAPTER NINE

I barely left the château for days.

It would have been different had Mizar boarded the Valkyrie. At least then I would have gained something from the conflict. I busied myself cataloguing the little material I had backed up prior to the mission, and tried not to think of the potential repercussions from my superiors for the loss of Mizar. I saw little of Shard, though I made a point of interviewing the other fighter aces, what little good that did me.

Flight Commander Talzin Nocter of Falcon Squadron was clearly nervous, perpetually fussing with his hair, or leaning back and forward in his seat. He answered my questions, and his responses would have garnered the approval of the most pious drill abbot. But his voice was hollow and inauthentic, as though he sought the correct answer to each question rather than revealing his own views on the war. His words were just another echo of a score of earlier picts.

The same could not be said of Flight Commander Orthox

Gradeolous. His file indicated a distinguished career, with victories against some of the Imperium's greatest foes, and he was presentable enough, despite his slightly brutish manner. But I did not like his smile, framed as it was by beautifully waxed whiskers. When he spoke of his glories there was a glint in his eye, not so much a disdain for human life as an ambivalence. I had been surprised to learn his squadron were designated the Sharks, as I understood this to be a reference to an ancient and aquatic Terran creature. However, having subsequently reviewed the mural adorning his fighter, with its razor teeth and cold, blank eyes, I could see a resemblance. A predator.

In contrast, few sought to speak with me. Flight Sergeant Plient was the first to knock on my door, arriving cap in hand and offering his condolences.

'So sorry to hear about your loss, sir,' he said. 'Is there anything I can do?'

If it were anyone else I would have thought they were mocking me, but he looked genuinely sorrowful.

'I doubt it,' I replied, tone sharper than warranted. 'Unless you can solve a conundrum. How does one create a pict when aircraft are moving at supersonic speed hundreds of miles above the swamp? Particularly as Mizar, my seer-skull with the best optics, is now lost.'

It was a question I should have given more time to prior to landing on Bacchus. I assumed there would be spare capacity in the fleet, or a vantage point from which commanders viewed the battle. I had been foolish, and in my anger I directed this at Plient.

But he did not take offence at my words, merely nodding.

'I will try, sir,' was all he said before departing.

My second visitor surprised me. Not that it was anyone of consequence, merely a member of Wing Commander Prospherous' staff. But he carried a note signed by the wing commander himself. Apparently I had made a positive impression on Tempestor Taton, and Prospherous was persuaded that I could perhaps accompany Flight Commander Shard on additional missions, on a discretionary basis.

I crumpled the note, tossing it towards the disposal bin. I missed, and had to rise to collect it, a challenge given the comfort offered by my chair. Like the rest of my quarters it was luxurious, a significant upgrade on the prior lodgings. I had three rooms including a balcony that offered a spectacular view of the grounds, were one to ignore the wreckage and promethium spills. The bed was wide enough to cater for a party of four. More importantly, it also incorporated a discreet data-point and a power output that did not leak foul-smelling fluids. I was charging my remaining seer-skulls and assessing their optical capabilities when it occurred to me to review the old footage. I told myself it was a petty whim, brought about by overindulging in the governor's wine. I am not much of a drinker, but I decided that afternoon to remedy that.

'State your name.'

I glanced up at the voice, though the speaker was not visible in the pict. The focus was a young woman, her eyes cold, face pale as moonlight.

'Lucille von Shard,' she replied, her voice betraying neither fear nor joy.

I had seen the feed a thousand times. It was but one of many interviews conducted with Flight Commander Shard during her training in the schola progenium. A time before she joined the Aeronautica Imperialis and surrendered to cynicism.

At least, that was what I thought. But as I replayed the footage, I found myself wondering. Even then, without the scar, I saw the beginnings of the sneer behind her eyes.

The interviewer, I assume a drill abbot or equivalent, was now praising Shard's family, listing the myriad achievements of the von Shard line. She nodded occasionally, her eyes fixed on something unseen. I drained my glass, grimacing slightly at the aftertaste.

It was odd. The schola progenium's precise methods were, mercifully, beyond my rank and ken. But I knew the result: war orphans born of the Imperium's greatest heroes, forged into iron-willed servants of the Imperium, loyal only to the God-Emperor and the Golden Throne. That was how the Scions were trained, along with manifold priests, administrators and soldiers. But I also knew the whispers, that such dedication was imparted by chemically stripping the students of their identities, leaving blank canvases onto which the drill abbots could work their art.

I understood the reasoning behind their methods, even if the thought of enduring such a process made me shudder. But it seemed not the case with Shard's family. I had met two of her brothers, Confessor Maric von Shard and Commissar Tobia von Shard. Both took pride in their family's history and siblings' achievements, and both were exemplars of their roles. I had assumed Shard was likewise. At least, until I met her.

The holo-pict was still running, the drill abbot recounting Colonel Horotha Shard's glorious victories and accomplishments. I had seen the footage numerous times, but my focus was usually Shard, trying to get a sense for the angles of her face, how she moved and how best to frame a pict. But I'd met her now, and I saw the girl in the chair as if for the first time. There was defiance in her stillness, even as the interviewer recanted her family's accomplishments.

Except *interviewer* was not the right word, for the drill abbot asked no questions, never veering from their script. Proclaiming her family's glory, over and over. Like a liturgy.

I was missing something. Perhaps, had I listened longer, I

would have discovered what. But at that moment the image vanished. Seer-skull Iwazar had cut the connection, replacing it with a repetitive beeping. Inebriated as I was, it took me a moment to discern its meaning. But when I did so I suddenly felt very sober indeed. This communication had been scheduled prior to planetfall, as it depended on Bacchus' orbit aligning with neighbouring Elis. I smoothed my hair and attempted to look presentable as the link was established.

At first, all I could see was searing light and a barrage of explosions. But the hololith flickered, my seer-skull compensating for the glare. As the light dimmed, shadows coalesced into the imposing figure of an Imperial commissar, his greatcoat billowing in the wind, his peaked cap emblazoned with a winged skull. I could only just make out his eyes, but they carried the same steely determination I had witnessed during the Palatine Crusade. His jaw was carved in a grim line, but his manner bore not the righteous fury of the priest or penitent. Contempt was the only emotion I had seen him express. Contempt for those who opposed the Imperium, or those who failed to serve it to the best of their ability.

I did not wish to fall into the latter category.

'Commissar von Shard?' I said.

He glared at me. The link quality was still suspect, but I thought I could make out troops manoeuvring into position behind him.

'Propagandist Simlex,' he said. 'I trust you have arrived safely on Bacchus?'

'Yes, sir. Thank you for your concern.'

'Thank only our God-Emperor,' he replied curtly. 'Has my sister seen my letter of introduction?'

'Yes, sir. I handed it to her myself.'

'Good.' He nodded, glancing past me to something unseen. 'Sergeant Vilma! Recalibrate the artillery! Focus on their left flank!'

'Sir, if this is a bad time, I could–'

'*It is no matter.*' The commissar shrugged. '*There is unlikely to be a better time. Not until we have broken these treacherous dogs.*'

'Yes, sir.'

'*Is the work progressing to an adequate standard?*'

'Yes, sir,' I replied. 'Though it might prove more challenging than I anticipated.'

'*Why?*'

'Some logistical issues. Local politics,' I answered, unwilling to mention Shard's name.

'*Then rise to the challenge, Propagandist Simlex,*' the commissar said. '*Remember, you obtained this assignment due to my own personal recommendation. I do not offer such endorsements lightly. You will not disappoint me.*'

'Yes, sir. I will do my best.'

'*No, you will do better than that, for whilst I–*'

His words were eclipsed by a deafening explosion. The image fractured, only to meld into the commissar, chainsword drawn, urging his men forward.

'*For the God-Emperor!*' he bellowed, his voice carrying even over the roar of his blade. It was difficult to follow what happened next, as his servo-skull was sprayed by a shower of blood, staining the lens crimson. Some moments passed whilst the vid-feed was restored, during which I was treated to blood-chilling screams punctuated by Commissar von Shard's chainsword.

Abruptly, his face coalesced into view, the cap now askew and stained red. Behind him, the Guardsmen were surging forward, the battle apparently won.

'*My apologies, Simlex,*' the commissar said, adjusting his uniform and wiping his cheek. '*I thank you for confirming your safe arrival and look forward to judging your final works.*'

'Thank you, sir. You will understand if I await your judgement with a little trepidation.'

'I won't pretend you don't have your work cut out for you,' he said, cleaning his blade on a torn shirt. *'She is a wilful one.'*

'I am sure she will prove every bit the hero, sir.'

He paused in his labours, glancing at me. His face was blurred by the fading connection, but he carried an expression I had not seen before. Surprise. Or perhaps concern.

'Propagandist Simlex, do not misunderstand me. I respect your work. It tolerably serves the Emperor's cause, which is a damn sight more than most of your ilk. But I did not vouch for you because I thought you would make my sister a hero. That is a lost cause.'

'Sir?'

'Your duty is ensuring she does not sully her family's name,' he said as the vid-feed faded. *'I do not care how. Make her a background player. Overdub her speech. Remove her entirely if necessary. But do not let her drag the rest of us down. Her failings will remain her own.'*

CHAPTER TEN

My conversation with Commissar von Shard did little to lift my spirits. I tried to focus on my work, obtaining background material and immersing myself in the base's operations. Kikazar's lenses were sharp enough to capture the aircraft's take-offs and landings, and our link strong enough for it to survey the swamp surrounding Governor Dolos' estate. I took to cataloguing these recordings in the hangar, where Plient conducted repairs, assisted by a corroded pair of maintenance servitors.

If asked, I would say I sought his company because his sanguine nature was a balm against the sting of recent setbacks. And that is true enough. But there was another reason, though it now lay in pieces, the engine disassembled and strewn about the workshop.

Shard's Lightning. *Black Griffin*, the name taken from the von Shard family crest emblazoned on its wing.

At least, I took that to be its name, but when I spoke it aloud Plient frowned at me.

'Black Griffin?' he said.

'Her plane?' I nodded. 'It's famous across the subsector.'

'Never heard her call it that.'

'What did she call it?'

'I don't know. Something in High Gothic. *Mendax Matertera*? Something like that.' He shrugged, returning to his labours.

Plient's work was predominantly patching holes and applying purified oils to the Lightning's delicate mechanisms, the servitors attending to the refuelling and reloading. But there were times I caught him shoulder-deep in the partially dismantled engines, or employing an arc welder to fuse cables and circuits.

I have dealt with the Adeptus Mechanicus. Before a single seer-skull was entrusted into my care, I had to memorise the catechisms of repair and perform the rituals of maintenance. I do not know to what extent the tech-priests entrusted these rituals to the common soldiery, but I suspect Plient's work went beyond whatever had been sanctioned, perhaps bordering on tech-heresy. But then I would see him cheerily chant psalms of sacrifice as he laboured, paying thanks to the God-Emperor each time an aircraft left the hangar. It seemed impossible such a devout soul could harbour heresy in his heart. No, the reason he laboured was simple: there was no one else to complete the repairs.

We were losing the war.

I had not realised this when I first arrived on Bacchus, assuming the flurry of activity indicated a thriving base that supported vast forces. But it was the same faces I saw each day, and they hurried and bustled because there was too much to do and too few of them doing it.

And it did not take a logis to calculate that when the aircraft took flight, not all of them returned.

Governor Dolos' personnel were also stretched thin, though I cannot say their labours contributed much to the war effort.

An inordinate amount of time was dedicated to beautifying the estate. A futile act, given the conflict, but they persisted. I saw work teams scraping the walls and attempting to patch the section of roof damaged by the errant Valkyrie. Steward Stylee oversaw it all. He did not sleep as far as I could tell, driving the servants day and night.

But his work paid dividends, for I awoke one morn to find the upper level of the château in full bloom. I could see the blossom from my window, the flowers an unreal-looking, vivid blue. I stepped outside for a closer view, and found I was not alone. A small crowd had gathered, some ground crew, others the governor's staff. But they were united in their admiration of the spectacle, and at their centre stood the beaming Stylee.

'Good morrow to you, my lord,' he said, bowing as deep as his ageing limbs would permit. Ever since the revelation of my apparent noble lineage, his manner to me had shifted. He now did an admirable job of hiding his disdain. Well, an adequate job, anyway.

'Good day to you as well,' I said, and nodded to him as Kikazar rose upwards, inspecting the flowers. 'This is certainly a spectacle.'

'It would hardly be the Harvest Banquet without mandack blossom,' he replied. 'To think, some claimed it would not flower this year! But even this dirty war cannot overshadow the passage of seasons.'

'It does this every year?'

'Yes, my lord.'

'Remarkable,' I murmured. 'I have never seen flowers blossom this quickly.'

'Well, I am glad we could educate you, my lord,' Stylee replied. His gaze was fixed on my seer-skull. It was still inspecting the tree, delicate limbs prodding the branches and dislodging a shower of blossom in the process.

I caught his expression and brought Kikazar to heel, though I could not help note that the petals clinging to its sides were dry, almost desiccated, as if they had wilted as soon as they fell.

'And how go your preparations, my lord?' Stylee asked.

'Tolerable,' I replied. 'I have pieces of footage, though there is much to do.'

He managed an almost inaudible sigh. 'No, my lord. I meant how go your preparations for the Harvest Banquet?'

I did not take his meaning at first. Apparently, my expression conveyed this.

'You have not forgotten, my lord?' he said, suddenly sounding alarmed.

'I am not sure I follow.'

'The banquet, my lord!'

I had been aware of the preparations. It was hard to miss the footmen buffing the château's walls and floors with purified waxes, rendering the wood so slick that it became a hazard to the hurried staff. Even Dolos had been occupied. I received periodic notes apologising for her absence and detailing the myriad responsibilities involved in hosting the lavish gala. I had disposed of these and thought no more of it. But, at some point since my arrival, my status had shifted from distant spectator to prized attendee.

Sadly, I had not been informed of this.

'But we sent you the robes! A full itinerary of events!' Stylee protested.

In his defence, I had received a bundle of orange fabric in a hand-woven wicker basket, but given the volume of material I had assumed it was fresh bedding. There may also have been a poem of some kind, a meandering sonnet on the wonders of the God-Emperor's bounty. I read half but, finding it uninspired, crumpled the composition and left it in the refuse.

My confusion was not well received. I could not tell if Stylee's face was white with fear or crimson with fury, the shades playing sequentially, but the other onlookers took a step back from him, as though he were primed to explode.

'I would be grateful to attend,' I said, but this did not placate him. He was swaying, and I was suddenly aware of his age and frailty, how accustomed he had become to the rhythms of the estate. To him, the risk of a potential faux pas was far more troubling than a horde of orks rampaging through the surrounding swamps.

'You don't understand,' he wailed. 'This is a formal affair! It is one of our most sacred rituals! The governor made special allowances to facilitate your attendance. You would be of the inner circle, and there are steps you must memorise and customs you must observe. Do you even have an escort? You cannot attend alone!'

'Why?'

I recognised the voice, and turned.

It was Shard. At some point she had joined the crowd, or perhaps she was there from the start, her face hidden by a broad umbrella emblazoned with the von Shard crest. It had not rained since my arrival, so I could only assume she carried the parasol to protect her pallid skin from Bacchus' unyielding sun. Her other hand was propped on the pommel of her sabre.

Stylee seemed momentarily stunned by her question.

'Wh-what?' he spluttered.

'Why do guests require an escort?' she asked innocently. 'Don't tell me this is a… fertility festival?' She raised an eyebrow.

'Certainly not!' he snapped, indignant. 'It is a celebration of the harvest and cycle of life. There must be even numbers – each honoured guest must be paired, like the sun and moon. When midnight comes those select few will flank the entrance to the throne room, where–'

'So it's basically a dance. Got it,' Shard replied, cutting him off before turning to me. 'In that case, as an act of charity, I will permit the propagandist to escort me.'

She smiled. It was not cruel, but neither was it kind.

'You wish to go with me?' I asked.

'That's a little strong,' she said, wrinkling her nose, as though she had smelt something unpleasant. 'But my superiors are of the opinion that we may work together again, so I am bound to assist you. I was attending anyway, all the officers do, but if we go together then I get to sit at the top table. I hear they're serving real meat. Can't miss that.'

I am not sure Stylee supported this plan, given his expression. He looked torn, unsure whether it was worse to endure the botched seating plan, or Shard sitting with the nobles.

And I?

I do not know how I felt, other than enjoying Stylee's discomfort. But it was in my best interests to establish a working relationship with Shard.

I shrugged. 'Then it would seem the matter is settled.'

'Once again I have saved the day,' she said, with a sliver of a smile. 'Now, if you will excuse me, I need to get out of the sun. I have a delicate complexion.'

She turned away, though her gaze lingered a moment on the blue blossom adorning the governor's abode.

'I can't say I'm impressed by the display this year,' she said. 'Damn flowers almost look stuck on.'

The morning of the Harvest Banquet I awoke with a skull-splitting migraine, interspersed by broken images of swamp water and barbed vines.

I hoped it was Mizar, data-fragments transmitted from the errant seer-skull. But they could just as easily have been aftershocks from the forced separation. I nevertheless spent the day trying to triangulate its location using the remaining two seer-skulls. It was tiresome and ultimately fruitless work.

My engraved, if slightly smudged, invitation stated it was some hours until the banquet, so when there came a knocking on my door, I chose to disregard it, assuming it was merely a servant. But it came again and again until, finally, I could ignore it no longer. I rose with a curse, flung the door open and found myself standing face to face with Flight Commander Lucille von Shard.

She was an impressive sight in her dress uniform – the double-breasted tunic a vibrant blue adorned with brass buttons, her epaulettes woven from gold thread. A grey half-cape was slung over her shoulder, the corresponding hand resting on the pommel of her sabre, and upon her head rested a peaked cap adorned by a crimson plume. She would have looked every inch the consummate Imperial officer, bar two notable flaws.

The first was that sneering smile. And the second was the foul-smelling buzzard perched upon her left shoulder. Though it was a scrawny and hunched thing, its beak was the length of a flick-blade, and its yellow eyes glared at me with a predatory hunger.

'Flight commander?' I said, glancing to the wall-clock. 'Why are you…?'

But she was already inside, inspecting the décor.

'Not bad,' she said, gaze lingering on the bottles of wine gifted by the governor. 'Well stocked too. You don't mind?'

I would have said I did not, but she had already snatched a bottle. My offer of a glass was rejected by a wave of her hand. Instead, she flicked the seal and took a long swig.

'Swear this used to taste better.' She frowned, glancing to the bottle. 'This planet is really going to the dogs. I hope the food is good tonight, it's the only reason I got dressed.'

'Do you often attend such lavish events?'

'I've been to a few,' she said. 'When you liberate a planet they sometimes treat you to a modest repast, or occasionally a ceremonial fast. It's important to pay attention during the briefings.'

She took another swig before belching pointedly. She must have caught my expression because her face split into a broad grin. I think that was the first time I saw her real smile. It might have been pleasing on the eye had her amusement not been founded on my discomfort.

'Is this how you intend to present yourself this evening?' I asked.

She rolled her eyes. 'Oh, please. This is not my first soirée. I know how to play my part.'

Her heels clicked together. Suddenly she stood tall and proud, her gaze steel and her jaw rockcrete, uniform unmarked by crease or blemish. She was at once a perfect soldier. It was uncanny. Even the scar on her lip was in keeping, a keepsake earned in combat.

Except the bird, of course. It seemed content to cling in place, but since its arrival an unpleasant smell had pervaded my suite. I was unsure whether the fowl was flatulent or if it had relieved itself on Shard's shoulder.

'That's an unusual creature,' I ventured. 'Is this the regiment's mascot?'

'God-Emperor, no! This is a noble raptaw. The von Shard family have bred them for centuries. It is customary for the eldest daughter to keep one for hawking.'

'And for bringing to formal events?'

'Indeed.' She nodded. 'I researched that quite thoroughly.'

'So, it is trained?'

'No. Just decrepit. He can barely fly, so the damage he can inflict is limited. Keep some distance, mind – he likes eyes.'

'Has he ever injured you?' I asked, my gaze flicking to her scarred lip.

She frowned. 'Not that I can think of. He's a loyal companion.'

She tilted her head, smiling benevolently at the bird. It was now balancing on one leg, the spare limb clawing the side of its head and spraying an alarming volume of feathers.

'My brother did not speak of it then?' she asked.

'Pardon?'

'I heard you've liaised with my brother Tobia,' she said. 'Not from him, obviously, but my sister Josephine keeps the family abreast of each other's activities. Providing it amuses her.'

'Commissar von Shard wished to check in with me about my project.'

'I'm sure he did,' she said. 'I assume he could only speak briefly? Because he was in the midst of some epic battle? You know he does it on purpose, so it seems he is always on campaign? I mean, how hard is it to schedule a ten-minute conversation? Most of the commanders are so terrified of him they would do whatever he asked, and nobody on the front line would miss him.'

'You do not care for your brother?'

'Why would I? I barely know my siblings. In fact, I don't think we have all been together since our mother's second funeral.'

She must have caught my expression.

'When they actually found the body,' she explained. 'Dug it out of the ruins, or dunes or something. We younger ones were dragged away from the schola progenium for an afternoon, and my elder brothers granted temporary leave from their duties. Just so we could stand around the sarcophagus looking noble and unified. I'm sure you've seen the picts?'

'I have. They feature prominently in some of our materials.'

'Well, I barely spoke to my brother that day. Or any of them. Wasted my time conversing with my aunt.' She shrugged. 'Since then, our duties keep us apart. Only Josephine binds us together. Her and the family name, I suppose. So why did you reach out to Tobia?'

'I did not. He requested my presence on this assignment and wanted to check its status.'

'Did you tell him what I thought of his letter?'

'No. I did not wish to offend him as I offended you.'

'There was no offence. I just have zero interest in what he has to say.'

Her tone was not convincing, but before I could reply her gaze fell to the bundle of orange fabric folded on the bed.

'This is what you are wearing?'

I could not deny it was an audacious piece. The silken robe was spun of auburn threads extracted from indigenous arachnids that weave their webs between the gnarl-vines. It was vast, the sleeves draping to the floor, and came with a headdress wider than my shoulders and primarily comprised of preserved insect parts.

Then there was the bodice. It was a well-crafted piece, the shaped carapace studded with gold and inlaid with jade. But having briefly tried it on I had to conclude its primary function was restructuring internal organs. Either that, or the original inhabitants of the planet who inspired the fashion were eight feet tall and possessed no ribs.

'It is what they provided,' I said. 'I assume military exemption is the reason you are not clad similarly?'

'Naturally,' she replied. 'A soldier does not have time to prettify themselves. I would make a start if I were you, though.'

'I'm not even sure how to,' I said. 'I hope Stylee will be willing to assist when the time comes.'

'The time came and went.'

There was something in her tone. She sounded amused, but I detected no note of insincerity.

'My invitation says eight,' I said, reaching for the parchment.

'Which means you must be there by five,' she said. 'It's called etiquette.'

'How can it be etiquette to provide an incorrect time on an invitation?'

'Because only the noble classes with an appreciation of social mores would know the distinction between when something starts and when one must attend.'

'That seems needlessly confusing.'

'It's entirely necessary. Without established codes of conduct, how would nobles separate themselves from the common citizenry? Besides their money and life expectancy of course.'

She glanced to the pile of cast-offs Stylee had provided.

'Well? Put them on.'

I hesitated. She sighed.

'I have zero interest in seeing beneath your robes,' she said. 'But very well – I will preserve your modesty.'

She turned, presenting her back to me and the stain the bird had left on her cape.

The robes were nonsensical to me, containing at least six armholes and assorted ties. I spent an age struggling with them, and kept expecting her to spin around just to provoke me. But she kept her word, remaining a statue, even when I pulled the last tie and found my legs abruptly bound together, the floor rushing up to meet me. I would have put my arms out to protect me, but they seemed caught in the silken folds.

The subsequent impact could best be described as bone-shaking, mitigated only by the padding provided by my robes. To her credit, Shard did not react.

'Can you move?' she asked, when it had become abundantly clear I could not.

'No.'

'Do you require assistance?'

'It would seem so.'

'Are you sure?' she asked. 'There is a not insubstantial risk I may catch a glimpse of your armpit.'

'I think it is an acceptable risk. Also, there is a possibility I might be slowly asphyxiating.'

She turned, tugging at the binds, her bird assisting with its beak.

'Honestly,' she said. 'You would think a propagandist would have a better understanding of the importance of a first impression.'

CHAPTER ELEVEN

I half suspected Shard had deliberately dressed me as an imbecile, until we stood at the top of the main stairwell, the other nobles mingling below. All wore variations of the same bizarre robes, the numerous folds hindering movement, and billowing sleeves posing a considerable risk to Dolos' more delicate ornaments. All had pinched waists, the nobles stoically enduring the discomfort. Though a slight fellow, I felt like the corset was impeding my renal system.

Stylee made my introduction and took his time about it. There was little reference to my achievements, but an inordinate time dedicated to my ancestry. The words 'siring' and 'betrothing' were frequently employed. I found myself swaying, unbalanced by the ornate headdress. I might have fallen had Shard's elbow not steadied me. She was far surer on her feet. Perhaps such poise was her birthright, but I suspect even she would have struggled in those ceremonial shoes. Wearing footwear constructed from mandibles was unsettling, and I felt as though my feet were on the cusp of being devoured. As Stylee concluded his introduction and we descended, I kept expecting disaster. I could not even see far ahead, not with the headdress tipping into my eyes, but Shard was my rock. She held me until we reached the bottom, where she offered a short bow.

'Well, propagandist, I will take my leave.'

'You'll take what?' I asked, panic creeping into my voice. Figures were already approaching from the crowd.

'It's custom,' she said. 'We separate and mingle for a time before coming back together later in the evening. Then we do that bit about the sun and moon.'

Perhaps this was true. I could envision such a code of conduct as a means for noble couples to enjoy the absence of each other's company. But it was equally possible she was lying to me, intent on the banquet tables overflowing with food at the room's rear, where I noted a handful of officers had already taken residence.

Still, I was not quite alone. Kikazar hovered at my shoulder. I had thought it prudent to bring it, hoping the rambunctious atmosphere might loosen tongues.

'My dear Simlex!'

I turned to find Governor Dolos resplendent in auburn robes adorned with shining stars. Her headdress comprised almost a full exoskeleton, the fusion of insect parts extending to the base of her spine. She offered her hand. I had no idea what to do with it, but she quickly recognised this, pressing the tip of her thumb to my own and splaying my hand open with her remaining fingers. There was some twist of the wrist that followed, but I was completely lost at this point, having imbibed a little too much complimentary wine. Dolos did not seem concerned.

'It's wonderful to see you again,' she said, smiling. 'And you look splendid, every inch a member of Bacchus' aristocracy. Come, let me make some introductions.'

This was clearly a lie, but so are most exchanges at such events. As the orchestra played, their instruments hewn from a hodge-podge of spider silk and repurposed carapace, I was presented to the various nobles and dignitaries. I got the impression Dolos was attempting to manage my interactions. Either that or, just like their revered insects, the nobility of Bacchus operated as a hive mind. I undertook the same conversations a dozen times. Kikazar was ever at my shoulder, its sensors logging each exchange.

Lord Pompo was an exception. I became cornered by him when Dolos disappeared to attend to some late arrivals. He was a portly man of noble bearing, his nose raised skywards, forcing him to regard me from the corner of each eye in turn. They were remarkably widely spaced, and I found myself wondering if the gentleman had bovine genomes in his ancestry.

'So, you're the fellow who will rid us of these wretched green-skins, what?' he said.

'I fear that would be beyond me, my lord,' I replied. 'My duty is merely to document events.'

'Damn right,' the elder man said, bristling. 'Someone needs to show that those so-called soldiers aren't doing their job.' He paused for a moment as a servant refreshed his glass. 'This year's harvest has been a disaster. We are taking home barely half of what we once did. And the workers! Suddenly everyone is too busy whining about raids or about being conscripted to do an honest day's work.'

He was slurring. It was understandable. The wine was sweet and subtle, somehow conveying soft sunsets and lazy evenings. There was none of the bitter tang I had previously tasted. I had thought myself half-cut, but Lord Pompo's glazed eyes told me I somehow had the man at a disadvantage. At least, in theory. I suspected that even when sober his belligerence and self-importance would have made him an impenetrable conversationalist.

'Blasted xenos,' he murmured. 'Scum, all of them. Did you know I served? Fought them… What are the blue ones called?'

'T'au?'

'That's right,' he said, nodding. 'There I was, my personal guard ready to deploy and wipe the looks from their disgustingly bland faces. But then diplomacy broke out! I ask you, who talks with xenos filth? Should have exterminated the lot of them, along with those traitorous milksops who wanted to placate them. Half the planets in the Imperium have gone soft, that's the problem.'

I nodded, trying to gracefully withdraw, but he advanced as I retreated, mirroring each step. His voice was loud, and carried despite the cacophony of the room, and as Kikazar had synced with his speech, I was subject to his blithering twice. From over his shoulder, I could see Shard and some of the other officers filling their plates, whilst Governor Dolos seemed to be hurrying in my direction.

'Worst of all are those pointy-eared ones.'

'The aeldari?' I asked.

He nodded, draining his glass. 'I still cannot believe a group of them had the gall to attend our banquet!' he continued as Dolos swept in, taking hold of his arm. 'Claimed they were invited!'

'That's enough now, Pompo,' she said, an edge creeping into her voice. He was too inebriated to detect it, but I was surprised by her demeanour. Pompo must have carried enough influence that even a planetary governor needed to employ tact.

'I told you then,' he said, turning to her. 'Can't give them the slightest opening. Pretty ones are the worst, because they can confuse a man. Well, a weak one anyway. Least the greenskins and the blueskins have the decency to look repugnant. Not like those disgusting she-xenos with their cold eyes and bright smiles.'

He trailed off then, his focus shifting somewhere unknown to me, his face softening even more at the memory.

Dolos took her opening.

'Lord Pompo, we have just received some amasec imported from Ultramar. Some say it is the Lord Regent's preferred beverage.'

This got his attention, and he was happily led away by one of the servants.

'God-Emperor bless him,' she sighed. 'He's an old friend and a loyal one at that, but he does get confused.'

'He seems to think the aeldari attended a previous banquet?'

'I know,' she said. 'Poor fellow. Perhaps he is thinking of an old campaign.'

'Was he a soldier?'

'Not exactly,' she replied. 'His family oversee a vineyard to the east. A small army is employed to ensure the workers' productivity and oppose potential threats. I believe they engaged in the occasional skirmish to protect his interests, sometimes even off-planet.'

'Including against the t'au?'

'That must be from his younger days,' she said. 'Come. There are other people you must meet.'

She dragged me through a parade of what passed for nobility on that backwater planet. Each shifted at the mention of my name, their eyes suddenly alert. Most thanked me for my efforts, claiming someone needed to show how the military were squandering its resources, instead of taking the fight to the orks. A few regaled me with their own struggles with the greenskins a decade earlier, before it was deemed a military matter. The way they told it, combating the threat was akin to a hunting party. The swamp-skimmers, usually employed in harvesting the gnarl-vines, were outfitted with heavy stubbers and used to clear out the horde. I can only assume the creatures they fought were closer to the knock-kneed primitives than the savage brutes now plaguing the planet.

Kikazar tirelessly logged each conversation, though I doubted it was worth the effort. What struck me was the similarity between the accounts; the same story relayed from a dozen mouths. As the wine flowed their tirades degenerated into slurs and outbursts of shrill laughter, and it struck me that the spectacle of these supposed dignitaries did little to glorify the Imperium.

I was growing bored, and encouraged Kikazar's sensors to roam, latching onto conversations that intrigued its inquisitive machine-spirit. Though it lacked Mizar's sophisticated lenses, Kikazar had advanced audio sensors, as well as a gift for translation and interpretation. I caught snatches of indiscretion from the shadows, but the passions and infidelities of the nobles held little interest to me. Mildly more intriguing were the servants. They scurried like worker insects, labouring with tireless desperation to maintain the event's relaxed façade. I caught Stylee berating a younger man clad in the governor's livery over the flammability of the spider silk adhesive used in preparation for the festivities. At the time I assumed he referred to decorations.

But then I spotted Shard loitering by the banquet table, exchanging pleasantries with the other officers. I was surprised to see Wing Commander Prospherous in attendance, given his seemingly adversarial relationship with Governor Dolos. I imagined it was protocol: as commanding officer his attendance was a matter of propriety. His expression indicated he was not enjoying himself. In fact, none of the officers looked in good spirits. What smiles they offered were rare and rang false.

And Shard's plate was still full.

I watched for a full minute, but she touched nothing, though that damnable bird perched on her shoulder managed to snatch a few morsels. Despite her earlier claims she seemed wholly uninterested in the food.

Kikazar still hovered behind me, intent on a stately noblewoman who was regaling our group with her views on the best means of chastising slothful servants.

'Kikazar, focus to subject Shard.'

The seer-skull bobbed at the command, directing its aural recorders to the conversation on the far side of the room and deadening the cacophony between. Via my interface, I caught a snippet of the exchange.

'–found our missing plane.'

'And the rest?' asked Flight Commander Nocter.

'We can only assume they were destroyed.' Prospherous sighed. 'I wish that were the extent of our troubles. What worries me most is where we found them. You know the province of Whalic?'

'No.'

'It's on the other side of the planet.'

Shard shook her head. 'That's impossible. Even flying at top speed and refuelling on the wing, none of our fighters can travel such a distance in a few hours.'

'Tell that to the survivor, though I use that word loosely. He is currently in a medi-unit. Not sure he'll make it. Even if he does, I suspect he can tell us little. When they found him all he could do was mutter about green lightning, and monsters stealing his soul in the dark.'

'It's the Green Storm,' Nocter muttered, making the sign of the aquila. I had heard that name before. Shard pretended to laugh, throwing her head back before leaning in.

'We need to know what is lurking in those storm clouds,' she said. 'Let me take a squad and–'

Prospherous cut her off. 'No. The western storm front is not going anywhere. From now on we stay clear of it.'

'Those clouds stretch wide enough to hide an armada. We need to investigate.'

'We have been investigating – that's why I have so many dead pilots,' Prospherous hissed. 'For now, we have orders to avoid that storm front. Whatever danger lies within is not intent on emerging. There is a good chance it is a natural phenomenon, as dangerous to them as to us. It might even shield our flank.'

'Pardon my bluntness, sir, but that reeks of cowardice.'

I recognised the speaker as Flight Commander Gradeolous. I could not help note that Shard and he had positioned themselves at opposite sides of the table.

'You have a better suggestion, Gradeolous?'

'Yes, sir!' Gradeolous replied, snapping off a rigid salute.

'Please enlighten us.'

'Send everything we have, sir – every craft that is airworthy and every pilot who can fly. We move as one and wipe them out.'

'And our other fronts?' Prospherous asked. 'The Astra Militarum cannot hold out without aerial support. Those ork bombers will simply erase them. Then there are the travel corridors we are trying to keep open. If they find a way to sever our supply lines, we are lost.'

Shard sighed. 'It would be easier if we didn't have to babysit these inbred halfwits.'

'You think so, Shard?' Prospherous replied. 'Do you think I wanted a third of my command operating a glorified escort service, just so these people can indulge their pointless ritual?'

'Then why are we?'

'Because we have orders and we obey them. Understood?'

'Yes, sir.'

'You are sure?' Prospherous frowned. 'For you are adept at seeming to obey orders to the letter whilst simultaneously violating their spirit.'

'Thank you, sir.'

'It was not a compliment. In fact–'

Their voices were drowned by the screeching. I gasped, hands clasped to my ears as I sank to my knees. The noble addressing me bent closer.

'Are you quite all right?' she said, apparently untroubled by the sound.

I nodded but could not answer; the pain was too debilitating. Instead, I mumbled some vague words of apology before getting back to my feet and turning away, Kikazar trailing me like an overbearing nursemaid. I thought the seer-skull the problem, its aural recorders latching onto a feedback loop. But as I staggered away from the festivities the sound intensified until I felt my teeth would crack. I found an alcove and leant against the wall, struggling to control my breath.

'Kikazar, break connection,' I whispered.

For a second there was blessed relief.

Then the pain came again, not as sound but as a throbbing behind my eyes. Each time I opened them lightning thrashed inside my head, along with broken images I could not process: screams and fire, utter chaos all around.

I heard a woman shriek. With a supreme effort, I raised my head, following the sound. She was intent on the window, pointing to something unseen. Two of the burlier servants were already approaching the glass, though I noted Shard and the officers had not moved.

Something stared through the window. I caught a flash of a gleaming red eye, and a leering grin.

Then the glass shattered and a terrifying spectre burst into the room. It stood taller than a man, or would have if only it had legs upon which to stand, for its form was comprised of tangled vines and swamp filth draped in a vaguely humanoid shape. Its only true feature was the glowing red eye now surveying the room, seeking something.

It took a moment for me to recognise it.

'Mizar?' I whispered.

The swamp-stained seer-skull veered towards me, dragging broken gnarl-vines with it. I could feel its machine-spirit clawing at my thoughts, anxious to be reunited after so long apart. With a whine of anti-grav motors it flew closer. Kikazar demurely deferred to its sibling and ducked aside. Too late, I realised what was happening – Mizar was desperate to sync with me and share all it had seen.

It was too much, beyond what I could process. Hours of navigating the swamplands, pursued by vile insects and terrible beasts, the thud of gunfire and roar of explosions. All were forcibly driven into my mind, the memories supplanting my own. I tried to scream, but all that emerged was a rasp. I saw Stylee rush over, his face etched in horror, presumably at the festivities being threatened.

'Get him out of here,' he hissed, but I pushed him aside. I could not process it all, but one image was burned into my mind. I sought Shard, who was smiling, no doubt at my discomfort. I tried to speak, but I could not find my vocal cords. Instead, I pointed through the broken window to the skies beyond. I could see people were laughing now, perhaps taking the spectacle to be part of the festivities.

I focused on the grinning Shard, stabbing my finger wordlessly to the sky.

'Yes.' She nodded, as though addressing a child. 'Window. He came through the window. Can you say window?'

I shook my head, still unable to speak. Instead I did the only thing I could think of, thrusting out my jaw and mimicking tusks with my fingers. As I grunted helplessly, laughter erupted across the room

Except for Shard. Her smile had faded.

'Orks,' she whispered, glancing to Wing Commander Prospherous. I could not hear what she said next, only Prospherous' bellowed orders to get to the hangar. As Shard and the other pilots broke into a run, shoving the confused guests aside, I sank back to my knees. Mizar's machine-memories were still clawing at my consciousness, but I knew what I had seen: the ork craft accelerating, intent on the château.

As my eyes glazed, I heard the distant thud of Hydra flak batteries.

CHAPTER TWELVE

I cannot be certain when I regained consciousness. I remember being stretchered by two members of the ground crew, only for Stylee to reprimand them, insisting that I be taken to the governor's physician. The subsequent debate might have persisted indefinitely, were it not for the explosion that lit the sky. As shrapnel rained down, it was decided the discussion could be postponed, at least until they were under cover. I would have agreed if I could speak, but my motor control was still limited. Mizar, like an excited child, sought to transfer every scrap of data it had accumulated in its travels. As the sky was lit by las-bolts and flames, I was treated to flashes of its pilgrimage. I saw remarkable flora and fauna, as well as rusted cabins nestled deep in the swamp. They had once belonged to the workers, but those unfortunates were lost, their bones strung between the gnarl-vines, perhaps marking territorial boundaries.

A cracked ceiling of pressed flakboard loomed into view, suggesting the ground crew had found cover. But Mizar's eye was now drawn to the battle above. A squadron of Thunderbolts pirouetted through the invading orks, the lead claiming a greenskin fighter with every flash of its lascannons. I knew it was Shard, for who else had such precision? But Mizar was too awestruck by the carnage, and could not focus on any one target, its gaze flitting between duelling fighters. I tried to exert some influence, but the seer-skull took this as a signal to re-establish the data upload.

My head snapped back as the images assaulted me. Endless vines, their fruit swollen but marred by ugly black marks. A wreck languishing in the swamps, the water unable to ward off the flames slowly consuming it as the desperate pilot struggled against his jammed flight harness. Then there was the platform: a vast artifice of steel and rockcrete. It looked of Imperial construction, but debased by foul xenos runes and curious patchwork devices of unknown purpose. As Mizar drew closer, perhaps recognising the architecture amidst the chaos, its aural sensors picked up the savage cries of the orks. At the platform's zenith, two greenskins were engaged in a ritualistic duel, surrounded by a dozen other whooping orks. Both were huge beasts, dwarfing even the creatures I had seen on the airboats. Their blows lacked finesse, but the savage fighters had remarkable fortitude and surprising speed. Victory was finally decided by the whirling edge of a massive chainblade. It slipped past a well-notched axe, delivering a decapitating strike. As the corpse fell the surrounding orks roared in approval, the sound almost a cheer, the victor raising his fist in triumph.

Then, alerted by some unseen cue, the orks as one glanced skywards, their guttural cries coalescing into a howl of joy. Unfortunately, by raising their heads they spotted Mizar's unblinking eye. The air was suddenly thick with bullets but, mercifully, the seer-skull had the sense to withdraw. As it departed an image flashed across my eyes. I could not make it out, the blinding light temporarily disrupting the skull's viewer.

But for a moment it was as if the sky was torn by green lightning.

I awoke to further conflict, though this time between Stylee and an irate chirurgeon in bloodstained robes. My gaze lingered on the scalpel clasped in his right hand, and the way he was staring at Stylee's throat. The steward seemed oblivious, thrusting out his woeful chin, his finger jabbing at the chirurgeon's chest.

'The governor insists you release him into her care.'

'Then the governor can come down here and tell me herself,' the chirurgeon replied. 'Until then he is my patient. And I am not releasing him into the care of that sawbones who attends your workforce. I've seen how many of them are short a limb.'

'Agricultural work is not without risk. Infection must be cut away at the source.'

'Is that right? Because when someone enters my surgery with a stubbed toe and leaves with one leg, I consider that a failure.'

'The only failure here is your people failing to protect the governor's château. If this oafish off-worlder hadn't alerted us in time we would not even be having this conversation.'

He gestured to me to emphasise his point, only then realising my eyes were open. He flinched, left eye twitching as though heralding an impending seizure.

'I… You are awake, my lord,' he said, unsure how to converse when playing the parts of both sycophant and dissident. The chirurgeon suffered no such indecision and was already by my bedside. He retrieved a small device from his robes, shining a faded green light into each eye in turn.

'How do you feel?' he murmured, addressing a spot behind my ear. 'Headaches? Blurred vision?'

'I... Not any more,' I replied, struggling to sit. There was little discomfort, just exhaustion. Mizar's data-records were still rattling around in my skull, like half-forgotten memories from an evening of debauchery.

I felt the chirurgeon's hands move from wrist to throat as he checked my blood flow. I was surprised; such assessments are usually conducted via a diagnosticator. But a brief glance at the infirmary provided an explanation. The rockcrete, though clean, was well worn, and cracked where the strangling gnarl-vines had sought to gain passage. The beds were crude cots, presumably once used by the planet's workforce. Most were occupied. Some soldiers sat upright, talking in hushed tones as a medic checked their dressings. Others lay quite still, lost beneath a plethora of tubes and injectors.

'Are these all from the attack?' I murmured.

The chirurgeon shook his head. 'No. We endured that quite well. The anti-air defences held them long enough for the fighters to get airborne. They drove them off.'

'There were few casualties?'

'I wouldn't say that,' he murmured. 'But those who get shot down don't end up in here.'

'Is there another facility?'

'No, just a pit. The remains are dumped in there until there is time to burn them. I would avoid it if I were you, the climate speeds decomposition and the smell is quite oppressive.'

He caught my expression and shrugged.

'What did you expect?' he said. 'You can't bury anything in a swamp.'

Before I replied he moved on, intent on the next patient.

Stylee cleared his throat. It sounded deeply unpleasant, like some foul creature had taken residence in the wrinkled folds of his neck. I glanced to him. He offered a smile of dubious quality.

'My lord,' he said. 'I must apologise for the current situation. Governor Dolos was adamant you be treated by her personal physician. But these soldiers? Pah!' He spat the word like it was rancid meat. 'They dragged you here before I could stop them.'

'It's fine. I'm fine,' I said.

In truth I was not, my head still a jumble. Even sitting caused me to sway. But, surrounded by the infirm and dying, I was acutely aware the bed I occupied could better serve another.

'How is the governor?' I said, swinging my legs over the side and rising unsteadily.

'Unharmed,' Stylee replied, slinging my arm over his shoulder. A sour aroma clung to his skin. Unwashed sweat. It had not been apparent before. However else I could besmirch Stylee, he was fastidiously clean.

'And her guests?' I asked as he assisted me.

'All uninjured,' Stylee replied, his tone suggesting otherwise. I did not press the matter.

'I still cannot believe they reached the château,' he muttered as we made for the door. 'The Harvest Banquet is a tradition dating back millennia. This is the first time in recorded history it has been interrupted, and there will be consequences. Governor Dolos prioritised the safety of her guests last night, but this morning she will be demanding explanations. I have no doubt heads will roll.'

We progressed along a barely lit corridor. Men slumped against the walls, awaiting their turn with the chirurgeon, while Stylee continued his diatribe.

'Lord and Lady Pompo were astounded by what happened. But you know those two will spread whispers across the sector. It reflects badly on all of us, that's what those glory-seekers don't realise. After a fiasco like this they move on to their next little war, leaving us to deal with the fallout. Any time we offer our hospitality there will be whispers, snide remarks about whether the event will go ahead. As if any of them could have done better.'

He was quite animated now, his gazed fixed to a point unseen. I looked away, spotting Flight Sergeant Plient sitting beside a grey-faced young man whose breath was a shudder. He glanced up, offering a well-intentioned smile that did little to convince me anything was going well.

We were nearly at the bunker's exit, steps leading to a door framed by a halo. Beyond it, the sky was so bright I had to shield my eyes as I surveyed what remained of the grounds. Once a muddied field, it was but craters, the turf carved open by the cascade of explosive rounds. Ground crew were clearing the wreckage, but I found my gaze drawn to the château.

The structure was remarkably intact, the aged mandack wood proving resilient to the assault. But the blossom had been incinerated, leaving the outer bark scorched black. Blue petals were scattered across the grounds, perhaps blown clear by the initial explosion. I reached for a nearby handful, and was surprised to find they were stuck to the runway. The flowers were dry to the touch, desiccated, as though long preserved.

I glanced to Stylee. He was quite still, eyes misted. He no longer supported my weight, slipping from under my arm and taking a stumbling step towards the château. He must have been in the field hospital since before the sun had risen, and had not known the extent of the damage. The poor man. His meticulously managed world no longer made sense.

But there was no sorrow in his voice when he spoke, only barely suppressed rage.

'Someone must face judgement for this abomination!' he spat, turning to me. I was surprised to be included in his confidence. But I suppose whatever my other failings, I was not a part of the military.

'Can it be repaired?' I asked.

'Repaired!' he scoffed, glaring at me. 'You think you can repair–'

He must then have remembered my rank, for he hesitated, before smiling that odious smile.

'I mean, my lord, that it is not possible to repair a building such as this. It is a living thing, and will not regenerate until it enters its growth phase in the spring. And it will not bloom again until next year.'

'You think it will recover by then?'

'Oh yes.' He nodded. 'Each year, without fail, there is blossom on the tree. I ensure it.'

There was pride in his voice, and renewed purpose.

'I am pleased to know that,' I said. 'But if you will excuse me, I must return to my labours.'

'Yes, you must show them,' he muttered. 'Show them all what those bastards have done to the governor's home!'

As I departed, I told myself he was referring to the greenskins.

Flight Commander Gradeolous was waiting outside my room.

Though I had briefly interviewed the man I cannot say I was taken with him, and my pace slowed as I drew closer. Beyond the confines of his aircraft, he was a towering figure, broad enough that it must have been a struggle to squeeze into the cockpit of his fighter. He had clearly seen combat that night; his flight suit was stained by mud and worse, and carried the distinct aroma of promethium. But his face was scrubbed clean, hair swept back and smoothed into place, and his moustache waxed into dangerous-looking points.

He straightened as he saw me, stepping forward and extending a hand that enveloped my own.

'Propagandist Simlex,' he said with a broad grin. 'I believe thanks are in order. They say you provided the warning that allowed us to repel the orks.'

'I suppose.' I shrugged. 'Though it was more luck than skill.'

'Still, you did your bit. That's all any of us can do.'

'True enough,' I said, nodding. 'Though I wonder what else I can do for you.'

'Ha!' He threw his head back as if my remark were the height of wit, then slapped my back with his free hand. The force propelled me forward, and I would have fallen on my face were he not still clasping my hand.

'What can you do for me?' he chuckled. 'You, my diminutive friend, have already done so much. If you hadn't provided advanced warning of the greenskin attack, who knows where we would be? My sources say Dolos is quite taken with you.'

'Sources?' I asked as he released his grip and casually strode into my room.

'The servants,' he said. 'Honestly, it's pathetic how desperate they are for acknowledgement. Buy them a couple of drinks and regale them with a few stories and they'll tell you anything.'

As he spoke he surveyed the room. 'This is nice. You must be a man of significant resources.'

'I am a servant of the Imperium,' I said. 'I take what it provides.'

He nodded. 'Naturally. But, in His wisdom, the God-Emperor tends to provide the best for those He deems most worthy. I should know.'

He laughed again, the bellows echoing along the corridor. I waited for it to subside, my gaze flickering to my cases. The seer-skulls were mercifully in place, Mizar having had the good sense to join its siblings. I had yet to examine the footage it had captured, as whatever it had uploaded into my head was too disjointed to interpret.

Gradeolous clapped his hand against his knee, taking a seat on one side of the bed, the other lurching alarmingly upwards.

'Ha!' he exclaimed one final time, wiping tears from his eyes on his sleeve. 'But enough banter. I'm here to save you.'

'Save me?'

'Yes,' he said, nodding. 'It's no secret that you seek to document the glory of the Aeronautica Imperialis. A worthy goal, but one you will not achieve without a suitable subject.'

He offered a pained smile, as though regretting that circumstances required him to impart this self-evident truth. His hands were spread wide, expression suggesting he expected some response. I nodded, hoping this was sufficient. His smile widened, flashing a set of almost-too-white teeth. It occurred to me an ork performing a similar gesture would be issuing a threat.

'That's why I am here,' he said. 'Your pict now has its lead.'

I knew not how to respond. His record suggested he was suitable, and he was clearly keen to appear on the pict screen. He was presentable enough, despite his slightly brutish manner.

But I still did not like that smile. Or those cold dead eyes.

'I am currently collecting footage from a variety of sources, but when time permits, I would be delighted to conduct another interview–'

'No, that won't do,' he said, raising a hand to silence me. 'No need to be coy. I know of Shard's attempts to hog the limelight. I'm not surprised, the woman's ego is legendary, and Prospherous sadly favours her. Did you know I was to fly the Valkyrie on your first foray into the swamps? But she stole my position. That was nothing short of reckless. She was half-cut from the previous night, and her inebriation might have jeopardised the mission.'

'Perhaps. But it wasn't her idea, I–'

He was suddenly on his feet, towering over me, his vast frame blocking the sunlight streaming through the window. A weighty hand rested on my shoulder.

'I know it's complicated,' he said. 'All commanders have their favourites, and she has a certain brashness that some find… appealing. But following that mission I expect any appeal has waned.'

'Maybe. But at least I had some to start with.'

We both stiffened as we heard her voice, glancing as one to the door. Shard was leaning against the frame. She too wore a dirtied flight suit, and there was a freshly stitched scar on her cheek.

'Damn cockpit shattered,' she said with a shrug, acknowledging my stare. 'I miss my Lightning.'

'Shard,' Gradeolous said coldly, releasing his grip on my shoulder. 'What are you doing here?'

'Investigating,' she said. 'I thought I heard the mating call of the Donorian Fiend. I rushed to protect our propagandist from its vile attentions. Of course, it now strikes me that the hideous sound was probably just your self-congratulatory sniggering, presumably following an ill-conceived attempt at humour.'

She smiled, making no effort to hide her disdain. I glanced to Gradeolous, whose jaw was clenched tight enough to grind bonemeal.

'Now you've seen there is no danger, perhaps you should be on your way,' he said. 'There is probably a bottle somewhere requiring your attention.'

'If only,' she sighed. 'I'm here to collect our hero propagandist.'

I frowned. 'Hero?'

'I'm as surprised as you,' she said. 'A certain aristocrat has decreed that the only reason we weren't destroyed last night was your well-timed warning. Personally, I think the anti-air defences contributed something, as did my own peerless skills. But it seems both pale in comparison to mumbling like an idiot before collapsing into a foetal ball, no doubt soiling yourself in the process.'

'I did not soil myself.'

'I wasn't minded to check. After all, someone needed to defend the Imperium,' she replied. 'On which note, you need to come with me.'

'Where?'

'I don't know. It's classified,' she said. 'Either that, or I wasn't paying attention during the briefing. But, regardless, someone wants you stinking up my aircraft. Oh, and bring your skull-friend. That's the important thing, isn't it?'

'How? It will never keep up with us.'

'Oh, it will,' she sighed. 'Believe me, our mission will not be conducted at speed.'

CHAPTER THIRTEEN

I learned much on that flight, most of it concerning the anatomy of the various insects that thrived in Bacchus' humid climate. They were heedless of our passage, content to splatter against the cockpit. Many had wingspans of a foot or more, and the craft's clearance systems faced a constant battle to remove their bodies and maintain visibility. It felt a futile exercise; hundreds more of the creatures would congregate on the craft, and every few moments we were greeted by another seemingly suicidal invertebrate intent on dashing itself on the Vulture gunship's screen.

I had not seen this craft before, though its silhouette was reminiscent of the Valkyrie, and its capabilities similar. But it held no transport capacity and, besides the pilot, was crewed by only a single gunner. I occupied their seat, though Shard had placed restrictions to prevent me accessing the weapon systems – a policy I endorsed, as I did not want to accidently discharge the craft's twin Punisher cannons. They were huge, multi-barrelled guns, capable of a blistering rate of fire. In fact, I could not shake the thought that they seemed almost orkish in design.

Ahead of us, a convoy of Chimeras attempted to advance through the quagmire. We were to be their escort and support, but their progress was pitiful. The armoured personnel carriers were semi-amphibious, and capable of traversing even bodies of water. But the swamps of Bacchus were almost gelatinous, and moving at any significant speed invited snared tank tracks and obscured viewports. We periodically had to halt so squads could disembark and dislodge tangled roots or clear clogged exhausts. Though the Vulture was capable of hovering, Shard took any delay as an opportunity to accelerate away from our grounded comrades, claiming she was conducting reconnaissance or pursuing an unidentified blip on the auspex. It was those moments, when the acceleration pinned me back in my seat, that I finally felt an inkling of what it was like to be a fighter ace. What it was like to be Shard.

It was a mistake to voice this. She laughed, shaking her head, the sound devoid of humour.

'What?' I asked.

'Nothing,' she said. 'Of course you know what it is to be an ace. After all, it's been a couple of hours sitting in a chair, watching bugs perform mass suicide. What else is there to learn?'

'I never said that I knew what it was like.'

'You did.'

'No, I said I had an inkling of what it is to be you.'

'You really don't,' she said softly. 'No one does.'

The craft lurched to the left, jostling me, before we pirouetted back towards our allies.

I switched my view, syncing with Mizar, who accompanied the convoy, its anti-gravity motors easily keeping pace. I had dumped its memory into the storage case prior to departure, and the seer-skull seemed invigorated by shedding this load. Through it, I captured the Vulture soaring over the advancing forces, its frame glinting in the sun. It was a spectacular shot, but little more than filler footage. There was no narrative underpinning the drama, no stakes. I also needed to filter out the mutters from adjacent infantry, who did not appreciate the aerial theatrics and employed some rather gratuitous language deriding it.

It was whilst adjusting the audio that I heard the screams.

Mizar swung around just as a many-limbed creature burst from the waters. It stood taller than a man, its wings spanning near ten feet. Hideous compound eyes framed a bladed proboscis, and it was quick to sink this weapon into the nearest infantryman, lifting him from his feet even as he shrivelled, his inner organs eaten away as the monster supped upon his life essence.

'We are under attack!'

Shard flinched at the sound, glancing over her shoulder.

'You don't have to shout. Who's attacking?'

'Down there!' I said, as the creature tossed the withered corpse aside, already bounding onto its next victim before his comrades could bring their weapons to bear. A couple of las-bolts were fired, one ricocheting from its carapace.

'That's just a banner-bug,' she said. 'Like a big fruit fly. They must have disturbed its nest. Unlucky, those things are normally nocturnal. Don't worry, they'll deal with it.'

'Can't you do something?'

'Of course,' she said. 'I can swoop down and let rip with both Punisher cannons. It will turn that bug into a smear. Unfortunately, it will do the same to anyone within about ten feet. Might even take out the Chimera if it clips a fuel line.'

Two more soldiers died as she spoke, their bodies reduced to shrunken bags of skin and bone. But another hurled himself onto the beast's back, even as it lunged for a fresh victim.

His knife glanced from its armoured carapace, but the ricochet tore the insect's delicate wing membranes. Off balance, it suddenly pitched into the mud, twisting as it fell, a clawed limb disembowelling the attacker. But the squad was mobilised now. Another volley from their lasguns pinned it long enough for the squad's flamer to be brought to bear. Mizar's vox was struggling to make sense of the cacophony unfolding, but I swear the creature emitted an almost human scream as its carapace cracked under the heat. It crumpled into the swamp, and soon was nothing more than an untidy stain upon the waters.

'They got it,' I said.

'Good.'

'But we lost four soldiers.'

'Sounds about right.'

The survivors bent to retrieve their fallen comrades, but were stilled by a barked order from their sergeant. Instead, the dead were stripped of equipment and offered a short prayer before being condemned to the swamp waters.

'They left the bodies,' I said.

'The banner-bug might have left eggs,' she said. 'You don't want those hatching inside a Chimera. That's why it was feeding – they use our blood to gestate their young before injecting them into the desiccated bodies.'

'How vile.'

'It's only during breeding season. Most of the year they subsist on vine-fruit.'

'So, they are only dangerous when laying eggs?'

'Oh no,' she replied. 'They are irrationally territorial and extremely violent. But they won't eat you, just decapitate you. Or pull your guts out and leave them strung between the vines. Nobody knows why, but they can be quite creative with it.'

'Is this why they are called banner-bugs?'

'I've never bothered to ask.'

The Chimeras set off again, the dead sinking behind them. I mumbled a brief prayer to the God-Emperor to preserve the fallen's souls. Shard did not join me, though she had the decency to remain silent, a state that persisted as the convoy continued through the swamplands. There was little to break the monotony. The gnarl-vines grew in haphazard bunches, forcing the occasional course correction, and a few more insects attempted to intercept the troop carriers, only to find the Chimeras' hulls proof against their attacks.

That was why I was so excited when we stumbled across the downed craft.

It was Imperial, but beyond that I could not discern its origin, the fuselage torn and pitted with bullet wounds. The convoy halted and, after a brief examination of the wreckage, elected to burn it. When I asked why, Shard shrugged.

'Deny it to the enemy.'

'But it was a wreck!'

'To us, perhaps. But greenskins are exceptional scavengers. Where do you think they got the calibre of weapons needed to bring down that craft?'

'They salvage even this junk?'

'We're on a swamp. Other than raiding the distillery platforms, where do you think they acquire their weapons? That is their strength. Our losses become their gains, but even when they lose it just leaves scrap behind. The next wave of orks can forge it into a new generation of weapons.'

'Is that why we are out here?' I asked. 'A scorched earth policy?'

'No,' she said. 'We are here to reclaim lost territory.'

'When do we get to this territory?'

She laughed then, glancing back at me, the smile warm but no less cruel.

'I almost like you, Simlex,' she said. 'Your naivety borders on charming. Almost makes up for your weak chin.'

'I fail to see the humour.'

'I know. I like that too,' she said, pointing to the swamp. 'We have already recaptured territory.'

Through Mizar's unblinking eye I surveyed the expansive swamplands.

'Thoughts?' she asked.

'It would seem this territory has little value.'

'You mean because it cannot be easily fortified and has no strategic worth?' she asked. 'Or because we are already under-resourced and should not risk losing a Chimera or Vulture to an environmental hazard?'

'I suppose–'

'Or are you thinking of the logistics? That so much time and so many lives, not to mention promethium, are being squandered for such paltry gain?'

'All of the above, I suppose.'

'Well, you erred in your analysis,' she said. 'If war were an equation, and only worthwhile if the output's value exceeded the investment, this conflict would hold no worth. But there are considerations less tangible. Morale, intimidation, cutting losses and defanging potential threats. A costly war today is still cheaper than an extortionate war tomorrow.'

'And that's what this is?'

'No. This is because a noblewoman was embarrassed at her party and wishes to lash out.'

I shook my head. 'She cannot order this. She has no military power.'

'No, but her residence came under attack. She can demand protection, and has enough political capital to ensure she receives it. She wants the land swept clean. So here we are. Sweeping.'

'She cannot command your forces,' I repeated, adamant despite the current situation.

'No more than you can command me where to fly.'

'Could I command you?'

'It's an interesting question,' she mused. 'On the one hand, no, because I am a flight commander and you have no military rank. Then again, you could pull a gun on me, aim it at the back of my head. There is a fair chance that would work. Or I suppose you could produce a scroll or letter of support from Governor Zanwich, confirming he has invested his authority in you. Then we would be in a difficult situation. I could refuse you, but if the governor took offence, my life would go downhill very quickly.'

'Does Dolos have a scroll, or a gun?'

'Both,' she replied. 'Are you still attached to that seer-skull of yours?'

'Yes.'

'Can you separate a moment? I need to pull away and I don't want you having a fit and soiling your breeches again.'

'I did not soil myself.'

'There's no shame in it. Many fresh recruits find their bowels loose when they first see combat. It rarely comes up more than once.'

'Because they learn to master their fear?'

'No. They just tend to die in the first wave. Solves the problem.'

'How reassuring.'

'Are you free of the floaty-skull yet?'

'I have disengaged, left Mizar on reconnaissance.'

'Good. Because there's another blip on the auspex.'

We accelerated, the convoy disappearing behind us, leaving only the featureless swamps. The sun blazed bright and, blinded by its glare, it took me a moment to spot the burnt-out ruins rapidly approaching. All that remained was twisted metal blackened by flames, but according to Shard it had once been a refinery tasked with processing vine-fruit, the first stage of the production of Bacchus' wine.

'The orks destroyed it?' I asked.

'Destroyed, stripped for parts. There used to be dozens of these, one every fifty miles or so. Little infrastructure holds out now, at least not here. Few are still standing.'

'I saw one like this,' I murmured.

'I doubt it. The only one close to the château is Dolos' private vineyard. You wouldn't be permitted within a league of it.'

'I meant in Mizar's memory. I saw one in ruins. Two orks duelled upon it.'

'They kept it intact?' she said. 'I'm surprised. Then again, they need somewhere to forge their aircraft and their fanboats. Maybe that's why they've stripped these platforms, to assemble their own manufactoria deeper in the swamp.'

We circled the wreckage. It must once have been quite the sight. Once.

'There was no mention of this at the Harvest Banquet.'

'That would require the nobles facing some unpleasant truths. They cannot do that. Better to throw lavish parties and drink the last of the good wine whilst pretending there will always be more, and this will just blow over.'

'The situation is that bad?'

'For them? It's worse. Because it's not just the orks that threaten their interests. There's something wrong with the fruit. Have one of your seer-skulls take a gander at the vines. Might put you off those bottles they leave in your room.'

'You drink it.'

'I've consumed tuber wine brewed in a sack,' she said. 'You strike me as having a more delicate constitution.'

'What's wrong with the vine-fruit?'

'Disease,' she replied. 'Not sure what caused it. Maybe something to do with the orks? Or the war prevents them being properly tended? I don't know, but the gnarl-vines are infested with something foul that rots their fruit. The lords and ladies still have reserve stocks. But once those are exhausted? This planet no longer has value. Nobody wants to be governor of an ork-infested swamp.'

'Why did you show me this?' I asked, as we circled the burnt-out remnants of the distillery.

'You wanted to see the truth,' she said. 'This is it. We fight to protect rotten fruit, dilapidated infrastructure, and to ensure the governor remains in the manner to which she is accustomed. I admit it's not quite as catchy as shouting "For the God-Emperor!", but you're the propagandist – you tell me.'

'And that's it?'

'Hmm?' She frowned, as though forgetting. 'Oh, I'm also fairly sure I saw a runt-spotter.'

'A what?'

'A small dirigible, barely a couple of feet in diameter,' she said. 'Little greenskins operate them. They're pretty hard to spot and act as lookouts for the bigger orks.'

'Are we pursuing this spotter?'

'No,' she said. 'It went off in that direction.'

She pointed towards the horizon. I could see nothing of a dirigible, but the smoke trails were unmistakable.

'They are heading for the convoy.'

'Yes,' she said. 'Given the trajectory and estimated speeds, the two forces should clash about... there.'

She gestured to an innocuous stretch of swamp some distance hence.

'So, we have abandoned them?'

'Perhaps,' she shrugged. 'Or perhaps I have repositioned us

to the east of the impending battleground, so we can execute a flanking manoeuvre.'

'Like you did with the Valkyrie?'

'That required improvisation, but broadly, yes. The orks are like a hammer blow. They strike with speed and brute force. But once in motion they struggle to respond to sudden shifts in battle. Their bloodlust takes over, and they lash out at whatever enemies they see without taking stock of the overarching conflict. Speed and agility are the best approach.'

'They don't seem overly smart either,' I ventured.

'Yeah,' she sighed. 'What sort of idiots would risk their lives for an ugly scrap of swampland.'

I followed her gaze to the gnarl-vines, where fruit slowly rotted on the vine.

We struck the orks' flank moments before they hit the Chimera firing lines.

I took no part; the Vulture's weapons systems rerouted to Shard's console. Still, I would have made an adequate gunner, for the gatling cannons were not subtle weapons. There was little need to aim, beyond ensuring no friendlies occupied the lines of sight.

The aircraft shuddered as she unleashed the weapons, the nearest orks evaporating into a red mist, their airboats reduced to scrap by the bullet storm. As before, the ork vehicles struggled to engage the new threat, their charge faltering as they cut across each other, desperate to face it. A few took aim with their crude ballistics, but we were too swift and heavily armoured. Our disruption allowed the Chimeras to fire with impunity, and the armoured personnel carriers were well equipped for the role. Heavy bolters and multi-lasers reaped a grim tally, the embarked squads supplementing the barrage with lasgun volleys.

None of this discouraged the orks, their battle cries joyous and vicious all at once. There was no retreat, but then again how could there be? The airboats' momentum forced them forward. They had speed but no manoeuvrability, firepower without the ability to direct it. Through Mizar's eye I watched the Vulture soar over the ork line, Shard tilting the wing to neatly slice a greenskin's head from its shoulders. The seer-skull tracked its tumbled flight, the ork's jaws snapping open and shut, its slab-like forehead furrowed in confusion.

The lens panned to the Vulture as Shard slammed the turbofans into overdrive, the craft pirouetting on the spot, spraying swamp water in all directions. She opened fire again, but it was hardly necessary now. Flaming wreckage from the first wave of orks lay between the Chimeras and the fresh attackers. They made no effort to circumvent it, their craft bunching and colliding, the attack descending into farce. I saw two craft run together, their ork skippers trading insults and then bullets, only for the pair to be rear-ended by a third. A stray shot must have caught their fuel tanks, for all three were consumed by a ball of flame. Through Mizar's lens and the choking smoke, I saw them exchanging blows, even as the flames consumed them.

Few of their craft were still swamp-worthy, and the last stragglers finally accepted this battle was not in their favour. They began to pull away, but Shard pursued, the steady thud of her weapons chewing through swamp water and airboat alike. I shifted my attention back to the cockpit, and with some satisfaction watched as she reduced the survivors into flaming wreckage.

A few orks lingered, struggling against the quagmire, but they were dispatched by las-volleys. Shard brought the Vulture about as the Chimera squads disembarked, dragging the ork bodies together for disposal, and attaching krak grenades to those few airboats that remained unsunk. It seemed wasteful.

The orks profited from our war efforts, most of their equipment constructed from co-opted Imperial technology. But we could not retrieve it now, for it was xenos-tainted, and to salvage it would invite execution for tech-heresy.

Shard slowed; the Vulture hovered twenty feet above the ground.

'Did you get all that?' she asked, turning in her seat.

'I got enough,' I said. 'Was that fly-by for my benefit?'

'Thought you'd appreciate the footage.'

Her voice was flat, but I did not dwell on it. It was a relief to finally have something, short as it might be. The Guardsmen had struck down or driven off the greenskin attackers without a single casualty. Shard's approach had been flawless, her attack timed perfectly for maximum disruption. The ork confusion and infighting was precisely the material I needed, for it showed how we could triumph against them. For the first time since arriving on Bacchus, the world felt ordered. Yes, the orks were a threat. They were strong and savage, and far more capable than I first realised. But fearlessness made them headstrong. They lacked tactical acumen and subtlety, too anxious to close the distance and attack. They lacked guile.

My focus shifted to Mizar, who bobbed amongst the troopers, capturing their relief and joy in victory. There was even laughter, though the sergeant was quick to stifle it with an admonishing look. Still, I do not think his heart was in it. The troops needed a moment's levity, just sometimes. Just to stay human.

The ork dead were being dragged into a mound, the squad's flamer trooper preparing to incinerate them.

I glanced to Shard. 'Why burn the bodies? Why not just leave them to the swamp?'

She shrugged. 'Old superstition. If you don't burn them, they come back.'

'The bodies... revive?'

She laughed. 'No. Those are just stories. For the most part.'

'The most part?'

'That's a separate conversation. All you need know is you cannot get rid of orks. Were you to wipe out every last one, somehow they'd find a way back. I've heard old soldiers claim their fallen just sprout back from the earth like weeds. That's why they burn them.'

'You think it makes a difference?'

'I don't see the harm. They must come from somewhere.'

'Are there... ork females?'

'For all we know these are the females,' she replied with a smile. 'They're certainly tough enough.'

The pyre was almost complete, only one last ork still face down in the swamp. It was huge, perhaps the biggest I had yet seen, even with its left arm severed by a well-placed bolt-round. Three soldiers gathered around it, ready to haul its corpse to the pyre, each reaching for a limb.

Something stirred in the water. A clawed hand lashed out, seizing the nearest soldier by the throat as the ork surged upright, brandishing the choking trooper like a club and battering the others aside. Before they could react, it had already snapped his neck and drawn a notched blade, surging forward with a blood-thirsty roar.

The squad scrabbled for their weapons, but they were out of formation, firing lanes impeded by friendlies and smouldering scrap. It tore through them, blade reaping a bloody harvest.

I glanced to Shard, but what could she do? The Vulture's weapons were indiscriminate and would have inflicted just as much damage. The troopers were rallying, volleys of las-bolts striking the creature. I kept waiting for it to fall. It was the sergeant who finally delivered the death blow, discharging a bolt-round point-blank into its skull. As it slumped face down in the water, I counted seven bodies floating beside it. An eighth would soon join them, despite a medic's efforts to stem his blood loss.

'It must have been unconscious, only waking at their touch.'

I heard myself speak, but did not believe the words. Because I had seen the joy in the creature's face, and how quickly it had moved from corpse to threat. It had lulled us in, used its body as bait just so it could claim a few more Imperial lives before expiring.

It should not have mattered. Only a handful had been lost, barely more than those claimed by the banner-bugs. But I was uneasy for one simple reason. We had underestimated the beast It had set a trap and met death with a smile, not only because of the lives claimed, but because it had outsmarted us.

And if we could not out-think such beasts, what hope was there?

CHAPTER FOURTEEN

Flight Sergeant Plient smiled at me from atop the Marauder bomber.

'Nearly there, sir,' he said, wiping a smudge from his cheek.

I nodded my thanks before returning to the cascading images projected by Iwazar. They were set to low resolution, the picts transparent and ethereal, like gheists from a forgotten war. I did not want to distract Plient from his work, nor tip my hand too early. Not that I had anything resembling a pict yet, just a skeleton of the project.

It would have been easier to work in my room rather than endure the dusty hangar, but I had grown sick of Stylee loitering outside my door with invitations or subtle entreaties from Dolos. There were few places I could escape her influence. The château was her fortress, every inch beholden to her whims. But the hangar was a military installation, and granted me temporary respite. Plient was happy to have me, though like me he was anxious to conceal his labours. Still, his excitement was palpable.

I was less enthused. It was a struggle to splice a coherent narrative from the jumble of images. I was usually meticulous with my files, but in the chaos of war my inadvertent separation from Mizar had entangled the data. One moment Shard would be soaring through the onrushing horde, raining death like a righteous storm, only for the image to fracture into the swamplands at dusk. It was painstaking work, using Kikazar as an in-between to purge the data-core and transferring the relevant files. But focusing on it distracted me from the scenes I'd witnessed. A least for a while.

It was not the deaths; those were regrettable but necessary. But I found the idea that the ork had lain in wait unsettling. I could not forget its face. Though its fangs were bared I don't think it was angry, at least not how a human would understand it. The expression reminded me more of Flight Commander Gradeolous. It was like it had been smiling, the carnage and bloodshed a joyous event, unknowing or uncaring that it could die in the conflict.

'Iwazar,' I murmured, the skull twitching in acknowledgement at the sound. 'Recall files designated "Template" and "Warlord".'

The skull whirred as it processed the request. The projection was not quite seamless; for an instant I was treated to a bank of cloud illuminated by the moonlight. But then the images coalesced into a spear-wielding runt and the bloodied survivor of the ork duel.

I glanced from one to the other. There were similarities: basic anatomy, a lack of hair and slab-like jaw. And the skin, though it was notable that the larger brute had a darker complexion. But the contrast was marked; the duellist must have been over a foot taller than the scrawny greenskin, and several hundred pounds heavier. It almost seemed a different species, like when the Adeptus Astartes stood beside human soldiers, the gene-forged demigod towering over the human fighter.

Except the Astartes were originally crafted by the God-Emperor's own hand, using the finest technology and alchemic science. Whereas this beast had arisen unbidden from the swamps, forged only by war and death.

What if this was not the end? What if they just kept getting bigger? And smarter?

'Ugly looking things, sir!'

I glanced to Plient. He was beside me, wiping dirt from his face, his gaze fixed on the images.

'Yes, they are,' I agreed, turning back to the projection.

'That might be the biggest I ever saw. At least on this planet.'

I frowned. 'You've seen bigger orks?'

He nodded. 'Yes, sir,' he said. 'Spent a bit of time in the Argon Sector. Gosh, must have been ten years back now. There were thousands of them, and some of the larger ones could rip a tank in half.'

'You're serious?'

'Oh yes, sir,' he said. 'Of course, they wore armour, fully enclosed suits, so it was a bit hard to tell how much of it was ork and how much machine. But I saw one peel open a Chimera like a piece of fruit, before unleashing a flamer into the confines. Poor devils never had a chance.'

'Sounds terrifying.'

'It was a bit alarming, those brutes appearing from nowhere,' Plient said. 'Still, at least they were slow. Once we'd got over the shock we just retreated and poured fire into them. The blighters couldn't catch us, couldn't move much past a walking pace. They had guns of course, but none had particularly good aim. Eventually we wore them down.'

'I suppose that's one thing we don't have to worry about. Heavy armour would be a liability out here.'

'Exactly, sir.' Plient grinned. 'There won't be no armoured orks ambushing us in the swamp.'

'No,' I agreed. 'Shame we can't say the same about their aircraft.'

'True, sir,' Plient replied, his smile fading. 'I still don't understand how they snuck through our defences. Did a bit of damage, I can tell you. I've patched up as many craft as I can, but until Orbital Station Salus can deploy reinforcements we will be stretched thin.'

'When do they resupply?'

'Every day, sir, but most of the drops are for the front line. We have to wait our turn.'

'We are fortunate to be close to a forge world,' I replied. 'Though the reliance on a single orbital station for reinforcements seems problematic.'

'I wouldn't worry, sir,' Plient said, grinning. 'No ork fighter can breach the atmosphere. It's beyond their reach.'

'They said the same about the governor's estate,' I replied, my gaze returning to the pair of orks, one brandishing a crudely assembled spear, the other a forged chainblade. 'Flight Sergeant Plient?' I asked.

'Sir?'

'You said you'd fought larger orks? Heavily armoured ones?'

'Yes, sir. In the Argon Sector.'

'And they appeared behind your lines?'

'That's right, sir.'

'How?' I asked. 'Were they lying in wait? Or did some ork aircraft drop them?'

'I don't think so. They were just there suddenly. I didn't really question it – we were too busy panicking and trying to bring them down. Perhaps they dug their way out of the ground? Or... were camouflaged in some manner?'

He did not sound wholly convinced. Neither was I.

'Do you remember anything unusual?'

'Smoke.' He shrugged. 'And... lightning.'

'There was a storm?'

'No. Just green lightning. All around us, so bright it was blinding. At first, I thought it a weapon of some kind, but it did not strike us. But when the light cleared they were there, making their attack.'

He looked thoughtful, or close to it.

'I did wonder...'

'Yes?'

'Well, sir, the God-Emperor's technology allows the Adeptus Astartes to appear from nowhere.'

'That is true.'

'I found myself wondering, as blasphemous as it may sound...'

'You may speak freely, Plient.'

'Given we can teleport our troops in such a manner, and given the orks appeared in a similar way...'

He averted his gaze, his hands fidgeting with a cloth.

'Yes, Plient?'

'I wondered if maybe... one of our tech-adepts had inadvertently transported the orks by mistake?'

He would not meet my gaze, fearful his words would be deemed treacherous.

'I suppose that is possible,' I said. 'Errors do occur.'

He nodded, relieved. 'Yes, sir. I'm sure it was just a one-time error, and the one responsible was suitably chastised.'

Chastised was putting it mildly. If such an incident had occurred the perpetrator's execution would only have been delayed long enough for their superiors to devise a suitably violent and ironic method. But, though I know little of teleportation technology, I am aware of its limitations. An object cannot simply be plucked from one spot and moved to another, it requires a bespoke platform, and it is all but impossible to transport something significantly larger than an armoured Adeptus Astartes warrior.

The idea that our technicians could have inadvertently deposited a squad of orks behind enemy lines was absurd.

But I knew why Plient clung to it. For the alternative was worse, and to suggest the orks harboured technology that could surpass our own was heresy.

I glanced to him. He had returned to his duties, whistling a toneless tune.

'Iwazar, play back file designated "Duel".'

The holo-image collapsed into beams of light, reassembling into the spectacle of two orks battling atop the desecrated platform. Why had they been fighting? A challenge for dominance? Squabbling over spoils? It could be both, or neither. Perhaps, in the absence of opponents, they merely fought each other for practice. Or fun.

But it was not their struggle that had piqued my interest.

The duel concluded, the victor raised his head to the sky, his followers howling in triumph. What did they see in the sky above? I would never know, for Mizar fled moments later. But as the seer-skull dodged the volleys of gunfire, its lens flicked across the darkness.

There.

'Freeze image,' I murmured, peering at the spectacle. The resolution was still set to low, the image bleached of colour.

Except for emerald-green lightning parting the sky.

Flight Commander Gradeolous glanced up from his meal. His expression was not welcoming, and I found myself wondering again whether this was a mistake. But I needed answers from someone I trusted to speak the truth. Or, to be more precise, someone who lacked the wit to hold their tongue.

'Flight Commander Gradeolous,' I said, bowing. 'Pardon the intrusion. I wondered if I might speak to you?'

He glanced from me to Kikazar, hovering behind my shoulder.

'I thought you preferred speaking to Commander Shard,' he replied as I took a seat opposite. The mess hall was reasonably crowded, the flight crews wolfing down their nutrient pastes, which is frankly the only way to keep the stuff down. But Gradeolous' table was notable for the vacant chairs.

'I do not always get the luxury of choosing my subjects,' I replied. 'I have my orders.'

'As do we all,' Gradeolous replied, tearing off a hunk of black bread. It seemed his repast was a little above the standard fare. Perhaps the privilege of being an officer, or perhaps he had a connection within the kitchen.

'Might I conduct a short interview?'

'Here?' he said, frowning. 'Whilst I'm eating?

'Yes, it grants authenticity. Shows that even a hero such as yourself still eats and speaks like a normal man.'

'Very well, a few questions then,' he said, wiping his chin. 'But be quick. I am set to fly once the craft is refuelled.'

'How often do you see action?'

He shrugged. 'As often as I can. I'd prefer to be out there now, except we have a shortage of fighters. And pilots, come to think of it. That damn ork attack was a serious setback.'

'I'm still amazed they got this close.'

He tutted. 'If you only knew.' He retrieved a case from an inner pocket, flicked it open with his thumb and extracted a miniscule moustache comb.

'I take it you cannot tell me?'

'There are operational matters that are beyond you,' he replied, teasing the corners of his moustache into place. 'Let us just say it was a close one. Closer still, had you not raised the alarm.'

'That was but luck,' I said. 'I would hate to rely upon it.'

'True enough.' Gradeolous nodded, returning his comb to the

case. I thought his grooming concluded, until he produced a battered tin and commenced smoothing wax onto his whiskers.

'Do you think the orks are becoming more aggressive? Or increasing in numbers?'

'Hard to tell,' he replied. 'There are more in the air. But I suspect it's more that their focus has shifted. Without the Aeronautica Imperialis, the ground troops would have been long overrun. We've been bombing them into oblivion – it's no wonder they strive to meet us face to face, assuming you can mistake their ghastly visages for faces.'

'And how formidable are their craft?'

'Not as robust as ours, but savage enough I suppose,' he replied. 'The trick is to engage head-on, match them shot for shot. It's why I favour the Avenger. Some think it a ground attack craft, but for one with the right fortitude it can be a formidable fighter.'

'You sound as though you don't fear the orks.'

'Of course not,' he snorted. 'You cannot let fear dictate your battles. I have been outflanked, outnumbered and faced the most terrible foes the sky can offer. But I never flinch, never retreat. Why, I was shot down three times this campaign alone, but I never let it affect me. That's why I'm the best pilot we have.'

'You fear nothing?' I persisted. 'I've heard some whisper about something called the Green Storm.'

'Cowards, the lot of them,' he sighed, rolling his eyes.

'You do not fear it?'

'Fear what?' he said. 'There have been no confirmed reports, just a couple of so-called pilots who met their match and cannot accept it. They flew into a cloud, claimed there was green lightning everywhere, and that the sky rained bullets. Nonsense, or at worst an unfortunate combination of bad weather, poor navigation and a surprise attack. A quick raid would be sufficient to assuage such unfounded concerns.'

'I see,' I said, nodding. 'And is that what you would propose? A more aggressive campaign?'

He was still tending to his moustache, but his expression had shifted. Suspicious was not quite the word, but I could feel him reappraising me in light of the questions. His gaze shifted to seer-skull Kikazar, who was silently monitoring our exchange.

'Is this part of your pict?' he asked.

'I'm just looking for quotes and soundbites,' I said. 'I might, for example, play your comments about being fearless over a shot of your craft sweeping into combat. It can help set the scene.'

He nodded slowly, his gaze fixed on the skull.

'And that device is reliable?' he asked. 'It looks on the verge of falling apart.'

'Oh, believe me, this is a prized relic. The skull used to belong to Propagandist Vite Kikazar. He was known to give voice to the voiceless.'

'Is that right?' Gradeolous frowned, closing his moustache case and tucking it into his pocket. 'Because it strikes me that the voiceless should remain so for a reason.'

'Kikazar disagreed,' I said. 'He would mingle with the dregs of society in the hive slums and shanty towns. There he would patiently hear any grievance or tirade, offering only a sympathetic ear and a glass of amasec. He believed that only through such patience would the traitor and heretic lose their guard and reveal their treachery. In this way he served, and through his tireless efforts thousands of potential heretics were burned before they could even commit an evil act.'

'Hmm,' Gradeolous replied, still intent on the yellowed skull, and the metal studs holding its cranium together. 'Looks as though he had an unpleasant end.'

'Kikazar made the mistake of lending his ear to a cult of witches. Whatever they told him resulted in his head exploding.

The skull had to be rebuilt from shards. Still, his cogitator is invaluable. He can register the subtlest nuances of accent and language, and translate almost any dialect.'

'I'm sure that is a valuable utility,' Gradeolous replied, rising from his chair. 'But this is war, and the only language an ork understands is the thud of auto-fire, or the shockwave of an explosion. Perhaps your focus should be there.'

'You are correct, of course,' I said. 'I thank you for your time.'

'A pleasure. For you,' he replied. 'But in future, focus on capturing my combat skills, domination of the skies. Good day.'

I watched him stride away, the remains of his meal strewn about the table. I could not decide if I had learnt little or much from him. I had no means to verify his words, but I did not get the impression he was lying, and a brief consultation with Kikazar's cogitator confirmed it had detected no indication of falsehoods from his biorhythms.

But that did not mean he spoke truth, only that he believed in his cause.

CHAPTER FIFTEEN

I spent that evening by the window, nursing a glass of questionable wine, my gaze affixed to the distant sky and the storm that squatted in the west. I swore it was creeping closer. Had it been there when we first deployed? I remembered mist; perhaps that had concealed it. Or had it gathered since my arrival?

I had little else to do while I waited. I had requested to vox with Confessor Maric von Shard, and his itinerary indicated the priest's ship was docked at Hedon for resupply. But my request only made it as far as his subordinate, and I doubted it would be relayed before his ship departed. Iwazar hovered beside me, poised to act as receiver. I doubted Maric would even pick up. Gregarious as he was, it was unlikely the priest would remember our time working together.

As the light faded I tried to get drunk, but struggled to finish a single glass. Dolos was generous enough with her bounty, at least in terms of volume. But I was beginning to suspect the quality depended on her current disposition. The bitter aftertaste suggested I was not, at present, well favoured. Still, the indigestible wine was probably for the best. I had already been half-cut before one of Shard's siblings and did not wish to repeat the experience.

Iwazar stiffened, its eye flashing as the holo-projector whirled, an image materialising in the window frame and blotting out the clouds. I straightened, glancing for somewhere to place my glass as the feed coalesced into a figure clad in the vestments of a priest, his shoulders adorned with a white cassock, a golden cincture straining against his waist. The chain slung around his neck supported a modest aquila, cast from humble copper, and his sun-blushed face was drawn in a broad smile that almost encompassed his rounded cheeks. He was not exactly corpulent, but there was a softness to him, especially when compared to his sister.

Except for his eyes.

'Confessor von Shard,' I said, bowing. 'I thank you for making time for me.'

He spread his hands. *'How could I refuse? Any man who earns my brother Tobia's respect is at least worthy of my time.'*

'I am grateful, confessor. We have met briefly. I don't suppose you recall–'

'The Gigerian Cleansing?' he said. *'Yes, of course I remember. Your picts helped rouse the Imperial citizens against the threat posed by their so-called ruling family. The God-Emperor was pleased by your work. As am I, His humble servant.'*

He bowed his head, doubling his chins in the process.

'Thank you,' I said. 'I am sorry to ask for your aid now, but I am not sure what else to do.'

'Oh?' he said. *'Do you fear for your soul?'*

'On occasion. But this is not about that. There is a situation developing here. I fear that conflict between the governing forces on Bacchus and the military will–'

'*Is it a spiritual conflict?*' He spoke softly, but his eyes were hard.
'No.'

'*Then I cannot assist you. The Ecclesiarchy does not involve itself in local politics. Unless there is evidence of spiritual corruption. Or heresy.*'

He spoke with such self-assurance I almost believed him. He was still smiling, the expression almost apologetic.

I sighed. 'I have not seen evidence of either.'

'*Unfortunate,*' he said. '*If you do, you must inform me. But unless you find proof of corruption, I cannot assist you. At least, not directly.*'

'So, there is something you can do?'

'*Of course,*' he said. '*I will pray for a swift resolution. You have my word.*'

'Thank you.' I sighed again, forcing down my disappointment. 'Well, I will not take up more of your time. I–'

'*Nonsense,*' he said. '*If I cannot offer my services to a troubled servant of the God-Emperor, what sort of priest am I? Is there anything you need to confess?*'

'I do not think so.'

He smiled. '*It might surprise you how many hold that view, until they find themselves in the penitent's chair. But I will take you on your word. Tell me, then, how do you find my little sister, Lucille?*'

'I... She is a fine warrior, and–'

'*Come now,*' he said. '*You can be honest. She's my kin, remember?*'

'It has been somewhat challenging,' I said. 'She is... I'm not sure how best to phrase it.'

'*Wilful? Obstinate? Foul-mouthed?*' he offered with a wry smile. 'I would prefer not to say.'

He laughed, his voice rich and sweet as molasses. '*I know her flaws. I will hardly condemn you for recognising such.*'

'I was just surprised how different she was. From both you and Commissar von Shard.'

'*Well, families are like that,*' he said with a shrug. '*She always had a rebellious spark. For a time it concerned me. I was worried she might not graduate from the schola progenium.'*

His tone was casual, but I had no doubt that the penalty for those who failed the programme was considerably more severe than a demerit.

'Those were troubling times,' he continued, his hand straying to his aquila. *'I remember during my first ministry I received messages from my former drill abbot – we had established something of a bond during my studies. It was informal, of course, but as the eldest brother he wanted me to know how close she was to failing.'*

'I take it you spoke to her? Set her on the right path?'

'Oh, I wanted to,' he sighed. *'But I had so many duties, and we did not see each other frequently. It wasn't until our mother's second funeral that I had a chance to meet with her in person.'*

'And she listened?'

'No. Unfortunately there were pressing matters that day and I could not find the moment. She spent most of the wake talking to her aunt.'

'Lord-Captain Elsbeff von Shard?'

He smiled. *'You really do your research. Yes, though I cannot say I approved of their exchange. The last thing one wants for a wayward child is a lecture from a rogue trader whose remit involves pilfering the galaxy to line her own pockets.'*

His smiled faded as he spoke. I understood why. Rogue traders explored the edges of known space, ostensibly at the behest of the Imperium. In truth, they operated with unparalleled autonomy, masters of their own fate. Not, perhaps, the best role model for the rebellious young Shard.

'Still,' he said. *'The God-Emperor works in mysterious ways. I do not know what our aunt said that day, but Lucille was a different student from then on. She began buckling down and working hard. The drill abbots still did not like her attitude, but at least she made efforts to conceal it. The rest you know – she showed a talent for flying and,*

*in time, became perhaps the finest fighter ace the Imperium has ever
known. It just goes to show, sometimes the most unlikely of tools can
be an instrument of His will.'*

He smiled at me.

*'Tell me, do you think my sister is involved in this conflict you
spoke of?'*

'I do not think so. But all of us are caught up in it.'

'Unfortunate,' he said, tapping his chins. *'Still, the God-Emperor
has a plan. I am sure He has equipped you with what you need to
overcome this challenge. I will pray that, through you, His will shall
be done.'*

I am unsure if it was Maric or my experience with the armoured
convoy that spurred me into action. Perhaps I do myself a dis-
service, and the impetus came from a desire for the truth.
Regardless, the following days were spent interrogating both aces
and ground crew about the conflict. When I asked of the Green
Storm, they were quick to dismiss this threat as just another ork
making a name. Like the rest, he would fail against their aces.
None of them claimed to have been near the storm front. Or
seen green lightning.

I even attended the medi-unit, interviewing those worst afflicted
by the conflict. Many were proud to display their wounds and
share their stories. But the chirurgeon was less welcoming. He
limited my interactions to those enthusiastic young soldiers keen
to return to duty, or else directed me to grizzled veterans who
spoke rehearsed lines with dour conviction. I was not permitted
to approach the rearmost medi-bays, where the sickest resided,
though their sobs and sighs were all too audible.

I did not think to speak to Plient again, assuming he was
too busy toiling in the hangar, maintaining the few craft still
sky-worthy. I was surprised when he sought me out in the mess

hall, smile so broad I feared he was muddled by inhaling too many promethium fumes. He insisted on dragging me back to the hangar but would not tell me why. Not until we were standing before an amorphous shape covered by a large cloth.

'You ready, sir?' he said.

'I hope so,' I replied, with some trepidation. It was not that I doubted his intent, rather that I feared disappointing him. He had laboured long on a project he hoped would assist me. I had no idea what it was, other than it smelled of burnt wires and could be concealed by a large drape.

'Ready, sir?' Plient repeated, taking hold of it with both hands.

'Whenever you are ready, flight sergeant.'

He swept the drape aside, revealing his handiwork.

I am not sure what reaction he expected. It might have helped if I had the faintest idea what I beheld. It looked like a section of an aircraft's carriage, containing a modified hard point roughly the size of a human head.

I glanced to the expectant Plient and shrugged helplessly.

'Don't you see, sir?' he said. 'Remember what you said, about not being able to capture the conflicts? Well, I've jury-rigged a housing for one of your seer-skulls. This is from a Marauder bomber, *Hephaestus*. The hard points are normally used to integrate weapon systems, but it should now be able to house the seer-skull. I think I could refit any of our craft now I've got the hang of it.'

He was beaming with pride. I could only stare.

'But… is this a sanctioned modification?' I frowned. 'Has a tech-priest approved it?'

'Ah,' Plient replied, smile slipping a shade. 'Well, sir, not exactly. But our enginseer, Calov-7C, sanctioned us to make repairs and necessary modifications to craft, subject to his inspection and approval.'

'And you think he will approve this?'

'I doubt it, sir.'

'That does not trouble you?'

'It would trouble me more if he did. The last I saw of him was when his transport collided with an ork fighter. The explosion was so fierce that it baked a mile of swampland dry.'

'Then… you complete the repairs alone?'

'Oh, me, a few others,' Plient replied. 'It's mainly replacing armour plates and patching up holes. Wing Commander Prospherous says I'm proof that any imbecile can do it.'

He seemed unduly proud of this fact.

'You aren't worried about what happens when a new enginseer is assigned to the unit?'

'I was a little, sir,' Plient replied. 'But Wing Commander Prospherous reassured me.'

'Did he now?'

'Oh yes. He said that by the time we see another tech-priest, it is unlikely any of the planes I've worked on will still be here. And I'll probably be gone too.'

'You think this good news?'

'Of course,' he said. 'It means we must be close to victory. And to tell you the truth I'm looking forward to redeployment. I don't like the climate here, it's too muggy.'

I could not think what to say and merely nodded, my gaze flicking to the panel. The design was familiar.

Could I trust his work? The mysteries of machine-spirits were beyond me. I had received training and sanction from an adept to maintain and attend my seer-skulls. The principle here was the same, though the execution sounded rather suspect. Plient was a trustworthy fellow and would only have the best intentions. But he was tampering with devices beyond either of our ken.

But what choice did I have? If I wanted to really fly, this was the only way.

'I… thank you, Plient,' I said. 'Did Wing Commander Prospherous approve this?'

'Oh yes, sir,' said Plient, nodding. 'The wing commander said I should do whatever it took to get that… to help Propagandist Simlex. Honestly, I was a bit surprised sir. I did not think he cared for you, but after that Valkyrie mission he changed his mind completely. He really wants to get you in the air.'

This surprised me, and felt wrong. But I was too elated to dwell on misgivings. For I finally had a means to see through an ace's eyes, to capture their battles as though I were a true combatant.

In my excitement, I neglected to give due consideration to what that word meant.

CHAPTER SIXTEEN

I will never forget the morning of that flight.

The sky was crisp, even if the air was muggy, and the morning dew gleamed from the fuselage of the Marauder bomber designated *Hephaestus*. It was a colossal aircraft, the largest I'd seen, requiring a crew of six and carrying sufficient payload to wipe out an armoured convoy. I could just spy Mizar, nestled on the underside of the craft thanks to Plient's handywork.

Hephaestus, along with twin sister bombers, dwarfed the squadrons of Thunderbolt fighters that would provide an escort. It was a majestic sight beholding the invincible force, and my heart swelled to be a modest part of it. Even the stench of promethium was somehow invigorating, for it bore the sweet scent of humanity's industry. I slowed to take in the scene, but Shard's elbow jarred into my back.

'We have a schedule,' she snapped, pushing past me.

I did not reply; her expression did not warrant one. Her perpetual sneer was today a snarl, her gaze seeking fault wherever it fell. The rest of the aces and flight crew said little, I assume to appease her. Still, their expressions were not as reassuring as the sight of the planes had been. They were hardened and stoic, but shared none of the savage joy of our xenos foes.

Wing Commander Prospherous struck a more positive note. He and two senior officers oversaw our departure. The soldiers saluted as they passed, and I attempted to do likewise, but he beckoned me over.

'Propagandist Simlex,' he said, offering his hand. 'I wanted to personally wish you good luck. You are a brave man to fly into an active warzone.'

I shook his hand. 'Your soldiers risk their lives daily for the Imperium,' I said. 'I am no fighter, but how can I risk any less in fulfilling my duty?'

He smiled. 'Let us hope it does not come to that. You are, after all, flying with the very best.'

I followed his gaze to Shard, who was clambering into the cockpit. From my vantage point, I could not see what caused her such offence, only that she snatched something from the console, berating one of the other soldiers before hurling it into the mud.

'Clean up after yourself,' she spat, as the man clawed at the quagmire, I presume to retrieve his discarded property. Perhaps it was a good luck charm, or token from his family.

I glanced at Prospherous. 'She does not seem in best spirits.'

'A bomber is not her preferred assignment,' he conceded with a wry smile. 'But do not let that concern you. She is still the best, irrespective of the craft.'

'I do not doubt it,' I said. 'Wing commander, I wish to thank you. I know my presence is an imposition. I am grateful for your indulgence and support.'

'I was too harsh when we first met, and the circumstances were not ideal,' he replied. 'But since then, I have realised my error, and how much you have to offer. Your vision is a vital part of the war effort, and I thank you for it.'

I nodded, too dumbstruck to reply. He smiled again and motioned me on board.

As *Hephaestus* soared skywards I synced with the seer-skull and, for the first time since my arrival, Bacchus was truly laid out beneath me. Admittedly, it was a rather uninspiring spectacle, a world of burnt orange threaded with black vines, but all I saw then was possibility. More possibility than Plient had intended, it transpired, for I quickly discovered Mizar was directly interfaced with the bomber. I could not only view the world through its lenses, but also each of the gunner's sights, though without picters I could not capture actual footage through the targeting overlays.

I decided to remain quiet on the matter. For Plient's sake, I told myself.

As we ascended the mire faded into a featureless blob, an expanse too vast for even Mizar's sensors to capture as anything but a blur. Ahead, a violet band of light separated Bacchus' atmosphere from the void. I shifted my view to the upper turret, watching through its targeting lens as stars blossomed into view.

Yet still we climbed, assuming that is the right term. I do not know at what point altitude ends, and one merely becomes an object floating in the void. But I know we passed this barrier, for the weight eased from my frame. I would have drifted from my seat were I not restrained by the flight harness. The sensation bore a stark contrast to my arrival on Bacchus, where we near burned a hole through the atmosphere. This was akin to sliding into water.

I shifted my view through the craft. From the upper turret, I could just make out the sun glinting from Orbital Station Salus. At this distance it resembled three silver blades suspended on a golden halo, the point of each directed at the planet below. Those were the launch bays, from which a fresh squadron was promptly departing, the craft glowing like embers as they pierced the sky and descended into the storm gathered below.

I was reassured by Salus' presence. It was a reminder that the Imperium spanned countless stars, and the world below was but one in the billion, the ork horde nothing more than a terrestrial threat. If all else failed, we could always flee, let them enjoy the foulness that was Bacchus.

The vox crackled into life, gunners and bombardier confirming their readiness and offering short prayers to the craft's machine-spirit.

Shard barely grunted in response. Her back was to me, and her face hidden by the pressure helm. But there was a stillness to her, a quality I cannot quite articulate. The vox continued to crackle, but she did not seem to hear it. We drifted in near silence, lifting towards the stars.

'Flight commander?' I eventually asked.

She glanced over her shoulder. 'What?' she said, irritated.

'The vox?'

'I'm taking a moment. It can wait.'

'A moment to what?'

She sighed pointedly. 'A moment to look out across the stars and muse upon the myriad possibilities contained therein. A moment to marvel at the stark beauty of cold void, to frame humanity's petty struggles against its majesty. But, apparently, the God-Emperor will not permit even that respite. Go on. I'm sure you have an annoying question.'

'I do.'

'Well?'

'Do you think you would have preferred a life out there? As a void captain? Or rogue trader?'

She did not answer immediately, and I did not press, settling into my seat and waiting.

Finally, she responded. 'Perhaps,' she said. 'Still, the duties probably do not differ greatly. And one does not get to choose how one might serve, despite any assurances otherwise.'

Before I could reply the vox crackled again, one of our squadron requesting a mission update. Shard's response was brief and foul. But with that exchange the moment was gone. She barked orders, and we pivoted from the canopy of stars, gliding back towards Bacchus. The craft shuddered, buffeted by the bleed between void and air. Until that moment, I had not appreciated the smoothness of our weightless flight, not until gravity once more found purchase.

I shifted my view to Mizar, but there was little of interest beneath, the landscape the same monotony of swamp and scrub. The meteorology was just as uninspired as the geography, the clouds little more than wisps of smoke.

Except for the storm front.

It was below and to the west of us: a seething mass of dark clouds that spiralled like a slothful tornado. I kept Mizar trained on it, half anticipating a flash of green lightning. But there was none, and the more I looked at it the less remarkable it seemed, merely another atmospheric anomaly.

'Are storms common on Bacchus?' I asked.

'Yes. No. What does it matter?'

'You are not concerned about that burgeoning storm front?'

'That is an entirely separate question,' she replied. 'And, at present, no, because we are moving away from it.'

'Does it concern you?'

'It's not my job to be concerned unless ordered otherwise.'

'You must have an opinion?'

'Not if I don't want to. My duty is to fly, not have opinions.'

'Gradeolous thinks you should commit to an all-out attack.'

'Attack a storm front?' she laughed. 'Does he hear himself?'

'At least he is forthright. And honest.'

'Honesty is commendable unless the speaker is an imbecile. Then it is just an idiot perpetrating a falsehood.'

'You don't know his reasoning.'

'I do. I just don't care.'

'Then what do you say?' I asked. 'I heard you dismiss this mythical pilot known as the Green Storm when you were bragging to the troops.'

'And what would you have me say?' she snapped. 'That we have lost fighters to an enemy we cannot even see? Do you think that would reassure them? They need a focus for their hate. You want the truth of war? The truth is we face endless greenskins. For morale's sake we need to designate special targets. Then we crow that the Bringer of Flame is brought low! A victory! We celebrate their demise, pretending that a dozen more ork fighters won't soon take to the skies, each seeking to make an even greater name. It never ends, and no single pilot really makes a blind bit of difference.'

'Including you?'

'Oh no, that's different. Flight Commander Lucille von Shard can single-handedly liberate a planet with two hunter-killer missiles and half a tank of promethium.'

'I see. And does she always refer to herself in the third person?'

'When the mood takes her,' Shard replied. 'Now pipe down, I need to concentrate on the mission.'

She would not speak further, so I chose to focus on my own project, recording our flight. But the initial excitement was waning. Besides the ascent and brief excursion into space, there was little worth capturing. The Thunderbolts were below us, but they remained locked in formation, and one pict of them was sufficient. We were so high the ground was a blur to even Mizar's sensors.

After perhaps an hour I made the mistake of raising this issue.

'Is there a chance we could briefly fly lower?' I said. 'I cannot capture much from this altitude.'

Shard stiffened. She flicked a few switches, engaging the automated pilot systems, before turning fully in the chair, unclasping her faceplate so she could look me in the eyes.

'Descend?' she said.

'I merely meant—'

'Do you understand how bombers work?' she continued. 'The guiding principle is you fly very high and drop bombs on things far below. Do you understand?'

'Obviously. I merely—'

'Are you certain?' she persisted, raising her hand to eye level and manoeuvring it as though it were a plane. 'Because this, my hand? This is us flying.'

Her fingers swayed back and forth, whilst she made accompanying sound effects. I knew better than to interrupt and extend my suffering.

'The bombs come out here,' she said, using her other hand to indicate the release of an explosive. 'Once we start dropping them the greenskins tend to notice. They shoot back, or send up their own craft. Our best defence is maintaining altitude and hoping their engines stall before they reach us.'

'But… we are armed and armoured. Surely a—'

'We are slow and ponderous,' she replied. 'The Thunderbolt fighters will do their duty, but if an ork gets through, you better hope the armour holds, because we carry about two thousand kilos of high explosives. If one of them is even clipped, we are done. So, for that reason, we stay as high as possible, at least until we have sighted our target.'

'And what is our target?'

'That would be classified.' She smiled, turning away.

I shook my head, syncing with Mizar and surveying the feature-less void beneath. It made the cold vacuum of space positively appealing. At least there were stars to enjoy.

I cannot say how long we flew, for I fear I drifted, lulled by the warmth of the cockpit and hum of the engines. It was never a full slumber, for that is near impossible when synced to a seer-skull, but abrupt cuts in the footage suggest I was not paying due attention. I kept experiencing flashes of data-scraps, dragged from Mizar's deep storage: bubbling swamps and green lightning, the images spliced with the cockpit and surrounding craft. I heard Shard murmuring through the vox, her voice low I could not pick out all the words, something about uncooperative cargo.

Suddenly the craft lurched to the side, my head slamming against the headrest. I glanced up, blinking, to find her facing me.

'Oh good, you're awake again,' she smirked. 'Pleasant dreams?'

'I was merely cataloguing some of Mizar's files.'

'That would explain the snoring. Did you find anything useful?'

'Useful?'

'In your little skull. Has it seen anything interesting?'

'Why do you care?'

She shrugged. 'I'm bored. I merely seek to pass the time.'

'I would have thought you sufficiently occupied preparing for the mission.'

'Yes,' she sighed. 'Well, between you and me, when I say "class-ified", I mean we are undertaking dynamic tactical interdiction with limited visual capabilities.'

'You are flying blind and hoping to find a worthwhile target?'

'I did not realise you had such an appreciation for military ter-minology. Yes, we are flying through hostile territory hoping to uncover something worth destroying. You would think it would be easy, but the damn greenskins have got better at hiding. They used to break cover when we soared over, firing those little guns of theirs, heedless that we were far out of range. It made it simple to cull them.'

'What changed?'

'They built planes. And discovered tactics. And stealth.'

'Like hiding? I can't really picture an ork lurking in the bushes.'

'You'd be surprised,' she said. 'This is not my first war against them. Most prefer a direct approach to violence, but there's always a few who appreciate the finesse of knifing someone in the back.'

'You think the orks are hiding somewhere?'

'You have the fancy sensors and scanners on your skulls. You tell me.'

It was not quite a command. But neither was there humour in her voice.

And she had a point. I synced with Mizar, and found the landscape had altered significantly. We still flew over the swamp, though it was now a more rusted brown. But the waters were barely visible, the view obscured by the tangled mass of gnarl-vines, the undulating vegetation forming peaks and valleys. It was impossible to say what could be hidden beneath the canopy, assuming anything could carve out an existence amidst the barbed vines.

As Mizar's lenses tried to pierce the thorned barrier, the fruit-lessness of our assignment dawned on me. Those precious resources Shard had mentioned – personnel hours, fuel, strategic resources – all squandered on something amounting to armed reconnaissance.

'This is hopeless,' I said. 'How do you spot anything through those vines?'

'We sometimes use a Thunderbolt fighter to fish for them,'

she said. 'It swoops sharp and low, as if in danger of crashing. They can't help themselves, and swarm to take potshots. Their guns have some teeth, even though they can't aim a damn. Still, twelve-barrelled gatling cannons are pretty forgiving in that regard.'

'I can't imagine that is a popular assignment.'

'It's fine if you are quick enough. The trick is a rapid descent. They rarely adjusted for the acceleration, and kept firing on where you were, rather than anticipating where you could be. But once they opened fire the bombers would have their targets. Still, it's a bit like trying to kill wasps with a hammer. You might swing it through a couple of bushes and crush a few. But sometimes you hit a nest, and then you have a problem.'

'Is that why you aren't employing this strategy?'

'No. It stopped working once they learnt to fly.'

She was silent a moment. But again, I did not press.

'I wonder if we were their teachers, however inadvertently,' she continued at length. 'They had no other means to truly engage. If this world was of rock or steel, perhaps they would have built tanks and transports instead of claiming the skies. For a time, we had a numerical advantage, as well as the superior craft. But we've long since lost the former, and the latter is now debatable. We can rarely press this deep, and only now because other squadrons are drawing ork attention elsewhere. We haven't culled them in months. For all we know, thousands more have been spawned deep in the swamps. Who knows what they have been up to?'

'Is that our real mission then?'

'It would be if we could find them. But our auspexes are near useless out here because of the swamp's ambient energy. I assume you've had the same issues?'

I had, of course. Even now, Mizar was strained to the limit trying to pierce the gnarl-vine canopy, unable to distinguish disparate life signs in the festering waters. On a whim I drifted through the electromagnetic spectrum, the swamp in turn sparkling or growing dark as a tomb.

Something glinted.

It was some distance to our flank. A sickly pulse of energy that flickered like candlelight.

'There... I see something,' I murmured.

'What is it?'

'I am not certain,' I said, squinting at the flickering light. It was unpleasant to look upon, like a grain of sand was lodged in my eye.

'Is it below us?'

'No. Some distance.'

'Which way?'

'Over there,' I said, gesturing vaguely in the direction. As I did so I felt the bomber shift, Shard muttering something into the vox.

'Is it ahead of us now?'

'I suppose.'

'Don't suppose,' she snarled. 'You're sitting in the navigator's seat. Do a better job, for Throne's sake.'

I flinched, startled. Her voice was hard, with an edge previously unknown to me. She turned immediately to the console, flicking switches and making preparations. I could just make out background vox-chatter as the vessels coordinated their positions.

'Adjust five degrees to the left,' I said.

She did so, and through Mizar I saw our escort do likewise. The formation seemed to be shifting, the Thunderbolts spreading out beneath us and accelerating.

'How far are we from it?'

'I... I don't know how to judge distance at this altitude.'

'Is there anything on the landscape?'

'You see that bulge of vines? The mound with tumour-like tendrils?' I said, pointing to the viewscreen. 'Whatever I'm seeing lies in its shadow, on the side nearest us.'

'Can you tell me anything else?' Shard asked. 'Do you see more than one light?'

'No.'

'How big is it?'

'I… I cannot really describe it in those terms. The source might be the size of a candle, but its glare is blinding.'

I thought this answer might irritate her, but she merely nodded before asking a final question.

'Is it stable?'

'No. It flickers and flares, energy spilling from it. Is this craft rad-shielded?'

'Yes. For all that it matters,' she replied, gaze fixed ahead.

The vox flared again. Most of the exchange was meaningless to me. But Shard responded to each squad, sounding them by name and wishing each good fortune.

I did not find it reassuring, nor did I enjoy Flight Commander Nocter's murmured prayer to the God-Emperor.

The light was drawing closer. I did not want to look at it, shifting my view to the surrounding planes, the Marauder bombers and the Thunderbolt fighters. One peeled off, almost dropping from the sky, its engines flaring as it descended towards the once-distant light. I could not think why, until I recalled Shard's story of sending a lone Thunderbolt as bait for their guns.

As it did so, light flared.

'Something is happening,' I said, but the warning came too late. Multiple beams of energy erupted from the undergrowth. They swung wildly through the air, seemingly at random, until one shone upon the descending Thunderbolt. The instant it did, the craft was wrenched from the sky, plummeting like a rock.

I did not see where it fell, for the sky was now filled with bullets and explosions.

CHAPTER SEVENTEEN

I had seen war. I had witnessed Imperial convoys clash with vile heretics, and captured the brutality of the killing ground between them. But even as the bodies fell, there was an order to it, lines ebbing and flowing as dominance was sought. There were feints and flanking manoeuvres, but these are time-tested tactics, another part of the great game of war.

I am sure it was different on the front lines, where the bullets were flying and bodies piling up. But even that would have seemed a coordinated conflict compared to the madness that unfolded a mile above the swamp. The ork fighters appeared from nowhere, hurling themselves towards the bombers, as though seeking to ram them. The Thunderbolts ran interception, their autocannons spitting a hail of shells and tearing the orks from the sky.

But an instant later another wave would be on us.

'I need an eye down there!' Shard bellowed. 'Where are they coming from?'

It made no sense. There were no runways below, not with the encroaching vines. I had shifted Mizar to more conventional optics to better capture the battle, but there was still a glimmer from that strange energy source.

'Whatever it is, it's almost below us,' I said.

Shard swore. 'Screw it. We're diving. Keep formation. Nocter, you have the lead.'

The view shifted as *Hephaestus* swooped downward, the sky receding as gnarl-vines flooded the viewscreen.

Then suddenly they were gone. There were no vines, or rather those that lingered were confined to the edges of a vast platform that dominated the swamp. Its construction held an echo of the vine-fruit refineries, but monstrous in size, having been assembled from the corpses of a dozen lesser platforms. Upon it was crafted a strange effigy: a crude orkish face welded from scrap. It was angled towards the sky, grinning with metal fangs that were embedded in a jaw wide enough to swallow *Hephaestus* whole. Beneath it, orks were scrambling to their aircraft, while strange cannons crewed by greenskin runts hurled beams of light that seemed to rob the Thunderbolts of their momentum, along with quite a few of the ork planes that became caught in the crossfire. Whether this was due to the weapons' innate inaccuracy or because the runt gunners were unperturbed by friendly fire, it was impossible to say.

Shard engaged the vox.

'Squads Raptor and Arrow, clear a path. Nocter, stay in reserve. Bombers, you have your target. Save the payload until we are closer. Wait for my signal.'

We were fortunate the greenskins were still taxiing their fighters. Indeed, I was surprised so many were already airborne. Though the platform was large enough to accommodate runways, they were poorly arranged. The ork pilots jostled their fighters into position, the inevitable collisions resulting in wrenched cockpits and howled accusations amid the explosions raining down on them. Despite the carnage I felt a flicker of hope: there was no way they would fully mobilise before we struck.

Mizar whined, alarmed. It had seen something. I flicked through the energy spectrum, even as Shard was poised to deploy the bombs.

Blinding light. It emanated from the ork effigy. Shard swore, for whatever was happening was now visible to her too. Green lightning danced between the monstrosity's metal fangs, erupting in a storm of vile energy, and a squadron of ork fighters vomited out from its gullet.

They seemed almost as surprised as us. One flew directly into those momentum-sapping beams, spiralling into the swamp. Two others nearly collided, their pilots only averting disaster at the last moment. But the rest flew straight at us.

'Nocter. You know your duty.'

Falcon Squad surged forward, intercepting this threat. But they paid for it, now surrounded and at the mercy of the ork guns. Through Mizar, I watched as one by one their craft were reduced to scrap by overlapping fire-lines or dragged from the sky by those strange weapons. I should have mourned the pilots, those brave soldiers who did their duty despite the obvious risk. But all I could think was how our casualties would soon feed the ork war machine. Their edifice was well chosen, those huge jaws embodying not only their savagery but also their appetite. They sought to swallow the world, repurpose every scrap to aid their conquest.

Sparks once again writhed between those metal fangs, as whatever foul contraption lurked within powered up, no doubt intent on unleashing another score of fighters.

We were heading right for it, Mizar staring down its yawning gullet. Beyond the thrashing lightning were images I could not decipher. Merely glancing at them made me nauseous, the sensation worsened by the rapid descent. Inertia pinned me to my chair, unable to scream or lambast Shard for our suicidal dive. *Hephaestus* was on the cusp of breaking apart, buffeted by our foe's guns and the foul energies emanating beneath. Shard was screaming something at our bombardier, but the pressure in my ears stole her words. It was like being trapped deep underwater.

There was no way we could pull up in time. The monstrous effigy would swallow us, like it would swallow this world. I could do nothing but mumble a short prayer to the God-Emperor, for what little good it would do.

I should have had faith. In Him, and in her.

Shard wrenched the flight stick back, *Hephaestus* screaming in protest as she dragged its nose up. Any moment I expected us to snap in two, torn apart by our own momentum, but we endured, the view shifting from that terrible edifice to the inviting sky.

Mizar was clawing at me, demanding my attention. I relented, syncing with it just in time to witness the Marauder dumping every one of its high-explosive bombs into the edifice's awaiting jaws.

We had moments before detonation.

Shard was well ahead of me, accelerating across the canopy of gnarl-vines. She did not attempt to ascend, despite the comparative safety it might offer, focusing solely on putting as much distance between *Hephaestus* and the impending explosion.

I wanted to close my eyes, but Mizar would not let me. Through our rear gunner's sensors, I saw the ork base disappear as we fled the bubble of the techno-sorcery that had shrouded it from view.

Seconds and a lifetime passed as we awaited the detonation.

At first it was a flicker, the full spectacle concealed by the ork technology. Then half the swamp was simply gone, torn apart in a searing storm of green lightning and high explosives. The energies arced across the waters, leaving torn sections of the platform in its wake. Some materialised high above the swamp, before shattering into shards and falling like rain. Clumps of vines appeared beside them, along with gallons of swamp water compressed into churning bubbles that burst like blisters. Two of the bubbles were inexplicably frozen into blocks of ice, and a third boiled into vapour, the cloud stripping the outer hull from a pursuing ork jet.

For they were still on us. The explosion had decimated the horde along with their effigy, but many fighters were already airborne when the blast struck, and some had escaped its aftermath. They were gaining on us, and even at top speed the Marauder had no hope of outrunning them.

'Clear our six!' Shard roared, though her words were swallowed by an explosion that almost took our wing. But *Hephaestus* was tough, its fuselage enduring the onslaught. We were ascending now, the climb ponderous and our pursuers unyielding. I kept waiting for the Thunderbolt escorts to intercept, only to finally realise none were left.

We were alone.

I shifted my view to the rear gunner, his weapons discharging a barrage of bolt-rounds into the swirling mess of ork fighters. It was an impossible task, at least to my eyes – like trying to kill flies by flinging toothpicks.

I heard Shard's voice through the vox.

'Leric! Kill them or drive them off, but get rid of them. *Hephaestus* can't take much more.'

'*The Emperor protects,*' was the only reply, the voice seeming so close that it was almost as though I spoke the words.

Perhaps faith was the answer, for our closest pursuer was

abruptly torn from the sky, the explosion swallowing the attackers. For an instant I thought it had claimed them, until five more aircraft burst through the smoke. None were alike, each a chimera cast from scrap and malice, but they shared a sole purpose. I could almost hear the ork battle cry.

It was hopeless. But still we climbed, and the first of our pursuers fell away, smoke even thicker than usual pouring from its engine.

If we rose high enough they could not follow. But only if *Hephaestus* maintained structural integrity. I could hear a whistling, no doubt air seeping from a fracture in the fuselage.

'Seal your pressure suit!' Shard screamed, her head flicking round for an instant. 'We are void bound!'

Panicked, I fumbled with my suit's seals, unsure if I had loosened them during the flight. Mizar still tugged at my consciousness, anxious to share the carnage unfolding to our rear. Only two planes remained, and the nearest was struggling. Though the pilot was equipped with some primitive rebreather, the engine could not function in the thinning atmosphere. It fell behind, leaving only a single pursuer. And they too were slowing, engine spluttering and failing as the altitude increased.

We had almost cleared the atmosphere. I could just make out a violet halo framing the horizon, obscured by inky smoke.

As the last ork fell away, Shard opened the vox, checking the crew's status. I set Mizar to scan the void, seeking survivors, a single Thunderbolt or Marauder that had made it through the maelstrom. But I found none. Those unclaimed by the ork guns must have been consumed by the explosion, or ripped apart by the energies unleashed by the ork edifice.

Who knew the orks could construct such a machine, its terrible jaws vomiting aircraft, seemingly from nowhere? Yes, we had destroyed it, but there was no reason not to think that more of them lurked somewhere in the swamp. The unexpected raids, the ork jets sneaking through our defences: if they could appear from nowhere, it all made a horrible sense.

By now, Shard had levelled the plane, slumping in her seat and closing the vox. Her back was to me, and I could not see her face. But I saw the shudder that ran through her shoulders, and how her head fell into her hands.

Perhaps she had forgotten me, or in that moment did not care what I saw. I wanted to reach out, rest my hand on her heaving shoulder, but what reassurance could I offer? The best I could do was pretend I saw nothing.

Mizar still nagged at me, its cogitator registering something of interest. I ignored it, tired of indulging its incessant need for attention. On our return I would have to pick through its data-records, relive the whole horrible experience once again. I wanted a moment of respite. I wanted to remember the dead who had brought us this pyrrhic victory.

There was a beeping in my ear. I thought it was Mizar, but soon realised it was the vox, relayed through my void helm. Shard did not respond. Perhaps she had disengaged hers entirely.

I was reaching for her when the blast struck, knocking *Hephaestus* off balance and back into the planet's gravity well. As Shard tried to stabilise the spiralling craft I synced with Mizar.

We were not alone in the void. The ork aircraft I had too eagerly dismissed had caught up with us. Though its engines had failed, it must have been equipped with some secondary propulsion system, for green lightning was arcing across its fuselage, the energy field somehow both propulsion and weapon.

'Shard! Our pursuer. You see it?'

'Can barely see anything,' she bellowed. 'Everything has gone haywire.'

'It's the Green Storm,' I said. 'It has to be! Just look at it!'

She grunted something, focused on the console. I shifted my view to the rear gunner, only to find the target lock hanging curiously to one side. I thought it a malfunction, until I heard Shard screaming through the vox for Leric to return fire.

No response. Perhaps the ork's attack had ruptured his pressure suit, or the shockwave snapped his neck.

The craft shook again, sirens wailing. Shard had no choice but to turn our fall into a dive, the ork in pursuit. This was no controlled descent, and I felt the heat rising as we tore through the atmosphere.

'Leric, return fire! What are you doing back there?' Shard snarled through the vox.

She didn't know.

I synced to the rear gunner, praying he had revived. But the target overlay still hung useless to one side.

I did not want to die, so I reached out through Mizar, who was intent on the pursuing craft. Teeth gritted, I forced the seer-skull's machine-spirit into the rear gunner's sensor. It was difficult, Mizar protesting all the way. But I secured it in the rear gunner's console, banking on Mizar's obsession to force it into repositioning the gunsights.

Nothing happened at first. I worried the mechanism was damaged, that there was no means to realign the weapons. But then the bolters swung about, Mizar framing them against our pursuer. We had re-entered the atmosphere, and I watched flames licking against its fuselage. None seemed to reach the craft, shielded as it was by a crackling field of green lightning. It was so close I could pick out the strange nodules and gubbins bound to its hull. On its nose was a device resembling a pincer with a glowing spear tip clenched between its jaws.

It fired, and the energy arced across the sky like a poorly tamed lightning bolt. It was an inaccurate weapon, and this is what spared us immediate destruction, but even the backwash was enough to play havoc with the internal systems. And the ork only had to be on target once.

I had no idea how to fire the heavy bolters, or even if I could. Via the interface I could perceive pictographs representing Mizar's sensors. I sought anything unfamiliar as the images shifted, the seer-skull's and *Hephaestus'* systems struggling for supremacy. All the while the Green Storm was charging its weapon, power coursing along the fuselage and coalescing at the spear tip. I swear I could feel it even from within *Hephaestus*, my palms itching and teeth tingling as the power waxed bright.

I ignored it, cycling through the symbols, cursing that I was not a tech-priest.

There. A flickering pictograph I could barely make out, as though Mizar was equally perplexed by its meaning.

I engaged, and the heavy bolters spat a hail of shells. I could not direct them, but this did not matter as Mizar treated the targeting sights as just another picter, and sought to train them on our pursuer. But the bolt-shells burst about it, warded by the energies engulfing the craft. The power still coalesced at the weapon's spear-like tip, forming a pulsing ball of blinding light.

With supreme effort, I compelled Mizar to focus directly on this point.

Right when the weapon fired.

There was a small explosion, accompanied by the faintest flicker in the energy field as if something had shorted out. The shield failed, and suddenly the ork was exposed to the heat of atmospheric re-entry. Its hull glowed red, then white as it tumbled. Seconds later it was nothing more than a cloud of molten metal.

I disengaged from Mizar, slumping in my chair, exhausted. My hands were shaking, and I could not find a way to stop them. Shard said nothing as we levelled out, reducing speed and peeling the rebreather from her face before she glanced at me from over her shoulder.

'That was you?' she asked.

I could only nod.

'Good work,' she said, but her voice was flat with no hint of the bombastic fighter ace.

She was still looking at me, and I wondered if she had more to say. But instead she turned away, back to the console.

Hephaestus limped home towards the château and I breathed again. We had bested the Green Storm, and I had been there to capture it.

But it did not feel like a glorious victory.

Ahead of us the sun was setting, but its light was already obscured by the storm front gathering beneath the shining light of Orbital Station Salus.

CHAPTER EIGHTEEN

Our return flight was undertaken in near silence. Shard and the surviving crew managed the occasional monosyllabic exchange concerning airspeed or distance. Ironically, I occupied the navigator's chair, my very presence adding an additional challenge to our return. But they found the way, perhaps using the glimmer of Orbital Station Salus as a beacon.

I was cold in the cockpit, despite my borrowed flight suit. My hands were still shaking, and I clasped them together. But it made little difference.

I had felt this once before, during the Gigerian Cleansing, where the squad I accompanied stumbled across the bodies of those slaughtered by the heretics. The perpetrators did not differentiate between the young or old, and the victims' flesh had been desecrated, carved with foul runes that stung the eyes. I had not been able to look at it for long, turning from the sight, my stomach heaving. I took solace that even some of the hardened soldiers had a similar reaction.

Little of that footage survives, my superiors deeming it too disturbing for the Imperial citizenry. I wondered then how they would view my latest escapade, opening with Imperial aircraft soaring majestically to war, and concluding with a solitary bomber limping home.

We were lucky to survive. I suppose we were lucky to have blundered into the ork base, though it did not feel that way at the time. Even its destruction could not really be celebrated, because it left me wondering how many similar edifices lurked in the endless swamps.

I sighed, glancing to the cockpit's window. The sun had almost set, its dying light bleeding Bacchus' sky a deep purple. It mirrored our outward journey, except now I felt despair, not hope. So much had changed. Then, my fear had been an uneventful flight, our mission having no assigned objective or target, that we might be wasting time and resources.

I frowned, my fingers drumming the armrest. Ahead of me Shard was occupied with the controls, bearing us towards the comparative sanctuary of the governor's château.

I re-engaged with Mizar, currently transfixed by the flight of insects, perhaps attracted by their iridescent shells. Through it, I reviewed the footage, though I was unable to play back any sound. I knew Shard had told me we sought targets of opportunity, and there was a soundness in this tactic in a conventional war, where potential targets included cities and supply lines. But how did it make sense in a featureless swamp?

Unless they knew there was something out there…

It was difficult to catalogue our flight path from the images Mizar had captured, but it seemed after take-off we had flown true, at least until we were deep within the swamp. Just before we discovered the ork base.

Before I discovered it.

It had not occurred to me until then, but Mizar's archaic sensors had been the only means of identifying the anomalous energies employed by the orks. The same had been true in the swamp, during my first mission with Shard and the Scions.

Wing Commander Prospherous had said my vision was vital for the mission's success. Arrogantly, I had assumed he was talking about my picts.

There was no hero's welcome. The runway was clear when Shard brought us down, a handful of ground crew swarming *Hephaestus* as it slowed, assessing damage and holes needing to be patched. I saw her detach the pressure helm, her shoulders slumped. But as the cockpit lifted she straightened, nimbly vaulting clear of the craft, as though embarking on a morning's calisthenics.

'Are the others behind you?' the lead mechanical asked as I emerged.

She glanced over her shoulder, that sneer marring her face.

'Oh yes,' she said. 'Several miles behind. It's hard to give exact coordinates when the wreckage is scattered so widely. Good news for you, though, only one aircraft to patch up.'

She patted the man on the shoulder, her gaze falling on the Valkyries being taxied into the far hangar.

'How was everyone else's hunting?' she asked. 'I'd hate to think someone bested my tally.'

'We lost two squadrons over the western front. Squad of orks emerged from nowhere.'

'Sloppy but not unexpected,' she said, before rounding to face me. 'And how is our favourite propagandist? Was that the sort of battle you were hoping for?'

'I hope to never witness something like that again.'

'Then you're not as stupid as you look,' she replied, before frowning and scrutinising my face. 'Then again, maybe you are, it amounts to splitting hairs. Which I can do, incidentally, assuming the lascannon is properly calibrated.'

'It was fortunate we stumbled across that ork nest. Or unfortunate, depending on how you look at it.'

'Quite.'

'And how lucky that Mizar was able to detect it.'

'Was that what happened?' she said. 'I don't really recall. I was too busy saving our lives. Isn't that right, my loyal crew?'

She turned, addressing this last remark to the disembarking gunners and bombardier. The nearest, Filmont I believe, offered a terse smile before slinking off.

'That's right, head to the officers' mess. And don't forget, the drinks are on you,' Shard called after them, but they did not make for the château, instead heading to the rear of the craft.

I had forgotten Leric, their fallen comrade. So had Shard, or at least she acted that way. As the soldiers bowed their heads and made the sign of the aquila, I wondered if I should capture the moment for posterity. It seemed ghoulish, but also important. He had died defending us. His loss should be mourned and remembered.

But I had no idea how to disengage Mizar from *Hephaestus*. Plient had handled the installation but had neglected to inform me how to detach it. The seer-skull was tugging at its restraints, the machine-spirit on the verge of panic. I hushed it, powering down the device before turning to the ground crew.

'Where is Flight Sergeant Plient? I require his expertise.'

'Ah... I am sure I can assist, sir,' the closest replied. 'What is your need?'

'I need Flight Sergeant Plient. Where is he?'

The man hesitated. From the corner of my eye, I saw Shard glare at him.

'Well?' she said. 'Spit it out.'

He sighed. 'Perhaps you should come with me. There has been an… incident.'

'How did it happen?' I heard myself say, my gaze fixed upon the broken body lying on the medi-slab.

'They had just made planetfall,' the chirurgeon replied. 'Him, and the reinforcements from Orbital Station Salus. Then the storm caught them. None of the others survived, but he managed to limp the craft back and execute a controlled crash. He was barely conscious when we got to him. Since then, he's been like this.'

Plient's eyes were closed, his breathing laboured. Though bandaged and bruised, his flesh was less scarred than one might expect. Providing you ignored the stump that was once his left arm.

'When will he wake up?' Shard asked from the doorway. She was leaning against the frame, her gaze fixed on the wall opposite.

'When the Emperor wills,' the chirurgeon said with a shrug. 'We had to sedate him to remove what was left of the arm. I did my best, but we have limited supplies. And the conditions are not sanitary.'

He shrugged again. So dismissive a gesture. Bile bubbled up inside me. But he was right; the hovel that constituted a medi-bay was barely hygienic, the swamp's miasma permeating the very air.

'What are his chances?'

'I do not think his injuries life threatening,' the chirurgeon replied. 'Infection is the risk now, and I have little with which to treat it.'

I nodded, for I had no words. That a soldier could complete his mission despite such injuries, only to succumb to Bacchus' toxic filth, was obscene. Vile. But I recalled the Scion from my first mission, the lesions that infested his flesh after a mere day's exposure to the swamp. At least Plient had been in the cockpit, his wounds shielded from the foetid waters. That surely counted for something.

'Is there anything else?' the chirurgeon asked, tone brisk. I once again suppressed the urge to snap at him. Instead I looked away, gaze falling on the medi-slabs and cots where the fallen lay in various degrees of infirmity. The medicae had a job to do, I reminded myself. My presence was disruptive to it, and the only assistance I could provide was departing.

'Thank you,' I said. 'Please inform me if his condition changes.'

The chirurgeon nodded in response, before turning away, intent on his next patient.

My gaze lingered on Plient. Without that well-meaning smile, his face looked older, haggard. Then again, I probably looked the same. I glanced to the doorway, expecting it empty, but Shard still lingered, seemingly intent on the far wall.

'You think it was deliberate?' I asked.

'You mean the orks shooting at him?' she replied. 'I expect so, they're a disagreeable bunch.'

'I meant the orks targeting our reinforcements,' I said. 'The same thing happened when I arrived. As soon as we broke atmosphere they were on us.'

'Impossible,' she said. 'The orks are a bunch of slack-jawed savages who can barely get airborne and are incapable of strategic planning. There are senior officers who would take great offence at any suggestion otherwise.'

'Is that what you think?'

'Flight Commander Lucille von Shard's duties are to maintain the family's good name and standing, and to bring death to the God-Emperor's enemies,' she replied. 'She is not obliged to think. In fact, it is actively discouraged outside of combat scenarios.'

'That's all you have to say?'

'We all have our duty, propagandist,' she replied. 'Mine is to rule the skies. Yours is to extol my virtues. And since visiting hours are concluded, I suggest you get on with extracting that skull-thing of yours from *Hephaestus*, and go back to making your little picts.'

'It's called a seer-skull. Its designation is Mizar,' I said. 'You must know this. Why do you insist on pretending otherwise?'

'I don't answer to you,' she said with a sneer. 'Get back to the hangar. I'll round up some mechanicals to assist you.'

'No, I do not think I will,' I replied. 'Mizar is powered down and will be quite secure. I cannot imagine *Hephaestus* will be fit to serve any time soon. I will make do until Plient can assist me.'

'Don't be ridiculous,' she began, but I pushed past her, continuing along the corridor.

She called after me.

'I know how dependent you are on those trinkets.'

'Perhaps,' I said, slowing. 'But they are my trinkets, and I do not answer to you either. Unless there is something else you wish to say to me?'

'Of course there is,' she said. 'But it involves language inappropriate for a medical setting.'

'I meant about the flight,' I replied, my back still to her. 'Why I was brought along.'

'Because those were my orders. And your request.'

'I was there because Mizar can perceive the ork energies,' I said. 'I'd wager you had a fair idea there was some base out there in the swamps. But you couldn't find it. Not without Mizar.'

'Huh,' Shard said. 'That's a possibility. You'd have to take it up with high command.'

'I could have died.'

'You asked to fly.'

'Yes, and if that cost me my life then so be it. But you owed me the truth about why I flew.'

I turned, glaring at her. She was framed by the doorway, arms still folded, staring intently at nothing in particular.

'Well?' I said.

She looked at me. There was a spark in her eyes, something akin to anger. But then she smiled, and all I could see was the sneer.

'You have the audacity to play the victim?' she said. 'Because I risked your life to fulfil my duties? This from someone whose raison d'être is watching others suffer so he can collect their final moments and turn them into picts? So he can bask in the reflected glory of their demise?'

She was no longer smiling, her eyes cold as the void.

'Hypocrisy becomes you, Propagandist Simlex.'

CHAPTER NINETEEN

I avoided her from then. Perhaps she avoided me too. Then again, there was little time to fraternise, for we had our duties. She flew her missions whilst I revised my footage. Despite my bluster, it was soon necessary to extract Mizar from the Marauder's fuselage, just to access its data-memory. Plient was still unconscious and, fearful of causing damage to the integrated systems, I requested that the entire panel was cut from *Hephaestus* and relocated to my quarters. I could not face going back to Plient's hangar.

I toiled there for days, lost in fashioning image and sound from data-scraps, as I wove the tale of the Aeronautica Imperialis' raid into ork territory. The result was dramatic, and inspiring, providing one romanticised sacrifice over success. But I thought the work a questionable recruitment tool. The destruction of the ork edifice provided cinematic spectacle but, no matter how I spliced it, few would see the appeal of being caught in that nightmarish battle.

Still, I was content in near seclusion, cloistered within my quarters. I ignored all messages from my superiors requesting updates, and even a bespoke invitation from Governor Dolos was laid on my dresser, unopened. Two further invitations arrived in the following days. Both were ignored.

On the third day, after several minutes' incessant knocking, I opened the door to find Steward Stylee.

'My lord.' He bowed, presenting me with an engraved letter adorned with the governor's personal seal. 'I would advise you attend,' he warned before departing.

I read the note. It invited me to join Dolos that afternoon for an excursion to a nearby distillery. The request was framed in casual language, but repeated reference was made to how I had been enjoying the governor's hospitality, the implication being that it could be swiftly withdrawn.

So, that afternoon, I met Stylee at the château's rear as instructed, accompanied solely by Kikazar. The invitation had been unclear as to whether the seer-skull was permitted, but I gambled that Dolos would be reluctant to interfere with my duties, and probably desired to show something of importance.

Steward Stylee bowed at my approach, his tapered hat flopping over his face. It was a curious article of clothing, a quality it shared with the long sleeved black robe that swallowed his scrawny frame. In a different setting, perhaps a dungeon with flanking firebrands, he might have cut a sinister figure. But in the fierce heat of the afternoon sun the garment seemed incongruous, bordering on farcical.

'Lord Simlex. So glad you could attend,' he said, his tone at odds with his words. 'The governor's private yacht awaits. I will escort you, just to ensure you do not become lost.'

I ignored that last barbed remark, following him across the grounds, my gaze flicking to the bunker where Plient lay comatose. I had broken my isolation to speak once with the chirurgeon, but Plient's condition was unchanged. The medicines and narcotics utilised by the infirmary were distilled on Bacchus using traditional methods, and their potency could vary significantly.

That was his claim anyway. It was equally possible that he bungled the dosage. How would I know?

The château's rear grounds held an echo of the estate's former glory. Two horticultural servitors were trimming the remnants of an ornamental hedge maze. It was a pitiful sight, the mindless cyborgs meticulously shaping the foliage, heedless that half the labyrinth had already been torched, leaving only mud, black stumps and a rather obvious route to the centre.

But we then passed a thick line of trees, and in doing so entered another world.

Or perhaps an older world, one from before Bacchus was at war. The grass was a lush green, the flame-leaved trees trained to form an archway and canopied passage, their leaves offering blessed shade from the sweltering heat. We crossed a glimmering bridge of polished stone, beneath which flowed a stream of crystal-clear water, populated by scarlet fish with shimmering scales. The flow must have been hermetically sealed from the surrounding swamp, but the work was flawless and I could see no join.

Beyond the bridge was a simple but elegant dock carved from mandack wood, its supports engraved with the busts of Imperial saints. But a faint scent of mildew clung to the bark and, though it had been painted a brilliant white, faint patches of mould were visible beneath the emulsion.

Still, I did not pay this much thought, for at the dock's end hovered one of the most ostentatious pleasure yachts I have ever seen. Superficially, it was sleek to the point of minimalism, but the opulence lay in subtle details: the gems glittering along its pulpit, and the silken cushions upon which its occupants could recline during the journey. There was no obvious means of propulsion, the anti-gravity generators cunningly concealed within the hull, the only evidence of their presence the boat's unwillingness to touch the water, and the slight distortion in the waves beneath it.

The vessel was manned, the servant at the helm clad in pristine white robes, two other crew members lurking towards the rear. But the cushions were notably unoccupied, and though a gangplank was lowered, I suspected this was a test of etiquette. I was expected to await my host, and she would take the opportunity to keep me waiting some time.

Kikazar, who had bobbed behind me all this while, approached the vessel, only veering away at the last moment, its motors skittering uncertainly.

'Your familiar has good instincts,' Stylee observed, as a small insect, no bigger than my hand, glided lazily towards the yacht. It was a foot from the hull when it abruptly burst into flames, an energy field of blue light flaring at the point of impact.

I glared at Stylee. 'A warning would have been appreciated. I could have lost my seer-skull.'

'My apologies,' he said with a faint smile. 'It must have slipped my mind.'

It was sweltering on the dock, with no trees to provide shade. I felt sweat pooling in the small of my back and beneath my armpits, an unpleasant sensation at the best of times, and worse when one is about to share a confined space with an aristocrat. I already knew I had lost Dolos' favour, but I would have preferred not to offend her with my smell. Stylee was untroubled by the heat, and I began to re-evaluate his choice of robes, suspecting they had properties that shielded him from the sun. I directed Kikazar to position itself to shade my face.

According to my timepiece, we stood there for the better part of an hour, until a barrage of horns proclaimed Governor Dolos' arrival. We turned to see her striding down the tree-lined path, flanked by two guards who rivalled Adeptus Astartes in height, their lumbering frames no doubt the result of gene-forging. A score of attendants and lesser nobles followed, but I ignored these, my focus on the familiar figure of Flight Commander Gradeolous at the rear. He was clad in his dress uniform. At least, I assumed that is what it was, for I doubted the outrageously large plume adorning his cap would have fitted the cockpit of even the most spacious aircraft.

Governor Dolos had never been more radiant. Her diaphanous robes shimmered like mirrored silk, and beneath she wore an elegant gown that sparkled like starlight, her headdress tapered into two wings of spun gold. She shone so bright that to look upon her risked blindness. I bowed, averting my gaze. I hoped this was respectful; I remained fearful of Bacchus' social mores.

'Ah, Propagandist Simlex. You decided to join us,' she said, as if seeing me for the first time. There was no mention of her tardiness, or the pointed invitation. She treated me as though we had blundered into each other by chance. Gradeolous simply ignored my presence, his focus on the skies above.

Stylee nudged me aside so Dolos could ascend the gangplank. I waited until her entourage had done likewise before following, the steward trailing in my wake. The moment I boarded the heat rescinded, no doubt screened by the same force field that incinerated the insects. The cool would have been refreshing if the folds of my robes weren't sodden with sweat.

Dolos took her seat amongst the silken cushions, her courtiers and guards assuming their places around her. Gradeolous, I noted, chose to stand, hands clasped behind his back, chest puffed and chin thrust out, his whiskers bared like the horns of a beast.

Dolos glanced to me, smiling as if we were old friends.

'Come now,' she said, patting the cushions beside her. 'Sit and we shall be on our way.'

I bowed again, and lowered myself to the offered spot, still mindful of the sweat clinging to my robes. I prayed to the God-Emperor there was no smell, but if there was Dolos did not acknowledge it.

Kikazar settled in my lap as our helmsman's hands glided over hidden controls and, silently, the craft began its passage along the river.

I had not travelled south of the château before. The territory ostensibly belonged to Imperial forces, and remained relatively untouched by the conflict. We sailed through rows of neatly maintained vines, the yacht gliding across the swamp water, its anti-gravity drives offering far smoother passage than the rather frenetic aircraft with which I was so recently acquainted.

The day was clear and warm, the sun's ferocity dampened by the craft's force field. It also shielded us from the more vora-cious insects, and by the God-Emperor there were enough of those. Each exploded into a miniscule pyre moments before it reached the vessel, the incessant flickers like tiny fireworks. I wondered what would happen if one of the larger banner-bugs attacked the yacht, before deciding it was better not to speculate.

We were not alone on those waters. Smaller vessels, crafted from wood and bound by stretched vines, were dotted amongst the foliage, their crews hacking at the gnarl-vines, seeking the sweet vine-fruits nestled amidst the barbed stems. Whatever they collected was deposited in the boat's midsection and covered by a tarpaulin. The crews themselves had no such protection; they wore short robes similar to Stylee's, but these provided only par-tial defence against the swarms of stinging insects.

I glanced to Dolos, but she paid the workers no heed. She

had been quiet for most of the journey, her entourage filling the silence with idle chit-chat. When not feasting on those purple berries she so enjoyed, she spoke only to request more refreshments, or to instruct the helmsman to make minor course corrections. But her manner was pleasant enough, at least for a noble of her stature.

I found my gaze shifting to Gradeolous, but the man had barely moved since our departure, hands still clasped to the small of his back. He did periodically glance to the sky, as though keeping watch, or waiting for something.

We reached an intersection, a junction cut across the rows of gnarl-vines, and turned left, cruising past the seemingly endless vineyard. I caught glimpses of the agri-workers, their hooked sickles prising at the plants, which seemed to flare their barbs in response. Ahead, I saw one man impaled in the shoulder by a foot-long thorn. Blood spurted from the wound and he fell, but before he could strike the water we had sped past, almost ramming a vessel emerging from one of the gullies. It veered aside just in time, spilling a score of the vine-fruit into the waters. It was overburdened, and I worried the wave brought by our passage would capsize it, but I lost sight of the vessel as we sped on.

'I'm worried for you, Simlex.'

I turned. Dolos was addressing me, though her gaze was fixed ahead.

'Governor?'

'You seem ill at ease,' she continued. 'Something troubles you. And, if I may be blunt, you were lax in responding to my solicitations.'

'My apologies, Governor Dolos,' I replied, bowing my head. 'I have been preoccupied with my work. When undertaking a pict of this significance I become inward-focused and forget the outside world. Please forgive my rudeness. I meant no offence.'

'Please, no apologies are necessary,' she said, dismissing my contrition with a wave of her hand. 'I also dabble in artistic pursuits and quite understand how one can get lost in the process.'

'I had no idea, governor. May I ask your medium?'

'Painting,' she replied. 'Stretched canvas with oil and brush. Somewhat antiquated, I realise, but on Bacchus we appreciate traditional methods.'

We were both staring straight ahead, conducting the conversation from the corners of our mouths. She too must have seen the empty boat bobbing in the water ahead of us, a single oar floating forlornly beside it. But she said nothing, instead placing a purple berry on her tongue.

'I would love to see your work,' I said. 'If such a thing were permitted.'

She laughed lightly. 'Oh, I could not present it to someone of your calibre. It is simply an indulgence for my own pleasure, or an outlet for frustration, depending on the day. But I understand how absorbing the pursuit of art can be, sometimes to the artist's detriment. For I heard you had a rather dangerous encounter in the swamps. I gather your aircraft was the only survivor?'

'That is sadly true. We encountered a significant ork force concealed in the swamps.'

'Unfortunate.' She frowned. 'One would have thought some light reconnaissance could have uncovered such a threat.'

'I believe we *were* the reconnaissance. At least of a sort.'

'I have heard similar,' Dolos replied.

Gradeolous, standing behind her, was rigid as a statue.

'You should not be risking yourself on the front line,' she continued, holding out her hand, a glass appearing in it a fraction later. 'You are in line for succession. Technically.'

'I think there is little risk of that.'

She shrugged. 'Perhaps not. But it would reflect poorly on my hospitality if you were to die in the conflict. Governor Zanwich might never speak to me again.'

'With respect, milady, I have been tasked by the governor to complete the project. That involves a degree of risk.'

'But you must have enough material now,' she persisted. 'You have undertaken half a dozen assignments already. That is surely sufficient?'

'There is volume enough. But I lack a narrative thread. There have been battles but no resolution. I do not see this war ending soon.'

'Sadly, I agree. Not the way it is currently being fought.'

We sped past a couple more of the smaller skiffs, each propelled by a standing oarsman and overburdened with vine-fruit. I could not help but note the cargo was pockmarked, the yellowed flesh infested with dark stains. The colour reminded me of Dolos' blushed berries. The smaller vessels were converging on a distant structure I could not quite identify. I caught the glint of metal etched by the unyielding afternoon sun, but it was behind the structure, condemning it to shadow.

'Might I offer a suggestion?' Dolos asked.

'Of course, governor.'

'Perhaps you should rethink your approach? Perhaps there is no final battle, but you could instead conclude your pict by showing the brave citizenry of the Imperium, and how the common agri-workers are valiantly persevering, despite the hardship. Those are the real heroes, my brave serfs.'

'That is a possibility.'

Her motive was transparent. She cared not for honouring her people, only that they appeared industrious and productive. But I had no better answer. And, despite what I said, I did not fear the war with the orks would be without end. I now feared that ending was imminent, and it would be safer if I completed my work off-planet. But the storm gathered beneath Orbital Station Salus made that impossible.

Dolos handed me a tapered glass brimming with amber liquid.

'Picture it – the thrill of aerial combat and the bravery of the God-Emperor's soldiers juxtaposed against the idyllic setting of Bacchus. There, even with the xenos threat, the populace continue to brew Subsector Yossarian's most desirable wines, fermenting their wares with the same traditional methods employed for millennia.'

As she spoke the metal structure loomed closer. It was an ugly slab of iron grey, walls pitted with corrosion, quite incongruous with the surrounding vegetation. But I recognised a distillation platform, the first I had seen that had not been sundered by the orks. Boats entered via a yawning set of doors, depositing their cargo before exiting on the far side. A steady stream of them bobbed in the water, awaiting their turn and perhaps enjoying a respite from their labours. But they were forced to manoeuvre from our path, for our helmsman did not slow, and the tip of more than one oar was singed by the yacht's protective shield.

We did not use the main gates, instead mooring at the distillery's rear, where a platform jutted from the structure. Dolos, Gradeolous and I descended the gangplank, Stylee scurrying behind, whilst the rest of the entourage remained on the yacht. Kikazar hovered beside me, sensors sweeping every facet of our surroundings. Whilst it lacked Mizar's range and sophistication, it possessed an exceptional eye for details, and enough sensitivity to register even minor fluctuations in biorhythms.

A welcome committee waited to greet us. Their robes were reminiscent of the workers', though the weave seemed finer, and the garments were unstained by blood or the juice of the fruits. They bowed, nervousness transparent even without Kikazar's refined sensors.

The lead figure, presumably the overseer, stepped forward.

'Governor Dolos, blessed is your presence. Thank you, Bringer of Harvests, for the bounty you bestow.'

Dolos rolled her eyes, glancing to me.

'Yes, yes,' she said, feigning embarrassment as the man bowed his head. 'No need to stand on ceremony. Overseer Willem, may I introduce Propagandist Simlex? He is here to speak to you about life on our beloved planet. You may address him freely, and need only speak the truth.'

Kikazar chirped a warning, the sound audible only to me. But it was unnecessary. I did not need the seer-skull's biorhythmic sensors to know she was lying.

Governor Dolos was on good form as we sped back towards the château, her entourage fawning over every attempted witticism. The excursion had gone exactly as desired. The agri-workers had extolled the virtues of her administration and their faith in their produce, despite the fact none of them had tasted it.

Serfs praising their planetary governor was hardly surprising. Similar would have occurred on any well-run planet in the Imperium. But this was a more comprehensive farce, as I was shown vast distilleries where the vine-fruit was pulped into a slurry, and the vats which fermented it into wines and spirits. I sampled the produce as offered, and the fruit was indeed succulent, its flesh firm, juicy and quite unblemished. The workers, though low-born and simple, appeared healthier than one might have expected, given the nature of their labours.

But Kikazar could feel their pulses quicken as they spoke, and a brief scan of the boats waiting to offload told a different story. Those workers' skin and produce was marred by purple blisters and black swellings.

Governor Dolos was laughing. I glanced across. Her head

snapped back as she cackled, spilling wine across the servant standing beside her. There she was, ruler of a dying world. Oblivious or uncaring to its plight.

I did not begrudge her the subterfuge. All citizens sought to present themselves as favourably as possible, she merely had better means than most. No one would care for the deception, for all that mattered was the planet was loyal and paid its tithes. Of course, if the wine was now tainted, paying tithes might become more problematic. But that was her concern, not mine.

I glanced to my glass. Amber liquid glistened within, with no trace of the taint.

That was what irked me. Dolos, like Shard, thought lying sufficient. She must have known how transparent it all was, for she had sent a dozen tainted bottles to my room. But why should she care, for none would dare refute her. My pict would show rustic agri-workers toiling at the vines and proclaiming the orks would never halt their labours. It was a nice touch, even if the delivery felt contrived.

That was the narrative now, whether I believed it or not.

The most depressing thing was I had no better story. At least, none that would appease my superiors.

Another burst of laughter erupted behind me. I did not bother turning, keeping my gaze ahead, Kikazar resting in my lap. I had already thanked the governor for the informative tour, and advised her I would need to process the files on the return journey. It was a small, solitary lie, and therefore easy to tell. Most importantly, it meant I could sit in silence and apart from her sycophants without arousing suspicion.

We were riding against the flow of traffic now, the smaller boats deferring to the canal's edges. Their wares were as blighted as before, but more troubling was the discolouration of their hulls. The wood was bleached a sandy yellow by the swamp water, but its boards were marred by ugly black stains. It made me think of the governor's château, and the discolouration I had discovered behind the hidden panel. It was as though something was slowly poisoning this world. Except the orks, who seemed to thrive despite the blight.

I felt footsteps behind me, but did not turn, maintaining the pretence I was absorbed in my work. But a heavyset figure squatted down beside me, his presence forcing me to shuffle along. I glanced across, and found myself staring down the imposing whiskers of Flight Commander Gradeolous.

'Not enjoying the festivities, Simlex?' he asked. It felt an odd question, given the sternness of his manner.

'I am calibrating today's pict files,' I replied, though I doubted he was listening, or that my answer mattered overly. He had addressed me to initiate a conversation, and knew where it next led. If I had told him I was too preoccupied by his dashing moustache to enjoy the festivities I'm sure it would not have had the slightest impact on what he said next.

'Do you still enjoy flying with Shard?'

'Enjoy is a strong word. I have obtained useful footage. That is sufficient.'

He grunted in response. He seemed to stare straight ahead, but from the corner of my eye I saw his gaze flicker to the empty sky.

'You do not seem to be indulging with the rest,' I said.

'I am on duty. I do not fraternise,' he replied as he unscrewed the cap on a battered hip flask and took a long draw. 'The governor requested I provide protection for this excursion. I have no time for chit-chat.'

A greenish insect, its wingspan the width of my shoulders, smashed into the field before us. It was unclear if the encounter was by chance, or the creature sought to attack us, but either way its body erupted in a neat plume of flame.

'I would have thought us already well protected,' I said.

Gradeolous shook his head. 'From petty annoyances? Perhaps. But greater dangers lurk in the skies above.'

I followed his gaze, though saw nothing.

'Forgive my ignorance, flight commander, but how can you defend us from down here?'

'Because I am more than a fighter, I am a commander,' he replied, pointing upwards. 'Observe.'

I followed his gaze while he whispered into his vox. Something glinted in the sky.

'My squadron, the Sharks,' he said. 'They are ever vigilant, but you may relax. This airspace is clear and far from the hotspots.'

'I was unaware we were being monitored.'

'They maintain a high altitude. Governor Dolos would prefer her excursion was not soured by aircraft roaring overhead, and some of these vine-pluckers might react poorly to seeing a military craft. It makes them think they are in danger.' He nodded to one of the boats bobbing beside us.

'And you coordinate their actions from here?'

'Just as Wing Commander Prospherous oversees our combined efforts. A commander does not have to be on the front lines to orchestrate the battle.'

'I see.'

He leaned closer. His breath reeked, and I wondered what was in his flask. Raw promethium?

'I hear one of our mechanicals found a way of transporting your recording devices by attaching them to our craft.'

'Yes. Sadly, he is now confined to the medical bay.'

'Unfortunate but irrelevant. My point is you do not need to risk life and limb flying with a maverick like Shard. You entrust your devices to me, and I will ensure you have eyes on every significant conflict going forward. I'm sure the governor would prefer that. She thinks you too valuable to risk.'

He clapped his massive hand onto my shoulder, the impact almost driving me into the bench.

'Something to consider.' He smiled, his eyes bright as blades.

CHAPTER TWENTY

The chirurgeon never informed me of Plient's waking. Perhaps he forgot, occupied by more urgent cases. Or perhaps he did not want a propagandist sniffing around his medi-unit. After all, we all have secrets.

I heard only by chance, for I was still toiling, having just spliced a crude cut of the final pict. I was particularly pleased with the opening shot of the ork attackers, having chosen the duel Mizar witnessed on the sundered distillery platform, where the two orks had engaged in brutal combat for dominance. It nicely invoked the savagery and threat posed by the beasts, whilst also underlining their mindless brutality and self-destructive impulses. Against my better judgement, I had tweaked the image a little, enlarging the tusks and broadening the shoulders of the victor, until the ork appeared the embodiment of greenskin savagery. From there the focus shifted to footage of the agri-workers, each proclaiming their faith and decreeing that no greenskin would prevent them fulfilling their duties to the God-Emperor.

Unfortunately, at that point the narrative began to unravel. I had enough recordings of aircraft gunning down orks, but the best shots portrayed the battles as chaotic brawls where our pilots barely held their own. That left Shard gunning down footsloggers in her Vulture, which was neither dramatic nor conclusive. It invited the viewer to question why the ork threat was so significant, when a single pilot could wipe out swarms without retaliation. I was beginning to sympathise with my predecessor who had cobbled together the original pict. Perhaps it was better to portray our forces as inherently superior and leave it at that.

Dissatisfied, I paused the playback, and had begun to organise archived files, ostensibly to free up some data-storage, when I stumbled across a pict of the young Shard.

It was from her mother's second funeral. Shard looked one of the youngest, her brothers towering over her. The elders of the group were clad in their robes of office: a slimmer Confessor Maric von Shard in his Ecclesiarchy vestments, Commissar Tobia von Shard in his greatcoat and peaked cap, Prefectus Josephine von Shard in the regalia of the Administratum, and Inquisitorial Acolyte Rile von Shard, who looked particularly sinister in his dark robes. The younger siblings, including Shard, still wore the modest attire of the schola progenium, their training incomplete and roles unassigned.

It was a curious group to look upon. One family, encompassing the many arms of the Imperium, unified in their dedication to the God-Emperor and humanity. But as I glanced from Maric's tanned face to Shard's almost ghastly skin, it struck me how little resemblance there was between them all. It was more than mismatched uniforms. Though bound together in grief, they did not look like a family.

There was a commotion outside. Well, perhaps commotion is

a stretch, but Shard's voice had a way of carrying, particularly when she was irritated.

'–don't care if the spirit of Saint Sanguinius is available, I am still the one who flies that damn mission.'

The muffled retort was inaudible, though Shard's subsequent expletives carried easily enough. I wrenched open the window, struggling with the runners, before glancing to Kikazar hovering beside me.

'Go listen. But be discreet.'

The seer-skull clicked in acknowledgement, darkening its lenses before disappearing into the evening's gloom. As I closed the window one final remark from her carried.

'You think Plient imagined it? That boy doesn't have any imagination. I've met servitors with a greater gift for abstract thought. What makes you–'

I closed the glass, muffling the sound.

Plient was talking? Awake? I had to see him. I owed him that much. Kikazar was capable of cataloguing Shard's ranting, but in that moment it held no interest to me. I muted the exchange, throwing on my robe and summoning Iwazar to escort me to the medi-unit.

It ceased playback, and the von Shard family faded from sight.

'Hello, sir! It's so good to see you.'

Plient beamed as I entered, awkwardly raising himself to a sitting position with his good arm.

'I'm glad to find you in such spirits,' I said, perching on the side of his cot. 'I was concerned you might not recover.'

'Oh, don't you worry about me, sir,' Plient replied. 'I'd be back patching aircraft today if they'd let me. The chirurgeon is a fine fellow but, between you and me, he fusses.'

I nodded, picturing the grim-faced surgeon who confronted

me at the medi-unit's entrance. He had refused admission at first, and I had been required to remind him whose interests I served. He relented, but I wondered how many more times I could play that card. If the situation continued to deteriorate, would anyone care whether I was under a distant noble's supposed protection?

'How are you feeling?' I asked.

'Not too bad, sir,' Plient replied. 'Well, except my arm of course. Not that it hurts, just… itches. Where my fingers should be. Odd, that.'

He looked crestfallen for a moment, but quickly rallied.

'Did my modifications to *Hephaestus* work?'

'Yes. You excelled beyond my expectations.'

'Thank you, sir… though perhaps you should not mention what I did too widely. I'm starting to wonder if I should be messing around with sacred technology. Maybe I offended the God-Emperor. That might explain… well…' He lapsed into silence.

'What happened out there?' I asked. 'They said you were the only survivor.'

'I'm not sure,' he said. 'What I saw… I don't know. It didn't make much sense.'

'You must have been in a hell of a firefight. I saw the damage to your craft. They had to scrap it. The outer hull was too riddled with bullets to salvage.'

'It rained.'

'I'm sorry?'

'The bullets. They fell like rain. I couldn't avoid them because they were all there was. That and the clouds and the lightning. It was all I could see.'

He spoke very quietly, I had to strain to hear him over the hiss of ventilators and groans from wounded souls.

'Lightning?' I said.

He nodded. 'Except… it was green.'

'This was from the storm? How did you get caught in it?'

'I was to escort the new fighters back to the château. We had just dropped in from Orbital Station Salus when the storm rolled in beneath us. It moved so quickly, our momentum was too great to avoid it. We decided to go full power, blast through it as quickly as possible to minimise risk. But once we were in there, navigation stopped making sense. It was like everything was over-charged. My hair stood on end. I felt it tingle in my teeth. I still thought it was the storm but… there was something in there.'

'Ork fighters?'

'I don't know. I never saw any. Just the gunfire. And the light-ning. It struck one of the Thunderbolts. The surge just… It was like the rear of the vessel was gone. In an instant. No wreckage. It just… wasn't there any more.'

He faltered, voice fading even as he spoke, the jovial tone that once warmed his words departed. It was like conversing with a machine.

With a gesture I urged Iwazar closer. The seer-skull bobbed forward.

'Replay file designated "Duel", minimal scaling, last thirty seconds,' I whispered.

The holo-projector flickered, before displaying the final moments of the two orks battling on the desecrated platform. As the victor roared, displaying the head of his decapitated foe, the image panned upwards, just as a surge of lightning tore the sky.

'Freeze image.'

Iwazar obeyed.

'Is this what you saw?' I asked, turning to Plient. 'I have more images from a more recent flight, though I have yet to cata-logue them.'

He was quite still, eyes fixed on the emerald light. His arm trembled. He opened his mouth to speak, but all that emerged was a plaintive sob, more akin to a wounded animal than a man.

'Plient?'

The sob became a cry, then a scream. I barely had time to collapse the image before the chirurgeon appeared, stabbing an injector into the now convulsing Plient's shoulder. Mercifully, his struggles slowed, his eyes flicking closed.

The chirurgeon turned on me, eyes lit with righteous fury.

'Get out.'

'I did not mean–'

'Get out now, before I violate my oaths,' he snarled. 'He is not a plaything for your picts. None of them are. Parasite.'

The final word was spat. I could not think of the last time someone had addressed me so. My cheeks flushed with anger, and with shame. I wanted to berate the man, for I was visiting a comrade, a man to whom I owed my life. But what purpose would it serve? And did it really refute his point?

I turned stiffly, marching away, Iwazar trailing in my wake. As I left the medi-unit and advanced along the corridor, I could not dispel the image of the weeping Plient. He was once unshakable in his conviction, but now was as broken as any of us.

I ascended to the bunker's entrance, trying to think of something I could do. There should have been a priest attached to the unit to provide words of comfort. But I had seen no sign of one, yet another indication of how thinly the Imperium's resources were spread. And that was before reinforcements had been cut off.

It had to be coincidence. However much we underestimated the greenskins, surely they could not weaponise a storm, or use it to orchestrate their attacks? Such tactics seemed more in keeping with the treacherous aeldari, or one of the other ancient races. No, the storm gathering beneath Orbital Station Salus had to be a quasi-natural phenomenon, perhaps exacerbated by the space station's proximity to the planet.

Yet wasn't that our eternal failing? To dismiss them as dull-witted brutes, ripe for ridicule in our picts and propaganda? To not recognise the threat they posed until its blade was pressed to our throats?

The bunker door swung open, and I found Shard standing on the far side. Her uniform was stained by the God-Emperor knew what, though the smell suggested some xenos secretions. She had her sword slung on her hip, and her cap was missing, as was Kikazar. Though I had assigned the seer-skull to discreetly monitor her conversation, there was no sign of it.

'Been visiting the infirm?' she asked. 'Or just taking a few picts?'

'I am not in the mood,' I replied, attempting to push past her. But her arm shot out, seizing my shoulder, the grip unbreakable.

'Soldiers do not have the luxury of moods.'

'I'm not a soldier.'

'Perhaps. But neither was Plient. Not really. He was a simple soul who was inspired to serve the Imperium despite lacking the ruthlessness or sadism the role requires. In a well-ordered universe, he'd toil away in some quiet backwater mending broken things. But the Imperium required otherwise, and someone like you convinced him his place was here.'

'I do not have to answer to you.'

'No,' she said, nodding to the medi-bay's entrance. 'But you must answer to him.'

'I answer to my superiors,' I replied, tearing free from her grip. 'I have a duty just like you. Perhaps my work will condemn some to the infirmary or worse. But there are wars that must be fought. This whole planet is proof of that.'

She smiled. How I had grown to hate it.

'And how are your superiors?' she asked. 'Do you think they will be satisfied with your work? I heard you enjoyed a nice boat trip the other day. What a scintillating pict that will inspire.'

'What do you want from me? You think it wise to reject an invitation from the planetary governor?'

'No. But neither is acquiescing to her whims. No matter how charming she is, or how appealing she looks in those robes, you should not trust her. Believe me.'

'Are your whims any better?'

She made a sound that might almost have been a chuckle.

'Do you know what I want?' she asked.

'Enlighten me.'

'To end this,' she said. 'To lead the assault on whatever lurks within that storm and eliminate it. This so-called Green Storm has claimed the lives of so many pilots, and nearly killed Plient. He might be an idiot, but he's the only one around here who I trust to keep me airborne.'

'How noble,' I sneered. 'Do you expect me to believe you? That you are motivated by altruism? You just desire another scalp for your collection.'

'What if I do?' She shrugged. 'The result is the same. I would be the hero who quashed the Green Storm, saving countless lives in the process and avenging my fallen comrades. And you could be the one who captures the climactic battle. Surely that would be a better conclusion for your little vid? The valiant Flight Commander Lucille von Shard, triumphing over the ork pilot responsible for so much death? Seems a little pithier than shots of rotten fruit and pampered aristocrats.'

'So now you fight for the benefit of my pict?'

'It's possible to have more than one reason for doing something.'

I was loath to admit it, but she had a point. Such a battle would be a more cinematic ending for the pict, and present a more positive conclusion. It would please all my masters, or at least offend none of them. Even Commissar Tobia von Shard would have to be satisfied with his sister's victory.

Still, I did not trust her.

'So, you wish me to accompany you? To capture your daring triumph?'

'That is up to you,' she said. 'Either be there when history is made, or stay here and pout. Whatever you choose, I am leaving now. Decide quickly.'

She spun on her heel, marching towards the hangars.

I hesitated, plagued by doubt. Where was Kikazar? Had she disabled the seer-skull? I could not find it. Maybe it had misinterpreted my orders, and was even now hovering outside some window, monitoring a scandalous tête-à-tête and ignoring its assigned target. It would not be the first time; it had a nasty habit of taking initiative in the field, as well as powering down and running silent when it detected a possible threat. Sometimes it took hours before I could sense it.

More pressingly, was Iwazar up to the task? It had pict recorders, but its primary function was holo-projection. It lacked Mizar's sophisticated sensors, but Mizar was still attached to the panel cut from *Hephaestus*.

Shard was still walking away but had slowed, her gaze creeping over her shoulder.

'You are coming, aren't you?' she asked. 'Otherwise it really undercuts my dramatic exit.'

'I... I don't–'

She sighed, meeting my gaze.

'Sometimes, Propagandist Simlex, one must take risks. You do not trust me, and I do not blame you for that. But you have seen my skills. Trust them, and trust my need to succeed against the odds. Isn't that something we share? Don't you also aspire to excel in your duties?'

'Yes.'

'Then let us bring an end to this war.'

CHAPTER TWENTY-ONE

I knew something was wrong. Why did we slink towards the hangar, scuttling from shadow to shadow? As we entered, I caught sight of Shard's Lightning suspended on chains, though at least its engine was no longer strewn across the floor.

She glanced to it, her step slowing a fraction, before continuing on towards an Avenger strike fighter at the hangar's rear. It looked a similar design to the Lightning, though the turbofans were located further along the wing, and a multi-barrelled Avenger bolt cannon was slung beneath the nose. Most notably, it had a rear-mounted cockpit, and the capacity to carry two personnel.

'Is this it?' I asked.

Shard didn't reply. Instead, she seized Iwazar. The surprised seer-skull barely had time to bleep in alarm before she'd twisted it about and rammed it into the modified hard point beneath the Avenger's wing.

'What are you–' I began, but she shushed me with a hiss.

'Quiet,' she said. 'We don't want to attract attention.'

'Why? And what the hell did you just do? Did Plient show you how to do that?'

'Sure,' she replied, barely hesitating. 'Now get in.'

'Am I to be in the rear carriage?'

'Unless you feel like flying?'

With her help I clumsily scaled the craft, clambering into the cockpit while Shard attended to the hangar doors. The flight harness was snug, though a shade more familiar now. I glanced to the control panel, oblivious to the dials' functions. A heavy stubber was mounted on the craft's rear, presumably to fend off enemy fighters. I hoped Shard would not rely on me to fire it.

My back was to the entrance, but I heard the doors creak open, and felt the weight shift as Shard vaulted onto the craft. There were distant cries as well, but they were soon drowned out by the roar of the twin turbofans.

'What is it? What are they shouting?'

'*Do not give it a thought,*' Shard said through the internal vox. '*Once we have tamed the storm it will not matter.*'

I synced with Iwazar. Through its eye, I could see figures waving their arms, intent on blocking our passage. Shard gunned the engines. The Avenger sped forward, heedless of their presence. At the last moment the ground crew flung themselves aside, the craft racing from the hangar, accelerating all the while.

'What are you doing?' I screamed, my voice barely carrying over the turbofans. 'Do we have authorisation to fly?'

'*Of course not. Why do you think we were sneaking around?*'

'But... what will they do? Shoot us down?'

'*With what? We have not yet been resupplied from the ork raid. Most of the Hydra flak batteries could not fire if they wanted to. Besides, this is the sort of thing a maverick fighter ace does. And all that really matters is results.*'

I tried to respond, but she cut the vox. I watched the grounds disappear as we soared into darkness. For an instant I wondered if the seer-skull was wired into the craft in the same manner as *Hephaestus*. Could I somehow override Shard, seize control of the vessel?

But what would I do? It was one thing aiming a targeting array, a task not dissimilar from taking a pict of a quick-moving subject. But I had no idea how to pilot the craft, and a single miscalculation would see us falling to our deaths.

No, such thoughts were pointless. Instead, I took a deep breath, trying to slow my pounding heart. I needed to place my trust in Shard, though that would have been easier if she had not just stolen an aircraft.

The governor's château disappeared, the only flickering light in the shadow beneath us. The Avenger was still climbing, piercing the thin layer of cloud veiling the void beyond. The stars blossomed, reminiscent of the insects that haunted the mire below.

I felt the craft slow. The last time we had breached the atmosphere, Shard had seemed absorbed by the stars. But with the vox disabled I had no idea what she was thinking. Whatever the case, the delay endured but a heartbeat, our craft banking left and accelerating. It was an unpleasant sensation when sitting in the rear cockpit. Normally the velocity pushed one into the flight seat, but instead I was pitched forward, the harness cutting into my shoulders. All I could see through the armaglass were the stars fleeing from us, as though anxious to be far from our impending fate.

Perhaps I should have taken Gradeolous' offer and kept my feet firmly on the ground, I thought. The governor had cautioned me against such risks. I wondered if, on our return, I could blame Shard, but she had a gift for skirting consequences. In fact, it would not be beyond her to lay the blame at my feet, claiming I evoked the authority of Governor Zanwich and commandeered her fighter to obtain footage.

It did not sound plausible, but neither did the idea of Shard wanting me on the flight. Who knew what she would do on our return?

Our return. Laughter bubbled up through me, a coarse cackle I could not contain. Soon I was rasping for breath, my chest heaving with each bellowed sob.

'What is wrong with you? You sound like you've been huffing hallucinogen grenades.'

I jumped at the sound, or would have were I not pinned by the harness. Still, the shock sobered me a little.

'I thought you had switched off the vox,' I said, voice finally under my control.

'I did, but I could hear you through the damn wall. What is wrong with you?'

'Nothing. Something amusing occurred to me.'

'Please share it. I could do with a good laugh.'

'I was sitting here, contemplating our return and whether you would blame me for this ill-conceived plan.'

'Hmm. I suppose that is funny. Shall I claim you overpowered me with your steely muscles? Or charmed me with your ravishing looks? Which is more believable? Or rather, which is even remotely believable?'

'That's not it. It merely struck me that I should welcome a possible execution for treason, because it would mean we somehow survived this suicidal flight.'

'Well, now you're just being hurtful.'

'You think you can take on a foe that bested three squads of reinforcements? Single-handed?'

'Of course. You forget two irrefutable facts. Firstly, they were blindsided and thus unable to defend themselves. Secondly, and more importantly, Flight Commander Lucille von Shard is the greatest fighter ace alive. The fallen were call-ups barely considered competent for deployment.'

'You're delusional.'

'We're both delusional, old chap. Otherwise, why did you tag along?'

'You said you were leading an assault.'

'So?'

'So, I assumed there might be a couple more aircraft involved.'

'There are two of us and I'm in charge. By definition that counts as leading.'

I knew she was baiting me. And, though it was irritating, I drew some comfort from it, for it meant she was at ease and unconcerned by an impending demise. Perhaps, I told myself, it was not arrogance, but confidence born from skill and experience. I had never witnessed her falter, or show fear.

Except in *Hephaestus*. Then, for but a moment, her facade had slipped. But that was only after the battle, when the adrenaline faded. During the engagement she was as close to invincible as anyone I had seen.

I synced with Iwazar, its unblinking eye picking out the darkness in muted greens, sensors struggling with the low light. Mizar would not have struggled. But I only needed to capture a little of the conflict. Assuming we survived it.

The storm front swelled as we hurtled towards it, its darkness visible even against the night sky. I have a limited understanding of meteorology, but seeing it so close dispelled any notion the cloud bank was a natural phenomenon. It seemed to spiral, its lower tip forming a few hundred feet above the swamp. As it rose, it grew, a vortex of smoke and shadow, never deviating from its assigned spot, suspended in place despite its size. Dimly, I saw the light of Orbital Station Salus looming above, the storm its shadow.

I expected ork planes to pour from the clouds at any moment.

The vox hissed. *'We're getting close. What can your little skull-thing see?'*

'Not much. The light is too poor.'

'Hilarious, but not the time. What energy emissions are there? Is it the same as the concealed platform?'

'I don't know. I can't tell.'

'Stop pouting and do your job. We need to know what is in there!'

I shivered, for there was the barest hint of concern in her voice.

'I cannot tell,' I repeated. 'Iwazar's sensors are nowhere near sophisticated enough to detect anything from this range.'

'What the hell is an Iwazar?'

'The seer-skull. It is all that remains of Fiwel Iwazar, a pict-forger who specialised in–'

'I don't care if he's the Ecclesiarch's lead trumpeter! I need to know what's in there.'

'I cannot tell you. Not without Mizar.'

She swore. 'Why in the Throne's name didn't you mention this?'

'You did not tell me that you needed sensor readings! You said you wanted to help complete my pict.'

'You must have known I was lying! Who gives a damn about your pict? The only reason you are here is because for some inexplicable reason you have the capacity to sense the orks' energy signatures. You think I wanted you here? Because of you I'm lumbered with flying a damn Avenger to accommodate the extra seat.'

There was anger in her voice, even betrayal. But I was angry too, and with my back to her it was easier to bite back.

'This is all on you,' I thundered. 'If you were honest from the start I could have told you Iwazar was not suitable for this mission. You should have told me.'

'Your stupid skulls all look alike!'

'So do your planes! Why should I care which you pick? I never asked for this mission. You came to me. All of this is on you!'

Silence. For a moment I thought she had cut the vox, but I could still hear her breath. It was not a reassuring sound.

'Listen. We should turn around,' I said. 'We can collect Mizar and a few more craft. Just tell them this was reconnaissance, or–'

'*No.*'

'No?'

'*Flight Commander Lucille von Shard does not run from a battle.*'

'But we are ill-equipped and this is the wrong type of aircraft, you said so yourself!'

'*It doesn't matter. A von Shard does not retreat. We will get closer so you can get the damn readings.*'

'No one could fly through that thing.'

'*I can, because I am Flight Commander Lucille von Shard. She is the best. I am the best. I can do this.*'

But, as we plunged into the maelstrom, I could not ignore the faint tremor in her voice.

CHAPTER TWENTY-TWO

I know not how Shard navigated the storm, the Avenger buffeted all the while by the unnatural winds that bound the tempest. A lesser pilot might have fought against it, and found their craft torn asunder, but she somehow rode the maelstrom, following the cyclone deeper into the darkness.

I was too terrified to sync with Iwazar, and could only gape from the rear of the craft. Through the cockpit I saw shadows in the storm, scraps of metal suspended by the vortex. Their angular lines were all too familiar, the shattered remnants of Imperial aircraft. It was as if we were flying through a graveyard of lost fighters.

At any moment I expected the Avenger to break apart. Nothing could last long in that storm, though at least that meant no enemy could oppose us. Plient's tales of malicious lightning and rains of bullets must have been delusions, imparted by the nightmare conditions. Perhaps the bullets were debris tearing at his craft, and the green lightning merely an ionic discharge.

Perhaps it was all a natural phenomenon, magnified by Orbital Station Salus' presence high above. Or possibly our aircraft puncturing the atmosphere had caused it, their cumulative arrivals from orbit somehow propagating the vortex.

I muttered a prayer for the God-Emperor to preserve us from the storm, but given the number of craft lost in its winds, I doubted He would pay my words much heed.

If Iwazar's data-core survived the tempest, would some enterprising young propagandist complete the project, earning their name through my labours? If enough of my cranium endured the crash, would I be fashioned into a seer-skull? Given my current successes, I doubted my superiors would consider me worthy of the honour. And in that moment I could not say I cared either way.

But just as I accepted the inevitability of our demise, the view suddenly cleared. From my position at the plane's rear, I saw us burst through the clouded vortex, the turbulence dissipated, supplanted by a calm that was almost eerie after the tempest. I could not believe we had endured, passing through the storm and emerging on the far side. I gave a great sigh, slumping into my seat.

'Thank the Emperor,' I murmured, engaging the vox. 'Shard, please tell me you don't intend to dive into that storm again.'

No response.

'Shard?' I murmured, clicking the switch. I thought I could hear her breathing, but she did not speak.

'Shard? Are you well?'

The silence smothered any good spirits. I tapped the vox a couple more times, before attempting to crane my neck. Pointless, of course, as I had no means of seeing through the cockpit. It took me a moment to remember Iwazar suspended beneath the plane. I synced with the seer-skull, and for an instant thought it had malfunctioned, some corroded data-fragment lodging itself in the optics.

Because what I saw was impossible.

The cyclone of cloud still spiralled miles around us. We had not flown through, but rather found the storm's eye, where the winds fell silent and even the tempest was cowed. And I could see why.

For the metallic monstrosity suspended within the storm was beyond anything I could have imagined, a mad fusion of shattered planes and rendered infrastructure, welded into a towering edifice of ork ingenuity. The central tower stood at least twice the height of the governor's château, four runways extending from it in a crude cross, each ending in a vast turbofan that provided lift, the whole ensemble mounted on a vast brass orb that thrummed with power. At the tower's apex, a series of exhaust pipes vomited black smog, the fumes drifting towards the upper atmosphere before being syphoned into the spiralling storm clouds.

I had no doubt this was the sky-fortress that had birthed the tempest.

This was the true Green Storm.

It was far from unoccupied. The fleet of fighters was still under construction, but at least half of them looked operational, to my inexpert eye. And even that was a force greater than anything I had seen the Imperium muster on Bacchus. They had yet to attack. I can only assume whatever crude sensors the edifice possessed were directed skywards, intent on intercepting the next batch of reinforcements. But I could make out diminutive figures racing across the runways towards the ork jets. Someone had seen us.

'Emperor's blood,' I heard myself murmur. It sounded like another's voice, my consciousness caught between my body and the seer-skull. Perhaps this was why I did not faint, or soil the cockpit. Either would have been reasonable, especially when I realised we were on an intercept course.

'Shard. We need to get out of here!' I said, my thumb stabbing at the vox-channel. 'Shard!'

'There's no point.'

Her voice was flat, holding no swagger of self-assurance. It was an echo of the young girl who listlessly repeated the drill abbot as he praised her family's pedigree.

'Are you mad? They will kill us! We must retreat before–'

'We cannot escape. We barely made it in. You can see them scrambling. I can't outrun all of them. It's over.'

'I refuse to accept that!' I thundered, rage repressing my fear. 'You're Flight Commander Lucille von Shard! You are the greatest fighter ace in the Imperium. For Emperor's sake, you have bragged of it often enough! You brought us here. You must do something!'

'I will.'

We accelerated, angling towards the nearest turbofan. Through Iwazar's eye I saw a flash of light as the Avenger's lascannons obliterated one of the nearer ork planes.

'You're attacking?'

'Of course,' she murmured in that cold, dead voice. *'How else would Flight Commander Lucille von Shard meet her end?'*

The vox cut out. I could only watch the flying fortress swell before Iwazar's eye. We were close enough now to pick out individual orks racing for their planes, whilst scrawnier greenskin runts rushed to the anti-aircraft guns. As the air filled with bullets and discharges of vile green energy, I found myself fixated on the cranes and drill heads mounted along the walkways. It was like some vast workshop, churning out squadrons from scrap. I had wondered how the orks acquired their craft, struggling to visualise the savage creatures employing spanner and arc welder. It seemed I had my answer.

Shard unleashed the Avenger's bolt cannon, the shots tearing into the scrambling greenskins. I confess my heart leapt as both ork and fighter were shredded by the barrage. But it was as nothing against the horde, like spitting into the ocean.

The craft shuddered as we took a hit. The armour held, at least that time, for it seemed the orks were struggling to mobilise against so small a target. But more of the runts were directing cannons at our craft, and they appeared marginally better shots than their larger brethren. Shard made little effort to avoid their fire, the bullets thundering against the fuselage. Perhaps she saw no point in manoeuvring through such a barrage, like trying to dodge raindrops in a storm. Or perhaps survival was no longer her goal.

Through Iwazar's eye, I saw two of the diminutive greenskins pushing a bizarre device into place on a ramshackle platform. It held a central cannon, flanked by four smaller rods that pulsed with power. Only as the energy coalesced did I remember the curious weapons employed against our bombing run, those beams that dragged planes from the sky.

'Shard?' I bellowed, but the vox remained silent.

The beam struck us, stealing all momentum, the Avenger now a dead weight. We plummeted, tumbling groundward. As we fell, the path of the beam was blocked by the hull of the sky-fortress, and suddenly power was restored, though we were still trapped in a death spiral. Shard regained control, but the Avenger now swooped beneath the colossal structure. I could see rows of cannons above us, but none were firing, the vessel's crew still struggling to mobilise their defence.

'This is our chance!' I yelled. 'Dive! Maybe we can slip out from under them!'

She paid no heed, accelerating towards the brass dome that squatted beneath the sky-fortress. As we closed on it, I could see that the sphere was neither smooth nor a single piece, the metal bearing the mark of numerous hammer blows, and threaded with copper-coloured wire that seemed to quiver in anticipation. We were close enough to pierce the heat haze surrounding it. Emerald sparks arced along its surface.

'It's charging!' I said, the hairs rising on my arms.

'I can still take it out,' I heard through the vox. *'If I hit it now, it might cause a backlash. Maybe destroy the whole thing!'*

She sought to convince herself as much as me.

She fired. The twin lascannons unleashed a pulse of white light, like the rays of the sun. It struck the dome, though I could not tell if any damage was inflicted. The blast was too blinding, overloading the seer-skull's sensors.

Then a surge of green lightning tore along the lascannon's beam. I assume the discharge was unintended, otherwise I doubt we would have survived it. But the backwash struck the craft, and I lost my connection to Iwazar, the seer-skull's holo-projector flaring in alarm. A dozen picts torn from its data-memory seared the sky. I saw Shard's face suddenly loom large across the clouds, her mouth set in that sneering smile the width of a Baneblade. The image shifted to the young woman being interrogated by the drill abbot, before that was obliterated by the snarling visage of a triumphant ork.

Shard's attack must have done something, though, for the dome was now flinging searing arcs of lightning in all directions. I saw one strike one of the turbofans supporting the sky-fortress, seemingly vaporising a part of it in the process. The monstrosity lurched violently to the side, orks and aircraft pitching from its runway. For an instant I thought Shard had done it, that her daring attack would drop the Green Storm from the sky. But it clung there, the remaining three turbofans sufficient to defy gravity.

'I'm taking another shot!' Shard snarled, bringing us about, the Avenger screeching in protest. I could almost feel it breaking apart around me.

'Are you mad?'

'Of course, it's part of my training. Why don't you try helping? There is a gun back there.'

An echo of confidence had returned to her voice. Perhaps she truly thought we could win.

I glanced down the gunsight of the rear-mounted heavy stubber. Though a high-calibre weapon, it seemed a tiny thing, barely bigger than the armaments carried by the ork soldiers. I reached for the controls, when green lightning suddenly flashed before me. I expected an explosion, but there was nothing so flamboyant. The rear of the craft simply disappeared, as if sliced clear by a vast blade, the heavy stubber and my cockpit all that remained.

'Shard?' I murmured, as we began to pitch down.

'What happened? What did you do?'

'Nothing. The lightning... removed part of the aircraft.'

'What? That makes no–'

A second blast struck the Avenger, this time a direct hit. For a heartbeat we were engulfed in its lightning.

Then the sky was gone. The world, too, as we tumbled through a void. Except this was not the darkness of space. Instead, it was a shadow forged from screams and blood. There was no sense of time, nor direction, only the terrible certainty that my fears were now manifest, and would soon crawl from my ears and devour my soul. I tried to scream, but the sound sought to strangle me.

I cannot say how long the madness lasted. Something between a microsecond and a lifetime. But suddenly we were falling again, and the swamp loomed rapidly into view, less than a hundred feet away from us.

I could not even move, consumed by the nightmare, but Shard tried to break our fall, wrenching the nose up. She levelled us, but we were moving too fast to escape that dive.

True darkness claimed me. I welcomed it.

CHAPTER TWENTY-THREE

I do not know how long I lay trapped in the wreck, only that I stirred at the rising of Bacchus' sun. Its light pierced the blessed oblivion, and brought manifold agonies. The worst was the wet throbbing from my shattered lower leg, and stabbing chest pain every time I took a breath. Perhaps my ribs were broken. My leg certainly was. Worse, the flight harness cut into my chest, constricting my ribs further. I could not scream, managing nothing more than a choked cry.

It was too much. I succumbed to darkness, seeking the comfort of nothingness. But it was no longer a sweet oblivion, for I now endured the pain from a body I was bound to. I did not crave death, though I was sure it would soon claim me. But I could not face the bleak impossibility of the situation. Even if I could overcome crippling pain and debilitating injuries, escape was impossible. Better to surrender to the nothing, await my end and perhaps the God-Emperor's salvation. I had served long. It was my time.

But all I could picture now was that terrible storm sundering our fuselage, the impregnable ork sky-fortress unleashing its vile lightning. The terrible fall that lasted forever, where the world went missing and a hellscape stole the sky. I knew then that, however brief or long I might live, I would never forget that nightmare. A part of me would always be trapped there, being stalked by my own inner daemons. Death was preferable to returning to that terrible place.

The light shifted above, a shape blocking the sun. The pressure of my harness eased, though this relief brought a renewed stab of pain as blood rushed to the constricted flesh. I gave a shuddering sob and thought I heard a reply, though the words were lost.

Then my broken body was hauled upright. Instinct compelled me to stand, but my leg was a bloody mess and could not support me. The pain drove me down and away and I fled my body, syncing with Iwazar, who was still embedded in the craft. The pict quality was dreadful, the skull struggling to focus, but through its eye I surveyed the wreckage.

The remains of the Avenger lay half-submerged in the quagmire. It had been torn to scrap, the fuselage cracked and wingless, the tail absent. There was some problem with the image, the sky in place of the swamp. It took me a moment to realise the seer-skull was inverted, as was the shattered wing in which it was secured.

A figure was bending over the rear cockpit, attempting to retrieve my body from the wreckage. Given the pict quality I would have struggled to identify her, were it not for the torn flight suit and sabre bound to her waist. It was curious observing her dragging my prone form. Perhaps it was Iwazar's influence, but I found I was rather unattached to that sack of skin and bone. The adepts of the Mechanicus disdain the flesh as weak, revering the machine as its superior. In that moment I understood their creed. Nestled inside Iwazar's neural network, I was untroubled by shattered limbs, the skull's own damage registering as nothing more than an inconvenience to standard operations.

I wondered how long I could linger there. If my body were to expire, would I die too, or persist as some electronic gheist? Would it even be me, or an echo wrought by the machine?

Shard had somehow dragged my body over her shoulders. She was breathing heavily, and favouring her left foot, but was able to haul my slight frame. I was surprised she had bothered retrieving me, particularly as there was nowhere to go. But I watched as she trudged through the swamp, its waters lapping at her waist. Slowly, she waded from my field of view. I tried to rotate to follow her, but something jammed the hard point, and she slipped from my sight, taking with her my link to the world of flesh. I could feel it tug on my consciousness, just as it had when I abandoned Mizar in the swamp. Only this time I would not be drawn back to that prison of pain. I would remain a detached observer, awaiting the expiration of Iwazar's power reserves with stoic acceptance. Then I would blink from existence. It would be the cold oblivion I craved. My fears would not find me then.

But that separation never quite came. Propagandist Simlex's body clung to life, persisting like a fly I could not quite swat. She could not have taken it far enough. That was easily deduced given the number of return trips. I had nothing to do besides watch her scavenge the crash site for whatever she could salvage.

Iwazar's internal chronometer must have been damaged, for I could not sense the passage of time by anything other than the shadows shifting. But night was approaching, and it was some time since Shard had hauled her last load of scrap. It was a shock when her face suddenly loomed into view, skin scorched red by the burning sun, nose peeling and cheeks marred by dirt and blood. Her eyes were bright and brittle as ice, and I feared they glimmered with a hint of insanity.

'What do we have here?' she whispered, staring straight into Iwazar's lens. 'Still functional? I suppose they build you to last.'

A blade flashed in her hand. I am unsure what she did with it, the weapon flicking from my view. But I felt a surge run through the seer-skull, and with a wrench I was torn from its housing and once more condemned to darkness.

I smelled the fire before I heard the crackle of fuel, but did not open my eyes. Would not, in fact. Because once my eyes were open, I would have to face my fate. And I did not see how it could be anything good.

The pain had lessened, the blade in my ribs now merely an ache, my shattered leg a distant annoyance. But the tingling in my fingers and dryness of my mouth indicated a sedative was responsible. That was mildly encouraging. It suggested medical support was available. Then again, my bed was hard and nobbled as rock, and the campfire blazing close by was not indicative of a medi-unit. I reached out for Iwazar, but could not find it.

'Good evening, Propagandist Simlex.'

I knew Shard's voice well enough. But it carried an edge that was neither familiar nor reassuring.

I risked a glance through narrowed eyes. The firelight barely etched the contours of our abode. It appeared almost a cave, except the walls had an organic, bark-like texture. We were, in fact, nestling in the hollowed roots of a mandack tree. The fire had been set at its entrance, most of the smoke billowing into the swamp beyond, though the air was thick with the stench of the burning wood.

There, silhouetted by the fire, sat Shard. She did not look at me, her focus the darkness beyond the cave. Her flight suit was torn, the exposed flesh reddened by Bacchus' harsh sun. The sabre was laid out beside her, but she held a smaller knife, using it to shave a length of wood.

I tried to speak, but coughed instead.

'There's water beside you. Don't try and guzzle it. Small sips.'

I groped for the canteen, unscrewing the cap with shaking fingers. Though recycled and stale, it tasted as glorious as anything from Governor Dolos' vineyard. But my throat rebelled, almost expelling the vital fluid. I held it in my mouth, allowing a trickle to pass at a time.

'Better?' she asked.

I nodded.

'Good, because we don't have much left. I salvaged some filtration packs, but I doubt they would cope with the swamp, and it's a couple of months until the rainy season.'

Her voice had that dead quality again, like before the attack. My memory was in pieces, the flashes interspersed by the nebulous hellscape. Perhaps the orks' weapon produced some mind-altering effect, inducing hallucinations or psychosis. I clung to that, for it meant what I had seen wasn't real, even if my aching soul told me otherwise.

But what did it mean for Shard?

'I'm... surprised we survived,' I said, the words blades to my throat.

'You can thank the swamp. It absorbed most of the impact.'

'You do not claim credit?'

She shrugged. 'How can I? I have never been shot down. I have no frame of reference for what one is supposed to do.' She continued to carve as she spoke, the blade sliding against the wood.

'What are you doing?'

'Making a splint,' she replied. 'Or maybe a stake. I haven't decided yet.'

'A splint?'

'You need to be mobile.'

'I cannot walk.'

'Then you will die here,' she replied. 'Perhaps we both will.'

'You think it will find us?'

'The Green Storm? No. We are miles from it.'

'That's impossible. They shot us down. We fell.'

'Whilst you slept I located Orbital Station Salus with my magnoculars. We are at least a hundred miles from both it and the storm.'

'Could the tempest have moved? Perhaps following Salus?'

'I doubt it could get far missing an engine. It's us. We were transported here.'

'The lightning.'

'Yes. It's some sort of teleporter. Almost like warp travel. That might explain… what we saw in there…'

She trailed off, gaze falling to her feet. Her knife slowed.

'I have traversed the warp many times in my travels,' I said. 'I know there are tales of its dangers, but I've never seen anything like that.'

'That's because warp craft have Geller fields,' she replied. 'They shield the vessel during the passage. You ever been caught in a warp storm?'

'No.'

'Well, I have,' she said. 'I was spared the worst. But some of the crew… Let's just say the galaxy has horrors worse than orks. We were lucky to escape with our souls intact.'

I considered her words. Not the nonsense regarding warp travel, which struck me as a tall tale of dubious validity. But the orks clearly had a means of launching raids without warning, and during the bombing run I had seen them appear as if from nowhere. Perhaps they did have such a device, and we had been flung miles from the sky-fortress.

'Do you think you crippled it?' I asked.

'What?'

'The ork's sky-fortress! The Green Storm!'

'Oh. No, I doubt it,' she said, rising to her feet. 'If it did not immediately plunge from the sky then it won't soon fall. I have damaged it, perhaps slowed their plans. But nothing more.'

'What plans?'

'You saw. They are building a fleet. And cutting off our reinforcements. In fact, the wreckage from our fallen craft is probably feeding the manufactoria. One has to admire the efficiency. I wonder if I should paint myself green and see if I can switch sides.'

'Do not speak such heresy, even in jest.'

She laughed, the sound high, sharp and barely controlled.

'You intend to tattle on me?' she asked. 'Perhaps vox Maric again? Yes, I heard about that. Or will you record some fresh footage for your little project? Add it to the data-scraps of my childhood you've been carrying around?'

She glared through me, but I could not take my eyes from the knife in her hand.

'I had… For a project such as this I needed to thoroughly research–'

'It seemed very thorough,' she said, drawing closer. 'At least, those moments I saw flash across the clouds, right before the orks shot us down. I'm impressed you dug up my old school record, but I was never an exceptional pupil. Unlike my siblings. Did one of my brothers provide what you needed?'

'I have sufficient clearance for such files.'

'They do have such fond memories of their time in the schola progenium,' she continued. 'Well, I say memories, but it's hard to be certain. The drill abbots poke around our heads, editing out inconveniences like our past. Their mindscaping techniques are quite robust, all that remains is what they choose to leave.'

She squatted down beside me, blade picking at the dirt beneath her fingernail.

'Siblings are a sometime exception,' she continued. 'They like us to know about our familial connections. Not so we can draw comfort from them, but so we will compete to honour the legacy. That's why I'm lucky enough to have siblings, so there is someone to overshadow me.'

Her voice held nothing but contempt.

'Still, you cannot argue with results,' she continued. 'The von Shards excel in every field. The survivors, anyway. It sounds like a propagandist's dream actually, having a perfect family to hold as an exemplar. One might even say that if such a family did not exist, it would be prudent to create it, don't you think?'

I did not reply and would not meet her gaze. I did not wish to provoke her. But she would not let me be silent.

'I asked you a question,' she said, tapping the flat of the blade against my side. 'Aren't you interested in my story? Isn't that the real reason you're here? Because I fascinate you so?'

'I don't know what you want me to say.'

'Just be honest,' she replied. 'Seven orphaned siblings, their parents two of the Imperium's greatest heroes. They are raised by the schola progenium to become the finest servants of the Throne. Each wildly different but exceptional in their own way. The charismatic priest, unflappable commissar and maverick fighter ace. Such an inspiring story. It's what drew you here, right?'

'If I have offended you–'

'Everything offends me,' she spat, rising. 'Because I am Lucille von Shard, the brash fighter ace who rarely toes the line but always gets the job done. That's what they chose to make me. And that's why I take offence.'

She turned back to the fire, throwing a handful of dried

leaves onto the blaze. It flared as though doused in promethium, releasing a plume of smoke, most of which wafted from the cave's entrance.

'Is that wise?' I asked.

'Unless you would prefer to freeze to death?'

'Won't it attract the orks?'

'Oh yes,' she said. 'Once the sun has risen, they will come for us.'

'And then what?'

'I will defeat them, obviously,' she replied, her back to me. 'It should only be a dozen or so, no match for the esteemed flight commander Lucille von Shard.'

'Even without an aircraft?'

'I have my blade and my wits. Actually, where is my sword?'

'By the fire.'

'Ah. Thank you!' she said, retrieving the weapon. 'For a moment I was concerned.'

'When did you last wield it?' I asked as she fastened the sabre to her hip.

'All the time.'

'Really?'

'Of course. Opening bottles, removing stray threads, carving expletives in the walls of the governor's mansion.'

'I meant in combat.'

'Not often. It's darn difficult to get close enough when flying. But I was trained by the finest fencing instructors of the schola progenium. I even came sixth in duelling one year.'

'Sixth?'

'Yes, though there was a sickness going round. Still, I'm sure I'll pick it up again fairly quickly. You hold it by the handle, right?'

'Where did you get that sword?' I asked, for in the firelight I could see the scabbard was marked by the von Shard crest.

'It was my father's. Not his best one, but the balance is tolerable.'

I could not tell if she was mocking me, or was broken by what had happened. She wore a smile, but it was worse than her usual sneer. There was a cold resignation to it, as if she no longer cared for our fates.

My own expression must have been similar.

'You look worried,' she said. 'I know why.'

'Do you?'

'Of course. You fear that you will be unable to capture my victory. Well, fear not. I found your little friend.'

She reached into the shadows, dragging free the grime-strewn seer-skull, holding it by the cables running from its spine.

'It hasn't been the best company,' she said, examining the dangling skull. 'Maybe you can patch it up? It will make it seem like you're useful.'

She tossed it to me. The skull landed in my lap, a stab of pain flaring from the impact. Then she turned from me, eyes fixed on the sky.

Awaiting the dawn and the death that would come with it.

CHAPTER TWENTY-FOUR

I could not sleep, but neither did I wish to. For if the dawn was to be my last, it seemed imprudent to waste it slumbering. But how should one spend their last night?

I see an argument for hedonism and debauchery. But I was crippled and trapped in a rotten tree deep in a perilous swamp, my only company a woman who detested me, even before her grip on sanity began to slip. Opportunities for indulgence were limited.

I considered praying, offering my soul to the God-Emperor. But there was no priest to hear my confession, nor abbot to exonerate my sins. And I felt a just deity should judge their servants on the life they lived, not their attempts to mitigate past transgressions in the final hours.

So, I spent the night as I would many others, attending to the seer-skull as I prepared to shoot one last pict. Iwazar had endured an impressive amount of damage, its survival a testament to the adepts of the Mechanicus. Though sanctioned to conduct repair and maintenance rites, I could not pretend I understood the device. I had never dreamt it could project such vast images across the clouds, a phenomenon I could only attribute to the power surge caused by the orks' lightning. It did not seem to have inflicted systemic damage, but the light was poor and mechanisms stained by the swamp. I could not be sure without testing it, but I feared doing so might rouse Shard. Her mania had receded, and she seemed content to doze by the fire. I do not know if she truly slumbered or merely waited. But either way, she did not desire my company.

The pain worsened as the night receded, and the effects of the sedatives waned. I did not ask Shard for more, not wishing her to know I suffered. Besides, there was a poetry in my pain. Propagandist Fiwel Iwazar, the deceased propagandist whose skull I was presently clearing of silt, was familiar with infirmity. His front-line duties had ended when an errant frag grenade severed his spine. Some would have been diminished by such a setback, but Iwazar had taken confinement to a hoverchair as an opportunity to advance his craft. Unable to obtain his own footage, he became the master of splicing and manipulating existing data-files, retelling tales of the Imperium's heroes, unconstrained by the limitations of facts and events.

I had once resented his flexibility with the truth. But I was coming around to his view, and not only because sitting in a warm room in some civilised part of the galaxy sounded quite appealing. For, as I watched her doze, I realised I had captured only facets of Shard. With but a few tweaks and choice omissions I could present whatever version of her I desired. I could show a hero, the Imperium's shield against the ork offensive. Or a soldier who took on every challenge without fear, leading the fightback, and only falling against impossible odds. The woman who had almost turned around the war single-handedly, and laid down her life for the Imperium, refusing to yield and inflicting a bloody nose on the ork offensive.

But it would be as simple to paint her as a cynical career soldier who cared solely for her own advancement and indulgence. Skilled enough that her superior officers ignored her insubordination, drunkenness and repeated derelictions of duty. But her hubris led to her disobeying orders, stealing a fighter and launching it into a raging tempest, where her body was lost to the swamp.

I could elevate or destroy her. If I was not condemned to die in obscurity.

I debated recording a final, vindictive message and dispatching the seer-skull. Perhaps it would find its way into Imperial hands. But what would be the point? Her legacy was no doubt already tarnished by her unauthorised assault against the Green Storm. I doubted her siblings would take it well. Perhaps they would have her record erased, or at least sealed. Then there could be six von Shard children. Six heroes, without a prodigal daughter to mar their good name.

I sighed, trying to focus on my work and ignore the itching in my leg. I wanted to scratch it, but I could not bring myself to peel back the dressing Shard had applied whilst I slumbered. I did not want to see those purple blotches on my skin that marked the onset of Vintner's Blight. Better to die with the pretence of purity.

I sealed Iwazar's panel, whispering the liturgy of activation. The seer-skull bobbed into the air, stretching its tiny appendages, as though awakened from a pleasant sleep. Tentatively, I attempted to sync my consciousness with it. It was difficult through the pain, but I managed to connect to it.

Just in time, too. The flickering fire was dying, but I could see the first rays of Bacchus' sun crest the horizon. As if on cue, Shard yawned, arching her back as she rose to her feet. She glanced to the cave's entrance and the encroaching day, before tossing another armful of leaves onto the fire. The flames greedily swallowed them, unleashing a plume of smoke which I noted was tinged green.

She had claimed the fire was to keep us warm. But I wondered if its true purpose was to summon the orks. Perhaps Shard preferred a death in battle over succumbing to thirst or disease. Or perhaps she truly imagined she could defeat them.

I whispered to Iwazar. The seer-skull whirred in acknowledgement before soaring from the cave's entrance, taking position in the sky above, ready to capture her last stand. I owed her that. She had saved my life several times. It was fitting I would capture her death.

That day I learned first-hand of a term familiar to military officers across the Imperium: *timore tedium*. My terror rose as the sun ascended, for I feared an attack at any moment. But as the hours drifted by, the sun continuing its path, I began to yearn for it. Anything was better than waiting. I just wanted it done.

By midday, the sun was so strong Shard had to retreat from the cave's entrance, shielding her skin from its glare.

'It's too bright,' she said. 'The glare from the water is almost as bad as the sunlight. Can your skull see anything?'

'Nothing dangerous.'

I had spent that morning using Iwazar to familiarise myself with our surroundings. We were indeed embedded in the bark of an aged mandack tree. I think it was dead, or close to it, the bark blighted by the taint that seemed to have infested the whole planet. Its vast bulk at least shielded our rear, the spiralling limbs and barbed roots forming an almost imperceptible wall. But Shard's smoke clearly revealed the crevice's entrance.

From this vantage point, I could just spy what remained of the Avenger. It lay half-submerged in the swamp, barely a hundred yards from us. Shard had hastily concealed it with branches and leaves, but I knew the orks would find it once they had dispatched us. More scrap for them to salvage. It struck me as irresponsible of Shard to leave it intact.

'No smoke on the horizon?' she asked.

Her voice carried, dreamlike. Weakened as I was, I had to focus so as not to lose myself to the seer-skull's machine-spirit.

'No,' I whispered. 'Are you so anxious for our demise?'

She did not reply, but from the way the smoke thickened she must have thrown more leaves on the fire. There was no doubting the green tint now, though I wondered why she bothered. Though the beasts used the colour as a signal, surely they would investigate any plume for salvage purposes? Perhaps she had no choice, the colour merely a by-product of the fuel. There was little else to burn.

I directed Iwazar higher, straining against the tug of my body. But there was nothing of note in the squalid swamp beyond brackish water and the tangle of gnarl-vines. The sun had begun to dip now, intent on the horizon, and the long shadows gave the twisted plants a sinister edge. Still, they seemed more uniform than usual, reminiscent of the vineyard I had visited in Governor Dolos' yacht. But, while plentiful, the vines were sickly. I saw signs of the blight, and a curious, tendril-like bindweed wound between the branches, choking the life from the plants. I thought I recognised its puckered pink flowers from somewhere, but there was no time to dwell on it, because it was then I stumbled across the boat.

It was one of the smaller vessels used to harvest the vine-fruit, and was capsized, perhaps due to the gaping hole in the hull. But the swamp had little current, and it was unlikely it had drifted far.

I swept Iwazar's sensors over the expanse, seeking evidence of human habitation. If we were close to a distillery, they could send a boat, or even contact the governor and dispatch a relief force. Perhaps she was in residence even now, with Flight Commander Gradeolous and his squad of fighters. Without Mizar's advanced sensors my visual range was limited, and I could only make out an indistinct shape on the horizon. It might have been the distillery, a particularly statuesque mandack tree or yet another ork fortress. But I could travel no further, having reached the limits of my connection. Dimly, I heard Shard's voice. I could not follow her words, but she sounded alarmed.

It was then that I saw the smoke. Orks. Not their ramshackle aircraft, but those fanboats the greenskins so favoured. I counted half a dozen, though perhaps there were more, their silhouettes shrouded by the smog spewed from their engines. They were racing towards our hideaway, our own thin plume of smoke pathetic in comparison.

I could hear Shard's voice again. Closer now, but still distant. I shifted from Iwazar, coughing as I took residence in my prison of flesh. A haze of smoke clung to the hollow, for Shard had doused the fire. She stood by the cave's entrance, blade sheathed at her side, peering through a cracked set of magnoculars.

'You still with me?' she asked.

'For now.'

'Did you see anything?'

'They are coming. I presume you know that.'

'Yes. But these lenses are terrible. I don't know how many.'

'I counted half a dozen boats.'

She swore. 'Probably forty at least,' she whispered. 'That's not good odds.'

'You think if it were a mere thirty you could best them?'

She glared at me. 'Is this the time to be flippant?'

'You mean in the face of certain death? I suppose not. Only a callous sadist would adopt such a tone.'

She did not reply. I enjoyed that silence, despite everything. Minutes passed, the orks drawing ever closer.

'What are they doing now?' she asked.

I synced with Iwazar. The seer-skull had drifted closer. I could see the orks drawing in, but since Shard had doused the flames they had slowed, their beacon faded. They did not seem to be taking this well, exchanging grunts and snarls, sounds I would have once dismissed as the tongue of beasts. But from the way Iwazar was attempting to compile it, the seer-skull considered it a language of sorts, though one quite beyond its ability to translate.

'They are close,' I murmured. 'They seem to be squabbling and have slowed to a crawl.'

'How far are they from us?'

'Less than two hundred yards.'

'Can you see the Avenger?'

'Yes.'

'And have they?'

'No. But the largest beast seems to be restoring order.'

The hulking greenskin on the foremost craft was bellowing at its followers, waving a brutal cleaver the length of my leg. The sounds would have been harsh upon a human ear, but Iwazar processed them in the same detached manner as it would the screams of the dying. There did seem to be repeated patterns and I wondered if a more sophisticated auditory processor would be able to decipher the ork tongue.

There appeared to be some disagreement between the creatures. An ork from an adjacent boat suddenly vaulted onto the lead craft, brandishing a pair of jagged blades that looked as though they might once have belonged to a Valkyrie's turbofan. It snarled a challenge, and the lead ork bared its tusks in response.

Or possibly it merely smiled; I am unsure whether the distinction is meaningful.

'They seem to be fighting amongst themselves. Well, two of them.'

'Pity the rest are not inclined to join in. Is one the leader?'

'Probably. It's bigger, and its armour has more skulls nailed to it.'

The two fighters circled one another, snapping exchanges in their crude tongue. The challenger suddenly lunged forward, knives bared like the claws of a mantis. The larger ork sidestepped the attack, bringing its cleaver around in a two-handed swing that could have pierced a battle tank. But the boats bobbed in the water, causing the challenger to half dive and half fall from the weapon's path. It recovered quickly, unburdened by the heavy cleaver, and drove one of its knives into the larger greenskin's thigh.

But the brute was unperturbed by the attack, twisting its body and dragging the still-embedded blade from the challenger's hand. In the same movement, it brought the great cleaver down. The attempt to parry was futile, the force of the blow shattering the remaining knife and pulverising the beast holding it.

The larger ork dragged the knife from its leg, the blade now stained a deep red. It licked it clean, studying the weapon for a moment before tucking it into its belt.

'It's over,' I whispered. 'The challenger lost.'

'And now?'

'I'm not sure. Their leader is yelling at the others. They seem to be dividing into groups. He might be trying to coordinate a search.'

'Have they seen the Avenger?'

'No.'

'Damn greenskins. Even an ork should be able to spot it. Get their attention.'

'How?'

'I don't know! Play them a vid-feed or something. But draw them to the Avenger.'

A vid-feed, she said. I, who had entertained nobles and clergy, reduced to playing recordings for an audience of orks. My career had truly reached its nadir. I did not know if the holo-projectors even functioned; they were temperamental at the best of times, and that had been before our encounter with the Green Storm.

I focused, willing Iwazar to engage the projectors. I did not know what pict it would summon, half expecting Shard's face to materialise. But instead we were greeted by the snarling visage of an ork. The projector was clearly damaged, the oversized face twisting and flickering, but it was hard to miss in the crepuscular light.

As one, the greenskins faced it, weapons raised.

But then there was silence. I had not expected that. I had assumed they would attack, or at least be amused or enraged. But the looped image of the roaring greenskin, its face plastered across the vines, was treated with a near reverence. The ork leader muttered something, the others following suit. It sounded almost like a word.

Gork.

Or possibly Mork. It was hard to tell.

'Are they taking the bait?'

'I don't know. They are just staring.'

'Move the image deeper into the vines. Draw them in.'

I did as bade, though I had not anticipated the orks' reaction. They snarled as the image receded, as if affronted it had shrunk. A few took a half-step towards it, sniffing the air like dogs, their gaze slinking to the undergrowth, perhaps seeking the source of the deception.

'I don't think they liked that,' I said. 'They are getting suspicious.'

'Well, in fairness, they damn well should be.'

I heard the click of a switch.

The Avenger's lumens flared bright as its systems roared into life one last time. Only the Emperor knows how Shard coaxed its machine-spirit into life. It was still crippled, and I doubted its electrical systems would last more than a few moments in the corrosive swamp water. Its lascannons were wrecked, torn clear along with its wings.

But it still had the bolt cannon.

The weapon screamed into life, the recoil lifting the front of the craft from the swamp. As it thrashed in its death throes, a hail of bullets tore into the orks. I drew Iwazar from the barrage's path as the nearest fanboats were torn apart and the ork crew shredded. Strangely, this did not dissuade the survivors. Instead, they surged forward, hurling themselves at their attacker. They were but a dozen yards from the downed craft, but each step cost them dear. I suspect none of the beasts would have survived had the weapon not jammed at that moment, its mechanisms clogged by the pervasive swamp.

The orks swarmed the craft, their jagged blades hammering into its hull, desperately seeking vengeance on their unseen attacker.

'Good boys,' I heard Shard whisper, as she flicked a second switch.

A single Hellstrike missile remained mounted on the Avenger's wing. Of course, that wing was no longer attached to the fuselage, and the release mechanism was non-functional. Instead, the missile flared, straining against its housing for a few agonising seconds, before detonating and releasing dozens of incendiary submunitions. The conflagration engulfed not only the shattered craft but also the attacking orks. I am not sure if the promethium tanks caught, or the vessel had already shed its fuel into the swamp, but the blaze erupted into an explosion that swallowed the horde. Even Iwazar was forced to retreat, a dozen warning pictographs flashing across its sensors as they registered the intensity of the inferno.

'By the Throne,' I whispered. 'You did it. You killed them all.'

But as I spoke, shapes burst from the water. Their hide was scorched and riddled with shrapnel, but this only seemed to enrage the beasts. Their leader tore clear his shoulder guard, flames still licking across the metal, as he roared in defiance.

'You had to tempt fate,' she sighed.

'You think he sees us?'

'If not, he soon will,' she replied, striding from the hollow. Through Iwazar, I saw her emerge from the crevice in the mandack tree, adopting a duellist's stance, though her blade remained sheathed.

'I am Flight Commander Lucille von Shard,' she bellowed, voice carrying across the swamp. 'Who wants to die?'

The only reply was that terrifying roar, the snarls merging into a battle cry that struck like a hurricane. It buffeted Iwazar, the seer-skull struggling to focus on the onrushing greenskins. Even Shard was pushed back by the wave of pure fury, stumbling and almost falling.

No, not stumbling. She was dashing back to the cave entrance, hauling a familiar-looking weapon into place. The heavy stubber, once mounted on the rear of the craft. It was not built to be portable, and she struggled to raise it into position and brace it between the tangled roots of the tree. The orks were surging onwards, their charge slowed by the swamp. But they were perhaps a dozen yards from her.

Less even, before the gun roared.

It was impossible to aim, and the recoil was sufficient to require a weapon mount. But at that range it was also hard to miss.

Rounds thudded into the orks, slowing but not stopping them. Then one's head was shorn from its shoulders, and two more fell, legs crippled by the barrage.

But the lead ork proved indomitable, wading through the bullets like rain on a summer's eve. It was close enough to seize the barrel, tearing it from Shard's grip with one hand and tossing it aside, even as it raised its crushing cleaver.

I urged Iwazar to it, focusing the holo-projector into the tightest beam, aiming it squarely at the ork's beady eyes. It howled at the blinding light, staggering, its blow tearing into the rock-like root inches from Shard's shoulder. She was already rising, unsheathing her sabre, the blade a thin and fragile thing against the marauding greenskin.

Until her thumb slid across a switch, and a halo of blue light engulfed the sword.

The ork abandoned its wedged cleaver, reaching for the knife tucked into its belt just as Shard swung her blade two-handed, the blow aimed at the creature's side. Strong as she was, I doubt it would have penetrated more than an inch if not for the power field wreathing the blade. Instead, it tore through the towering ork, carving deep into its sternum.

Its fist lashed out, knocking Shard sprawling and into the swamp. As she disappeared beneath the waters it sought the blade embedded in its side. Steam was rising from the wound, but the beast's bulk made it unable to reach the handle.

It gave up and glared at the swamp water, seeking some sign of Shard. But the sun had almost set, and the foetid swamp was opaque in the half-light. As it searched, the beast did not see her crawl beneath the surface, circling behind it. It did not see when she rose from the quagmire, uniform stained black but eyes blazing. One of her arms hung limp, perhaps dislocated by the ork's blow, but with the other she seized the sabre's handle, twisting it savagely. The ork roared in pain and fury, blood bubbling from its wound as it sought to turn and face her. But she matched its movements, staying behind it even as she wrenched the blade back and forth, tearing open the ork's flank. It spun sharply, almost lifting her from her feet, but still she clung to the blade, driving it deeper. She must have reached the lungs by now, but still the beast refused to die.

Suddenly it surged forward, tearing the blade clear. Shard fell back, scrabbling to her feet even as the monster turned, its chest a bloodied mess. It lunged towards her, but she clambered up the tree's massive roots, her feet slipping against the bark, one shoulder still hanging useless.

The beast tried to follow, but it too was reduced to one arm, the other nearly torn clear by her bladework. It attempted to haul its massive frame onto the root-branch, but she slashed the sword across its knuckles, severing two fingers. Still it scrabbled with a stump-like hand, refusing to surrender.

But the movement had slowed, its roar dying as it slumped over the root. It seemed dead, but she took no chances, stabbing the tip of the blade into its hide and twisting. The beast did not react, but still she was hesitant, slicing at its remaining arm as she crept closer, poised to retreat if it gave any sign of life. At last, she took a chance, leaping forward and driving the blade into the beast's neck. It shuddered as the power sword pierced the vertebrae, then was still.

Shard deactivated the sabre, sheathing it on the third attempt before collapsing to her knees. Her breath was beyond laboured, her arm useless. But she glanced up at Iwazar, who was still surveying the scene.

'Get a good look,' she said, each word preceded by a shuddering gasp. 'I told you. I am Flight Commander Lucille von Shard, and I will not–'

I have no doubt it would have been a stirring speech. But at that point she doubled over, and the next few minutes were spent emptying her stomach of the putrid swamp water.

CHAPTER TWENTY-FIVE

We were fortunate one of the ork fanboats remained swamp-worthy, despite the bullet holes riddling the hull. I was reluctant to use a xenos vessel unsanctioned by the Adeptus Mechanicus. Perhaps the craft felt likewise, for Shard struggled to engage the engine. But, as she pointed out, it had been salvaged from stolen Imperial parts and was as much ours as theirs. And, since the alternative was waiting to die, my principles yielded to pragmatism.

I pointed Shard in the direction of what I hoped was the distillery, and we limped along the gnarl-vines, shuddering at barely a walking pace, the pair of us half-crippled and our transport little better. Only Iwazar seemed relatively unscathed. Despite all it had endured, the seer-skull whirled happily beside us, its lenses capturing the expansive swamps.

I drifted in and out of consciousness, and could not judge the passage of time or distance. Dimly, I saw the shadow of the refinery falling over us, but I was fading then. We must have made quite the sight as we drew up to the docks. I only later learned that we were not shot on sight because our craft had moved so pitifully slowly we had been initially mistaken for one of the work crews hauling vine-fruit.

By then I was unconscious, and only know what happened next from reviewing Iwazar's data-core.

I was carried from the fanboat by a work crew not dissimilar to those I had interviewed a few days prior, but Shard was less fortunate. Armed guards awaited her, part of Governor Dolos' security detail. I doubt they knew she was coming, but the orders for her arrest had been dispatched to all serfs. Iwazar's footage showed a brief exchange between Shard and the guards, though the dialogue was inaudible. I do not know why they struck, the blow doubling her over and to her knees. To Shard's credit, she still managed to mutter something cutting enough to warrant a rifle butt to the back of the head. After that they dragged her away.

I knew nothing of this. Not then, as I could only alternate between pain and darkness. I remember the stinging caress of a scalpel, as the flesh was carved from my leg. I must then have slept, for I dreamt of the disastrous flight through the Green Storm.

But, through Iwazar, I gradually made sense of my surroundings. Flashes of the room were revealed, its opulence surprising. The walls and floor were the same pressed flakboard as the rest of the facility, but they had been scrubbed to a buff finish. Quite an achievement, given the pervasive layer of sludge that contaminated the distillery. The furnishings were also ornate: I recognised a bedside reading-lumen that had been manufactured on Hedon, and the bedding and sheets were soft as spider silk. But the most glaring anomaly was the triptych of paintings hung opposite the bed. Iwazar was captivated by the display, its unblinking eye drawn to the image whenever my focus ebbed.

Collectively, the work showed a trio of figures standing in

an idyllic clearing, the flora a glorified interpretation of the gnarl-vines pervading the swamps. Through sun-kissed branches, the three seemed to be caught in a momentary indiscretion. The image was not sordid or graphic, particularly as each participant was divided by a separate canvas, but the tilt of a head and the placing of a hand suggested an intimacy beyond that captured in the painting.

The figure on the far left was easily identifiable, the oversized robes and distinct headdress reminiscent of the many guests who had attended the Harvest Banquet. But the other two wore robes in a style unknown to me, adorned with runes unlike any I had seen. That alone meant little; the Imperium comprises a multitude of worlds, each with its own unique language and culture. The figures could have represented a district of the planet, or characters from myth or folklore.

That might have explained their inhuman quality. Both were too tall and slender, though it was difficult to discern their forms beneath the enveloping robes. Their faces were angular, the ears tapered and cheekbones pronounced, and their expressions quite inscrutable. They were too androgynous to discern gender, though each was beautiful, I suppose, in a strange, hollow way.

In time, my fever ebbed. I still ached, but the cocktail of stimms managed the pain tolerably. Perhaps two more days passed before I found my eyes open, and felt myself to be fully in the room.

The physician, who was examining my dressings, lurched up in alarm.

'You're awake, my lord,' he said, bowing his head. 'I did not think... I was not sure you would recover. You have been quite unresponsive. I feared the worst.'

'I was close to death,' I murmured, tongue thick. 'I commend your skill.'

'It was nothing,' the man said, bowing again. He seemed nervous, or perhaps just startled. 'Thankfully, the black rot had not fully set in, and the break was clean. But... you must understand I have limited resources, sir. I cut away the diseased flesh. There will be scarring to the leg, and without further treatment I fear you will struggle to walk unaided.'

'That does not matter.'

He visibly sagged in relief, wiping his hand across his face, his fingers slick with sweat.

'Good of you to say so, sir,' he said. 'I confess I recognised you from her ladyship's last visit. I suspect a man of your station is accustomed to a standard of care greater than I can offer.'

'I travel in varied circles. You saved me, and that is all that matters.'

'May the Emperor bless you, my lord.'

'What of Commander Shard?' I asked. 'Is she recovered?'

A frown marred his face. 'Who, my lord?'

'Flight Commander Shard. She piloted the boat that brought me here.'

'Ah,' he said. 'She was well enough when I last saw her. But the governor's guards had orders, sir. She is a fugitive. We dispatched her back to the governor's château.'

'Fugitive?'

It should not have surprised me. In undertaking the ill-omened flight, Shard had broken a plethora of rules and regulations. The fact the governor's guards were ordered to detain Shard, even those situated far behind enemy lines, spoke volumes. I pressed the physician and he told me what he could, though he was reluctant, perhaps fearing his words could be used against him. I felt sorry for him, and eventually feigned fatigue, thus giving him the excuse to depart he so desperately craved. But before he left, he told me he would dispatch a message that I was recuperating.

As the door closed, I wondered why he had not done so sooner. Perhaps, had I expired, they would have condemned my corpse to the swamp, claimed I was dead on arrival. It did not take an investigator of Kikazar's skill to realise the physician was terrified of displeasing Governor Dolos. This was hardly surprising, but it did not seem a hypothetical fear of a distant, unknown ruler. Rather, he had seemed familiar with her, at least to a point.

I wondered how often she visited this site. I had thought our prior excursion for my benefit, to present a favourable view of Bacchus in rather trying circumstances. But perhaps it was more than that. Many planetary governors had their own bizarre hobbies. I had heard tell of some who enjoyed stepping into the arena, trading blows with hardened cyber-gladiators for the chance to bask in the elation of the crowd. Such contests were rigged of course, whether the governor knew it or not, but it was not uncommon for nobles to develop such eccentricities, to treat the toil of lower ranks as a pleasant diversion from the business of running a planet. Perhaps Dolos enjoyed playing the provincial wine maker, running her private boat out to this rustic but spruced refinery, taking her turn pressing the vine-fruit and then retiring with a glass in the evening.

It would certainly explain the room. Too refined for any labourer, it could only belong to Dolos.

I must have drifted, as I was woken by a commotion outside. Iwazar was already at the window, its lenses focused on the scene. Flight Commander Gradeolous was dressing down a man who, from his uniform, I took to be one of the refinery's overseers. I could not quite make out their exchange through the glass, but Gradeolous' fury was palpable. He stood inches from the man, towering over him and forcing the slighter figure to crane his neck just to maintain eye contact. The pilot's finger stabbed at the man's chest, each thrust accompanied by another exclamation of fury.

Beside him stood a figure in simple white robes, adorned with the twin-snaked symbol of the Officio Medicae. He was a physician, though clearly one of higher rank and standing than the poor fellow who had tended my wounds, and was accompanied by a medi-servitor, as well as two guards adorned in Governor Dolos' livery.

They had come for me.

CHAPTER TWENTY-SIX

By the time I was presented to Governor Dolos I had begun to suspect they had nursed me back to health merely so I could be formally sentenced and executed.

There was little conversation on the journey back to the château. At least, none with me. Governor Dolos' physician inspected my wounds and dressings, scanning them with a diagnosticator. For the first time I saw my twisted leg, the flesh vivisected by the surgeon's blade in his desperation to clear the taint. But there was no sign of the blight, and I felt only a sense of relief.

I spent most of the voyage watching Flight Commander Grad-eolous. He acted as captain, bellowing orders to the crew, and I suspect he would have employed a lash if one were to hand. He barely acknowledged my presence, and when not admonishing the others his gaze was drawn to the skies. I could not help note his whiskers were unwaxed, the limp moustache smeared across his lips, and his flickering gaze lacked its former self-assurance.

Though no one spoke I knew where we were heading. As we

sped along the canals I reminded myself that Dolos had provided her personal physician and yacht. It was certainly better treatment than Shard had received. But I had ignored her warning, and I knew there would be consequences.

She did not keep me waiting this time. A hoverchair had been prepared for my arrival. They pushed me briskly from the docks, through the botanical archway, towards the château. As we passed beneath the trees it struck me the leaves had thinned since my last excursion, and the painted dock was clearly marked with ugly, dark splotches.

I was taken to the château's rear entrance, Iwazar hovering along beside me, and then through a twisted web of passages and corridors. Many were in desperate need of repair, the bark malformed and cracked. Tools were scattered, and I saw one footman had chiselled out a five-foot-long section of wood and was now using chain-link gloves to haul out handfuls of tendril-like roots.

We did not slow, not until we reached a gleaming set of great doors, the wood relentlessly varnished to a mirror-like sheen. There we halted, the party shuffling around me, conforming to a protocol unknown. Two positioned themselves beside the doors, pressing their shoulders to them and heaving with all their might. They took some moments to open, the warped wood chewing at the floor.

Still, that gave me ample time to admire the throne room.

It had not occurred to me Dolos might possess a throne. Despite her title, she rarely chose to present herself as a monarch, more a steward of the planet and people.

That was no longer the case.

She sat on what might have been a lavish throne, but it was difficult to tell, as little of it was visible behind the silken folds of her crystal-blue robes. They bunched to her shoulders and cascaded across the floor like a tsunami. Her headdress was even more neck-strainingly elaborate than usual, adorned with the fangs of a dozen banner-bugs arranged like the points of a crown. Even the faceplate was formed from the head of such a beast. Its savage features had been tempered to appear vaguely humanoid, which only made it more terrifying. Her right hand clasped a spear-sceptre, the barbed end presumably made from the insect's stinger. The weapon looked ancient, but its tip still glistened with a sickly yellow glint. I found myself praying it was purely ceremonial, though it struck me that such ceremonies could include ordering an execution.

She said nothing until our party had marched into the chamber and bowed, though confined to my chair I could do little more than nod my head. I hoped she would not find this disrespectful, but I doubted it would make much difference to my final fate.

'Propagandist Simlex,' she said, her voice muffled slightly by the mask. 'You did not heed my warnings.'

'Sadly so, my lady,' I said. 'I should have trusted your guidance.'

She ignored the clumsy compliment, rolling her weapon between thumb and forefinger.

'Still, you survived.'

'Yes. Thanks to Flight Commander Shard.'

'Shard?' she hissed, leaning forward, the spear resting across her lap. 'That renegade almost got you killed. Do you have any idea how poorly it would reflect on me if I allowed a relative of Planetary Governor Zanwich to die on my watch? Did you even consider that?'

'I did not. I am sorry.'

'Spare me,' she said. 'She will be taken care of. You are the only loose end from this ghastly enterprise.'

I did not know what to say. Dolos was in no mood for charm or platitudes. I know not what had transpired whilst I was trapped in the swamps, only that her knuckles whitened as she clasped the spear-sceptre, her anger palpable. I did not speak, fearing anything I said would invite retaliation.

She waited a heartbeat longer before continuing. Her voice had softened slightly, but still held a malicious edge.

'Poor Simlex,' she said. 'I'm sure she made all kinds of promises to persuade you to fly. You are lucky to still be breathing.'

'Yes, governor.'

'And I intend to keep you that way,' she continued, motioning to her physician. 'My medicae has made some modifications to your quarters. Under his watchful care I am sure you will recover. In time.'

'Thank you, governor. I am already feeling stronger, and I am sure a few days–'

'That will be the decision of my physician, not you. Make no mistake, Simlex, I will no longer permit your life to be risked needlessly. From this day forward you will be constantly monitored, and guards will be posted outside your quarters to ensure you are not press-ganged into another ill-conceived flight.'

'Thank you, Governor Dolos,' I said, bowing my head.

'Stylee?'

The steward was suddenly beside her. He must have been hidden by the folds of her robes.

'Take the propagandist to his room.'

He bowed low, skuttling behind me and steering the hoverchair away. Iwazar made to follow, but one of the guards seized the seer-skull by its spindly limbs. It whined in alarm as he dragged it away.

'Wait!' I said, trying to turn. 'You cannot take–'

'For your own sake, be silent!' Stylee hissed, quickening his pace.

'But I need the–'

'Governor Dolos has decreed the device be detained until adepts of the Mechanicus can conduct necessary repairs and data-scrubs.'

'Data-scrubs? What exactly does she think it has seen?'

'It does not matter,' he said as we exited the throne room. 'It is beyond your ken or concern. Do as you are told and the governor will ensure you have everything you need to complete your work. Focus on that and forget anything else you think you saw, unless you want to end up like your friend.'

My quarters had undergone renovations. The silken sheets and luxurious bed had been replaced by a medi-cot that would not have been out of place in the bunker. The tables and chairs had also been removed, and the windows reinforced with iron bars crudely nailed into the wood. Mizar was still present, wedged into the panel carved from the Marauder bomber, but there was no sign of Kikazar.

As prisons went, it was not so awful. The physician attended me regularly, applying healing balms and monitoring my vitals. I was soon back on my feet, albeit with a borrowed cane and pronounced limp. Not that there was anywhere I could go. The door was guarded, and any request I made to leave the chamber was deemed against the physician's advice.

I had a vox-unit, but my attempt to contact Confessor Maric von Shard was unsuccessful, as I could not access an external link. My conversations were limited to the kitchens and servants, neither of whom were particularly attentive to my summons. Meals were simple things: black bread and a mulch stewed from roots and some of the softer insect parts. This restricted diet complemented my convalescence. That's what they told me, but I suspect it was another subtle punishment. Tellingly, my penitence included a bottle of wine with my evening repasts, though if I held it to the light, I swear I saw thin veins of black threaded throughout the liquid. Each day, I made a point of pouring it out the barred window.

In fact, the window was my chief entertainment for a time. I would watch the aircraft streak by, and peer at the horizon, where either insects or flyers duelled above the swamp. But my focus was the compound. I watched the ground crews sweep the runways, clearing rubble and wreckage. I watched the governor's servants' ongoing battle to maintain the creaking château. I would surge to my feet when the sirens wailed, intent as the pilots raced for their planes. All except Flight Commander Gradeolous, who seemed unwilling to proceed at anything faster than an evening stroll.

But I never saw Shard.

I had made enquiries, but the servants would not speak on the matter. In desperation I attempted to hack into the vox, but only succeeded in damaging the unit. Stylee accompanied the mechanical tasked with repairing it, glaring at me whilst they worked.

'I do not know why you busy yourself sabotaging the governor's facilities,' he muttered. 'Shouldn't you be completing your pict?'

'I smelled something unpleasant,' I replied, my back half to him, staring from the window.

'So you began fiddling with the wiring?'

'I thought it came from the casing. There was something similar in the first room you gave me – a black mould around the power unit. It smelled like that.'

From the corner of my eye, I saw him stiffen.

'Impossible,' Stylee replied. 'There are no outbreaks in the château. Certainly not at this level.'

'I'm sure I imagined it.'

'Yes, you did,' Stylee replied, marching over to the mechanical and examining the vox-set. He pulled the unit clear, peering at the polished wooden wall.

'There, you see? No sign of it,' he insisted. 'Now stop fussing at matters beyond your concern and complete the governor's pict.'

'I wish I could. But I have no means.'

'You have your seer-skull device,' Stylee replied, nodding to Mizar, still embedded in a section carved from *Hephaestus*.

'But I cannot use it. Its systems are still integrated into the wing.'

'That is your problem.'

'Indeed,' I agreed. 'And I am incapable of fixing it. You have seen what I did to the vox. If I do not receive assistance, Governor Zanwich's pict will never be completed.'

Stylee flinched. I wager I knew his thoughts. He would be happy for me to fail and earn Dolos' further displeasure. But what if Governor Zanwich truly cared about the project? If he subsequently took issue with Dolos and demanded an investigation, she might choose to blame Stylee's inaction for my failure.

He glanced to the mechanical. 'When you are done, attend to… this.' He waved at the wing-section propped in the room's corner. The mechanical glanced from it to Stylee.

'I… This is military technology, sir. I am not sanctioned to interfere with it.'

'Just pull the damn skull out!'

'Sir.' The mechanical bowed, approaching the device cautiously, his arc welder shaking slightly.

I waited until he was a finger's width from it before sending an impulse to Mizar. I was not sure the unit would be responsive, but it had been crafted by the finest artisans of the Adeptus Mechanicus. The seer-skull's unblinking eye pulsed red. Once again, it tried to liberate itself from the housing, except this time it was no longer attached to the bomber, only a carved section of wing. Its anti-gravity unit flared as the machine dragged itself skywards. It could not hold the weight, and the metal housing sliced down, almost bisecting the mechanical before embedding itself into the floorboards.

At the sight of this, Stylee near leapt from his skin, racing over to inspect the damaged floor, shoving the bleeding mechanical aside.

Mizar was not done, though, thrashing against its prison, the panel slicing deeper into the wood. Stylee skittered backwards on his hands and knees as I rushed over, whispering the deactivation rites that would power the unit down.

I glanced to the mechanical. 'Are you well?'

The man nodded. I turned to Stylee.

'You see the issue?' I said. 'This technology requires a specialist sanctioned by the Mechanicus. Without it, I will not be able to complete the governor's pict. Unless you could restore the skull you seized?'

'Out of the question!'

'Then there is no solution.' I sighed. 'I wonder if I should just tell Governor Zanwich now. Do you think he will show mercy if I explain the circumstances?'

Stylee shifted his weight, frowning uncertainly. 'Who completed the initial work?' he said.

I made a point of furrowing my brow, as if struggling to recall.

'It was one of the mechanicals of the Aeronautica Imperialis,' I said. 'A specialist. Plient? I think that was his name. Bright chap. Missing an arm.'

He threw up his hands. 'Fine. I will see if he can be dispatched to complete the extraction,' he said. 'But cease interfering with the operations. Remember, you are the guest here. Be respectful of that.'

* * *

I was sipping tea when I heard the knock at the door. Somehow I knew it to be Plient, for the knock was both cheery and apologetic, as though he did not wish to disturb.

I rose, shuffling to the door with the assistance of a cane. Plient smiled as I opened it, before catching himself, offering a salute instead. It was good to see him up, even if one of his sleeves was tied off. Behind him, a servitor was dragging a large crate, presumably housing his equipment, my guards flanking them. They were doing their best to be suspicious of the visitors, but it was challenging; there are few faces in the universe more trustworthy than Plient's.

'Sir!' he said. 'I'm so thankful you're alive!'

'I share your sentiments.' I smiled as I ushered him into the room, the servitor following. 'And by the Throne it's good to see a friendly face.'

'I'd heard rumours you had returned, but no one knew for sure. I'm… I'm so sorry about your leg though, sir, that is shocking poor luck.'

I glanced from my injury to Plient's missing arm.

'I think you had the worse of it.'

'I suppose, sir,' Plient said with a shrug. 'But I joined up knowing the risks. I'm not going to start complaining now. That's no way to serve the God-Emperor.'

'Indeed not,' I said. 'But should you be on duty? Given your injuries?'

'Oh, I'm not going to let my comrades down, sir,' Plient replied. 'We need every hand we have, no pun intended. It's… it's not good out there, sir.'

'The orks?'

'There are more of them and less of us. I heard whispers that high command think they've established a base near the… near where the storm is. We would have pulled back, but the governor says she will not abandon her home.'

'Does she not fear the orks?'

'I don't know. I only hear what the servants say, and they seem to think she has powerful allies who will save us all. Do you think that is the case, sir? Maybe she can call upon the Adeptus Astartes?'

'I doubt it.' I sighed. 'But I know less than you. At least you are privy to whispers. Without my seer-skulls I feel almost blind.'

'Ah, then let me help you with that, sir,' Plient said with a smile, shuffling over to the section of wing.

'Do you need assistance?' I said, glancing to the servitor. 'I could perhaps hold some of the tools, or–'

I did not get a chance to finish. I don't know exactly what Plient did. He seemed to merely brush the hard point with his fingers, and suddenly Mizar fell free, bouncing on the floor and rolling towards me.

'Sorry, sir,' Plient said. 'I should have put a cushion down or something. Is it undamaged?'

'It has seen far worse,' I said, stooping to retrieve the seer-skull. Its eye flared bright and it slowly rose, scanning its surroundings before settling into place beside me.

'I thank you, Plient,' I said. 'Despite everything, it is a relief to have Mizar freed.'

'Happy to help, sir. I'm just sorry I was unavailable before. I was... not at my best, sir.'

'None of us are, at present,' I replied. 'Shard and I certainly had some... challenging moments.'

'Yes, sir.'

'Plient, I hate to put you on the spot but... do you know what happened to her?'

Plient shook his head. 'Wish I did, sir. I've only heard rumours. Some of the ground crew saw her being dragged away, but the officers are keeping quiet. Gradeolous seems happy, though, so the news is probably bad. You should watch him, sir – not only is he after her spot, but he keeps making enquiries about your seer-skulls. Seems he wants to know how they interface with the aircraft. I can't really lie to him, sir. He outranks me.'

'I understand, Plient,' I said. 'But what of Shard? Is she to be executed?'

'I don't know, sir. I doubt it – I think I'd have heard something.'

'Dolos wants her dead.'

'Perhaps. But she's not commanding officer. Then again, I don't know if Wing Commander Prospherous will fight for her this time, given how she ran off and disobeyed orders.'

'Does he usually support her?'

'I'm not sure. There was some incident last year. I don't really know the details. But he ended up in the infirmary, and she took command for a time. It got a little dicey, but we came through.'

'And he holds a grudge for this?'

'Doubt it, sir. He lost his memory from the injury. Heard it was a head wound. Or seizure or something. Either way, he didn't remember there was a problem, and no one mentioned it much after that.'

'Well, it strikes me you need every pilot you have.'

'Yes, sir. We do,' Plient said. 'In fact, I should get back to the hangar.'

'Then I thank you for your help. Though it seems your equipment was not needed.' I nodded to the servitor and the crate it hauled.

'Ah, thanks for reminding me, sir,' Plient replied, turning to it. He tapped a code into the control panel, and the crate suddenly yawned open, a red eye glinting within.

'Kikazar?' I said.

The seer-skull emerged cautiously, surveying the room as if assessing possible threats. It then sidled towards me, like a returning stray.

'I found it in the hangar a couple of days ago,' Plient said as I examined the device. 'Not sure what it wanted, looked almost as if it was hiding. I was surprised it let me near it, but I thought I should keep it safe until your return.'

'It is a wilful old soul,' I said, and smiled. 'Perhaps the hangar was a familiar space, somewhere safe. I was saddened to think it lost.' I glanced to the beaming Plient. 'Thank you again, flight sergeant. I only wish I had something to offer in return.'

'No need, sir. I only do my duty,' he said, as the servitor lifted the now-empty crate.

'I will find a means to repay you, flight sergeant.'

'You already are, sir,' he said with a smile. 'You're inspiring the next generation of soldiers to defend the Imperium. Why, without people like you I might not even have signed up!'

As the door closed behind him, I turned to the seer-skulls. Mizar, finally unshackled, hovered expectantly. But something was off with Kikazar. It flitted from side to side, as though desperate to relieve itself.

I beckoned it over, frowning as I saw the flashing light on its lower carapace. *Data full*, it indicated. I was surprised, as the machine's memory was measured in days. I had directed it to eavesdrop on Shard, but it had somehow lost her, or she it. Yet there were days' worth of recordings.

What had it heard?

CHAPTER TWENTY-SEVEN

I listened.

'I don't care if the spirit of Saint Sanguinius is available, I am still the one who will be flying the damn mission.'

Kikazar had recorded the words, so it must have been monitoring Shard even before I dispatched it, its cogitator apparently deeming her speech important. The pict quality was poor, but I watched the seer-skull descend on the pacing Shard. It was only when it drew closer that it registered the other speaker. He spoke softly, but with no less authority for that.

It was Wing Commander Prospherous.

'There is no mission,' he hissed, glancing over his shoulder. 'And for Throne's sake keep your voice down.'

'There is something in the storm. We can't keep ignoring it.'

'We have orders to stay clear until the phenomenon can be assessed.'

'You think Plient imagined it? That boy doesn't have any

imagination. I've met servitors with a greater gift for abstract thought. What makes you–'

'That's enough!'

His voice rose but a fraction, though it was sufficient to silence her, at least for a moment.

'We don't know what Plient saw,' he said. 'There is no evidence at present beyond the ravings of a traumatised mechanical.'

'Except the bullets embedded in his craft.'

'Orders are orders. Even were we to disobey, what action do you propose? Sending our depleted forces into that hurricane, which may or may not house ork fighters? It's a suicide mission.'

'The alternative is to wait for them to attack and wipe us out.'

'Then we die either way,' Prospherous replied. He did not seem aggrieved, unlike the pacing Shard. In fact, now her voice had lowered, he spoke as calmly as though discussing more conventional weather.

'If we attack now, we can catch them off guard.'

'Or fly right into a trap. Our orders are to secure Governor Dolos' summer residence and await reinforcements.'

'Reinforcements?' Shard frowned. 'When will they be sent?'

'Not until Salus completes analysis of the storm.'

Shard swore at this, but I was more enraged by the château being referred to as Dolos' 'summer residence'. The servants spoke of it with such reverence that it had not occurred to me this was only a temporary abode, and that she probably had a far grander and more secure palace on the other side of Bacchus. We had lost lives defending the place, just so she maintained access to her seasonal retreat.

'Sir, half our intelligence is in Governor Dolos' pocket. If she wants, she can keep us here indefinitely. We need high command to recognise the threat the storm poses.'

'You suggest I flout our orders? Do as I see fit?'

'I think sometimes one must separate the spirit of the order from the letter.'

'I see,' he said. 'So, you feel the spirit of our orders would be to take your little propagandist and fly into the maelstrom?'

Her pace slowed. She glanced at Prospherous. 'What does this have to do with him?'

'If you're going in there, we need a record of what is happening. He's the only one who seems able to detect the greenskins' technology, and he certainly has suitable recording equipment. If you wanted to find evidence the orks are hiding something, he would be a useful resource. Hypothetically speaking.'

She looked at him, though from the angle of the pict I could not see her face.

'Yes, sir,' she said after a moment.

'And then, assuming you could provide evidence of the threat, we could petition for additional resources.'

'Yes, sir.'

He nodded. 'Good, then it's decided. Obviously, you can't do that, because that would be treasonous. But at least now we understand exactly what you mustn't do, don't we, flight commander?'

'Yes, sir.'

'Good.' He smiled. 'On that note – are you on patrol tonight?'

'Yes, sir.'

'Delegate it to someone else. I'm relieving you of duty. Just for tonight.'

'Tonight, sir?'

'Yes,' he said. 'I'm sure you can find something to occupy your time.'

I ceased the playback, resting my chin in my hands, my gaze flicking to the tainted wine provided by Dolos. It might have been tempting, if I was not already sick of that blight-ridden vine-fruit.

I did not know what to feel. Betrayed, I suppose. And manipulated. But I just felt like a fool. I should have seen through her, seen through them both, for Prospherous was just as bad. Worse, in fact, for at least Shard risked her own life alongside mine. It seemed he preferred to abdicate all responsibility to a supposedly renegade pilot.

But I could not fault them, for they were right. Stellar politics had somehow overridden cohesive military strategy. I knew what was hidden in the storm front: an aerial fortress that dwarfed the governor's château and grounds. I had said nothing, for I had no one to speak to and no evidence to provide, with Iwazar confiscated. And I feared what they would do if I spoke up.

But Shard had no fear. She must have said something. If they had let her.

I resumed playback, watching Shard disappear into the shadows. It was then Kikazar's error became clear. I had not instructed it to eavesdrop on any particular individual, merely a conversation, and when Shard had departed it elected to shadow the wing commander instead.

I doubted I should watch further. His private conversations were not for my ears. But I needed to know what had happened to her. So, I accelerated the recording and cut the audio, instructing the seer-skull to restore standard playback in the event Shard's name was spoken aloud. I saw Prospherous race at ludicrous speed around the compound, bellowing silent orders as the seer-skull watched from the shadows.

I tried to keep focused, particularly when the playback slowed at the mention of Shard's name. But Prospherous dismissed any questions concerning her with a shrug, advising the other officers he had provided an evening's leave. As the mention of her name became less and less frequent I found my eyes glazing.

I do not know when I fell asleep, only that I awoke to a

thumping at the door. The pict was still playing, but the wing commander had retired at some point, Kikazar taking residence in the shadows outside his dorm, perhaps through some strange sense of propriety.

The hammering continued, the door shaking under the flurry of blows. I recognised the braying voice accompanying it, and feared Flight Commander Gradeolous was poised to put his fist through the wood.

I ceased playback, the image collapsing as I hobbled to the door. It opened stiffly, revealing Gradeolous accompanied by a trio of armed ground crew. Governor Dolos' guards were stood facing the far wall, having inexplicably chosen that moment to inspect the bark.

'What took you so long?' Gradeolous thundered as he barged past me. 'There is a damn war scheduled for the morn and you are making me tardy.'

I had barely woken and could only blink in response. Not that it mattered; he pressed on, his finger stabbing at Kikazar.

'Give me that pict-thing.'

'I'm sorry?'

He glared at me, but my sleep-addled brain was slow, and fixated on his untrained moustache. He did not respond well to my reticence, eyes narrowing. For a moment I thought he might strike me. His knuckles were already stained red, as was his sleeve.

'My apologies,' I said. 'I retired late as I was working on the pict. I am a little dazed.'

'That is why I am here,' Gradeolous snapped. 'I am to be the subject of the piece, as agreed.'

'I'm not sure–'

'Governor Dolos insists,' he said, cutting me off, his gaze falling on Kikazar. I had no doubt he could simply snatch it, and I could not allow that, for there were days of footage I needed to see.

'Wait,' I said, retrieving the recently liberated Mizar. 'Take this one. It is fully charged.'

I did not want to surrender it. But I had backed up Mizar's memory already, and I needed to know what other secrets Kikazar had uncovered.

Gradeolous reached for Mizar, but it surged from his hands, hissing, its sensors flaring a warning red. He jumped, startled, before rounding on me, cheeks flushed.

'Make the device compliant!' he blustered.

I called the seer-skull to me, murmuring words of reassurance.

'Do your duty,' I said, before whispering the liturgy of compliance. It relented, the light dimming as it dutifully fell into place beside Gradeolous. The fighter ace still glared at the machine, suspicious.

'Do you need assistance?' I asked.

He bristled at the suggestion. 'Of course not. One of the mechanicals can make the installation. Just be ready to put the pict together when I get back.'

As he marched from the room, I knew somehow I would not see Mizar again.

I suppose that also meant I would not see Gradeolous again, though I cannot pretend that concerned me.

As the door closed I glanced back to Kikazar. 'Resume,' I said, and the seer-skull obliged whilst I busied myself making a cup of recaff.

The footage began with it still loitering outside the wing commander's quarters. There was little activity. Occasionally it would detect a voice, its advanced audio sensors zoning in on the sound. But it never heard anything important, just servants going about their business.

As I listened my gaze was drawn to the activity outside the window. There were still days of footage to review, and I did not

know how long I had left. Aircraft were scrambling in the quagmire below, their landing gears chewing up what remained of
the grounds. It was chaos, fighters being dragged into the path
of bombers, the limited ground crew relying on servitors for
the heavy work. Though capable of performing the tasks, the
machines could not organise themselves. In a strange way, the
chaos reminded me of the orks. Except they were increasingly
well coordinated, whilst we devolved to their level.

It took two pilots squaring up on the runway for me to realise
the extent of my naivety. For it had always been that way. Only
our conflicts were usually resolved behind closed doors in clandestine chambers, where military needs were weighted against
the nobles' coin. Perhaps the ork way was better: disputes were
settled face to face by blade and blood, the strongest ruling by
right of conquest.

I saw Gradeolous stride from the château, Mizar trailing in
his wake. He roared at the combatants and they lowered their
fists, avoiding each other's gaze. But this was apparently insuffi-
cient. The nearest of the pair, perhaps the instigator or simply the
closest target, was backhanded across the face. It was an impressive blow, launching him several feet. And it certainly helped
restore discipline amongst the warring troops.

'Get on with it, you cur!'

I stiffened at the sound. I knew Stylee's voice well enough,
its range straddling obsequious toadying and ill-concealed contempt. But here he sounded furious.

I turned my attention back to the pict. It still showed the corridor, but the shot was moving now. Kikazar had also recognised
the voice, or was perhaps attracted by the aggressive tone. Either
way, it had rounded a corner, tucked high and close to the wall.

There was Stylee, accompanied by two footmen. They had
peeled away the bark covering on the far wall, and were clawing

at it with barbed hooks. Even with the subdued light and questionable pict quality, I could see the wood was infested with the fungal blight. The footmen tore sections clear as they sought to cut away the rot. I do not know why, for it was clear the wood was beyond saving. But still the two laboured, peeling out rotten sections, replacing it with an emulsified paste whilst Stylee paced.

'Faster,' he snapped. 'We have to tear out this whole section by morning. The governor intends to take a craft and visit the botanical garden. She always takes this route when attending the gardens. It needs to be spotless, every hint of rot must be torn away.'

'If we clear it all there will be no bloody walls left,' one of the footmen muttered. He hadn't raised his voice, but neither was he quiet.

Stylee swung to him, quivering with rage, and for a moment I thought he would strike the man. Perhaps he intended to, but the footman was a stout fellow with a jaw like rockcrete. This could be why Stylee relented, or perhaps fatigue sapped his ire. Either way, he sighed, leaning back against the wall and reaching into his gown for a flask. He took a swig, hesitating just a moment before offering it to the others.

'We just need to hold it together until she leaves for the winter,' Stylee said. 'Then we can strip it clean without interruption. It will recover by spring, it always does.'

'Maybe,' the footman mumbled, taking a drink from the flask before handing it back to Stylee. 'I've never seen it this bad.'

'We always treat the lower levels.'

'Yeah. But as a preventative measure. I've never actually seen it penetrate the bark, let alone reach the upper levels. And those strange root-tendril things? Where in the Throne's name did they come from?' The footman glanced to the wall, stroking his fingers across the bark as though petting a loyal hound. 'I think the château is dead,' he murmured.

Stylee, who was swigging on the flask, nearly choked.

'It should have blossomed by now,' the man said, continuing over Stylee's spluttering.

'It did blossom,' Stylee snapped. 'Ask anyone.'

'I know. I was on the roof the night before gluing on the flowers, remember?'

'It's those damn orks,' Stylee spat. 'This disease is one of their tricks. But you wait. Once the seasons shift, this old place will recover. It's stood for thousands of years, it's not falling now to some greenskin filth.'

The third man muttered something. Kikazar struggled to capture the words, but Stylee bent his head, glaring at the man.

'What did you just say?'

The footman sighed, glaring back and mulling over whether to repeat his words. In the end, he snatched the flask out of Stylee's outstretched hand, taking a swig before replying.

'I said, it ain't the greenskins who did this. It's those pointy-eared freaks that Dolos fawns over. The aeldari.'

'You watch your tone!' Stylee warned. 'The governor will not be addressed in that manner.'

The man looked around. 'I don't see her here,' he said. 'And you know I'm right. The orks have been there for years in some fashion. This' – he nodded to the pox-marked wall – 'only began after she started cosying up to those dirty aeldari witches. Least the orks are honest monsters, pure and simple. But those degenerate freaks strut around like they're human. I still can't believe she let them attend a Harvest Banquet. Sickened me, it did.'

'Be silent!'

'Tell me I'm wrong?' the man said, shrugging. 'Tell me you think it was right they set foot on our planet? That's what's caused this, their foul magicks.'

Stylee just stared at him, his face hidden from frame.

'The governor's job is complex,' he said eventually. 'Sometimes diplomacy requires dealing with parties one might prefer to steer clear of, like the aeldari.'

'Steer clear of?' the man sneered. 'Come off it. I've seen those fancy robes she hides in the back of her dresser, and that creepy plant she keeps on her table. Gifts from them.'

'Gifts! What would you expect a planetary governor to do when presented with gifts from foreign dignitaries?'

'Burn them. Not eat their food and play dress-up in aeldari clothes,' the footman replied. 'Do you know what I think? I think she wants to be one of them. I bet she'll be getting her ears tapered next. Damn xenos-lover.'

Stylee was on him. No warning, just fists flailing in all directions. The second servant tried to intervene, and was rewarded by a blow to the chin for his troubles. All three ended up scuffling on the floor, their allegiances unclear. Kikazar must have designated the situation a threat, for it retreated. But as it did so, its sensors caught sight of the painting hung on the far wall.

'Cease playback,' I whispered, approaching the flickering holopict. I suspected I had seen it before in passing. It was neither good nor bad enough to inspire much comment. But even with the questionable pict quality, I had no doubt it shared stylistic similarities with the triptych hung in the governor's room in the distillery. There was only one figure in this image, surrounded by greenery. Her headdress of antennae and mandibles suggested it was Governor Dolos, or someone of similar rank. But the robes were wrong, lacking the folds and layers common to the planet. It was close-fitted and adorned with unfamiliar runes that echoed those from the distillery.

Except... they were not quite unfamiliar. I had seen something like them once before, on an assignment to Segmentum Pacificus. I had been advised against making recordings of the pictographs for fear they might contain foul magicks. But I recalled the smooth lines and sweeping flourishes, these qualities carried over to the paintings.

The runes were aeldari in origin.

CHAPTER TWENTY-EIGHT

I watched Plient make the final adjustments to the vox. It still perplexed me how a simple soldier could demonstrate such proficiency at technical work. I had been taught only adepts of the Mechanicus could be entrusted to oversee the sacred toils of manufacture and maintenance. But Plient certainly put this tenet to the test.

I had summoned him on false pretences, claiming I needed assistance with the seer-skulls. But I had another idea in mind.

'There you are, sir,' he said. 'You should be able to connect with Orbital Station Salus. One of the subordinates on the station can grant you access to Departmento Munitorum records. It's not a strong signal, though. You might have to shout into the receiver, and you won't be able to connect with anyone off-planet.'

'Thank you, Plient. I am relieved you could spare a few minutes.'

He shrugged. 'Not much else to do, sir. All aircraft are in the air. We have to wait to see what comes back.'

'All of them?'

'Well, not quite. But we ran out of pilots,' he said. 'I offered to fly, even just to draw some fire. But I can't, sir. Not like this.' His gaze fell to the stump where his arm should have been.

'All of them?' I heard myself say, repeating the phrase as though it might inspire some fresh revelation.

Plient nodded. 'It's the Green Storm, sir. They have gone to face it.'

'Do they know what they are up against?'

'I don't think so. I said what I saw, but I am not a real pilot, and they place little value on my words. Shard spoke out, told them that the orks have built a fortress in the sky, but they didn't believe her. Said she was trying to justify being shot down.'

'Shard spoke? Is she still alive?'

'I... I cannot say, sir. I have orders. I don't disobey orders,' Plient replied.

'Do you know where she is?'

'I have orders, sir! Orders!'

'I understand,' I said, stepping back, hands raised. 'I'm sorry, Plient. I am just relieved you mentioned her name.'

'Sir.'

'Well, what about the governor?' I continued, changing the topic in the hope of calming him. 'Surely she cannot want her château left undefended?'

'I... I don't know, sir,' Plient replied. 'I hear things. I try not to listen because it distracts me, but sometimes they speak so loudly there is nothing I can do. I know her servants have been packing up during the night. Few of them are around this morning.'

'I did note my door had only one guard. I assumed the other was relieving himself,' I said, frowning.

Just one. Could I subdue the man and escape? No. He looked as though he could crush both of us, even if we were healthy.

'Thank you again, Plient,' I said. 'I bid you farewell.'

He nodded, offering a crisp salute before turning away. But he lingered at the door, his hangdog eyes meeting mine.

'Sir?'

'Yes?'

'I'm sorry about Mizar, sir. Flight Commander Gradeolous ordered me to install it into his Thunderbolt.'

'You did your duty, Plient. I am sure Mizar will do likewise.'

He nodded once before departing.

Alone, I took a seat at the vox and began the tedious task of connecting with the Departmento Munitorum. Plient had undersold the poor quality of the transmission. It took an hour to speak to a subordinate on Orbital Station Salus, and I could barely make out her words. Time was wasted inputting endless encryption keys, before I finally had access to the data-veil. Or a shadow of it, anyway; my clearance was limited, and I had the burden of a lagging connection.

I knew what I must do. But it took time to gather the courage, so I procrastinated. I first accessed Shard's file, but the 2208th Expeditionary Air Wing's records were months in arrears. My own attachment to the division was not yet even listed. Perhaps it was bureaucratic incompetence, or served some higher party's agenda. There was no way to know.

I next accessed Governor Dolos' file, but found little of use. However, from there I did locate some records concerning Vintner's Blight, also known as blackpox. It was classified a fungal infection not uncommon amongst the workers, but usually a minor ailment requiring intermittent treatment. There was a recent addendum, suggesting that incidents and severity had seen an upward spike and advising this should be reported to the Officio Medicae. I could not tell whether this action had been taken.

I closed the file, taking a deep breath.

The hard part. The aeldari.

There was nothing suspect about inputting the word itself. As a trusted servant of the Imperium, I was entitled to know our enemies. The files described the aeldari as an elder race, their bodies superficially similar to humans but tainted by their xenos origins. They were known for their devotion to witchcraft and deception. I cycled through images of their soldiers and weapons, as well as data-extracts of questionable quality suggesting means of spotting their malefic influence. The picts had clearly been spliced, but I had no time to review exactly what had been changed.

I tried cross-referencing aeldari activities with Subsector Yossarian, but my limited access uncovered only heavily censored reports of raids by aeldari pirates. There was little meat to these tales, though their prevalence was notable, historic records indicating a dozen incidents within the Hedon Cluster. But none had taken place within the last century.

I could have ended it there. But I needed to know more. There was a link between it all, disparate pieces of data that held a greater truth, some key that could tie it together.

I pulled the image of the governor's paintings from Kikazar's data-file. I regretted I could not access those from the distillery, which had been recorded by Iwazar, but those mounted within the château had similar symbols. I plucked the most prominent, tracing it into the data-veil and seeking additional occurrences. But I knew not what it meant, and therein lay the danger. Perhaps it represented a philosophical concept, or religious tenet of trivial importance. But if it were deemed a sanctioned glyph, merely searching for it could have severe consequences.

Then again, what were the chances of me surviving the next ork attack? I could at least die knowing the truth.

I sat back in my chair, uncorking my bottle of the governor's wine as I awaited the results of my search. I had no idea how long it would take, but it seemed the perfect time to overindulge. There was a good chance I'd be dead long before I had to endure the inevitable hangover.

What would happen if I overstepped my mark? Sought knowledge that was deemed forbidden? It seemed improbable I would receive a warning, a flashing red light or wailing klaxon. Most likely I'd be left staring at the screen, awaiting the search outcome even as assassins closed in on my position.

So I was surprised to suddenly find myself staring at the face of a young woman clad in the robes of the Adeptus Administratum.

'*Good day, Propagandist Simlex.*' She smiled, the expression not reaching her eyes, though admittedly the left was a mechanical device that glimmered a piercing red. It reminded me of the seer-skulls.

I stared back, the bottle touching my lips.

'*Now, I appreciate this has been a challenging few days,*' she continued. '*There was the storm, and the lightning, not to mention being flung halfway across the planet. And here you now sit, imprisoned, abandoned and powerless, awaiting near-certain death.*'

She leant forward, her eyes fixed on mine.

'*Let me calm your fears. For, however bleak your present circumstances may seem, you must believe me when I say they can get so much worse.*'

I shivered, despite the heat.

'*This conversation?*' she continued. '*Right now? This is the most danger you have ever been in. Do you understand?*'

There was no malice in her voice. She sounded almost sympathetic. Just doing her duty. Like the rest of us. In the distance, I could hear explosions, but they did not seem as threatening as her.

I opened my mouth but she raised her finger.

'*No. Do not say anything unless I ask first. You will only muddle through events. Just answer honestly. Assume I know more than you, because I do. Do you understand?*'

I nodded, silent. She smiled at that.

'*Excellent. Now, do you know what you were searching for?*'

'No.'

'*Then how did you stumble across it?*'

'I saw the image in a painting.'

'*I see,*' she said. '*Excuse me a moment.*'

Kikazar suddenly surged upright, its flickering projector spraying a flurry of images, seemingly at random. They were splashed across the walls before it stopped abruptly, having located the painting.

'*Oh dear.*' She winced as a dozen images manifested around it. I saw flashes of Shard facing the orks, a banner-bug lunging from the swamp, Dolos presiding over the Harvest Banquet in all her finery. Then there was a sound. A siren? My gaze flickered to the window, but I could see little from where I sat. And I dared not move.

My interrogator sighed. '*By the Throne, this is poorly organised. How do you complete your picts?*'

I shrugged.

'*That wasn't a rhetorical question.*'

'I... It has been difficult to stay on top of it,' I replied. 'Perhaps I can help if I know what you seek?'

She glared at me, before acquiescing. '*Why not,*' she said. '*So, who painted this? And these others?*'

The triptych from the distillery flared into view.

'I... How did you retrieve that image?' I said. 'Iwazar was taken. I did not have time to copy–'

'*Your other skull is still active. With my level of access to the network, it is trivial to transfer data from one node to the other. Look.*'

More footage. The sky-fortress at the centre of the tempest, Shard's Avenger bolt cannon tearing into scrambling greenskins. A sudden flurry of explosions.

'Does that satisfy you enough to answer my question? Who painted it?'

'I suspect Governor Dolos.'

'Suspect?' she said. *'A dangerous word to employ against a planetary governor. Do you have proof?'*

'Nothing concrete, but I believe it to be the truth.'

'Hmm.'

Kikazar hummed, and abruptly shifted projectors. I was treated to a dozen picts of the governor, her entourage, even her chambers.

'What is that?'

I glanced at the displayed pict. It was the outside of the château; a moment snatched from one of my recordings.

'I do not know,' I replied. 'What am I looking for?'

The image magnified a thousandfold, focusing on one of the upper windows. It was too blurred to see much, but she worked some visual wizardry, and the image cut to another and coalesced into the silhouette of a plant. I could just make out the amber-flecked leaves and puckered pink flowers. I recognised it easily enough.

'I do not know. It belongs to Governor Dolos, but the species is unfamiliar to me.'

'What did the flowers look like?'

'Pink. They are ugly little things, like mouths. And it has berries. The governor is very fond of them.'

She swore, her gaze flicking as she reviewed some file invisible to me.

'You didn't eat any?'

'No. Why?'

'And how long has it been there? Is it rooted?'

'I don't know,' I replied. 'I overheard it was a gift. I take it the plant is not indigenous?'

'No,' she replied, still not looking at me. 'Isha's Needle is not indigenous, in the same way a blade inserted violently into the sternum is not a natural part of the human anatomy. Do you know who gave this so-called gift?'

'Only what I overheard from the servants.'

'Well, it doesn't matter. It's obvious enough,' she said. 'By the Throne, the aeldari are a sneaky bunch. Destabilise an entire eco-system through one well-chosen gift. Where is the governor now? Assuming she still has her sanity? By the God-Emperor, the visions she must have seen.'

'I heard whispers she has fled this place.'

'Running away? Very sensible. Let me just make a record of that.'

A quill was plucked from somewhere, and she recorded a note on a scrap of scroll, etching the letters with a cartographer's flourish. She then sat back, triumphant, before glancing up at me. She looked surprised, almost as though my presence had been forgotten.

'Ah, Simlex,' she sighed. 'I cannot say I have enjoyed this conversation as I know it will result in a hive's-worth of paperwork. But it has been useful, so I should thank you for that.'

'What will happen to me now?'

'You?'

'You said my life was in danger.'

'Oh, it is. But not from me, thanks to your answers.'

'What about the Administratum? Will others come for me?'

'This is not strictly official Administratum business,' she said. 'I intercepted your little request before it could trigger any alerts or sanctions. No, this is me doing my family yet another favour.'

'Then I'm free?'

'Oh, yes,' she said, nodding. 'At least, free for the next thirty seconds or so. After that you will be arrested and incarcerated in a military prison. It's for your own good, though. And mine obviously.'

She smiled again.

I just stared back, confused, hoping this was some parting jest. But her expression said otherwise.

'Wait!' I said. 'What do you–'

'Give my sister my best.' She smiled as the image faded.

Moments later a hammering began at my door, the frame giving on the second strike.

CHAPTER TWENTY-NINE

I had expected soldiers in blacked-out armour, working at the behest of some clandestine branch of the Imperium. I was almost disappointed to find the attackers wore the uniform of the 2208th Expeditionary Air Wing. I think I recognised two of them, but it was hard to say because, even as I raised my hands, a fist met my face, knocking me to the floor. When I tried to speak, a rifle butt slammed into my head.

They tried to drag me upright, but I was dazed and fell as my unsupported leg caved. My head still rang from the blows, but I heard muttering before hands seized me again, pulling me to my feet, my arms slung over their shoulders. I was half carried, half dragged down the corridor. I could hear Kikazar hovering behind me, no doubt recording the whole exchange. I worried they might take a shot at it, but they seemed unconcerned by the seer-skull. In fact, their conversation was focused not on me, but the aerial battle apparently ongoing. I swayed, almost losing consciousness as we reached the main staircase. As we descended my foot struck against the steps, agony searing through my leg. I screamed but they did not slow.

Outside, the sun was blinding, my eyes weakened by the confinement. With my arms pinned I could not shield my face, but neither could I make sense of much. Shadows seemed to duel overhead, though I could not tell if they were fighters or distant insects.

Not until the ork aircraft slammed into the château.

I caught a glimpse of it passing overhead, right before the impact shook the world and hurled me from my feet. My ears bled white noise, and I could see little through the dust. But despite the flames and smoke, I could just make out the remnants of a xenos fighter embedded in the château's entrance.

One less greenskin in the air. That was technically a positive.

Then another blast flattened me. I knew not the source, only that the ground quivered and my face was sprayed with what I hoped was dirt. Strong hands grasped my shoulders, as my captors hauled me to my feet. I was surprised, assuming they'd fled for cover. But they did their duty, dragging me through the storm of fire and bullets.

Ahead lay the bunkers, still embedded like ticks into the governor's grounds. So far, they had weathered the barrage. The lead soldier kicked the door open, and I was forced down the steps and through the medical bay, the chirurgeon barely acknowledging our presence. Not that I could blame him; he clearly had his hands full. The injured lay strewn about, the ward well beyond full occupancy and reeking of blood and death. As I was hauled through, I caught sight of Wing Commander Prospherous. He was laid out in one of the cots, grey-faced, his eyes closed.

I was escorted past him, past all of them, even those in the rearmost ward where the critical lay dead or dying. Before me, there was the glint of iron bars.

They threw me inside, barely pausing to slam the door. The plascrete floor felt cool to the touch. I lay there a moment, wondering why I was still alive. It seemed an awful lot of trouble to move a man from one cell to another. Presumably they wanted me alive, though whether that was a good thing was less clear.

I felt buzzing over my shoulder. Kikazar. The guards had not noticed the seer-skull, or did not care enough to do anything about it. Unless Kikazar was incarcerated too, awaiting interrogation of its data-files.

I forced myself onto my hands and knees, rolling awkwardly onto my side and stretching out my legs. The left ached terribly, but I did not think it re-broken. That was something, but my head was ringing, perhaps from the shockwaves. The cell was dark. I could make out bars, though now I looked closer these seemed a late modification to the structure. Otherwise it resembled one of the medi-bays, lacking the diagnostic equipment but incorporating the fold-out cots.

It took me a moment to spot the figure reclining in one of the bunks, hands tucked behind her head. I could not make out her features, but I still recognised her.

'Shard?'

She raised her head and glanced across, as though seeing me for the first time, despite my memorable arrival moments earlier. I could barely see her in the half-light, but the swelling around her eye and cuts to her cheek were clear enough.

'Oh,' she said. 'What did you do?'

'I asked the wrong questions.'

'That was foolish. Still, if you are alive someone probably has a use for you.'

'Should I find that encouraging?'

'I suppose. Given the alternative.'

'Is that why you are alive?' I asked. 'You're still useful?'

'I exist in a state of both life and death,' she replied. My eyes were adjusting now, and I could just make out her face. It was bruised and cut, but she did not look pained or fearful. Her eyes were cold and empty as the void.

'Do you speak of some philosophy? I know little of such things.'

'No. I literally sit awaiting an impasse between your friend Dolos and military command. Obviously, my punishment should be the remit of my superior officer, but once a planetary governor begins exerting their authority the situation becomes complex.'

'I take it she has demanded your death?'

'Yes. I wasn't sure why at first. After all, I didn't steal anything from her. Then again, I did pilfer her pet propagandist.'

'She has tired of me.'

'Well, you are tiresome,' she conceded, gaze returning to the ceiling.

'Are you injured?'

'Only superficially.'

'Can you stand?'

'I imagine so. I could when I arrived, and I don't think much has changed since then. We'll find out once dinner turns up. Assuming it does. You should hear the fuss coming out of the kitchen.'

'The orks are bombing us.'

'That's probably why, then,' she sighed. 'I did warn them that might happen. But no, apparently I was lying about our attackers, because I didn't care to admit an ork had bested me. Which is demonstrably false, as my account clearly states that I was defeated by an ork. Granted, he was operating a flying stronghold supported by an aerial armada. And I had the wrong damn plane. Still though, their lack of faith is tiresome.'

'So, you admit no fault?'

'I made mistakes. I picked the wrong co-pilot for a start.'

'You still blame me?'

'You brought the wrong seer-skull,' she said. 'Which is this one, by the way?'

'Kikazar.'

'That doesn't help. What does it do?'

'Listens.'

'So, nothing, then?'

'Why does it matter? Did you have some daring escape planned? One that hinges on a different seer-skull?'

'No,' she replied. 'From the sound of things, I'm better off in the cell. Besides, I have orders.'

'Orders?'

'Yes, and I'm supposed to follow them,' she said. 'Wing Commander Prospherous was clear about that. The whole regiment bore witness to his rant about my failings. It lasted nearly an hour. He kept returning to how I had gone rogue, and that he never suspected I would do something so reckless.'

She smiled, before continuing.

'Still, he was adamant that my sentence should be postponed, for we had a shortage of pilots and need every fighter in the sky. Dolos held a different view. So, I was ordered to remain in this cell until the matter was resolved.'

As she spoke, a tremor rocked the bunker. Perhaps from a detonating shell.

'I saw the wing commander laid out in the medical bay,' I said.

She rolled her eyes. 'That man is such a shirker.'

'It did not look good.'

'He will be fine once the dust settles. Maybe some cuts and bruises, and a little selective amnesia.'

'I'm not sure any of us will survive this.'

'Possibly not.' She shrugged. 'Still, assuming I can reach my Lightning, I have a good shot at escaping off-world.'

'Does it have the range to reach a neighbouring planet?'

'No.'

'So, you would die out there?'

'Probably. But that wouldn't be for a few hours. And, until then, I would be free to do as I please. There are worse ways to die.'

Another shudder. A scattering of dirt fell from the ceiling, the foetid soil having seeped through the cracks between the plascrete. A sudden image of a landslide struck me, the swamp entombing us alive. Shard's proposed death did seem preferable.

'I recall the Lightning has only one seat?'

'Correct.'

'A pity.'

'You think I would extend an invitation to you?' she said, her smile without a hint of sneer.

'Not really. But, given the circumstances, I thought I would ask.'

'I'm surprised,' she said. 'I would have thought you'd dedicate your final moments to your friends. The skulls.'

'Kikazar is all I have left,' I said. 'Mizar left with the fighters. And Iwazar was taken by Dolos.'

'My condolences. I know they mattered to you.'

I nodded. I could not think what to say, and my throbbing head made conversation difficult. The pain came in waves, and at that moment one crested. I'd thought the ache a consequence of the blow to my head. But it was getting worse.

Shard was saying something, but I could not hear it. It was as though a great pressure was building behind my eyes. She glanced at me, something akin to concern flashing across her eyes. It was pleasant to see, but only lasted a moment, for the next thing I saw was the plascrete floor rushing to meet me.

I lay there, listening as Kikazar began to shriek like a dying beast. The seer-skull lurched upright and, had it possessed a lower jaw, I have no doubt it would have snapped open and shut. As it was, its spindly limbs thrashed in anger or pain. Through our connection, I felt its machine-spirit screeching a warning as it was beaten down, supplanted by an unknown force. I feared it would shatter again under the pressure, but I could not sync with it, only watch helplessly as something bent the machine to its will.

A pictograph flickered into life, jagged runes carved by a blade. They looked alien, and nothing like the aeldari symbols. This was something far more savage.

The holo-projector flared, throwing a crackling image of a hideous face. It resembled a greenskin runt, its snivelling visage all bladed ears and hooked nose. Even its chin was sharp as a dagger, and its lips were stretched into a broad smile of yellow fangs. It screeched some vile sound, though Kikazar mercifully deadened the cacophony. More of the runts appeared in the flickering image, chittering like excited rats as they eyeballed me in turn. One of them began crowing, as if summoning a superior.

We did not wait long. Something seized the projector, twisting it around. We were momentarily treated to a montage of scrap and scattered tools, before the snarling face of the runts' master loomed into view.

It was an ork, but worse, for it appeared half-machine too. Its jaw had been replaced by mandibles of jagged metal, and its right eye was a blood-red lens fused into the skull. It roared a barrage of guttural sounds, savagery on full display. It seemed impossible such a beast could master the simplest device, or possess the faintest understanding of the technology embedded in its skull.

But somehow it had taken control of my seer-skull and was broadcasting a message. Of sorts.

'Vile xenos!' I spat, though this bravado was only possible because I was far from the beast.

It surprisingly fell silent at my words, its slab of a brow drooping into a frown. Abruptly, it seized one of the diminutive greenskins, bellowing at it before backhanding the creature across the face. It scampered off, and returned dragging a cable. I am not sure where it was inserted, only that I felt a fresh stab of pain in my temple.

The ork bared its fangs and spewed another mouthful of abuse. But all I heard from Kikazar's vox was a monotonic voice.

'Query – summon/obtain Gork's Emissary.'

I stared at the twitching skull. It had never spoken before.

The ork roared again.

'Query – bring/challenge Gork's Emissary,' the skull repeated.

But it was then I realised that it was not the seer-skull who addressed us.

It was the ork.

CHAPTER THIRTY

I thought I'd gone mad. The greenskin leader, for that is surely what it was, continued to snarl like an animal. But Kikazar regurgitated its words, transcribing them into Low Gothic as best it could.

'Request/demand Gork's Emissary engages in battle. Refusal warrants sanctions/termination.'

I did not know what to say. Shard had propped herself on her elbows, but still lay in the bunk.

Was the ork even addressing us? Perhaps this was a feedback loop triggered by the greenskin hacking into the device.

'You are in no place to issue demands!' I said with feigned bravado.

Shard rolled her eyes. It was a poor line, as the ork was perfectly placed to issue all sorts of demands. I did not expect it to respond anyway. But, faintly, I heard a series of grunts and snarls synthesised by a mechanical voice that sounded almost Imperial in origin.

The ork certainly responded. A guttural rumbling emerged from its throat. I thought it a growl of anger, but then the beast threw its head back, the sound rising to a crescendo that might have caused my ears to bleed had Kikazar not deadened the sound.

'By the Throne, what is it doing?' I whispered, glancing to Shard.

'Laughing?' she offered with a shrug.

She was right. The diminutive greenskins were also cackling, their chirps a little closer to human. One of them was leaning against its master's shoulder for support. The ork, still laughing, glanced to the runt. The two mimicked a high, squeaking voice that bore little similarity to my own, before collapsing into further guffaws.

Even Shard was smirking. I glared at her.

'What?' she said. 'It was a good impression.'

The ork sighed, shaking its head, metal tusks still somehow grinning, the laughing runt half-collapsed against its shoulder. Then the ork's arm struck out, knocking the diminutive greenskin from view. It snarled, grunting a curse that Kikazar took a moment to translate.

'Power lies/resides in the hands/clutches of the children/soldiers of Gork/Mork. The weak/soft/human hold none/zero/absence. Bring Gork's Emissary/Summoner/Offering.'

Each phrase was a struggle, the seer-skull attempting to translate concepts as alien as the xenos beast itself. But I felt a glimmer of understanding dawn.

'Gork,' I said. 'What is Gork?'

The creature listened to my response. I could not have read its face, even if half of it were not replaced by machinery. It looked either appalled or puzzled by the question, and it struck me the translation was probably even more dubious at its end.

It snarled. A moment later Kikazar spoke.

'Gork the violent/shrewd, sibling to Mork the shrewd/violent. Gork the propagator/patron/destroyer. Gork the deity/god/archetype.'

'God,' I whispered, glancing to Shard. 'Gork is their god?'

'I suppose.'

'Then who in the God-Emperor's name do they consider his Emissary?'

I did not expect Kikazar would translate my words. But the ork heard me, and it seemed my words irritated it. The brutal creature lurched from my view, and for a moment we were offered a glimpse of the ork hangar, before the image was filled by greenskin runts making obscene gestures and waving weapons. Mercifully, this did not last long, the ork brushing them aside with a sweep of its massive hand as it barked something at the screen.

'No more weak/small/unworthy fighters. No more skirmishes/fisticuffs/playing.'

It held up a fallen figure. His face was a mess of purple bruises, eyes staring blank and dead. I might not have recognised him, were it not for the unwaxed moustache.

Flight Commander Gradeolous. Or what was left of him. But his appearance solved part of the puzzle. For if they had his body they must have brought down his plane. Perhaps they recognised Mizar's energy signature, and no doubt the seer-skull was in their possession, the greenskins having somehow adapted the device to communicate with us.

The ork tossed the body aside, still grunting at the picter.

'This foe/weakling/non-ork was not the Emissary/summoner, despite the same signature/scent/spore. Send the Emissary/summoner.'

'I don't understand,' I said. But then I thought of the swamp, when I had distracted the orks using the projected face of the snarling greenskin.

Gork. That was what they called it.

'Kikazar. Access Iwazar's data-files,' I murmured. 'Timestamp twenty-three seventy-eight. Play file.'

I doubted it would work, but it transpired my Administratum interrogator had transferred over the entire recording. The image spluttered into place, the seer-skull struggling against the invading ork's influence. But the pict was clear enough: the flurry of explosions as Shard waged a solo war against the monstrosity. There was a power surge and the image faded, but not before the ork had bent forward, its snarling face filling the projection.

'*Confirmation/exhilaration,*' Kikazar noted. '*Send/bring the Sky-Emissary to battle. Its death/subjugation shall commence the ascension/migration/war in the void.*'

I did not quite take its meaning. But I understood the demands. The greenskin wanted to face the one who had damaged its fortress. Perhaps it sought revenge and atonement for the loss. Or it thought such a battle was blessed by its vile god, mistaking the picts I had inadvertently plastered across the sky for a divine presence.

I glanced to Shard. She was quite still, intent on the flickering image.

'What if I can find you this emissary?' I asked. 'And what do you offer in return?'

The ork looked blank. Quite an achievement for a xenos monstrosity with bionic mandibles. It eventually spoke, the cadence slow, as though addressing a dull-witted child.

'*The Emissary will be slain/smashed/sacrificed in Gork/Mork's name. Then will come the ascension/migration/war in the void.*'

'And if the pilot cannot be found?'

'*The ascension/migration/war in the void.*'

I turned to Shard. 'What the hell does it mean? What is it offering exactly? Why did it even bother contacting us?'

'You don't speak warrior,' she said, and sighed, slipping her legs off the bunk. She stood and stretched, arching her back, hands pressed to her spine. Straightening, she glanced to the flickering image. 'You offer Gork's Emissary a chance to fight and die in battle. In return your god will manifest, and the war in the void will begin?'

The ork grinned. Perhaps it recognised something in her manner, or remembered her from the pict I inadvertently projected across the sky.

'Yes.'

'When and where?'

'The storm's eye. Soon.'

'How soon?'

'Before the sky is broken/breached/dominated.'

'I see. Consider your message received. Simlex, cut the signal.'

'I… am not in control of any of this.'

'Well, that's unfortunate. Because now I look like an idiot. Can't you just pull some wires out or something?'

I am not sure the ork followed this exchange, though it made a terrifying grumbling sound that might have been amusement. But there came an audible crash behind it, a trio of runts sprinting past, two of them at least partially on fire, bickering despite the blaze and subsequent minor explosions. The ork grunted something that, mercifully, Kikazar was unable to translate, before slamming its fist into the projector. The image went blank, and Kikazar fell to the ground, its lenses dark. I could see smoke seeping from the cracks in its skull.

'They really are ingenious creatures, aren't they?' Shard murmured.

'Shard, I… Do you even think you have a chance against it?'

'Perhaps a small one. Maybe. That is, if I could leave this cell.'

'There must be a way,' I said, inspecting the rather solid-looking bars. 'What if... Could we cut through the metal somehow? Or cause a distraction? I still have one seer-skull. Have you–'

I turned as I spoke, expecting to see her beside me. But she had returned to the bunk, laying her head upon the pillow, gaze fixed to the ceiling.

'Shard?' I said, still expecting something.

She raised her head, glancing at me. 'What?'

'What are you doing?'

'Waiting for dinner,' she replied, lying back again. 'I do hope they have some proper meat this time. I swear yesterday's stew was mostly carapace and antenna.'

'But... I thought you said you had a chance against it?'

'Yes,' she said, frowning. 'Sorry, I don't see how that's relevant?'

'You don't intend to fight it?'

'Why should I do that?'

I stared at her, incredulous.

'What about honour?' I blurted.

'I have orders,' she said. 'I was told not to leave this cell. And I have recently been reminded of the importance of obeying orders to the letter.'

'But... you don't follow orders. You just do as you please!'

'As I please?' she snapped, gesturing to the cell. 'You think this is as I please?'

'I doubt this is the first cell you–'

'Do you know what I wanted to be when I was a child?'

'No.'

'Neither do I. The schola progenium cleansed most of the formative stuff. I gather it's more efficient to shape your recruits from scratch rather than try and build upon past experience.'

'You remember nothing?'

'Some things, though I cannot tell if they are memories or something imparted by the drill abbots. Or maybe my own fantasies.

328

Either way, the schola progenium made me what I am, shaped every part of my being. How then, can I ever do as *I* please?'

She glared at me, and I at her. How long the impasse would have endured is hard to say, for in that moment of oppressive silence I heard a faint tapping at the bars of the cell.

'Excuse me. Sir? And, sir?'

Plient was standing outside the bars. He looked grey and thin, and a trio of fresh scars were carved into his head.

'Plient! Good to see you.' Shard smiled. 'Tell me, what's on the menu today? Yesterday's slop was almost palatable.'

'I… I don't think there will be anything, sir. I think the kitchens have been destroyed.'

'I see.' She nodded. 'And the wine cellar?'

'Buried beneath rubble.'

'Unfortunate. In that case, why are you here?'

'To release the propagandist,' he replied, unlatching a key from his belt. 'I'm very sorry, sir. I'm not sure why you are down here. A message was dispatched from high command stating it was vital you were seized and brought into custody.'

'Who sent it?'

'Hard to say, sir. It's no longer there. No trace of it,' he said, setting key to lock. 'I'm sorry they were rough, sir.'

I shook my head. 'It matters not. No doubt it saved my life. Is the war still raging?'

'No, sir.'

'Did we… win?'

'No, sir.'

He unlocked the door, but struggled to open it one-handed, the bottom bars catching on the floor and throwing up sparks. I stepped forward to assist. Shard remained on the bunk.

'What now then?' I said. 'If the orks have won, why are we still alive?'

'Because we're boring,' Shard replied. 'They've brought down our planes and firebombed the remaining ground targets. But following up and accounting for every survivor isn't how orks wage war, unless they require slaves. This lot seem more preoccupied with the next fight.'

'What's left to fight, sir?'

'Well, they could look for another airbase.' Shard shrugged. 'Or maybe some of our ground forces?'

'If you say so, sir.'

She sat up, glaring at him. 'Do you have something to say, flight sergeant? I might be in a cell, but I would remind you I am your superior. Yours, and everyone else's.'

'No, sir. Only...'

'Only they haven't gone anywhere,' I whispered.

I felt their gaze on me, but mine was fixed upon Kikazar. The seer-skull's lenses twitched, its projector throwing a flickering pict onto the cell wall. What modifications the ork mechanical had made to Mizar was unclear, but the signal continued to transmit. I could see ork aircraft swarming like insects. It was hard to be sure, as the quality was so poor, but I got the impression we observed them through a viewport, or perhaps a screen of some kind.

What was apparent was their numbers.

For we beheld an unassailable force, marshalled from across the planet. Even if we were at full strength, with every fighter ace in the air, there was no way we could stop them.

CHAPTER THIRTY-ONE

I don't know what the others thought, as we stared at that poorly rendered holo-pict. Plient's eyes were as wide as I'd seen them. Shard, ever guarded, appeared a casual observer to the aeronautical swarm. But something was happening behind her eyes. It was as though she were plotting the path of every plane, trying to make sense out of the greenskin horde.

'How... How would they even resupply?' I found myself saying, as if that mattered in that moment. But I clung to it, perhaps seeking a needle of logic in the chaos unfolding. For how could they refuel? And what was the purpose of so many craft in one spot? The Green Storm, that terrible sky-fortress, could have single-handedly flattened the 2208th Expeditionary Air Wing, and the château along with it. Why draw so many planes to this one spot? They had already beaten us.

What was their target?

They must have been summoned by the lightning, for even that sky-fortress could not have created such an armada from scratch. But, if that were the case, why were they still here?

Their mission was not yet over. I could see energy coursing around the brass dome mounted beneath the sky-fortress. It was hard to be sure from the flickering pict, but it did not seem to be coalescing with quite the same urgency as when we last fought.

Either that, or it was building a bigger charge.

'They're migrating. Like birds.'

Shard spoke softly, entranced by the spectacle. I glanced to her, then back to the image. She had a point. I had seen both avian and insect gather in similar numbers in preparation for a long journey.

'Why?' I asked. 'Where are they going?'

As I spoke an explosion lit the vid-feed, two aircraft colliding, or perhaps trading shots. The closest fighters dispersed, jostling for position before settling back into their continuous loop around the sky-fortress.

'You heard the ork mechanical,' she replied. 'They are looking for a battle and besides me, they have no competition left. Not on this planet, anyway.'

It took a moment to take her meaning.

'Salus...' I murmured.

'Yes. My guess would be they intend to take the fight to Orbital Station Salus.'

'But... that's impossible.'

'Of course it is,' she said. 'Orks cannot accomplish such a feat. Just like they cannot master matter transportation, or manufacture void-capable fighter craft. Right?'

Derision dripped from her voice, but I still could not fathom it. Orbital Station Salus dwarfed the ork sky-fortress and carried sufficient weaponry to erase it from the planet's surface.

Yet, Shard's words held a horrible truth. We continually

underestimated the greenskins. Worse, we actively underplayed their threat; my very presence was proof of that fact. Governor Dolos had used her influence to downplay the danger, concerned only by the damage a full Imperial crusade could inflict on her world, or fearful of the scrutiny that might accompany it. Her reluctance to face reality may well have cost the Imperium the entire planet. Perhaps even more, assuming the orks were able to establish a holding point in the sector.

'You think they can do it?' I asked.

She shrugged. 'I think they will try,' she said. 'The only question is whether they can stabilise a portal large enough. Otherwise, who knows what damage they will inflict? Perhaps everything for a hundred miles will be launched into space. Or Salus will be brought low and torn apart by the planet's gravity? I do hope we maintain this connection – it will be fun finding out how our lives will end.'

'What do we do, sir?'

I glanced to Plient, but he was intent on Shard.

'Who is in charge?' she asked, not looking round.

'I don't know, sir. Most of the officers are either dead or in the medical bay. I managed to speak to Lieutenant Quillte.'

'And he said?'

'Nothing much, sir. Nothing that warrants repeating anyway.'

'No actual orders then?'

'Not exactly, sir. Something about how I should do as I please because we were all lost and there is no hope.'

'That's it?'

'He was drinking, sir. Only spoke between mouthfuls.'

'Smart man that Quillte.' Shard nodded, still intent on the swarm. Two more planes had just collided. Unsurprising, given the volume of orks occupying the space.

'Sir?'

'I'm relieved of duty, Plient. You need not call me "sir".'

'Please, sir?'

She turned away, bowing her head, fingers clasped to the bridge of her nose.

'What exactly do you want me to do, Plient?'

'Save us?'

She sighed, glancing to me, as though addressing a co-conspirator.

'You see what I put up with?' she said. 'Save the day, Shard. Defeat impossible odds, Shard. Bring down the impossible enemy, Shard. As if it were that simple.'

'It might not be simple. But it strikes me as the sort of thing Flight Commander Shard would do.'

She glared at me. 'Simlex, is this a feeble attempt at manipulation?'

'No,' I replied. 'For it does not matter what you do. There is no way anyone could defeat that horde. Not even you. We have seen that already. The Green Storm is out of your league.'

'Last time was hardly a fair match,' she protested. 'I lacked my plane, I didn't–'

She trailed off, sighing, the anger dying in her eyes.

'Do you honestly think me this malleable?'

'Flight Commander Shard? Of course not. She would simply prove my misgivings wrong via some cunning strategy and daring skill.'

'I hate it when other people try and be clever,' she said, glancing skywards before turning to Plient. 'Did you ever get around to fixing my Lightning, flight sergeant?'

'I did, sir. Sorry it took so long. I had to adjust the hard points to facilitate the seer-skulls, and then–'

'Where's Prospherous?'

'In the medi-unit. Unconscious, sir.'

'Very well,' she said, reaching into her flight suit and withdrawing a rather crumpled envelope. 'Simlex, I assume you can read?'

I took the note, breaking the seal and extracting a letter written on Wing Commander Prospherous' headed paper.

'To whom it may concern,' I read, addressing them both. 'I, Wing Commander Prospherous, in the event of being injured beyond the capacity to command, immediately nominate Flight Commander Shard to act in my stead.' I glanced at her. 'How long have you had this?'

'A while. I need it back, mind. For next time.'

'It's undated...'

'Pays to be flexible,' she said, tucking the letter into her flight suit. 'Plient, get to the hangar. I need you to make some cosmetic modification to my Lightning. And Simlex?'

'Yes?'

'Is this the skull-thing that flew with us? The one that gave the orks that light show that has so inspired them?'

'No. This is Kikazar, not–'

'I don't care. Just get the right one.'

'Governor Dolos took it. I have no idea where it could be. She might have destroyed it, or taken it with her when–'

'We know she hasn't destroyed it because you showed its files to the ork. Go search whatever's left of the château. Look everywhere. We need it if this is going to work.'

'Dare I ask if you have a plan?'

'Please,' she said, rolling her eyes. 'Flight Commander Shard always has a plan.'

I was hesitant to step outside, my pace slowing as the bunker's exit loomed ahead. Two guards were posted on the interior, though it was unclear whether their role was to prevent desertions, or they merely thought it safer to guard the bunker from the inside.

They did not waylay me. What did my fate matter to them?

As the door creaked open, I half expected to find a courtyard brimming with rampaging orks, but the grounds were devoid of life. Whatever remained of the grasses and shrubs had been obliterated or consumed by flame. The earth was too sodden to maintain the inferno, but the air was thick with smoke. I could barely see, coughing as I staggered through the smog, the quagmire grasping at the cane I had borrowed from the medi-unit.

I knew the château lay ahead, but doubted it still stood. Surely the orks would have reduced the edifice to ash? But I could see a shape lurking in the smoke, vast, if diminished, and as I drew close the smog dissipated, and I saw what remained of the building.

Its outer surface was black, scorched by the terrible inferno unleashed by the orks' firebombs. I could see a one-armed servitor scraping pathetically at the torched bark, but there was no saving it. The mandack tree was dead. In fact, it had probably been dead long before the ork attack. For with the bark split, I could now see the threadworm tendrils that infested its innards. Somehow, they had proved resilient to the inferno, the outer surface darkened but the flowers still pink and puckered. They now hung distended from the shell of the great tree, like spilled entrails. The infestation extended into the earth as well, tendrils bursting through the cracked runways. No wonder the château had succumbed to the parasitic plant. By the end, it must have been wearing the great tree like a shell. Who knew how deeply it had penetrated the planet, or how far its influence had spread?

But it had survived. Which meant, perhaps, some of the interior had endured, if only I could access it. The governor's rooms were central, and would no doubt be reinforced against attack. But the entrance and walkways were both ruined and entangled by the new growth.

My gaze lingered on the servitor. I could not tell if it was the one who had first greeted me, that Plient had referred to as Garrie. They all looked alike. But perhaps it fulfilled a similar role.

'You there!' I said, approaching the lumbering automaton, which was still rasping pathetically at the blackened bark. 'Take this bag to the governor's room.'

It ignored me, assuming it even registered my presence. It was damaged, missing its arm and with jagged cuts scouring the grey flesh of its sternum. Perhaps its programming was compromised.

I tried again, forcing myself into its view and shoving a torn scrap of material into its hand.

'Take this bag to Governor Dolos' chambers!' I ordered.

It slowed, glancing at me with dead, grey eyes. I shivered, for I knew not how damaged it was. It could have lost whatever mechanisms prevented it from harming me. But I had no choice.

'Bag!' I said, hand outstretched.

It reached for it, grasping the scrap of material. It attempted to pass it to the missing limb, but instead dropped the scrap onto the ground before marching stiffly towards the rear doorway, now collapsed under the weight of burnt wood and sprawling vines. It barely slowed, its taloned hand reaching for the thrashing tendrils and tearing an armful clear. As it dug its way through, I followed in the servitor's wake, tucking myself tight and avoiding the flowers. For beneath their petals, I could see rows of thorns that seemed to gnash like teeth.

My gait was still slow, reliant on the walking cane, but the machine's pace was equally restricted by the ruins. We ascended the staircase, intact only because of the repairs overseen by Stylee. Now the bark was burnt away, whole sections were revealed to be recast in resin. Judging from the way it was layered, and in places aged, this must have been ongoing for months, as the mandack tree was slowly hollowed by the invasive tendrils.

We reached an impasse, where the stairs had crumbled. I half expected the glitching servitor to plunge into the abyss. But it slowed, twitching for a moment, before turning and proceeding along the corridor. There was something concerning about its gait; it stumbled at points and I could see curious marks on its grey skin, like tiny bites, the surrounding flesh swollen and discoloured. Though the servitor was lobotomised and immune to pain or discomfort, its biological components were still susceptible to certain toxins.

I followed tentatively, using my cane to ward off tendrils emerging from the cracked walls. Their pink flowers seemed drawn to me, perhaps attracted by my body heat. The damage was less here, at least from the fire, but if anything the infestation was worse. Perhaps the heat from the flames acted as a catalyst, or the death of the mandack tree had provided the opportunity for explosive growth. Either way, I swear the amber-flecked tendrils were attempting to encircle us.

I glanced back. Had the tunnel narrowed? Or was that paranoia? Both seemed equally probable, for I did not recognise the path we walked. I feared the deteriorating cyborg would lead us to a dead end and consumption by the encroaching plant, until it tore through the last of the roots, revealing a door at the corridor's end. Beyond was a metallic lift shaft, long carved into the wood, the stained metal untouched by the invasive tendrils. Pipes ran beside it, carrying promethium to the inner sanctum. It seemed this was the industrial heart of Dolos' rural retreat.

The servitor lumbered to the lock, engaging its implanted key on the second attempt.

As we stepped inside, I wondered if it was aware of my presence or had slipped into a comforting subroutine. But as the door closed and the lift ascended, it seemed to sag. Perhaps, as it was no longer in motion, the machine was conserving power, but doing so placed additional strain on its organic system. It slid into a gradual heap, its leg buckling until it lay prone. As the lift slowed and the doors ground open it tried to rise, but the mechanical components could no longer compel it, its remaining arm clawing at the floor. I would say it looked confused, but I am not sure its biological systems were even alive. Perhaps it was the toxins that had distorted its face into a scowl. I prefer to think that. It is better than wondering if some echo of humanity still clung to the dying machine.

I had been too preoccupied by the tendrils to dwell on what awaited beyond the doors. I would have guessed a standard service corridor, but the walls were patterned in teal and gold, and strangely unmarked by the parasitic roots. The paintings that adorned the passageway were of a familiar style, but I had little time to critique them as I hobbled onwards, intent on locating my seer-skull. The imagery evoked by the pictures reflected the planet's ecology, entrancing sunsets mirrored in the still swamp water, the insectoid motif prevalent throughout.

But as I pressed on the subjects changed. I do not know how the paintings were ordered, whether chronological or themed, but as I progressed those slender beings in curious robes crept into the imagery. I found myself slowing, my gaze lingering on the alien figures. Their appearance was consistent: androgynous features and flowing robes. Aeldari, I assumed, their prominence accompanied by a shift in style; the linework grew increasingly unrefined, the paint almost carved into the canvas. I wished I had a seer-skull with me, that I might have recorded what I saw.

Particularly the final image.

I saw echoes of the Harvest Banquet in the final painting, both in the clothes and pairings. But the silhouetted figures, framed by a waning sun, were like shadows writhing in flames. Their anatomy was painfully distorted, and I could not tell whether the revellers were cavorting in lust or indulging murderous whims. At the centre of the festivities a dark figure was suspended above the swamps, pale flesh peeking from beneath black robes. Its face was barely rendered in a flurry of brushstrokes, but there was something haunting to the eyes and terrible in the smile. Worse was its excess of limbs, additional arms emerging from a hunched back, and its dangling feet did not quite touch the ground.

I don't know why Dolos had painted this monstrosity. I could believe it a dream or nightmare, brought upon by overconsumption of her own tainted produce. But I recalled the Harvest Banquet, where Lord Pompo had complained about aeldari attending the previous festivities. Could this twisted creature be one of their race?

I tore my gaze from it as I emerged into a foyer. Dolos' portrait hung above an ivory-panelled fireplace that blazed cheerfully, its fuel supplied by the promethium pipes running parallel to the lift shaft. Perhaps this was her sanctuary, accessible only to the most loyal or mindless of retainers. If so, she might have hidden Iwazar somewhere within the chamber.

I tried to sync with the seer-skull. I could feel it. Close. But it saw only darkness.

'Playback, random file,' I murmured. I had hoped to catch sight of a flickering image, but there was nothing.

Still, I heard a faint sound, barely a whisper.

'Play back file designated "Shard",' I said. 'Maximum volume.'

There it was: the monotone intonations of the drill abbot. I followed the sound through a gilded door and found myself in the suite where Dolos and I had once breakfasted. It was dishevelled now, drawers and cupboards ransacked in her sudden departure. The plant still squatted on the table. A body lay beside it, flesh marked by those puckered bites.

Stylee.

I doubt I could have identified him without his robes, for his flesh was desiccated, clinging tight to his bones. The plant's tendrils were still wrapped around his hand. He was clutching a billhook, I assume intended to be used against the plant. He could have slipped, found himself entwined in its tendrils. But by then I was certain the plant possessed some malign instinct. Indeed, the flowers were dripping resin, as though salivating at my presence.

I moved warily, following the drill abbot's voice through to Dolos' bed-chamber.

The bed had been lifted, the hidden panel beneath exposed. The servants had left it open in their haste. Trinkets and treasures were scattered about the room, but I ignored those, intent only on the casket. It must have been too heavy to carry, for the wood was thick, although not thick enough to muffle the drill abbot's voice.

I undid the latch, and Iwazar rose unsteadily. It was in a sorry state, charred from the storm and stained by the swamp, but it fell in behind me as I departed the chamber.

The plant had swollen in my absence, continuing to ripen even as I watched. The remaining purple berries fell from its puckered flowers, darkening and shrivelling in the air, the last drops of their juice staining the wood black. The markings reminded me of the Scion's pox-ridden flesh.

My gaze slid to Stylee. Why had he not fled with his mistress? Had she abandoned him, and he decided to take out his frustration on the plant? Or was he here under her orders, to kill the wretched thing and perhaps remove any evidence of its existence? I would never know. Still, snivelling creature that he was, he did not deserve this fate.

Carefully, I bent down and retrieved the billhook, retreating before the flowers supping at his wrist could reach for me, their thorns glistening. I stepped back, debating whether I should attack the plant, hack it to pieces before it spread further. But its roots had already burrowed deep beneath the château's shell, and by now had infested the swamp. Killing it was beyond me.

I turned away, activating the billhook's oscillating blades, praying to the God-Emperor it would be sufficient to carve a path back.

CHAPTER THIRTY-TWO

I returned to find Shard in the main hangar. It looked odd stripped so bare, every aircraft it once housed already sacrificed to the ork threat.

All bar one. Shard's Lightning. *Mendax Matertera.*

Or rather, the vessel formerly known as *Mendax Matertera*, for its proud silhouette was now plated in scrap. I could not tell if the patches were cut from ork or Imperial craft, or if the distinction mattered any more, but the haphazard placement certainly gave it an orkish silhouette.

Shard raised her head as I entered, frowning at the sap staining my robes and the billhook's blades.

'Success?' she asked.

I nodded, Iwazar gliding into view beside me.

'Did you have fun?'

'It does not matter,' I replied, gaze lingering on her craft. 'Is this supposed to be ablative armour?'

'Not exactly,' she said. 'But we still need to install your minion. Plient?'

A head emerged from somewhere within the fuselage. Plient's face was stained black, and one of his eyebrows was missing. But his smile had returned.

'Well done, sir,' he said, beaming. 'I'll have it installed momentarily.'

'I do not see the purpose of this,' I muttered. 'Your craft looks barely sky-worthy, and has space for only a pilot. What use is a seer-skull?'

'Because I need backup. And that's your job. You need to operate the skull.'

'But there is no space in the vessel.'

'Then you do it from the ground.'

'I cannot. They do not have sufficient range.'

She raised an eyebrow, nodding to Kikazar. It was laid out beside the plane, its holo-projectors intermittently flashing picts of the sky-fortress' interior.

'That is some sort of xenos techno-sorcery.'

'Are you saying the orks can do it, but we can't?' she replied. 'Because that sounds suspiciously like heresy. I may have to shoot you.'

'Go ahead. It makes no difference. We do not have the means to replicate what they did. Believe me, I have been trained by the adepts of the Mechanicus and know every oath of activation.'

'I see.' She frowned, glancing to Plient. 'What do you think, flight sergeant?'

'Not my place to say, sir.'

She smiled. 'Indulge me. That's an order.'

'Well, maybe if I connect the Lightning's locator beacon to the seer-skull's transmitter it could boost the connection range considerably. Burnout might be an issue, but given it endured the ork lightning it should hold out for a time. Assuming the cogitators share an interface.' He glanced anxiously at our blank faces. 'Or something like that.'

I met Shard's gaze. 'Did you understand what he said?' I asked.

'It isn't my duty to understand it.'

'But you are certain you can do this?' I asked, turning to Plient.

'For a time,' he said, smile retreating. 'But Iwazar has already endured much. I don't know how long it will hold together. I'm not Mechanicus. I'm not supposed to tamper with things beyond my ken.'

His gaze fell to his feet, whilst Shard's drifted skywards.

She sighed, rubbing her eyes. 'Plient, what did Wing Commander Prospherous' letter say you should do in the event he was incapacitated?'

'Follow your orders, sir.'

'So you do follow orders?'

'Yes, sir.'

'Then, by the God-Emperor, I order you to do whatever you just said you were going to do. With the boosting and wires and... so forth.'

He saluted. 'Sir! Yes, sir!'

'How long have you had that letter?' I asked as Plient fired up his arc welder.

'What year is it?'

'Never mind.'

'Would you prefer to be in charge? Because I'm due a latrine break.'

'No.' I winced as Plient cracked open Iwazar's casing and teased out wire and cable. 'You think he can do this? He is no tech-priest.'

'True. But I'd wager he's at least as smart as an ork, and they managed it.'

There was then a loud hiss of steam, followed by a muffled curse as Iwazar's lens flared red. I looked away, my gaze following Shard's, who was intent on the flickering image of the sky-fortress. The ork mechanical was moving down a corridor, dragging the seer-skull with him. I caught the occasional glance at the chain binding them together.

'I take it you can't connect with it?' she asked. 'Perhaps arrange for it to bash our foe about the head? Or self-destruct?'

'No. If I try, I become overwhelmed. All we can do is observe.'

As we watched, the image shifted, the seer-skull drifting towards a viewport. Despite its enslavement, it was still obsessed with the whirlwind of ork jets, its sensors drawn to the frenetic energy. The rim of the brass dome squatting beneath the fortress was barely visible, sparks of green lightning flaring from it.

'Do you think they will wait for Gork's Emissary?' I asked.

'Orks are not renowned for their patience,' she replied. 'They might be able to build things, but they are quite poor at sitting still.'

We watched another explosion tear the sky. Not a collision this time, as Mizar tracked the hail of bullets that claimed the craft. Perhaps the attack was provoked by boredom, or an ork pilot decided to settle an old grudge. Either way, it did not go unpunished. I heard bellowing grunts, presumably the ork mechanical demanding retribution. As we watched, energy coalesced around the copper dome, and a surge of lightning lashed out like an overseer's whip. It ripped the sky asunder, the energies tearing a score of aircraft from the sky. Presumably this included the perpetrator, though I struggled to see how they could be identified in the chaos. It reminded me of the worst of Imperial justice, where punishing the crime takes priority over identifying the perpetrator.

'If we leave them long enough, do you think they would destroy each other? Descend into civil war?' I asked.

'Maybe. But we do not have the time.'

'But what chance do you have? Alone against that?'

She smiled. 'Oh, I won't be fighting alone. The Two Thousand Two Hundred and Eighth Expeditionary Air Wing will fly with me.'

Plient and I watched as *Mendax Matertera* ascended.

I had offered her a salute as she made the final checks. I still held the pose, despite her only response being an eye-roll followed by an obscene gesture. It was Plient who eventually took hold of my arm, gently lowering it to my side.

'Come on, sir,' he said. 'We've done all we can. I'll brew some recaff.'

He was wrong, though. Plient had done all he could by getting the Lightning airworthy. I still had my duties. As he made for the hangar's miniscule kitchenette, I glanced to Kikazar. The seer-skull's anti-grav units remained offline, but we had mounted it in a spare hard point, and I had improved the pict quality, albeit marginally. The ork mechanical was ensconced in the sky-fortress' bridge. I caught the odd glimpse of the craft's interior, ork warriors stationed at consoles, or intent on the viewscreen. It seemed incongruous that these brutal creatures could play the role of navigator or enginseer.

I looked away then, breathing deeply, seeking to sync my consciousness with Iwazar. We had tested the connection from the ground, but there was no way of knowing whether it would work once Shard was airborne. But I focused, reaching out, ignoring the fractious hissing from Kikazar.

I could not say I saw only darkness, for even darkness is a thing. I just felt nothing, like my hand passing through the void. But she was out there, racing towards the storm. I had to reach her. I tried picturing Iwazar, and when that failed, I pictured her instead, piloting the scrap-plated plane, alone against an airborne armada. Flight Commander Shard: the greatest fighter ace in all the Imperium.

It was then I caught a glimpse of storm clouds. It lasted an instant before the link was severed. But now I knew what I sought, its shape and feel, it was easier to find it again. This time I held it, and once more I was soaring through Bacchus' skies.

The storm front lay ahead. Shard did not slow, plunging into the maelstrom, casually riding its winds as she circled towards the storm's eye.

'Shard?' I said, speaking aloud, my voice's echo reverberating through the cockpit.

'About bloody time,' she muttered in response. *'I was beginning to worry the connection was impossible, and that you were right all along. Terrifying thought.'*

'I'm struggling to maintain a hold.'

'Be brave. I know how challenging it must be. If you just let me finish manoeuvring this patchwork craft through hundred mile an hour winds, on my way to almost certain destruction against impossible odds, I will be right there offering sympathy for your terrible burden.'

'Almost certain destruction?' I asked. 'Is Flight Commander Shard experiencing doubt?'

Her response was swallowed by a hiss of static.

'–never cared much for her. Hello? Simlex, are you still there?'

'Just about.'

'Good. Because we have arrived.'

She broke through. I remembered the momentary calm I had experienced the last time we crossed that threshold, before I knew the threat within. But this time was nothing like that. I could not process the chaos of circling fighters, but Shard plunged in, finding a place amidst the greenskins. I expected them to turn on her at any moment, but they did not, the scrap-plated Lightning resembling an ork craft just as well as any of the others.

As she completed her first orbit about the sky-fortress, I sought order in the chaos. There were moments when the greenskins seemed to function as a unit, circling as one. But all too easily it broke down, the ork fighters taking the opportunity to race against their rivals, weaving through the circling craft at maximum velocity. A few insisted on flying against the swarm, forcing other jets to evade or collide with them. I watched a score fall, either from flying too fast or taking one too many risks. But there were no further retaliations from the fortress. Perhaps it needed to conserve energy, for the green lightning was now arcing along it, flowing like water, its tributaries pooling at a single point at the base. Even through Iwazar's eye, I could not look upon it directly. It burned too bright.

'You have eyes on the ork mechanical?'

'He is on what I assume to be their bridge.'

'Any idea where that is? I could try taking a shot at him.'

'No. Somewhere central, I suppose, but it's unclear.'

'Pity. There is something wonderfully clean about dispatching an adversary with a single shot.'

'It might be too late. The energy is building.'

'I know. Are you ready?'

'As I ever will be,' I sighed. 'Shard, if this doesn't work, I just want to say that when I first came to this planet I never–'

'I know. I surpassed every expectation you had.'

'Actually, I wanted to say I regret ever meeting you, and I wish I never came to this armpit of a world.'

The audio feed crackled with her laughter.

'Fair,' she said. *'Now do your damn duty.'*

I closed my eyes, syncing fully with Iwazar. It was a struggle, the images flickering, the pictographs buried in its memory little more than blurred distortions. But I knew what I sought, having spliced the footage prior to take-off.

I wish I could have recounted the names of the brave pilots who sacrificed everything for the Imperium. But it was all I could do to keep myself there, to hold on to the connection.

'Stand by for reinforcements,' I murmured.

And all at once, the sky was filled with the 2208th Expeditionary Air Wing.

CHAPTER THIRTY-THREE

I wonder what went through the orks' minds when a dozen squadrons of Imperial fighters suddenly appeared in their midst, lascannons flashing and autocannons blazing. Admittedly, the weapons made no sound, and the fighters' silhouettes were some-what indistinct.

But it certainly provoked a response.

The orks, their bloodlust too-long suppressed and discipline already fractured, threw themselves at the interlopers, tearing free of the spiral holding pattern and unleashing the full fury of their guns. Of course, since orks are not known for their accuracy, they tend to compensate through volume of fire. The barrage of bullets passed harmlessly through the flickering holo-images, for there were simply no targets to strike.

Besides other orks.

The subsequent explosions rocked ork and pict alike, the Imperium's fighters spluttering as they were fractured by shockwaves and debris. But it did not matter; the orks were too enraged to disengage, chasing the phantoms and firing indiscriminately.

Shard remained to the outskirts of the chaos. Her lascannon flared intermittently, each shot dispatching an ork pilot, but it seemed incidental, like she was passing time.

'*Simlex? You still there?*'

'Barely.'

'*An update would be helpful. How is our ork mechanical enjoying the show?*'

'I have to focus... Plient? What do you see in the ork vessel? And shout, for Emperor's sake!'

His voice came to me as both yell and whisper.

'Not much, sir. They are arguing. I think some punches are being thrown. Hang on, we are moving to the viewscreen. Can't really see what's going on, though...'

'Shard? Not much. They seem–'

'Hang on,' said Plient. 'One of the big ones restored order. They're cranking levers and... By the Throne, their machines are strange. They're priming a device that looks like bellows. Something is about to happen.'

'Shard? Plient says they might be charging–'

'*Yes I can see that!*' she snarled through the vox. From the edge of Iwazar's vision I could see energy arcing along the brass dome. But it did not herald the ork ascension to the void. Instead, a scything blast of lightning wracked the sky. I could not say if it was aimed at the spectral Imperial fighters, or at the wayward horde. But a score of orks were torn from the sky, the energy jumping between them. Shard banked sharply, avoiding the blast, and I felt my stomach heave, a momentary reminder of my mortal body. There was a metallic taste in my mouth. Blood? Or some neural overlap from Kikazar? It was a struggle separating one from the other.

'*Intelligence, please!*' Shard's voice pierced through my fractured consciousness.

'Plient?' I grunted. My tongue felt heavy.

'I don't know, sir,' he replied. 'They seem angry, sir, but they always seem angry.'

'Plient thinks we have annoyed them.'

'*Oh, I intend to do far more than that.*'

Her lascannon flared, carving through the chaos, a single bolt claiming the lives of at least three ork planes. Again it fired, each shot wielded with the precision of a scalpel, severing wings and crippling engines. But their numbers were limitless, and she was but a blade against the swarm. I felt the craft shudder as something struck it, though the armour held.

'*This is a losing battle,*' she grunted over the thud of shells. '*I can thin them, but I doubt I have the ammo to take out even a third. And they only need one lucky shot.*'

'I am not sure how long I can maintain your reinforcements.'

'*They are barely registering now,*' she tutted. '*Keep flickering like ghosts. The orks are beginning to realise something is up.*'

I lacked her eye for war, but the explosions marring the sky had lessened. Perhaps the sky-fortress had a vox-system and had ordered them to stand down. Or perhaps sufficient grudges had been settled and anger tempered. Our plan had been to cause enough disruption that the orks' savagery would cause them to turn upon one another, and perhaps the sky-fortress too. But discipline seemed to be restored, the orks falling into line.

'*It looks like they're powering up again. Any ideas? Because I do not want to experience another ork teleportation.*'

I could not think what to do. My strength was fading, and it was getting harder to maintain the connection.

Then a thought struck me.

I had no time to discuss it and even less to focus, scrambling through Kikazar's pict-files. There was the duel, from which I had forged the ork archetype the greenskins mistook for their god. The second file took a fraction longer. It was one of the earliest. Not my work, but impactful in its own way. I had little time to splice the images, and was struggling to see what I was doing.

'I have something,' I whispered, voice weak. 'Be ready.'

She responded, but I could not hear it, the noise of the battle fading, darkness encroaching on my vision. But I focused on that one pict: the savage embodiment of the ork race, their god manifest in pixel lights.

I released it.

The snarling face filled the skies, its tusks mountains, its jaws wide enough to swallow the armada whole. I let it blaze for a few seconds, enough that every greenskin would see the pict. Then suddenly it shrank, collapsing into a diminutive creature. Still savage, and still an ork, but now a knock-kneed and skinny thing not dissimilar to a runt. Faintly, I could hear the narration overlaying it, though I suspect I was the only one.

'On the agri world of Bacchus, vile xenos beasts threaten the loyal citizens of the Imperium.'

There was no mother and child, just the creature brandishing its spear, right up until its head was taken from its shoulders by the Aeronautica Imperialis fighter.

Over and over. Each time bursting like rotten fruit.

I did not know how the orks would respond. A least, not until a blast of lightning tore the sky in twain. Literally, as it turned out, the discharge slicing fighter and firmament alike. Pieces of aircraft fell like rain, but still the lightning lashed through the armada, seeking to rip the blasphemous image asunder. Impossible of course, for the pict was composed of light, and though each blast twisted and distorted it, they could not erase it. Not unless they struck Shard.

But she weaved through the horde, slipping between craft, ensuring the defiled image of their god remained unobstructed. Still the lightning lashed the sky. Some I think tried to flee, taking their chances with the surrounding storm. But their cowardice provoked the sky-fortress into even more punishing volleys, the energy arcing through the clouds, its cannons thundering.

The sky was a tempest now, the power nigh uncontrollable. Blasphemous as it might be, I wish I knew the intent of the ork mechanical. Was he driven by blind rage, like a beast? Or religious fervour, believing that the shrivelled deity somehow reflected the failings of his followers? Or perhaps he saw through it all, and sought to silence the source of the deception, heedless of the casualties his own forces would suffer.

I would never know. For at that moment Shard launched her attack, flying straight at the lightning-spewing monstrosity, lascannon spitting bolts of searing energy, and tore into the fortress.

'Come on!' she roared through the vox. 'You see me! Look upon me, beast!'

It did, at that. The green lightning lashed out, but she twisted in the air, hugging the upper level of the fortress and using it to shield her from the lightning emanating from below. She fired continuously, blasting holes through the hull, but doing only superficial damage.

'Shard, you have company.'

Ork fighters were detaching from the chaos and launching a pursuit.

'I see them,' she said. 'Not sure they can keep up, though.'

Her autocannon ripped into the fortress, her craft soaring through the gap she had created. I could not make sense of the images from within, expecting any moment for Shard to hit some obstruction and be torn to pieces. But, impossibly, she ducked and darted, the manoeuvrability of the Lightning matched only by her skill. Emerging on the far side she banked sharply, blasting a new hole through the xenos structure and soaring within again, just in time to avoid the ork pursuers.

I could barely watch, but neither could I turn away. To sever the link might mean I could never restore it. Still, an image pricked the edge of my mind. It was faint, but the hunched silhouettes framing a pict screen were unmistakable. It showed schematics, presumably the fortress' interior, the pict crude but clear.

It was Mizar. My proximity had somehow reconnected me with the seer-skull. I could free it, perhaps allow it to escape through a viewport and trust its anti-gravity unit to bring it home. But there was no time, for as Shard burst through the hull once more I saw her registered on the screen, and heard the ork mechanical grunt as he ordered his crew to bring their weapons about. Fast as she was, skilled as she was, she could not do this forever.

And my role became clear.

Mizar, so long enchained, required little urging. I compelled it to drift from its captor, extending the chain to its maximum length. Then I urged it forward and round, so that the links wrapped about the ork's throat and pulled taut. The ork mechanical gasped, grasping at its neck, but the chain was forged by ork hands, the links thick as my wrist. It scrabbled, struggling against me, but I held tight, ignoring Mizar's manifold warnings. The ork's subordinates raised their weapons, either seeking to free their master or slay him and take his place. Bullets and searing bolts of energy tore through the air, but Mizar was a small target and the orks were no marksmen.

'Shard,' I managed. 'They are set to fire. There—'

'*I see them.*'

A shot clipped Mizar, and it tumbled from the air. But it landed facing the viewport, and through its dying eye I saw Shard's Lightning hurtling towards the bridge with terrifying speed. The lascannons flashed bright. My pain was momentary, if not my sense of loss. As Mizar faded I found myself syncing with Iwazar. But all I could see was lightning, tearing the sky apart.

'Shard?' I tried. The vox crackled, but I could not hear her.

The pict was fading, but I managed to rotate Iwazar. The sky-fortress lay both behind and beneath us, for Shard was accelerating vertically up the tower, fleeing for the safety of the void. Beneath her the Green Storm was consumed by its own malefic energies. And there were no orks to shut down the generators.

As she raced on, the clouds spun faster, lightning arcing between them as the storm began to collapse in on itself.

'Shard, it's going to–'

There was a blast of green light. And I lost her.

I rose to my feet, stumbling from the hangar, ignoring my aching leg and the blood in my mouth. In the distance I could see the storm dissipating, remnants of ork craft falling from the sky, so far away that it looked almost like rain.

I tried to find her, to reach out one last time. I caught a faint image of the Lightning suspended in the void, the cockpit dark and engines still, floating silently in space, like a broken boat drifting through Bacchus' swamps.

Then it faded, and I was left with only my own two eyes.

POSTFACE

The Glorious Martyrdom of the 2208th was fast-tracked into production, spliced from the files extracted from Kikazar.

It told the story of Flight Commander Lucille von Shard, who led the last of the 2208th Expeditionary Air Wing in an all-out assault against the ork threat hidden in a cloud. Despite terrible casualties, the armada was brought down, the greenskin offensive blunted by their sacrifice. Medals were awarded to the pilots, nearly all of them posthumous. Wing Commander Prospherous was heralded for his tactical foresight, conserving his forces for this last vital offensive. Not that he could provide an account of precisely what transpired, as he was injured in the ork raid, suffering a blow to the head. He could recall little of those days before the final battle.

This was not the account I presented to my superiors. It is not the truth.

But the truth was not to their liking. Nobody wants to dwell on our soldiers suffering. Not only from the ork guns, for that is their duty, but also from their rulers' failings and bureaucrats' indifference. A true Hero of the Imperium is stoic and loyal, unquestioning, adhering to orders. A true hero slays an ork blade to blade, not scrabbling in the dirt and stabbing it in the back. They should not possess an acid tongue and sour wit. They do not sneak, or drink, or care little for anything and anyone beyond themselves.

I do not blame my superiors for dismissing me. My pict would neither aid recruitment, nor reassure the sector that the ork situation was contained. Not that it mattered any more. The near miss on Bacchus finally spurred the Imperium into action, with Governor Zanwich assuming the role of temporary planetary governor for Bacchus in Dolos' absence. He in turn secured a company of soldiers from the death world of Catachan. They have been deployed to the front lines, and it is said they are pushing the orks back, though whether that is the truth is a separate question entirely.

As for me? For my failure I was sanctioned and demoted, reduced to cataloguing old files and cleaning poorly spliced data. My pict was coddled into something more palatable, the credit given to another. It suits me well enough. I am no longer dispatched to fantastic locations, capturing the glories and horror of our unending war. But I think I would struggle with my limp, and I no longer have the stomach for it, or the fire in my soul. Perhaps an after-effect of that terrible ork weapon, or a weakness of my character brought on by the things I saw. Either way, I am not the man I was, my ambition as diminished as my status.

Still, my work found an audience. For, one evening, whilst compiling the day's files, I received an unexpected vox from a Prefectus Josephine von Shard. I did not think I had met the woman. Not until I saw her face, for the bionic eye's housing was quite distinct.

'Scribe Simlex,' she said. 'I hope I find you well.'

'As well as might be expected.'

'I just wanted to let you know the family enjoyed your pict.'

'That cinema-pict release is not my pict.'

'I know. But I managed to procure a copy of the original. It's a little rough, but some of us are quite taken with it. Tobia went as far as calling it "tolerable", which is high praise indeed.'

'It is a pity those sentiments are not universally shared.'

'Indeed.' She tutted. *'It's a shame how it ended up for you.'*

'I made my choices.'

'Yes. And I'd say you did right by us.'

'May I ask a question?'

'I think you've earned that.'

'The doctored records stating I was cousin to Planetary Governor Zanwich. Was that your work?'

She smiled, her face the mirror of Shard's. Only without the sneer. *'You asked your question. I never said I would answer it.'*

'I think you did.'

'Would you like to know a better question?' she asked.

I nodded.

'Which planetary governor was recently apprehended attempting to flee the sector?'

'Dolos?' I said. 'She has been arrested?'

'Detained at the request of Inquisitor Ortis Atenbach.'

'Her crime?'

She shrugged. *'That is to be decided. But conspiring with xenos and importing contraband flora are distinct possibilities.'*

'Were you involved in this?'

'You already asked your question. Besides, you'd be better off speaking to the agent who actually intercepted her.'

'And who might that be?'

'I believe it was Acolyte Rile von Shard,' she said. *'And on that note I will bid you farewell.'*

'Wait!' I said. 'You said the family enjoyed it.'

'Most of them.'

'Did… did she think it fair?'

My former interrogator sighed. *'You'd have to ask her yourself.'*

The pict screen went dark.

I leant back in my cold metal chair, gingerly stretching my twisted leg. It ached, but the pain was dull now and familiar. I glanced to Iwazar, resting upon my desk. It too could no longer fly, crippled just like its master. They had allowed me to keep it as an act of charity, or perhaps as a means to hide it from the tech-priests, who would take exception to its sorry condition. It barely functioned now, its deterioration beyond even Plient's skills.

He had written to me, more than once. He remained on the front lines, assigned to the 183rd Fighter Wing. He was back working in the hangars, thanks partly to his shiny new bionic arm. The picts he sent show the man beaming, and I know he will derive great pleasure tinkering with it, assuming he is not arrested for tech-heresy first. Such augmentations are uncommon for low-ranking soldiers. But it seems his commander insisted. She trusted no other to repair her craft, and paid for the augmentation herself, drawing the funds from the von Shard fortune.

Because she survived. She always survived.

It had been close, her craft barely outrunning the storm, its backwash shorting its internal systems and leaving her floating dead in space. She was barely able to contact Orbital Station Salus, whose officers had finally woken up to the chaos beneath them and were poised to unleash weapons sufficient to flatten a continent. I suppose I owe her my life once more, though I've lost count of the tally.

I wonder what she told her superiors. Did it match my account, or was it closer to the fiction of the cinema-pict? I won't ever know. Just as I will never know exactly what her aunt said to her at her mother's second funeral. What promises were made, and subsequently broken. Why she only seems at peace amongst the stars.

Still, I do know that I have made my mark on her. For, according to Plient, she still has the broken remnants of seer-skull Kikazar embedded in her craft, despite his offers to detach it. A good luck charm, apparently.

But I wonder sometimes. For there are nights, as I drift into slumber, that I feel the thrill of acceleration. And it is as though I fly with her again, my soul bound into the seer-skull's shell, the sky stretching forever, the stars eternal. Is it a waking dream? Little else would explain it, for there is no possibility that we could be linked over such vast distance.

But in those moments I fly with her, and know what it is to be free.

ABOUT THE AUTHOR

Denny Flowers is the author of the novels
Fire Made Flesh and *Outgunned*, the novella
Low Lives and several short stories. He lives in
Kent with his wife and son, and has no proven
connection with House Delaque.

YOUR
NEXT READ

DOUBLE EAGLE
by Dan Abnett

The war on Enothis is almost lost. Chaos forces harry the defenders
on land and in the skies. Can the ace pilots of the Phantine XX turn the tide
and bring the Imperium victory?

For these stories and more, go to blacklibrary.com, games-workshop.com,
Games Workshop and Warhammer stores, all good book stores or visit one of the thousands of
independent retailers worldwide, which can be found at games-workshop.com/storefinder

YOUR
NEXT READ

STEEL TREAD
by Andy Clark

Under the fell light of the Great Rift, Hadeya Etsul must battle her demons
while her dysfunctional Leman Russ Demolisher crew struggle for survival
against the Ruinous Powers.

YOUR
NEXT READ

AVENGING SON
by Guy Haley

As the Indomitus Crusade spreads out across the galaxy, one battlefleet
must face a dread Slaughter Host of Chaos. Their success or failure may define
the very future of the crusade – and the Imperium.